CROWN SHYNESS

CURTIS GILLESPIE

© Curtis Gillespie 2007

All rights reserved. The use of any part of this publication reproduced, transmitted in any form or by any means, electronic, mechanical, recording or otherwise, or stored in a retrieval system, without the prior consent of the publisher is an infringement of the copyright law. In the case of photocopying or other reprographic copying of the material, a licence must be obtained from ACCESS the Canadian Reprography Collective before proceeding.

Library and Archives Canada Cataloguing in Publication
Gillespie, Curtis, 1960–
Crown shyness / Curtis Gillespie.

ISBN 978-1-897142-27-1

I. Title.
PS8563.I489C76 2007   C813'.54   C2007-902548-X

Editor: Jack Hodgins
Cover photo: Doug Hohenstein
Author photo: Bluefish Studios

 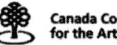

Brindle & Glass is pleased to thank the Canada Council for the Arts and the Alberta Foundation for the Arts for their contributions to our publishing program.

Brindle & Glass is committed to protecting the environment and to the responsible use of natural resources. This book is printed on 100% post-consumer recycled and ancient-forest-friendly paper. For more information, please visit www.oldgrowthfree.com.

Brindle & Glass Publishing
www.brindleandglass.com

1 2 3 4 5 10 09 08 07

PRINTED AND BOUND IN CANADA

for Cathy

Look, he says to his father and brother who have stopped to wait for him. Those tree branches never touch, up there at the top. See that?

His father stands beside him, also looking up. Crown shyness, he says. That's what they call it. Survival thing. At the top of the canopy, the branches don't want to hurt one another, so they developed this way to not touch at the tips when they're growing. Even in rough weather, they sway and blow all over, but they'll never damage one another, or at least not much.

— Rick Munk, 2006

ONE

Calgary

The jail was still an hour away. The only thing Paul could see out the car window was the prairie's vast flaxen austerity, and he chided himself for not bringing a magazine, a book, some work, even a pen and paper; it was wasted time, this leg of the trip, more so because his parents, seated in front, had let the conversation thicken and clot, so that the dominant sound was the drum of tires repeating their tread against the hot black road. Paul couldn't think of a single thing to say to loosen their compacted silence. He ought to have insisted on driving; it would have occupied him. Instead, as he stared out at wheat stubble and disked fields given boundary only by the deep horizon, he felt a mood seeking him out, a melancholy, slightly embittered feeling. He knew it was about Rick, about what his release might bring. But what he does, Paul told himself, is out of my hands. And always has been.

Half an hour from the jail they passed through the small town of Haddington, in which Paul counted three churches of different denominations for a population of two hundred at best. One of the churches, the Pentecostal assembly, looked as if it might once have been a small, plain community hall. On the scraggly, rectangular strip of baked brown lawn that ran the length of the building beside the road stood a large portable message board with blockish, yellow letters that read, THE ROAD YOU'RE ON WILL LEAD TO MY HOUSE. The word *my* was in red letters. Paul said, to no one in particular, "Actually, I think the road we're on leads to the Big House."

Paul's father laughed, a bit too loud, as if happy to have the reason to do so. He said, "Good one," but Paul's mother remained quiet, seemingly engrossed with tonguing something out of the tiny space between her bottom front teeth. A poppy seed, Paul figured, or maybe a chewy strand of orange marmalade rind.

"Speaking of," said Paul's father. Paul could see a purplish-black vein running down the side of his father's neck. From the side and back, it almost looked to Paul as if the vein was bulging and emptying, slowly, thoroughly, evenly, all of which seemed in keeping with his father's temperament.

Paul looked at him in the mirror, met his father's eyes.

"House. How much longer? Your place, I mean."

"Oh." Paul hesitated. The renovations to the apartment building he lived in weren't that intrusive or extensive—he could even have stayed, had no other options existed—but he'd used the renos as a reason to stay with his parents, to be around for Rick's return, just in case, though in case of what he couldn't exactly say. "Don't know. Another week? Ten days?"

His father grunted through his long nose, not, Paul knew, because he wasn't welcome to stay as long as he liked, but because it was his father's way of expressing disapproval, in this case over the hassle it had become "to get anything done on time and on budget" in Alberta, such was the cutthroat petro-boom free-for-all of the place. Paul's mother turned around. She had shortish brown hair (dyed to hide the grey), which spiked slightly and then moved across her forehead in gelled licks. The intended effect, Paul guessed, was to make her seem youthful and current, but to his eye it came off looking like she was papering over an experiment gone wrong.

"Don't worry," she said flatly. "You're welcome to stay as long as you like."

"Lisa doesn't mind having more people around?" asked Paul, referring to his younger sister, who was living at home while finishing grad school.

"Lisa?" said Paul's mother. "It's not her house, is it? Anyway, there'll be more people around with you or without you, now that Rick is getting out."

Paul nodded at her. *Now that Rick is getting out.* Part of him still found it hard to accept that his brother was even *in* jail, a feeling he'd had since the first time Rick had gone in. Paul remembered being in the courthouse eight years earlier when the first sentence had been handed out. He would never forget the angle of his brother's spine. Rick had tried to battle the shame by holding on to his posture, but the moment the number of years was spelled out he'd failed and stood bent like a cane, as if his head were too dead a weight.

Looking out the car window, Paul could see early signs that they were nearing the open geological book of the badlands, with its eerie capped hoodoos and haunted broken-clay bone yards. The land to the south and east rippled and then began to open up along sharp seams of erosion that had completed their work long ago, steep-sided gashes in the otherwise flat prairie that would quickly widen into deep, dry coulees winding down to the Red Deer River just a few kilometres to the southeast. Paul had never tired of investigating the badlands and never would. But they weren't going that direction. The highway veered north and the jail came up shortly after. Paul thought what he always thought when approaching the place, that from a mile away it looked as if it might have been a large technical college or perhaps a manufacturing plant, given its semi-industrial light khaki exterior and square lines; it wasn't until you got closer that the high chain-link double fence and razor wire emerged. They slowed on the highway, signaled, and turned right, onto the short runway of tarmac leading up to the jail grounds. It was two in the afternoon and the sun was charring its way across the day, blistering the sky's outer edges, turning them white and diffuse. At the entrance gate booth, a large sliding window glared like sheet metal. Paul's father put a deflective hand to his brow as they eased to a stop. A segment of window was noiselessly retracted.

"Rick Munk?" said Paul's father.

The guard examined a sheet of paper on an old brown clipboard, made a notation, then peered into the car as if following the beam of a flashlight into a root cellar. Paul tried not to stare back, but the man had a wide, pulpy nose, and it made Paul think of stepping on crabapples in the backyard when he was growing up.

"Who you got in the vehicle?"

"Me. Wife. Son."

"And you are?"

"We're his parents," said Paul's mother, leaning across her husband's lap to see out the driver's window. "We're picking him up."

"Are you now?" The guard took another glance at his clipboard. "You Maureen Munk?"

"That's correct, officer."

"I'm not an officer." He looked at Paul's father. "You're the father? Brother in the back?"

"Yes, I'm Brian Munk. That's Paul Munk behind me."

The guard grunted and motioned at Paul's mother. "Picture identification please."

She removed a wallet from her purse and passed the whole thing over to the guard. He received it with a low-grade irritation, as if it were a sandwich different from what he'd ordered. Asshole, thought Paul.

"In the plastic frame. My driver's license."

The guard glanced at the picture, and then returned the wallet. He wrote a few words on his clipboard. "I've only got Maureen Munk down here on my sheet."

"Well, so what?" said Brian, taking a hand away from the wheel. "We're not here to break him out. He's getting out today. What's the problem?"

The guard looked across the splattered bow of his nose into the car, meeting Paul's eye, pushing out his lips and nodding, as if a question that had been puzzling him for some time had just been answered. He put his clipboard on the desk behind him and then leaned a little farther out the window so that his chest was bisected by the frame of the window. Paul saw his black tie go taut, as though someone under the counter were pulling on it. "I'll ask you to stop on your way out, please." He spoke slowly. "You can proceed."

Brian put the car in gear, easing forward into the parking lot. "Mean son of a bitch," he said. "It's true what Rick says about them."

"Why give them anything?" His mother's voice was calm, but Paul could see the tendons rigid from the base of her skull down to her shoulders, as stiff as ropes holding a canoe to a car roof. "I think it's a mistake."

"Aren't we all trying to do the same thing? *Corrections.* Isn't that what they call it? Aren't we here to help, too? Aren't we here to get him back on track? To help? People don't need to be treated this way. He's not a criminal anymore."

"He's always going to be a criminal."

Brian slowed the car and glanced over at his wife, frowning. Paul said nothing because he knew that what he wanted to say—if that was how she felt, maybe she should have just stayed home—wasn't going to help here and now.

"Well . . . I'm sorry if that's not very empathetic," she said. "But jail doesn't erase what he did. Does it?"

The Processing Centre was a waiting room for families and friends. Paul went in first. The walls were brick, painted a tan colour. There were no posters or pictures hanging on the wall, no windows, just ten metal chairs and the concentrated stink of a bleachy disinfectant, which made Paul wonder what had gone on in there to require such a harsh cleanser. The space had been scrubbed clean of human warmth or enterprise, and clearly whatever processing went on took place somewhere else. There was a single wall-mounted intercom, above which was a set of instructions. Maureen announced their presence into the unit.

"Take a seat, please," came a disembodied reply.

Paul and his father sat side by side, and this close to him Paul felt he could have identified his father with his eyes closed; the old-man aftershave, the hair cream, the same deodorant he'd been using for thirty years. No one else smelled like his father. It made Paul nostalgic for his boyhood, and though the scent was not exactly pleasing, it was reassuring, no small thing in a place like this. A door leading into the guts of the jail opened. Paul's mother stood, pulled her top over the small bulge of her stomach, smoothed the fabric, played with her rings. Paul peered inside the other room, which was better furnished and obviously a place in which some genuine business was conducted. They went through the door. There was a guard sitting on a stool behind a small window opening in the wall, as if he were selling tickets to the movies. He ignored them as they stepped into the room. Rick was sitting on a metal bench seat against the far wall.

He turned his face up to them, but his expression didn't change much. Because he usually affected such a buoyant mood, at least around Paul, to see him so undemonstrative made him seem different physically. His skin was oily, his face slack and fleshy, and he sat slouched against the bench rail, which made him look like a bored young offender. Then he smiled, abruptly, and the air pressure in the room lightened.

"Rick. Here we are. We're here," said Paul, hearing his voice as if the words were coming from somewhere other than inside his own body. He went to his older brother, shook his hand, hugged him. "We're here." Paul felt the size of his brother, his bulk, his muscle; he'd added some weight while inside, none of it fat. Rick held Paul tight, but said nothing, just breathed loudly, hoarsely. Paul stepped away, let his parents move in. Paul's father shook Rick's hand, nervously, pulling as much as shaking, as if to say, Let's just get the hell out of here. Paul's mother put her tongue between her teeth and bit it, and then she stepped to Rick, embraced him, put her arms around his neck, her face against his chest. She stayed that way for a moment before pulling back and wiping away tears so she could gaze into Rick's face, as if needing to check one last time that it really was her son. The sight of her mottled skin and runny nose almost brought the same out in Paul.

"Mum, let's just go," said Rick.

"We don't have to do anything more?"

"I've finished all the paper work."

In the parking lot, Rick did a serpentine sprint for the car, which made Paul and his father laugh. But as soon as they passed the gate—where the crabapple-nosed guard smiled crookedly as he waved them straight through—Rick turned and looked back to the jail. He took a couple of moist breaths. "Jesus Christ," he said, and began to sob. He bent his head to his knees and cried like Paul had never heard him, or any grown man, cry before. Paul was sitting to his brother's right, so he reached up and put his left arm around his brother's shoulder, gripping the broad, round muscle with his fingers. Rick leaned into him a little, enough to make it seem to Paul as if he were consoling Rick for some piece of dreadful fortune—which, Paul thought, was perhaps the truth. Still, it felt awkward, backwards, the younger brother holding the older, but Paul couldn't think of a way to change it, and also he knew Rick would somehow read it wrong if he tried. So he stayed as he was. Paul saw his mother and father glancing back, fidgeting, exchanging a look. You could say something, thought Paul. It wouldn't kill you. But that was uncharitable, he realized, because as he thought it, he knew he didn't have anything comforting to say to Rick, either. They gained the highway and drove west, into the sun and dust.

They were driving past the board and message in Haddington—which had the same MY HOUSE mini-sermon on its eastern face—when Rick spoke up, addressing Paul, but loud enough that it was meant for them all to hear. "Hey?" he said. "You remember that pen pal I told you about, right?"

Paul's parents turned their heads slightly to the back seat and both nodded.

"The one in Montana?" said Paul. "Albertan, though? Something like that."

"What was her name again?" asked Paul's father, in an amiable and hopeful tone.

"Tammy," said Rick, pausing. "Tammy Vine."

Paul groaned. "Oh, right. How did we forget that?"

"And so," said Paul's mother. "Tammy Vine. What about her? You told us in one of your letters that she seemed a nice enough person. Though really something like that must be awfully hard to decipher from a letter, don't you think?"

Paul's father affected a surprised expression, eyes wide, mouth ajar. "Didn't you and I exchange letters for a year before we got married, when I was up north doing my teaching practicum?" He grinned at her, though he was doing it for his sons' entertainment, and that made Paul and Rick grin, too. Paul liked the way his father had always gently teased his mother, as if to try and help her take herself less seriously. Not that it had worked.

"Keep your eyes on the road. And that was different. You know it."

"Oh? How so?"

"Good question," said Rick. "How so, Mum? Because Dad wasn't in jail, maybe?"

"That's not what I meant," said Maureen, who had taken to facing straight ahead. Paul could see bits of spiky hair sticking up above the headrest.

"Whatever," said Paul. "So what about her, this Tammy Vine?"

"Well," Rick said, halting. "I . . . I think we're pretty close, even though she's living in Stennets, in Montana, right now. It's not far from the Idaho panhandle. You know that part of the world, hey, Dad? Isn't that around where you were born? Sandpoint?"

Paul's father nodded. "Well, Coeur d'Alene, actually."

"I thought you were born in Sandpoint?" said Maureen, looking at her husband with some surprise.

"Moved there before I was one. But I was born in Coeur d'Alene." He paused. Paul smiled, knowing his father was about to recite the line that was now the only reference he ever made to dodging the Vietnam draft. "Born in the USA. Alive in Canada, eh."

Rick didn't smile or laugh, but instead turned his attention to a pile of letters on his lap, which he'd removed from the small duffel bag at his feet.

"What are those?" said Paul. "Are those all her letters?"

Rick nodded. "They helped, a lot."

There were at least fifty, maybe more, and Paul was certain that the letters themselves were giving off a faint odour, the faded tones of a floral perfume. The letters appeared worn, not exactly grubby, but used, referenced, like a collection of favourite recipe cards. During his last couple of years inside, Rick had mentioned more than once that he had a pen pal, but he'd never hinted during previous visits, or in any of his letters to the family, that this Tammy was more than just someone he wrote to in order to pass the time and ease the deadly boredom he so often complained about.

"This was the first one," he said, meticulously locating the edge of a piece of foolscap within an envelope, as if the paper were ancient parchment in danger of disintegration if handled too briskly. He teased the paper from the envelope with his thumb and forefinger, and the care he took made him appear girlish to Paul, which Paul found ironic, since Rick wasn't that way at all, and typically, historically, went to great pains to prove it. It had been part of the mix that had twice put him in prison, first for assault, next for aggravated assault.

"It's only a page," said Paul, gesturing to the letter. "Not even on both sides."

"It was her first one. What's she going to do, spill everything on the first date?!"

"What does it say?" said Maureen. She didn't turn her head as she asked.

"Hello, mostly. Pleased to meet me. Explaining why she's writing. She says in the first one that she decided to write me because she heard we're lonely all the time. Well, the ones that aren't queer anyway. She says she likes writing letters and that she got my name from a mutual friend . . . a guy I used to know. . . . Anyways, she got my name, wrote, and look what happened. I mean, you don't think there's miracles? Listen to this: 'I make cups and mugs and plates. I'd be happy to send you one some day, if that's the kind of thing you think you could use. Are you allowed stuff like that in jail? Isn't that an awful thing, Rick, to have to ask that question? I mean, why wouldn't you be allowed a silly thing like a plate or a coffee mug? Anyway, you let me know if it's okay for you to have a coffee mug, and I'll send you one, okay?'"

"Did she send it?" said Paul. "The mug?"

Rick reached into his duffel bag, and sifted through an assortment of unfolded T-shirts, jeans, socks, underwear, magazines, books, and videocassettes. A deck of playing cards with the words *Survival: Be Prepared* on the box fell out onto the seat beside Paul. He picked it up and handed it to Rick, who tossed it back into the bag. Finally, he pulled out a long grey woollen sock. It was lumpy and heavy at the toe. Grinning like a Christmas party Santa sinking an arm into his gift bag, Rick reached into the sock and came up with the mug. He held it in front of Paul. After first instructing her husband to keep his eyes on the road, Maureen turned around to look.

It was a clay mug, bright red, thickly lacquered. *RICK* was looped around the surface in large lazy letters. The handle was shaped like a cell key. Rick stared at his mug as if it were an archeological relic, turning it this way and that, lovingly blowing away a speck of dust. Paul thought for a moment his brother might actually put the mug against his cheek and nuzzle it.

"It's cheery," said Maureen. "Sort of cute."

". . . Cool," said Paul.

"I used it every day."

He put the mug back in the sock, wrapped the sock in a pair of jeans, and then buried the whole bundle inside his duffel bag. After returning the bag to the floor, Rick put the stack of letters back on his lap, speaking as he pulled out the next one. "So, anyway, I wrote back telling her about me. Believe it or not . . . she still wrote back." He paused and let his eyes rest on the letters, as if he still somehow could not believe it had all happened. "I mean . . . I'm sure it's not going to work out," he said as if talking to himself. He peeked up. "Stuff like this doesn't ever really happen, does it?"

"Don't believe that for a minute," said Brian with mock sternness. "Why wouldn't it work?"

"Well, for starters they've never met," said Maureen.

The air in the car went stale, but Paul's father abruptly said, "I want to hear another letter. Tell us some more about Tammy."

Rick took another letter out of its envelope, a letter made up of two pieces of foolscap with writing on both sides. The letters, Paul sensed, were in chronological order. It was obvious Rick had arranged them carefully, whatever the criteria. And each envelope had been torn in exactly the same place, not along the top, but at the end nearest the stamp. Each opening was precise and clean, with no torn edges or shredded leaves. Paul noticed then that each envelope was numbered in the bottom right hand corner, in ink, in Rick's hand. Tammy herself must have also been an organized person; despite a correspondence of at least a couple of years, every letter she'd sent to Rick had come in the same size and colour of envelope, and each page of foolscap—so far—was of the same make. The stack was deeply substantial, and it seemed to Paul's eye that the letters toward the bottom of the pile—the most recent—were the thickest. What did that mean? Paul gazed upon them with a kind of greed in his heart. In his brother's lap was a life, a relationship, a connection of emotions he himself had experienced only once, many years earlier. How satisfying it would have been to have owned those letters. It almost didn't matter what was inside them. They contained something, and no matter what it was, it was a something Paul didn't have. And wasn't that basically all love was, learning how to cherish the something replacing the nothing?

Rick scanned the second letter, but must have decided it held nothing suitable for the narrative he was trying to generate. He folded it back into the envelope and began flipping through the rest of the stack, searching them as if he were trying to locate a certain LP from a cardboard box collection. He was concentrating. Paul was taken with the notion that Rick was reading from these letters only partly for his family's benefit, that the bigger motivation was that he wanted to read them for himself, now, to read them outside the walls for the first time, read them because he couldn't wait to see if they still carried the hope and magic they had inside. He kept fingering through the pile, and a third of the way through it he halted, pulled out a letter, examined the envelope briefly, then extracted the pages.

"Here's a good one." He cleared his throat again, wiped at the opening of his nostrils with his thumb and forefinger. "We'd been writing for about a year by this point. 'Hi Good Looking.'" Rick paused and smiled. "We'd exchanged photos."

Paul turned to the page of writing on Rick's lap. He could see long strings of words in blue ink on white paper. The handwriting was blockish, small and messy, almost as if she were hurriedly printing, rather than taking the time to write longhand to someone. It was not handwriting to make you fall in love with the person behind it. There were dashes, ellipses, and lots of exclamation marks. Paul wondered what Rick thought of her sloppy writing, since Rick had always done well in English and even used to talk of writing novels, though he didn't say those things anymore.

"'Hope you're doing all right these days!'" said Rick, reading from Tammy's letter. "'Keep your chin up . . . you're more than halfway through now, and I pray for you every day, for strength, for courage, for patience . . . especially for patience, Rick, because patience is what we all lack, it's what gets us in trouble. I don't mean to preach. Sorry. But you can't be impatient, because that will just bring you more unhappiness and trouble. I've been thinking about you and when you're getting out. That will be an important day. But you probably shouldn't think too much about it. Maybe you can hold it up like a light when it gets too dark for you to see. I think that's how I'd look at it if I was in your position. Like the lights at the airport, you know? Something that's maybe far away, but close, too, something I can see and count on, and put my trust in. Does that make sense? Something to . . . I don't know, to close on in.'" Rick stopped reading out loud, but let his eyes wander up and down the page as if he were trying to memorize it, or was testing how well he'd already memorized it.

"That is amazing," said Paul, though he was thinking how naïve this woman sounded. "Are these people paid by Corrections Canada?"

Rick laughed at the joke, but Maureen reached over to the radio and turned it on. "I hope nobody minds," she said. "It's just about time for the news." She turned the volume up so that it could be heard easily in the back seat. The CBC newscast came on and an authoritative male voice began discussing the political situation in Alberta and Canada, amid speculation about both a provincial and a federal election in the next year or so. Maureen leaned forward, as if this were a piece of news she'd been keenly awaiting. Paul also listened in, partly because the CBC tended to be his default station, but also because he was waiting to hear if the name Daniel Code came up—Code, who was heavily favoured to win the upcoming leadership vote of a relatively new but already popular western conservative breakaway party, was the subject of a magazine profile Paul was about to begin writing. A female commentator was introduced and offered the opinion that Alberta tended to bracket the content of debate in Canada, whether through the envy of its fiscal position or the derision of its social policy. "We need to bring moderation to the politics of this province," she was saying. "We cannot go on being seen by the rest of the country as rural Christian rednecks. This is in fact a sophisticated and highly urbanized province, and . . ."

"CBC!" said Maureen vehemently. "Lefties." She switched the radio to a classic rock station playing a tune by the Doors. She turned the volume up again, and seemed to have forgotten about everyone else in the car. Paul glanced to his brother. Rick, holding a letter from a woman he said he loved, a woman who'd said she loved him, was gazing at the back of his mother's head, his eyes unblinking, his cheeks hollowed out. He licked the corners of his mouth, then folded the letter carefully and replaced it in its envelope, after which he riffled through the stack to find the right spot for it in the arrangement. Paul was watching his brother, ready to offer him a smile if he happened to look up, but Rick didn't look up. As they drove through the stark, pure light of the late afternoon, like riders chasing the falling sun back to camp, Rick concentrated on the papers in his lap, reading for himself. He surfaced when they got close to Calgary, when their father said, as he had for thirty years returning on drives, "Thar she blows." Rick stared out the window at the panorama before them. Paul supposed that technically the city was a part of the prairies, yet it was encircled by such differing landscapes. The sharp granite tumbling off the Rocky Mountains in the west gave way to the foothills that eventually shook themselves out into a dusty prairie stretching a thousand miles to the east. Driving into Calgary from the east or northeast was always thrilling for Paul, as the skyline emerged out of the flatness of the prairie with the mountains as the backdrop, a skyline made up of the province's true spires of faith, the bank and oil towers straining skyward, forty, fifty, sixty storeys.

    This was a place he couldn't imagine leaving, though Alberta's oftenbackward political culture had turned him into a habitual ranter, usually in print. While his mother up in the front seat was adding nuance to her views about the neocommunist tendencies of the CBC, Paul gave himself over to recalling an essay he'd published a few years before,

"Albertans Anonymous," after the United States had invaded Iraq. In the essay, pretending to be at an AA meeting where he confessed how much he both loved and hated Alberta, he'd railed against the rabidly conservative provincial government for gutting health care and education solely so they could claim it wasn't working. He also condemned the premier for outrageous gerrymandering, pandering to the rural religious right, persecuting gays, denigrating the disabled, and even for offering to support George W. Bush in Iraq, despite not having the legislative authority to do so. This piece still held the record at *2.2.4.*, the magazine that employed Paul, for most Letters to the Editor.

"Hey Rick," Paul said, turning to face his brother, who was still gazing out the window. "You got the mag inside, right?"

"*2.2.4.*? Yeah, every issue."

"What did you think of my Albertans Anonymous essay?"

Rick widened his eyes to their limits, like some B-movie actor confronted by a giant bug, and then he started to laugh. "You're a commie, is what I think. Or were you just messing with us, like, satire or something?"

"You didn't agree with me?"

"Agree?!" He made a sour face. "Are you kidding? I almost had Mum and Dad do an intervention. It's a good thing nobody reads your magazine."

"It's true," said Paul's father, affecting a serious tone. "About the intervention, I mean. He did suggest it, but your mother told him I'd have to be carted away, too." Paul's mother didn't laugh, just nodded soberly, as if it had all nearly happened and might not have been such a bad thing.

Paul smiled at his father, and then turned to Rick. "And what do you mean by 'up here'?"

"Canada. I mean, Calgary's not so bad, but we still got a long way to go."

"To where?"

Rick snorted and shook his head. ". . . Later."

<hr />

They turned off John Laurie Boulevard into Edgewood, one of the bright, barren suburbs around Nose Hill Park high in the city's northwest. Giant homes on narrow lots glittered under the elemental Alberta sun, the late-afternoon light still surging, still angling hard off the metallic exteriors and large sparkling windows. Paul's father turned into the lane behind their house and touched the automatic garage door opener clipped to the sun visor. They pulled in and he shut off the car. Paul saw his brother looking afresh at the crowded space of the garage, and so he looked at it, too: his father's truck, an old extra freezer, a work table with tools scattered across it, bottles and cans jammed into one corner, various golf clubs leaning against the walls, an old box spring mattress, skis, poles, bicycles, a lawn mower, extension cords, and a step-ladder that for some reason was standing open near the door. There wasn't anything that didn't belong, but it was still disorganized and messy.

"This garage is a disaster," said Maureen, turning back to Paul. "A lot of this junk is yours. Didn't I ask you to clean it up so you can take what's yours back to your place?"

"I will," said Paul. "But I don't even live here. How can it be all my mess?"

"I don't care whose mess it is."

"So you're saying you want me to clean it up, even though I don't live here?"

"I'll give you a hand," said Rick, as he pulled his duffel bag over his shoulder. "I've got time, right?"

"Maybe you don't live here," Paul's father said. "But just because something isn't technically your responsibility doesn't mean you can't help."

"Let's just get inside," said Rick. "I want to have a cold beer and sit at the kitchen table. That's all."

They left the garage, with Paul bringing up the rear. He felt along the wall for the button to close the big garage door. A few weeks earlier he'd helped his father install a new automatic door opener, and the laser beam that crossed the garage entrance at shin height was sensitive to even the most apparently imperceptible of interruptions. They had tested it at some length. When they swept a hand through the beam the door reversed its action. When they broke the beam with a golf club it reversed its action. With a finger, a pen, a sheet of paper, even a pinch of sand; the same. Almost anything you could imagine using as an interruption was enough to make the door reverse its path. They hadn't had this new technology in place that long, and Paul was still fascinated by it. He found it strangely compelling that something he couldn't see could be so affected by a seemingly unrelated action. Paul allowed his forefinger to rest a moment on the small plastic button, and then he pushed once, which started in motion the surprisingly quiet gear and chain action. He watched the bottom edge of the heavy door move downward until, like a thick tomb door grinding closed, it met the concrete floor.

TWO

A bus driver locked in early morning traffic down on National Avenue leaned on his horn, and the high-pitched complaint split apart Paul's concentration. He looked out his second-floor office window and saw that the large message board of the End Time Revelation Church, half a block down on the other side of the street, had changed. Yesterday it had read, SUFFERING TRUTH DECAY? BRUSH UP ON YOUR BIBLE. This morning it said, JESUS: THE ULTIMATE WIRELESS. He laughed, took out his notebook, shook his head, and wrote the new message in the back part of the book. It seemed to Paul there had been in the last three or four years an increase around town of such message boards in front of this or that fundamentalist Christian church, and he'd been dutifully scribbling down their messages, though his reasons for doing so—beyond his harvesting impulse—were still something of a mystery to him. He closed his notebook and vowed, as he had about once a month since he began collecting the sayings, to simply walk down and meet the End Time Revelation person who'd been inventing and posting these catchy but often facile mini-homilies. Yet though he knew instinctively it couldn't fail to be a meeting worth having, he'd still not made it across the street.

Pushing his chair back, Paul stood up, slowly, letting his spine uncurl in articulated segments, like a half-length of rusty old bike chain. He groaned loudly, pleasurably; no one else was in yet. He'd been at his desk too deep into the night and then behind it again too early in the morning, and though he was always glad to be up to witness the dawn's pomegranate wash, his back ached and his thighs felt like sandbags stitched to his hips. Letting his feet drag in an agreeably listless way, he went down to National Avenue to pick up the one coffee he allowed himself during his morning's work, a strong double Americano that typically saw him through to the concentration desert of the late-morning. After glancing at a newspaper sitting on a table and chatting about the upcoming hockey season with the university student in the hip rectangular glasses who drew him his coffee every morning, Paul returned to his office, sat down, and looked up to find a person before him. It was Meena, and she was standing in his doorway, her black licorice hair and chestnut skin almost two-dimensional in relief against the linen white backdrop of the office space behind her.

"You don't look like you're doing anything important."

". . . I'm not. Why?"

"It's nine. We're waiting. For you and Harold."

"Nine?"

"9:10, actually." She jerked a thumb down the hall.

Paul followed Meena down the corridor to the meeting room. This was pleasing in ways he retained as a private distraction; Harold strictly forbade office romance and regularly threatened to fire any or all parties involved. Besides, Meena claimed to find Paul exasperating, and as a "friend" had often informed him he'd be a nightmare as a partner. "You're distracted and absent-minded," she'd said. "And you're sloppy. Not only that, you never quite say what you mean. Everything means something else. There's always a 'but' implied. I could never live with someone like that. It would drive me crazy."

Inside the board room, along the two inner walls, were framed covers from past issues, as well as scrolls celebrating the many writing and design awards 2.2.4. had won. The street noise—the honking of pissed-off drivers, the shrieks of traffic-dodging pedestrians, the shouts of construction workers—was muffled by the thick, leaded window glass, but the ambient background hum it created made Paul feel at ease the way he imagined a mother's intestinal gurglings might comfort a baby in the womb.

Su Li, the Art Director Harold had poached from *Currant* magazine in New York, looked at Paul, then at the thin-banded silver watch on her slim wrist. "On the phone?"

"Just preoccupied."

Su Li crossed her arms and pretended to be annoyed. "Gee, that's just not like you at all."

As Harold bustled and huffed his way into the board room, Paul smiled at his friend and mentor, then angled his head like a parent sarcastically welcoming a teenager late to the dinner table. "Nice of you to decide to join us."

Harold was sweating heavily, as was his habit. A fat man, Harold was hot in every season, and was constantly complaining about the heat in any room Paul had ever occupied with him. His fine, longish hair was in a state of moist disarray, as if he'd forgotten to comb it right after showering. "You were late, too," he said to Paul.

"How do you know?"

Harold looked to Meena and Su Li, who both nodded. He pulled on his shirt, tugging with a forefinger at the neck opening to introduce some cool air. "Where's the agenda?"

Meena passed Harold a sheet of paper. He took it and moved through a series of points on feature articles already assigned and in development, or ideas that had been proposed but not yet approved. Harold was always rather breezy and flippant in these meetings, a quality Paul admired, given the corporate and aesthetic pressures he was under. The disregard for formality and process, and sometimes even careful consideration, with which Harold seemed to make serious decisions was a condition Paul aspired to.

"So, Paul," said Harold, as he ticked through his list. "You're on top of this Democratic Alliance guy? Code. He's a priest?"

"Former pastor. At some rural splinter Pentecostal church. Neo-con. Old Testament. Sure winner in that party."

"Nutbar, I bet."

"Not that you're prejudging him," said Paul.

Harold made an exaggerated check mark on a sheet of paper and seemed to be preparing to move on to another item.

"Don't you want to know any more?" asked Paul.

"It's a good idea. It'll be a good story. It needs doing. What? Aren't you sure anymore?"

"I really haven't told you much about the guy. I do think we should do something pretty extensive on him. After all, he'll probably win the leadership."

"Okay."

"Except that I'm not completely sure I know what I'm doing on this one."

Harold fingered through a sheaf of papers, every bit of it unbound and messily gathered, as if he'd just that minute been forced to gather up pages from a warplane's propaganda drop. He pulled one page from the pile and looked at it. "One of the fall issues would work. Not December. October or November. Good time for a political piece. Take as much room as you need."

"Eight thousand words?"

"No."

"You just said to take as much room as I needed. It's complex. He's charismatic. He's dangerous. He's popular. It's about the interplay of ideas and personality. I need eight to do it right."

"We might get four or five thousand words in October before we have to run all those fucking Christmas perfume ads. Is that going to be enough? Five thousand?"

"No."

Harold looked around the table for effect, causing the others to smile at an exchange they had heard before, a thrust and parry that had become a kind of ritual. "We'll make it fit to five. You always write too much anyway, though this Code guy sounds like such a piece of work it might be fun to do more."

Later that day, as Paul was preparing to leave, his phone rang. It was Harold. "Come down to my office," he said in his usual wheezy voice. Harold had left Toronto eight years earlier, due, he told everyone, to the progressive worsening of his asthma. He'd walked around *The Upper Canadian* magazine gasping, often stopping in the office of a colleague just to catch his breath. It was a telling combination of the humidity and pollution in the city. The air quality index was murder. Toronto was killing him, literally. He was going to sue somebody. The mayor. City council. The premier.

Paul knew the actual problem was that Harold was fat and smoked heavily and made it a point of pride to engage in no activity that might be interpreted as exercise, going so far as to take the elevator up and down from the second-floor 2.2.4. office. Harold didn't have asthma or anything like it, though only Paul knew Harold had invented his condition. Harold had disliked Toronto but needed a different reason to leave, a reason he could use to avoid the discussions and looks and warnings and commiserations that were sure to ensue if he were to tell people he was moving west. Such was the ego of the cultural capital: leaving Toronto by choice would be viewed by everyone in the business as either intellectual entropy or an act of willful career suicide. In either case, he'd be regarded with pity, as one who had lost it or surrendered it. So he made up the asthma, and never told anyone, other than his ex-wife, until he told Paul a couple of years ago.

In the months prior to leaving Toronto Harold had received hundreds of calls of support and sympathy for his condition, as well as expressions of quiet horror at being forced to relocate to the colonies. He'd told them all he was starting a new magazine out west called *2.2.4.* (named in honour of Orwell's line in *1984* that freedom is being free to say 2 + 2 = 4, and that if that was granted, then all else followed. Orwell and Camus were Harold's moral headlights). For this small start-up, a magazine of ideas with national scope, his many friends in the business promised him support, advertising, editorial and story assistance, photography, design assistance, distribution, and frequent visits. A variety of friends Harold had made over the years while visiting Calgary, friends in the rampantly wealthy oil patch, helped fund the magazine at the start, as did a few establishment pals from Toronto. Paul appreciated that it was only because Harold was well loved that all this had come to pass precisely as he'd wanted.

Except the visits. None of Harold's friends from Toronto ever seemed to find the time to travel to Calgary, strangely, with the exception of his ex-wife, Margueritte, whose height and tower of jet-black curls had always made Paul think of Cher. She'd worked as a criminal lawyer and was now a judge. She visited two or three times a year and always seemed happy to do so, because, she'd told Paul on one visit when they were all out at dinner and she'd had a couple of glasses of wine, "Harold is a lot easier to love from a distance."

"So what's up?" said Paul, as he entered Harold's office. He slouched into a chair after moving a stack of books onto the floor, all of which seemed to relate to European film somehow, though Paul didn't look at them closely.

Harold moved a pile of papers away from the space right in front of him on his desk, as if he were making room for lunch. "How do you feel about this piece, on this kooky pastor who thinks he can become prime minister?"

"Good, I guess. I don't know. I'll know more once I meet him. I've just done background so far. It's worth doing, though. The guy could win this Democratic Alliance leadership. Then he's got a platform. Who knows, right?"

"No, quite right," said Harold, as he pulled harshly on his right ear lobe. "I'm sure he will win."

"He's got a percentage of the vote waiting for an election. The religious vote . . . well, the evangelical vote, anyway. The rural vote. Hard-line right-wingers. There's a lot of votes just right there, almost enough in itself. If he gets some real funding done, some ads, some cash to do some rolling polls . . . ," Paul shrugged. "I don't see him as a national threat, but he might get some real play."

"Listen, a goldfish would get a percentage of the vote. Fucking idiots out there. Anyway, I just wanted to bring you up to speed on a couple of things. They're not related to this Code character, but, I don't know, it just seemed like now was a good time to let you know what's going on." He pulled a manila file folder from his desk drawer and placed it on the space he'd cleared in front of him.

"What do you mean, *going on*?"

"I talked with Boar last night. We had dinner, a long and really unpleasant dinner. At Capo."

"Capo!" Paul rubbed a thumb and two fingers together in the air. "Nice . . . except for the Boar part."

"We had a great Amarone." Harold placed the tip of this tongue between his thick lips, as if picking out the last little hint of wine. "Boar was paying, obviously."

Paul called to mind an image of Jonathon Boar; tall, slope-shouldered, dark lank hair, big nostrils. Boar was a former staff writer for the magazine who now acted as both its publisher and as content liaison for the InfoTrue Group/West. When Harold had sold the 2.2.4. majority ownership (but not the editorial control) two years earlier during a severe revenue drought, it had been his old University of Toronto friend and InfoTrue CEO Edgars Stranga who did the buying. Stranga, for reasons Paul never understood, encouraged Boar to quit writing so that he could pay him to take an MBA while also, as Boar had once put it, "learning the ropes of the cultural asset business." About six months ago he'd resurfaced, in a very good suit, to act as "a link," said the press release, "between the corporate and intellectual interests of the InfoTrue Group."

"So, what message of asset-enhancement and synergistic collaborative emulsification was he spreading last night?"

Harold exhaled through his nose, grimaced. He pointed at the file folder before him. "Bad bottom line, apparently."

"Bad bottom line? We're running a super tight ship right now. How can he say there's a bad bottom line?"

"He was talking about InfoTrue." He opened the folder. "Memo here, for me to distribute to the staff."

". . . What?"

"They're hurting. Bad choices. Mistimed synergies. Bad angles of convergence. Acquisition miscalculation. 9/11 hangover. Et cetera Translation: major fuck-ups. Edgars isn't happy. He's going to roll some heads in the big smoke, is my guess."

Paul glanced around Harold's office to express his impatience and frustration, but then was caught up, as he always was, by what he saw—the shelves full of all manner of books and reference manuals, a framed poster of the Alan Rudolph film, *The Moderns*, fire-hazard calibre piles of magazines jumbled randomly in rows against the side wall—not just 2.2.4., but *The New Yorker*, *Harper's*, the *Atlantic Monthly*, *Alberta Views*, the *TLS*, *Granta*; it all spoke of learning and intelligence, but more than that—curiosity, investigation, critical thought, not just as a moment but as ongoing practice. What did synergy and convergence have to do with any of that? "Boar said all that, all that shit?"

Harold nodded deeply, insofar as his triple chin allowed it. "Well, except for the rolling heads part. But I know Edgars. He looks like a gentle guy, but he likes rolling heads." Harold closed the folder, then pulled his dog-eared leather day timer off his desk and onto his lap. "Anyway, Boar wants to meet the staff in a couple weeks, after we distribute this memo, just to talk about what he calls global frameworking, or some damn thing. He wants to tell people there might be cuts, there won't be raises, we've all got to do five per cent more with five per cent less. That sort of thing."

"Is that all it means to us?"

Harold shrugged. "Jonathon doesn't like me, though he pretends to because I've got friends he wants. But he knows I don't give a shit about InfoTrue."

"Who does?"

"Shareholders, apparently. Most of them live in Berlin. I just wanted to let you know some of this stuff was going on now. Didn't want you hearing about anything second hand, or missing Jonathon's meeting."

"I don't think it would bother me to miss it."

"He told me he wants you there."

"He said that?"

"He said, 'It would be useful to Paul to make it to the meeting.'"

"'To' Paul, or 'for' Paul?"

Harold stuck out his bottom lip, lowered his brow. "I don't exactly remember."

"And so what do you think that means? Wanting me there?"

Harold shrugged and broke open a smile for his friend, a smile Paul had come to love as much as anything about him; compact, the corners of his lips turned up just slightly into the thick fat of his cheeks, so that it almost looked as if those indentations were buttressing the bulge above.

"Good question."

They both laughed. "Hey," continued Harold. "How'd it go with your brother? He's back?"

Paul shrugged. "Yeah, he's back. We'll see. It's tough. For him. For all of us. You know."

Harold nodded and narrowed his eyes. "No, not really," he said. "Anyway, good luck."

"Thanks." Paul stood to go but stopped at Harold's door. He turned back to Harold and had the urge to tell him more about Rick, about growing up with his brother, with their problems then and now. But he hesitated, and then the impulse was gone. It wasn't that Paul didn't trust Harold. He wasn't Paul's best friend in the common understanding of the word; there was fifteen years between them, they didn't spend too much informal time together and didn't have much of a social history outside work. But he was someone Paul trusted, fully, and there was no reason not to share his thoughts and anxieties about his family. Paul knew Harold would have been curious, compassionate, supportive, and yet also clear and direct in his opinions on the whole mess. This was Harold's gift, or one of them, anyway.

"I might be in and out for the next little while. Just to be around home if I'm needed. You know, to help out. I don't know. Moral support . . . whatever."

Harold had picked up his phone. "You'll be good at that."

"Are you winding me up?"

Harold hit a speed dial number then looked back to Paul, his face plain, unexpressive. He put the receiver to his face. "No, I'm not. You'll be good at that. That's why I said it."

Two days later, Paul was seated at a table booked by Daniel Code's media liaison, a woman named Rachel. Code was twenty minutes late for lunch. From where Paul sat, he could see the lineup into the patio at Bravada. No Code. Paul returned to that morning's paper, the front page of which featured an interview with Code. In the piece, he stated that his plan for operating as a member of parliament and leader of the Democratic Alliance Party—should he be "fortunate enough to have the people, who are always right," choose him as leader—was simple: he was "going to let his conscience speak." Conscience was one of his self-described Code Words, a roster of platitudinous signifiers, with Honesty, Accountability, Responsibility, and Transparency forming the remainder of the quintet, a grouping he had further simplified to the over-referred-to and campaign-defining acronym CHART. His campaign workers wore and distributed blue on green buttons that read *The Code CHART*.

The provinces of western Canada, Code said in the interview, suffered from an alienation, an isolation, that he felt deep in his soul. He would address this without fear of reprisals from the nabobs who controlled the central Canadian power structures. Nor did he fear political correctness. It was an evil of its own sort, he said, and too many people were afraid to speak the truth for fear of being branded as intolerant or bigoted. Daniel Code, former pastor, did not fear such outcomes. "My heart guides me," he said. "And the Lord owns my heart."

Paul signaled to the waitress, who was a few tables away, and she nodded in his direction, smiling with such exceptional cuteness it could only be an artificial construct. After finishing with the table she'd been tending to, she came and stood over Paul. She had to be six feet tall, and looked like a pole vaulter—or at least how Paul, at this moment in his life as an unattached man who had not had sex for four years, imagined a pole vaulter might look in a white halter top and tight Capris.

"No phone call?"

"No. I hope your date shows up, though," she said, smiling wide and amiably teasing him. "Wouldn't that be just awful if you got stood up. I'll bring you another diet coke."

She turned and made her way back off the patio and inside the restaurant. She was shamelessly pandering for a large tip, but it was working. A couple of minutes later, she was back at the table with a fresh drink. "Hey, guess what? There was a call a couple of minutes ago. Your date is on the way."

"It's not a date," he said, feeling defensive and embarrassed at the same time. "It's business."

"Oh, sure. It was a woman that called."

Paul nodded and surreptitiously watched her sway through the tables, back inside the restaurant. He took a moment to check the surroundings of the patio again. It was not a perfect place for a first meeting, not a place he would have chosen. It was in the shade, which was good, but there were other tables a bit too close. Also, the traffic on Seventeenth Avenue was heavy, and occasionally a large truck rumbled by—making it difficult to hear, let alone tape. That wasn't too serious, though, since the recorder was mostly a prop, meant to help Code believe that Paul knew what he was doing (which he'd never yet fully felt in his six years writing for the magazine). Still, he always tried to project a persona when interviewing: competent, politely skeptical, and, above all else, amiable. Code, like any politician, would retreat if he sniffed a takedown. So Paul planned to work slowly, to act as an enabler. He'd yet to see a politician sprint off the plank, but he'd watched a few trip at the edge. Get Code's toes over the open air and be there to observe what happened next. This was Paul's job. He loved his job.

Paul was just about to get up and find the washroom when a shadow fell across his notebook and tape recorder. He looked up to find Daniel Code staring at him, smiling. "Paul," he said. "I'm so sorry I'm late." He held out a hand as he sat down. "Just a call I had to take. An organizer from Black Hills, my riding, had to have an answer about something for an event tonight."

"Not a problem," said Paul, half standing and taking Code's hand. It was a solid, fellow-citizen handshake—briefly held and firm enough, but not so strong and fiercely gripping as to calculatedly signal *strength* or *power* or *confidence*, which was the kind of handshake message most politicians thought served them best, especially when applied with a winning smile and words of respect for the views of one's constituents. Paul knew a communications consultant in Ottawa who offered half-day seminars, at one hundred dollars an hour, on the art and science of the political handshake, a fact Paul found personally galling yet was professionally thankful for, since he knew he would eventually get around to turning it into an uncomplimentary article.

"Anyway," continued Paul. "You're busy, what with the race and all, and so I just want to say thanks first off for taking the time to meet. I'm hoping to chat a couple of times with you over the next few weeks, and see you in action. I hope that will all be okay."

Code nodded. "Just check it all out with Rachel. Of course, it's always a pleasure to spend time with the media."

". . . Really?"

Code sat back, smoothly crossed his legs. "You're just people, trying to do the best job you can. I respect that. We're not so different, really. We have to communicate. That's what it's all about. I know how good you are at what you do, and I try to do my best at what I do."

Paul did a swift microassessment of whether Code was that audacious—to spin a writer so nakedly five seconds after meeting him. He decided it was too clever by half, and therefore more likely that Code was parroting one of the tropes drilled into him by his handlers, choosing from a selection of standard introductions in the same way a chess master with a quiver of openings will use the one that best suits the moment and the opponent. Paul studied Code's face. Already, it was blank. His eyeballs looked as if they had been scooped from a bowl of pectin, lacquered, and then squeezed back into his face. His neck, chin, and cheeks had been flawlessly shaven and smoothed over with emollients. His expression was bland and affable. There was genius in it, a political brilliance, to be able to give precisely nothing away. Code continued to smile benignly, but soon cleared his throat to signal that Paul's moment of physiological analysis had expired. Control freak, thought Paul.

"How was your little break from campaigning? You were away for a few days last week, weren't you? In Penticton, or Kelowna?"

Code nodded, angled his head, pushed out his bottom lip. It all looked natural. He was presenting a flawless impersonation of an actual human being. "The weather didn't help."

"Bad?"

"Rain."

Paul sucked on his teeth hoping this would project commiseration. "Shame."

"For the little ones mostly. I'm happy just having time off, but they go stir crazy inside all day."

"That must be tough."

"Do you have children?"

Paul laughed. "No."

"Why is that funny? Don't you want to have children?"

"I'd love to have children," Paul replied. "No partner."

Code gave Paul an avuncular smile. "I'm sure you'll soon find the right woman to share your life with. It's a joyous thing. I was married for nearly fifteen years before my wife passed away about fifteen years ago in a boating accident." He stopped and looked over Paul's shoulder, then back, his expression one of sadness and surprise. "I can't believe she's been gone now the same number of years we were married."

"You got married thirty years ago!" said Paul, reaching for his notebook and tape recorder. "Well, we might as well start here." He hit Record on the machine and started scribbling in his notebook. "I thought you weren't even fifty yet?"

"I'm not," said Code. "I'm forty-nine. Marjorie and I met in high school, and got married right afterwards. We were together until her accident."

"Incredible," said Paul, half under his breath.

"Why is that incredible?"

"No, I didn't mean that in a bad way. It's just that, well, to get married so young."

"Love and commitment aren't fashionable anymore, aren't cool. That's more a comment on our world, our modern ways, than anything, don't you think?"

Paul raised his eyebrows. "Umm, I guess so. I haven't really given it a lot of thought. Getting a date seems hard enough, so I usually just worry about that."

Code didn't smile along with Paul. "Well, perhaps you should give it more thought. It's important. Besides, it's a better way to live. Marriage was delightful and having children is a joy. We have three."

"What are their names again?"

"Kevin is the baby, he's twenty-two, studying agriculture at the university here in Calgary. Eric, he's twenty-five, and he's just finishing dentistry up in Edmonton. And I believe you've already had contact with our eldest."

"Excuse me?"

"Rachel is our daughter. She's twenty-eight, and is doing graduate work in political science at the University of Toronto, but she's taken time off to act as my media liaison. She thought the experience would be of value. She's doing a fabulous job, and I'm very proud of her. She's here with me today, but she's making some calls and catching up on other things right now."

"I thought you said before that the rain on your holiday made the 'little ones' go stir crazy. I guess I thought you were referring to your children . . ."

"Grandchildren," said Code. "I've got three."

The pole vaulter emerged from behind Paul, draping her hand across his shoulder as she moved to stand toward the middle of their table. "Hi, I'm back!" she exclaimed, turning to Paul and then Code. "I can see you were telling me the truth. You're lucky."

After she had taken their orders and moved off to another table, Paul explained, "She thought I was waiting for a woman at first."

"I'm sure she's delighted I showed up."

"It's her job to flirt. She works for tips."

"That's uncharitable, Paul. Toward both of you. I don't see what's not to like, on either side."

Paul placed his notebook on the table and scratched the back of his neck. The man was at once so formal and yet so personal it brought back to Paul a memory of his younger life, from an earlier version of who he was—an altar boy talking with the parish priest at St. Luke's in northwest Calgary.

"You know," said Paul, laughing through an exhalation, "I don't think I've ever started off an interview with a politician by discussing my love life."

Code nodded benevolently, as if to say, No problem.

"I'm just going to quickly use the washroom," said Paul, hoping it didn't sound cowardly or deflective. "Before our food arrives."

Code nodded again, and Paul got up, shutting off the tape recorder. After leaving the patio, he passed through the foyer and saw a woman sitting in a chair with a binder-sized datebook on her lap, a pen in her left hand, and a cell phone to her right ear. She was bent over slightly, as if straining to hear and write something at the same time. This image perfectly fit the profile of a media liaison or personal assistant, and he knew he was looking at Rachel Code, though her face was hidden behind a long screen of hair that was so luxuriously auburn it was almost black.

After finishing in the bathroom, he walked out to the foyer where Rachel Code was still bent over her book, on the phone. As he passed, she reached up and curled a flap of hair behind an ear, though she didn't look up. She's already given her parents grandchildren, thought Paul. It was incredible. She may have been twenty-eight but she looked twenty. It made him think of Rick and Tammy, and he wondered if they'd talked already about children, even though they still hadn't even met face to face. It wouldn't have surprised him. Judging by the letters Rick had read aloud, there seemed nothing they hadn't already shared with one another. A cloak of loneliness fell over Paul. His legs went heavy and dull, but he kept his pace steady through the foyer so that the Code woman wouldn't look up or notice him.

Paul stopped at the door to the patio. Not for the first time he wondered what his life might have been like with Emily. His memories were self-indulgent and melancholy—summer nights at their secluded spot on Nose Hill, making love, or not, lying out under the humbling starscape above—and when he gave himself over to this past, which he did too often, it suited his view of himself as some restless, existential character in a sombre European arthouse movie.

The patio door screeched open. Paul could see to the table where Code was seated. Their food had arrived, but he wasn't touching it, and seemed to be waiting for Paul to return. He was sitting quite still, with posture so crisp it was almost a kind of caricature. Paul had purposely taken the seat in the shade so as to leave Code staring into the sun, but Code had placed a pair of dark, chunky sunglasses over his eyes. He looked like a presidential bodyguard.

Paul sat down and before they started eating, he switched on the tape recorder and reached for his notebook. Looking down his roster of questions, he launched in with those easiest to answer. Today would be about building a rapport, now that he knew Code was amenable to multiple interviews and to having Paul follow him on the trail. There would be ample time to work toward questions of actual interest to Paul. That there was no rush would intensify the satisfaction of the process. The extraction of information when writing a profile was almost teasingly sexual; he would probe, advance slowly, move toward the payoff. The metaphor didn't extend past that point, however; Paul had not stocked his relationship pool with past subjects.

Over lunch, Code answered every question in unsurprising ways. Why did you choose to run for elected office? *Because I felt a duty towards public service.* What impact has the political life had on your family? *My family has been supportive and is excited by the challenge, but they recognize there is always a sacrifice to be made.* Where do you see yourself in five, ten years? *Impossible to say, though I want to remain vibrant and challenged, and able to serve my constituents, whoever they might be.* What are your priorities should you get into office? *Education, health care, and security for all. We need to go forward, yet protect those that need our protection.* What's your political style? *I'm not afraid to say what I believe as an individual, but I'm deeply committed to consultation and communication.*

Paul tried to divine whether Code was keeping his powder dry with genuine intelligence in reserve or was dull-witted, simply calling up rote answers to stay on message and out of trouble. It was difficult to tell. His answers were anodyne, but his manner was filled with hesitations and knowing looks, as if he were trying to signal to Paul that they were being watched by a third party and he was unable to speak freely. Paul decided Code was trying to project thoughtfulness and camaraderie, but he was no intellectual. This would hardly be unusual. Politicians who came equipped with a hi-test brain tended to burn out or get torn in two on the Manichean rack of public opinion. It wasn't as though most voters were thinkers, either.

Code finished the final bite of his sandwich, and moved an empty chair out from the table, as if he were expecting it to be occupied soon, which proved to be the case. The woman Paul had seen in the foyer strode to the table and sat down. She looked at Paul through small fashionable glasses.

"Hi, Paul. My name is Rachel Code. I'm the media liaison for the leadership campaign. I believe I left you a message, once, anyway."

She was tall, almost as tall as he, but with a body like a green sapling. She wasn't beautiful, exactly—misaligned teeth, a nose that had once been badly broken, thin lips—but in summer clothing she radiated a graceful physicality, a spare clean strength; this was a marked contrast to how Paul felt about his own body, with his nonexistent muscle tone, baggy clothing, always messy hair, plain glasses, his default distracted walk that Meena in the office had labeled "the Munk shuffle." All that saved him from physical ridicule, he was sure, was the lanky height he'd inherited from his father. It hid a lot of faults.

"Pleased to meet you," he said.

"No, the pleasure is mine. This is great that you're doing this. I told my father that I've read many of your pieces in 2.2.4. It's my favourite magazine."

"You're kidding?"

Displaying her irregular teeth, she gave Paul a confused smile. "Don't you think it's a great magazine? I mean, you work there."

"No, no. It's just that, I don't know, I don't hear that too often from the public."

"I find that hard to believe."

"We mostly get complaints or abuse."

"It's the same in politics, Paul," said Code, his tone so fraternal it almost made Paul laugh. "We hear the most from complainers or people who want something. When people are happy, they keep their mouths shut for some reason."

"Well," said Rachel, leaning back in her chair, ignoring her father. "I think that's a shame. I ought to go home right now and write a letter to the editor of 2.2.4. magazine saying that I think you're all doing a great job. How about that?" She paused. "Of course . . . I can't actually do that *right now*, today, given the situation here. But I will afterwards. I mean it."

Blocking out the smile, the rich brown hair, the laugh like bell chimes, Paul wondered how she could possibly be telling the truth. If she had been sincere about reading the magazine, she would surely have read his piece on Purves Mackie, the conservative federal MP Paul had eviscerated so completely that Mackie had threatened to sue 2.2.4. Or she'd have read his recent short essay on the political theory of Mavis Eichorn, the Democratic Alliance strategist Paul had likened to the love child of Margaret Thatcher and Augusto Pinochet. Had she read either of those pieces, she ought to have been a wreck at the thought of Paul doing a full profile of her father. But Paul reminded himself, again, that he was looking at it from only one side of the prism. He was always, *always*, surprised that politicians, or anyone really, ever talked to a journalist. But talk they did, politicians, and at length—more than any other profile subject, whether it was athletes, artists, business tycoons. Politicians talked because they always believed the process was theirs to control. They always thought the narrative they wanted told would get told. They were always mistaken.

Code stood up abruptly, twisting slightly and reaching behind to pull his wallet from his back pocket. As he did so, Paul noticed that Code's fly was wide open. It was an unsettling thought to consider it had been agape throughout lunch. Rachel hadn't noticed the open fly, but Paul thought a little male bonding could go a long way toward facilitating ongoing access to Code, so he cleared his throat loudly and made a nodding stare back and forth between Code's face and crotch. He cottoned on immediately, and looked down, at which point Rachel noticed as well.

"Dad," she said in a hissing voice. "For heaven's sake."

"Damn." As he discreetly zipped up, Code winked at Paul and said, "Old campaigning trick. Works every time."

They all laughed, and Code laid enough money on the table to cover the bill. He went off to the washroom, saying good-bye to Paul and telling Rachel he'd meet her at the car. Paul reached to the notes on the table and handed a twenty back to Rachel. "It's okay," he said. "I can expense it."

She took the money. "Whatever you say." She opened her date book and made a brief scan of the next few days. "You just let me know when you want to talk to my father again. He's obviously very busy, but we'll make it work."

"So you have three kids, hey?"

Rachel looked up from her date book.

"Your father said he has three grandchildren. I assumed, since he said you were the oldest . . ."

She smiled at Paul, but in a different way than before. There was no crinkle around the eyes, no show of teeth. "My youngest brother and his wife got married early, just like Mum and Dad, and they had a girl and then twin boys last year."

Paul reached for his notebook and pen in so transparent a gesture that he nearly abandoned it halfway. "So . . . so, you're studying political science, your father tells me. A PhD?"

"Yes, that's right."

"What area?"

"The collusion of the press and the political class in liberal democracies."

"Yikes," said Paul, trying to make her laugh, though inside he was busy parsing the ways in which simply the title of her thesis showed the degree to which she was smarter and tougher than he was.

Rachel smiled again, in a nicer way—probably, Paul thought, only to relieve him of his embarrassment.

"Anyway, yes, I'll let you know when I'll need to speak to your dad, I mean, to Mr. Code, again. Is it *Pastor*? He doesn't use *Pastor* anymore, does he. Anyway, it'll certainly be within the next week, and then I'll be at the leadership convention, and then I'll want to speak to him again after he wins."

Rachel raised her eyebrows and drew them together. "Do you think he'll win?"

"Don't you?"

She looked at him as if seeking his reassurance. "I don't know."

Paul was about to offer her that reassurance, but he stopped and saw immediately what he was doing, what he was letting himself fall into. People had roles to fill; what was left was fantasy. He now had enough material to make it work. He could stop collecting.

"I'll call you when I need to speak to him next."

Rachel stood up. She put her hand out, and Paul grasped it gently. It felt at first as light and delicate as one of the balsa wood airplanes he'd glued together as a child, but she squeezed with authority and it gave Paul the confidence to squeeze back. It's just not right, thought Paul. Feeling a sudden want, but to know it could never be returned. It wasn't the way things were supposed to work. Or was it? He knew what his sister, Lisa, would say about the whole thing, that attraction was and always would be about power. She might be right, or she might be wrong. But if Lisa was right about the way relationships worked—or didn't work—the one thing Paul knew was that he held no power, or at least none he was aware of.

He stayed behind as he always did after an interview, sitting by himself making notes. It was the part of an interview he enjoyed most, after the subject had left, and he was alone to collate impressions. After spending fifteen or twenty minutes with his thoughts, with regular and cheery coffee refills from the pole-vaulter, he picked up his Blackberry and checked his messages both on the cell and back at the office. Four messages total, two on the cell, two from the office.

The first, from Harold. "Paul. Harold. Meeting with Boar, and Stranga, on Friday, ten AM, our boardroom. You will attend, and you and I will both be prepared to quit if they challenge our autonomy."

The second, from his mother. "Hi, dear. It's your mother. Dinner tonight is around six. Can you bring a couple bottles of red wine home with you, if you get the chance?"

The third, from Stelio, the building manager of his apartment complex, who was also overseeing the renos. "Pole," he said in his old-world Italian accent. "Things not too bad so far. You come by to check if you like. All fine, yet there is always the unforeseen, heh heh. Right now, it is impossible for me to predict the unforeseen, but, of course, I will immediately notify you in the event that future unforeseen problems become foreseeable in the present."

The fourth message was from Rachel, who had been sitting beside him not twenty minutes earlier. "Hi, Paul. This is Rachel Code. I'm just doing a follow-up call to your meeting with my father. Please don't hesitate to give me a call at any time if you need any information about him or the campaign. You have my cell number, and I keep it on pretty much all the time. Oh . . . hang on a sec. (Paul could hear muffled voices in the background.) Hi, I'm back, sorry. Yes, let me know when you want to schedule the next interview. Things are filling up, but I'm sure we can work it in. Also, my father wanted to tell you that he's giving a speech at the Rotary club tomorrow morning at seven AM. He said you wanted to see him in action. Bye for now."

Placing his cell back on the table, Paul took a moment to compartmentalize the messages and consider them separately, rather than in a jumble. The meeting with InfoTrue was unsettling but not unpredictable. The only real variable was the level of Harold's bile. It could even be fun if the tone was right. Of course, he might not have a job at the end of it, though this seemed unlikely. It was ridiculous to think InfoTrue would toy with the only asset that gave it serious cultural cachet.

The second message, from his mother, was the most uncomplicated on the face of it, but what it alluded to—dinner—was a source of anxiety pasted to a sad kind of expectation. Paul wanted to see Rick. He wanted to be close to Rick again. He would do everything he could to make it happen, but there was an emotional murkiness to it all, a lack of clarity or certainty, that confused Paul. Why wasn't he excited, simple as that, at the thought of getting to spend time again with his brother? The dinner was also a chance to spend time with his mother and father and Lisa, and that wouldn't be unpleasant, though it would have been misleading to say he was looking forward to it.

The third message, from Stelio, was not overly worrisome. Paul thought about dropping by to check in on how it was going, and then discarded the notion; if he'd had any furnishings or possessions of value, or even if he lived in one of the nicer units in the building, he might have popped over, just to appear responsible and adult, but the only thing he owned worth more than a couple hundred dollars was his flat-panel TV, which he'd covered with bubble wrap and a quilt. Beyond that it was an IKEA futon, an IKEA couch, an IKEA table, an IKEA desk in the second bedroom, a couple hundred books on IKEA shelving, and the dishes his mother had given him when he'd moved out seven or eight years earlier.

Lastly, the call from Rachel. She sounded positive, not hesitant as she had during his clubfooted step into her personal space. He wouldn't make that mistake again.

The pole-vaulter stopped at his table. "How was your business lunch?"

"Fine."

"Good." She smiled and left.

Paul had to pay with a credit card because he had no cash, and when he opened the folder with the credit card slip inside, which had been sitting in front of him for fifteen minutes, he noticed that there was writing on the back of the bill. His heart stuttered, but it read "Have a super day!" She'd inscribed a happy face underneath.

Back at the office, he called Harold, only to find he was out. There was one message in his email inbox from CodeCamp. The subject line read, "Further." It was from Rachel Code. He shook his head and muttered, "Saturation bombing." He was disappointed. She was like every other media liaison he'd had to work with and through, every other corporate or political intermediary who existed solely to shield the primary target. Part of him had fantasized at lunch that she would not just follow time-honoured practices, that she was not simply another operative. But she was. Of course she was. It was a precondition to having the job.

Dear Paul,
Just sending an email on the address you gave me at lunch, so

that you have my email address if you need it. I've also noticed here that my father has some other speaking engagements that might be of interest to you, things like a fundraising lunch Thursday in TriGlen, if you're interested. It starts at 11:30. Call if you need to.
Rachel

He added her address to his contacts list. After rereading the message one more time, he closed the program and went home for dinner.

THREE

The road to Paul's parents' house from his office on National Avenue was merely an urban nerve line, moving uphill out of the city centre, into the northwest suburbs, past so many malls, past the football stadium, past the pell-mell construction of a city still in the greed grip of an oil and gas godsend. For him it was a road that led backward, toward his childhood and who he used to be.

When Paul was a child, Edgewood was virtually the northwestern corner of the city; now, twenty-five years on, it was considered a relatively central neighbourhood. The boomtown seemed to be metastasizing at every compass point, increasing in vulgarity and barrenness as it went; his love for his city dropped a notch every time he drove north out of downtown, up Crowchild Trail, turning onto either Shaganappi or Sarcee, because all he saw were treeless hills under the occupation of thousands of monster homes jammed side by side, literally inches from one another, like some phalanx of war machines waiting for the order to advance.

He turned the last corner to his parents' house, past the One Shepherd Parish. Its message board read, JESUS WAS EITHER A LIAR, A LUNATIC, OR GOD. YOU DECIDE. In the house, Paul put the two bottles of wine on the counter. Lisa was sitting at the kitchen table reading a book and drinking beer out of a glass. Turning her small oval face to her brother as he walked in, she almost smiled at him. It hit Paul that his sister was actually not unattractive from a purely physical point of view. But if you ever put any value on that, in front of her, she'd poke your eye out.

"Hey," she said, putting a mark in her book. "How's it going?"

"Good." Paul sat down and picked up Lisa's book, turning it over as he spoke. "Melanie Klein . . . poet? No wait. Food writer, isn't she? . . . Eggplant? Or does one say *aubergine* in the academy?"

Lisa retrieved the book with exaggerated gentleness and placed it on the other side of the table, out of Paul's reach. "You shouldn't play around with tools you don't know how to operate. You could hurt yourself."

"Where is everybody, anyway?" Paul looked at his watch. "I thought Mum said dinner at six?"

"She ran out of something, so she went to the store. Dad went with her."

"Where's Rick?"

"Downstairs. In his room."

"So . . . how is he today? How does he seem?"

Lisa shrugged, turned the corners of her mouth down. "He hasn't exactly pulled me aside to have a heart to heart."

"I said, how does he *seem*? Thereby implying that I was soliciting information based on observation and the intuitive qualities I assumed you possessed. Wrongly, it appears."

"According to the impressions I've been able to gather . . . he seems, to me, to be a bit down." She took a sip of her beer. "What a shock. What does he have going for him? No job. No money. No place to live. No plans."

"That's a bit harsh."

"Is it?"

"Yes." Paul picked up his sister's beer and took a slug. "How's school?"

"I'm in university. I've been in university for seven years. I'm completing a doctorate. I finished 'school' eight years ago."

"You like that word, don't you?"

"What word?"

"*Doctorate*. You like saying it. Doctorate, doctorate, doctorate. When you say it quick like that, it's like, doctor . . . it. You know, like you're faking something. That's weird, don't you think?"

Lisa gave Paul a look of heavy-lidded tolerance. "It's the correct word for what I'm doing."

"I'm sure it is." Paul stood up. "So I take it things are going okay? With your . . . doctorate?"

Lisa crossed her arms. "It's not about okay or not okay. It's a journey. I'm a traveller."

"A journey. Right. I'm going to journey downstairs and see how Rick is doing."

Paul went to the basement of the house, to the room his mother had assigned Rick for the duration of his stay. *Impossible to tell*, Rick had replied when she'd asked him how long he would be living at home. He needed to get settled, get a job, a credit rating, get set up with Tammy. There was so much to do, he'd said, weariness plaguing his voice. Outlining the conditions necessary to fully adopt his freedom, his face had gone slack, long and flaccid like a nearly empty feed bag. Paul's heart went out to his brother. What a fate. It must have seemed insurmountable, almost beyond him, to move from the inside, from this one way, not just of life, but of thinking and feeling and breathing—with no real autonomy—to suddenly having a radically different way of life handed to you, forced on you. It tested you both ways: on the way in and the way out. And on the way out, your new life got handed to you as if responsibility and freedom were simplistically positive, as if such things were a concrete bridge to a better, reformed, and productive life rather than the rickety, swaying, rotten-planked suspension bridge it must have looked to Rick. It called for tiptoeing, for one careful foot after another, testing every board, not the sprint to the other side it was too often made out to be. Recidivism was not without its own logic. Paul wondered, not for the first time, how he might have helped to make things different in his older brother's life. A word spoken, a different one left unspoken. But that was over and done with. Things had happened.

Paul eased his head into the space of the open door frame. Rick had parked himself on the side of his bed, hands together, elbows on his knees. His duffel bag was flat and empty, sitting on the floor like a punctured beach ball. It looked as if he'd just finished unpacking, and Paul wondered why he hadn't already done that. The rectangular room was dingy and small. Paul almost made the obvious joke but decided against it. This had been Rick's room thirty years earlier, when they'd first moved into this house. In Paul's mind, in the staging of his memory play, Rick's old bedroom was so much bigger and brighter. The same was true of his old room on the other side of the basement, a room he'd be occupying for the next week or two anyway. But these basement rooms were the scenes of so many incidents, so much fun and pain, so many moments caught in the driftnet of his memory, that he was now shocked to look back inside and see how tiny and deromanticized this room in particular really was. Rick seemed to fill half of it with his muscular body.

"What are you up to?"

Rick looked up from a spot on the floor that had been holding his gaze. "Not much. You know, just catching my breath a little. What about you?"

"Thought I'd come down and say hi, see if you needed any help, or . . . I don't know, do you need to get anything? We could zip out while Mum and Dad are out."

"What sort of help?"

"I didn't mean help getting unpacked or . . . whatever. I just meant generally."

Rick stood up, and Paul saw his head nearly graze the light fixture hanging from the ceiling. It was ridiculous. Had the house shrunk? Had Rick gotten taller in jail? "Been a while since I hung out in this room," said Rick.

"There's a room upstairs, isn't there? Why did Mum put you down here?"

"She doesn't want me upstairs. Not me personally, or at least I don't think. She thinks Tammy and I might be here for a bit, and she doesn't want us upstairs. It'll be better, I agree with her on that. But I plan on having a place for us pretty soon."

"That," said Paul, smiling, "is a very good idea."

They moved toward the door together and started to go upstairs, but Rick stopped by the TV room. Paul had spent a fair portion of his first twenty-five years slumped on the various pieces of furniture here, holding the remote, surfing. The thought made him smile. He'd never considered it wasted time, then or now. To this day, he loved TV and didn't trust people who claimed to despise it.

"You know, there is one thing you could do, one thing I would hugely appreciate, but it's asking a lot."

"What's that?"

Rick started upstairs again, talking as he went. "You don't have to."

"Run it by me."

Lisa was no longer in the kitchen, probably because she'd heard them coming up. The room was almost blindingly white now that the sun was slanting in hard from the west. The kitchen had once been a cluttered and welcoming room, earth toned, always warm, the place where the family met by design or accident. At least this was how Paul remembered it; but after he moved out and Rick went back to jail, their mother had renovated. Everything was white—the cupboards, the counters, the floor, the blinds—and it always smelled of a piney disinfectant.

"What I said before, about Tammy, well, it wasn't completely right."

"... She's a man?" said Paul, making his voice incredulous.

Rick briefly closed his eyes. "Funny. No, just that she's not coming here."

"But you read those letters . . ."

"What I mean is, she wants to come here. She wants to be with me. Man, I'm not saying this right."

"It's okay, Rick." Paul put his hand on his brother's upper arm.

"It's not that big a deal, but it's just pathetic, that I want help. But I told her I'd come get her. She moved there to be with her sister who was dying. Cancer of the uterus or some god-awful thing. Anyway, the sister is dead. Not that that matters. But she wants help, or support, or something. She doesn't want to move back on her own. She needs help moving stuff, I guess. She doesn't have a car, but she's got a fair bit of stuff. But I think she just needs, you know, support. And I guess I do, too."

A deep tiredness came over Paul. He was surprised by how much he did not want to follow this conversation. An old feeling returned, something he hadn't felt in years that he instantly resented—being asked to help sort out someone else's problems. Something occurred to him, but he tried to make a joke out of it, to ask the question but also to hammer in the tiny nail of bitterness poking out of him.

"So, what, you need me to sneak you across the border in my hockey bag, is that it?"

Rick looked at Paul as if mildly insulted or annoyed, briefly drawing his eyebrows together. "No. That's not why I'm asking."

"I know that," said Paul, quickly. "I'm kidding. Anyway, of course I'll go."

"Are you sure?"

"Sure. Why not?"

"Really? That's great."

"But what about the bus?" Paul asked.

"Hey?"

"What about the bus? Why doesn't she just take the bus?"

"The bus?"

"I mean, it's no sweat. I'll look forward to a little road trip. But how much stuff does she have?"

Rick held his hands out in front of him and frowned. "Now you don't want to go?"

"I said I'd go. I'll go. I'm just wondering why she can't come up on her own."

"Well . . . alright then. You don't have to. And I don't need you to, either." Rick closed his face up. "I just thought you might want to help."

Lisa came down into the kitchen. "What?" she said, smelling discord. She turned her head quickly from brother to brother. "What's up?"

"That's not fair, Rick," said Paul sharply. "You know that."

Rick ignored him and went back downstairs, a response that brought angry blood pounding up Paul's neck and into his ears and sinuses. He heard the TV roar on, a baseball announcer shouting something at the top of his lungs. Lisa was about to speak when the back door opened. Paul's parents came straggling in under the weight of a dozen bags of groceries. His mother barely breathed a hello before going to the drawer under the oven, from which she pulled a large cast-iron pan, a thing the size of a hubcap that was so heavy she needed two hands to lift it to the stove top.

"I'm going to make spaghetti for dinner. Is that okay? With my meat sauce."

"Excellent," said Paul, out of politeness rather than any great love for his mother's spaghetti and meat sauce, a meal he'd had once a week in this kitchen for twenty years and that, as a consequence, he hadn't made for himself more than twice in the years since leaving home.

"No mushrooms," said Lisa. "Don't 'forget' like last time."

"What's wrong with mushrooms?" said Paul. "How can you not like mushrooms?"

"They're a fungus. They taste like wet chalk. They grow in shit."

Later, over dinner, Paul said to Rick, "So what are you up to tomorrow, bro'?" Paul thought he'd try to remove the bad feeling left by their exchange before dinner and so he tried to make his question sound brisk and free of expectation, but Rick didn't respond with a laugh or a smile. He looked up from his pasta and brought his napkin to his face.

"Don't know."

Their father placed his fork on the table. He brought his bottom lip out and over his upper lip and rubbed his knuckles as if working through some arthritic throbbing. He took a deep breath, held it briefly then exhaled. Paul knew these signals to be preparation for a few words in the fathering-is-my-job mode. Nothing was wrong with that; his approach was less than passionate but it was solid, and Paul had come to appreciate it, because though the content was not always perceptive or enlightening—and was sometimes even downright clueless—the broadly supportive sensibility behind it never wavered. "I know you're not asking for my opinion," said Brian, "and I'm not here to say my opinion is everything, but I think the single most important thing is to look for work." He picked up his fork and spun some spaghetti in it, continuing to look at his eldest son.

"You don't have to feel worried about giving me your opinion. And you're right. A job is priority number one."

"A job doing what?" said Lisa, reaching for the grated cheese. "That's going to be a problem. You don't really have a lot of skills or anything."

"Lisa!" said her mother.

"What? I'm just saying what's true. What's the big deal? We're family. Aren't we supposed to be able to talk? Right, Rick?"

Rick was grinning and slowly shaking his head. "Like you've got just the skills society is looking for."

"Society? Spare me." Lisa put the cheese back in the middle of the table, and Paul watched her turn her hazel eyes and small mouth to Rick as she prepared to make sure he got her point, exactly. Paul couldn't help but smile at her manner, that combination of brilliant professor and pain-in-the-ass teenager, all of it caught in a short, slender, almost frail-looking twenty-five-year-old body. At times Paul thought she was like one of those freak kids who graduate from medical school when they're sixteen. She looked slight, pliant even, which she never failed to use to her advantage. "'Society' can't even spell *intellectual*, let alone know what to do with one."

"Hence, my point."

"Seriously," said Paul. "What does a person do with a PhD in . . . in . . . what are you studying again?"

"Paul," said his father. "Show some respect for your little sister. Don't make fun of something you can't do. You never hear her making fun of what you do, do you?"

"She makes fun of me all the time. She says I'm not even a writer, that journalists are just typists." Paul turned to his sister with the intention of insulting her further, only to see she'd put a zombie-eyed, cubicle-bound expression on her face and was silently mock-typing on the dinner table in front of her. Rick noticed and laughed at her, shaking his head. Paul laughed, too.

"Well, never mind," said Paul's father. "You know what I mean." He turned to Lisa. "I think it's terrific, Lisa. I'm always telling my friends down at the golf course about my sweet little girl who has grown up and is now doing a PhD in physiotherapy."

"Philosophy."

"By the way," said Rick. "Paul and I are going down to Montana to pick up Tammy next week. Tuesday, Wednesday, something like that. I guess we'll be gone a couple of days, and then we'll be back. Paul, and me and Tammy."

Lisa, who Paul knew was always on alert at moments of potentially extreme human behaviour, grinned and began looking around the table. "That is so cool," she said, her voice enthusiastic enough for Paul to know she was being sarcastic. "Really. I can't wait to meet her. Hey, Mum? What do you think?"

Maureen pressed an eyebrow with the tip of a finger as though staving off a headache.

Rick looked around the table, then settled on Paul. His face was so open, so completely stripped of defences, it almost made Paul want to cry. "Right, Paul? We're picking her up?"

"Right," said Paul. "Absolutely."

Later, after everyone else had gone to bed, Paul flopped onto the couch in the TV room and hit the remote. He flipped through the channels quickly, vaguely looking for stories having to do with Daniel Code and the Democratic Alliance, but also allowing his attention to be caught and released like a fish. He stopped once or twice at channels long enough to discover that he should have kept right on going. For a few moments he settled on a program documenting a major surgical procedure that appeared to involve a number of doctors and dozens of metal clamps holding in place lengths and widths of skin, with organs exposed deep inside a sliced-open body. Not only was Paul unable to tell what the operation was, but he was unable to distinguish which area of the body was being operated on, though it definitely looked visceral: large segments of shiny wet matter seemed to be throbbing or possibly convulsing. A canopy covered parts of the body not under consideration, and the section the surgeons were working with was so slick with blood and mucous it might have been a killing floor. The last thing on earth Paul wanted to be subjected to was the inner workings, or failings, of the human body. He was happy to know nothing about it, in the same way he chose to learn nothing about cars or computers. What was the point of knowing a little about something you didn't really know anything about? Partial knowledge merely reminded him of how tenuous things seemed. If it was all so complex—this life, this world—and if so many things were interdependent of one another, then to Paul it simply meant the more of a dillettante you were, the less faith you were entitled to. Not that faith, in anything or anyone, offered much comfort, either.

After leaving the blood and guts, Paul's scrolling through the channels took him to a twenty-four-hour news station that had been running a commercial the first time through. On his second jog through the channels, something on that same channel caught his eye, though he was moving so quickly he had to stop a couple of channels further down and tack back, as if he'd overshot the river dock he'd been navigating toward. It was a political story. Yes, there he was. Paul turned the sound up. Daniel Code was yammering away in some kind of media scrum, but it looked orchestrated, as if he'd been at a function and had then allotted a set time for the media. He was discussing western alienation, even the very nature of the country, the way in which "all Canadians in and of themselves as human beings" were like the west and east, the way we were made up of so many parts that had to work together or collapse. It was fabulous bullshit, but he made it sound as though he meant it, and he skillfully used his winning smile to flick away questions he didn't want to answer.

The camera panned backward to take in some of the surrounding crowd. Code remained directly in the centre of the lens, but four or five people were fully visible behind him. Rachel Code seemed to be listening intently to what her father had to say, but she must have sensed the camera, because she nervously put a hand to her face and tried to remove a strand of hair from her mouth. The camera treated her well, despite her nerves, and Paul had no doubt her father had planted her there for precisely this reason: to create a fully telegenic *mise-en-scene*. It was a given, and she was smart enough to be fully complicit. Perhaps she'd even suggested it. Paul leaned back against the couch, then he quickly shut off the TV. Pastor Code needed, deserved, his full and skeptical attention, but Rachel was inside his skull, and that wasn't going to help. He'd need her out to do his job properly. He sat in the silent darkness for a moment before deciding to head off to bed, back in his old room.

Lying in the dark, he saw Rachel on the screen in his mind's eye, her forefinger pulling away that strand of long, dark brown hair. She had short clipped fingernails, he remembered that. Nails polished with a clear lacquer. Clean hands. These hands moved toward his chest, underneath the white cotton T-shirt he wore to bed every night. The murmur of her voice slipped like a ropy line of smoke into the tunnels of his ears. He moved his hand as she told him to, following her movements, her guidance, her whispered urgencies.

FOUR

When Paul stepped unannounced into Harold's office twenty minutes before their scheduled meeting with Boar and Stranga, Harold closed his laptop with a brisk click and looked up as if he'd been expecting Paul at that precise moment. "How's it going with the nutjob preacher?"

"One meeting so far. I'll go watch him talk tomorrow. More interviews." Paul sat down after moving a pile of dictionaries off a chair.

Harold put his head back and stroked the folds of fat under his chin, as if preparing to offer a scholarly opinion. "Find someone who hates him. As a person, I mean. That'll spice it up."

"Sage editorial advice. Seriously, the thing I do have trouble figuring out sometimes is what's going through the heads of people late at night, lights off, head on the pillow. You know, a guy like Code is thinking . . . what? . . . like, is he lying in bed plotting to bring the death penalty back, about killing abortion doctors, about making sure 'homosexuals' can't marry? But, you know, it's actually the transition I've been thinking about. That moment. That's what fascinates me. That fulcrum. What leads up to or causes that moment someone goes from being one thing to another? Like, from being someone who is a religious individualist to some intolerant extremist?"

"Wrong analogy. It's not a fulcrum. More a train track."

"I like my fulcrum. I spent some time coming up with that. I was thinking of using it in the article."

"Nice. But flawed."

"I like it."

"It's without merit. It's not about a moment. Nobody has epiphanies anymore." Harold paused. "That just occurred to me."

Paul grinned. "Nope. You're wrong. People do have moments when the fulcrum tips. When they're one thing, and something happens to them, and then they're a different thing."

"Kind of poetic, but incorrect. And *so* wrong in politics. Come on. Think about it. Politics is a calculator that never stops processing." Harold looked at his watch. "We could probably head into the boardroom. Those two are in there by now, I'm sure."

Paul stood up. He felt more ready for a coffee and a muffin than a meeting with InfoTrue; but, there were things you could avoid and things you couldn't. Harold stepped into the bathroom and Paul went ahead. When he got to the boardroom, they were waiting: Boar and Stranga. Jonathon Boar was seated to Stranga's right and was maintaining a very erect posture, as if he were using his spine to clinch a hidden package against the back of the chair. He had a variety of colour-coded folders on the table in front of him. Stranga was half slouched in his chair, looking—appropriately, Paul acknowledged to himself—as if he owned the place. On the table in front of him there were no folders, no daytimer, no cell phone, just one sheet of blank unlined paper and one gold pen so slender and pointy it made Paul think of a poison blow dart.

"Paul," said Boar, standing. "Great to see you. I'd like you to meet Edgars Stranga, CEO of the InfoTrue Group."

Stranga smiled and nodded elegantly from where he remained seated at the head of the table with his hands together in front of him. He didn't reach out to shake Paul's hand, so Paul didn't offer his. Boar sat down and flipped his red-checked tie away from the folds of his jacket and shirt, smoothing it down so that it rested against him in an uncreased state. "So how's the writing going, Paul? The magazine is looking great, reading great."

"Yeah, pretty good, I guess."

"You guys are putting out a superb product. Makes me wish I was still writing."

Paul nodded, refusing to stroke Boar's ego.

"I miss it. I really do. I miss that edge, that creative expression. Of course, there are other manifestations of creativity, aren't there?"

What are you after? thought Paul. It can't just be that he wants a little flattery, told how good a writer he was or could have become. That was too simple, too straightforward. Simplicity was not a hallmark of interactions with Jonathon Boar. Stranga sat motionless, turning his gaze from Boar to Paul in turn. Paul found the contrast between the two striking. Boar was tall, pale, big nosed, and kept his hair slightly longer than business normally dictated (a last semblance of his "bullshit rebel self-image" Harold had said). He had a boil on the side of his face, almost on the point of his cheekbone. It was a red little hole, and he occasionally touched a finger to it.

Stranga, though, was dark and tidy. He was flawlessly suited, slight, delicate and fineboned, all of which seemed somehow incongruous with the fact that he was a very hairy man. Hairs as coarse as the legs of a black fly sprouted from the backs of his hands.

The door to the boardroom opened and Harold waded in, coughing. He put his papers down beside Paul and only then looked up to Boar and Stranga. He nodded without really saying hello, and Paul wondered if they'd already spoken that morning. It certainly appeared as if none of them were interested in formalities. Boar looked at his watch and applied a half smile to his face. "On the phone?"

Harold arranged some papers as he spoke. "On the toilet."

Stranga unclasped his hands and put his arms across his slender chest, but his flat expression didn't change.

"Right." Boar coughed. "Then I guess we'd better get started. Edgars has to leave before lunch to catch his plane back to Toronto. Here's the scenario. I had dinner with Harold last week and we talked about a lot of things: things to do with 2.2.4., and things to do with the InfoTrue Group. I brought Edgars up to speed on this meeting, and I believe, Harold, you told Paul about it."

Harold nodded while looking at the papers in front of him.

"So, here's why we're meeting today. We need you to start thinking about 2.2.4. differently. Revenues are down. A proliferation of outlets has splintered advertising dollars across the board. Consumers are using the Internet for information gathering and opinion molding instead of the traditional avenues of print and newscasts. Advertising and new entertainment streams have altered the collective attention span. All relatively old news, of course."

Paul could see an opinion bulging out of Harold like a tongue up against the inside of a cheek. "So," said Harold, "the 'consumer' views 2.2.4. as a quaint artifact. The rotary phone of the media universe?"

"No," said Boar.

"Yes," said Stranga, speaking the first word Paul had ever heard him utter.

"Finally," said Harold. "Finally, somebody around here is telling the truth. I mean, not the truth, but at least admitting to something he actually thinks."

"I didn't say I thought that, Harold," continued Stranga. "I said that's what the public thinks." He adjusted himself in his seat, and scratched the back of his hand, which made Paul think of that black fly rubbing its legs together. "And I'm not saying the public is right. But the magazine is small, and the world is getting bigger. InfoTruc doesn't own properties to run as hobbies. That's why Jonathon met with you, Harold. To start talking about ways of guaranteeing that 2.2.4. survives. That's the point. It's about increasing the flexibility of your business model."

"Oh," said Harold. "I feel so much better." He took a hankie from his front pants pocket and blew his nose, after which he wiped his forehead. Paul grimaced and looked away to avoid seeing the inevitable last act, wherein Harold jammed the whole damp bundle back into the pocket.

An hour later they were still talking about ways of ensuring the survival of the magazine, though it was conversation in an alien tongue—MBA. Stranga, and particularly Boar, used it like it was English, but it was not a language, Paul thought, understood by those on the ground, the front line. It was, Boar said, going to be up to Harold and Paul to *broaden and further commodotize the core asset's highbrow special sauce*. Paul had not heard a single idea from Boar or Stranga that had anything to do with the way the magazine was run on a daily basis. What he longed to hear from them was just one sentence that included a concrete suggestion.

"Doesn't it matter at all to you," Paul said at one point, "that we're trying to do something here? Something rare? Analysis, critical thought, ideas, elegance of expression. Don't these have any value?"

"Define *value*," said Stranga.

Just before noon, the conversation began to trickle away. Boar stood and bent to collect his things spread out over the table, but Paul spoke. "Jonathon?"

Boar trained his grey-green eyes on Paul. His gaze was full but dead, like a strikingly realistic piece of portraiture. A moussed hank of his bullshit hair hung almost to his left eyebrow.

"I'd like to know why I'm here, Jonathon. I mean, this was a meeting you've already had with Harold. And I wasn't particularly involved, or meant to be involved, in the conversation today."

Boar cleared his throat and said, "Well . . ." but he was interrupted by Harold.

"You're here," said Harold, "because they're worried I'll quit, now or later. Then they can offer you the job in the interim until they find the person they want, or until they kill the magazine. Edgars is just getting a read on you. That's why you're here."

Again Boar made to speak but this time he was cut off by Stranga. "That's not true," said Stranga in a quiet voice.

"It's okay, Ed. I'm not insulted."

"Paul is important to the magazine, which means, simply, he's important to InfoTrue. 2.2.4. is a value-added component to us. You do a good job with the magazine, Harold. An excellent job."

"I don't need you to tell me that I do a good job with my magazine."

"That would be true if it *was* your magazine," said Stranga. "Though I'd be happy to say it in any case." He broke into an open smile and began to chuckle. "Harold, Harold." Standing, he picked up his briefcase and leaned over to Paul and held out his hand. "A pleasure to meet you, Paul. Harold is Harold, we aren't going to change that. But you're lucky to be working with him, whether he believes I mean that or not." He turned to Harold. "A pleasure as always, Harold. I'd offer to treat you to lunch, but I have to get back. Rain check?"

"If you think that's something you'd enjoy."

"*I* would," said Stranga. "But that fact alone might be enough to make it hard for you to enjoy it." He smiled again at Paul, and left the room with Boar silently hovercrafting along behind him. Paul shut the door. He stood looking out the window for a moment, then sat down across from Harold, slowly shaking his head.

". . . That was a meeting about . . . ?"

"Ed wants to kill the magazine."

Paul frowned. "Harold. Weren't you listening? To all those compliments? And anyway, that wouldn't make sense. He even agreed that we don't lose money, though I guess we don't really *make* any, either. We have advertisers. We win awards. Why would they kill it? It makes no sense."

"What we do, Paul," said Harold, waving a hand around the boardroom, at the awards on the wall and out towards the other offices and cubicles, "means nothing to InfoTrue. It's not about how well we run the magazine, it's not about breaking even every year, it's not even really about the stories we write. It's about a corporate profile. This is a multinational with a market capitalization in the billions. The assets of 2.2.4.—the writers, editors, awards, reputation—those are all things

InfoTrue can co-opt without having to produce the actual magazine. Do you see what I mean? Nobody cares about 2.2.4., anyway. How many readers do we have? Ten thousand subscribers, and we sell another thousand copies on the stands. Each copy might pass through the hands of three or four readers. Let's say we have sixty, seventy thousand readers. So what? More people than that watch fishing on TV. All we possess is integrity, a kind of cachet. That's all. Nothing else. That's the only reason InfoTrue bought us. And once Ed figures out how to best transfuse that, we're gone. Then we're just something that can be trimmed, downsized to create a more streamlined reporting structure, greater efficiencies having people like you and me inside the beast. That's why Ed bought it when we were in trouble. So he could do this to me." Harold got up with a grunt and rumbled out of the room.

Paul sat staring out the window. His throat hurt and his eyes began to water. Harold was wrong. They wouldn't do it. He closed his eyes to concentrate, to create a positive vision of what was going to happen, to make it exist so that he would have it to move toward, so that it might pull on his instinct. It was about the stronger vision, he thought, the ability to see a purer, clearer result than one's adversary. But Paul had to cancel his vision for the time being—Stranga's hairy fly-leg hands kept coming into his mind's eye. The sun was spilling into the boardroom. Paul got out of his chair and stood at the window, where he could see by the pedestrians in shorts, bikers in tights, cars with windows down, that it was a hot, dry, parched day. He went to the corner of the office and drew the blinds shut.

FIVE

Since he wished both to surprise Code and convey seriousness, Paul attended the 7 AM Rotarians' breakfast at which Code was to deliver a few words and shake some hands. Such events meant ironing clothes and shaving, two things Paul didn't do without exceptional cause. It took a public meeting to bring Paul's iron out of the closet, and even this was only because Harold read him the riot act six months after he'd started. An advertiser in the magazine had seen Paul asking questions at some meeting; the same advertiser later applauded Harold for being progressive enough to hire the homeless for internships.

The Rotarians had advertised Code's event and promised a lively debate, but there were at least a hundred empty seats in the small basement auditorium of the northwest Rotary Club building. Paul had to admire Code's graciousness and sense of humour in the face of such a snub. He made a couple of jokes about the sparse turnout, asking the man who organized the event, and who had also introduced him in an overly apologetic way, if he wouldn't mind offering his organizational skills to Code's campaign opponents. This brought out a good-natured giggle from the ten or so people in the hall, a group sitting so upright and close together they reminded Paul of penguins huddling for warmth, a sense of uniformity enhanced by what Paul thought might be a Rotarian dress code: grey slacks, functional shoes, plaid short-sleeve shirt, tidy haircuts. Of course, it was also possible this was more the dress code of the demographic interested in the speaker. Code, after teasing the organizer about the attendance, also joked about the number of leftover pastries, saying that since there were so many extra he'd be happy to drop them off at the Food Bank on his way back to the campaign office. Everyone laughed again, but he stopped them dead, saying flatly, "I'm quite serious about that." They choked on their laughter, embarrassed, but then with perfect timing Code grinned widely, causing them to hoot with glee. *They ate it up, so to speak,* Paul wrote in his notebook.

Code delivered his standard CHART speech. Paul took no notes, having heard it before. There were a few questions, mostly to do with issues of social alienation, the homeless, youth crime, welfare fraud. Paul kept hoping someone was going to ask a touchstone question—capital punishment, abortion, gay rights—but no Rotarian went near it. Every question was handled easily and warmly by Code. After the meeting ended, Paul waited for Code at the back of the room.

"Hello, Paul. How are you, today?"

"Fine. You?"

"Vibrant. Exuberant. Big crowds always do that to me."

"Bit disappointing."

Code sat down. "You could look at it that way. But that's not how I choose to look at it. First of all, this Rotary club has a top Alberta PC party executive on their board, and the club hasn't always been sympathetic to my party, or me for that matter. I was surprised and delighted they asked me to come at all. Anyway, you can only change one mind at a time. Small crowd, big crowd. Doesn't matter. It's still soul by soul."

". . . You mean mind by mind?"

Code smiled. "Is this turning into an interview?"

Paul looked at his watch. "Sure, why not. It's only seven-thirty, after all. All these guys are going to work. We could probably sit here for a bit."

Code turned and looked up to the front of the room, where the organizer and another man were staring sadly at a huge tray of assorted pastries. "Donald," he said loudly. "Do you mind if we sit and talk for a while here?"

Donald waved back that it was no problem and asked if they wanted a danish: cherry, lemon, or apple. Paul took apple, and Code lemon, though Code stared at it a moment before biting into it, which made Paul hesitate. Code seemed to be considering it as some kind of offering, a votive pastry, instead of the crummy little slab of fat and sugar it was. Finally, he took a bite and Paul was able to do the same.

"We don't have to go too long or anything," said Paul, chewing, "since this is unscheduled time, and I'm sure you have other things to do. I don't want you to get in trouble. Then I'd have Rachel angry with me."

"And you don't want that, do you?"

"No," said Paul, unable to tell if Code was teasing him. But why would he? "Anyway," he carried on, "I'd be really interested to talk to you about your past, your family history, that sort of thing. It's not necessarily going to be a huge part of the profile, but it helps me get a sense of who you are, where you've come from, and so on."

"I think this might be a good time to tell you a bit of story?" asked Code in a low, conspiratorial tone. "What do you think?"

It was a peculiar and almost laughably dramatic setup, but Paul assumed Code was merely gearing down to a certain gravitas he used for shading narratives about his past. He half expected Code to cast a chin-to-his-shoulder scan around the room to make sure there were no eavesdropping Rotarians skulking about. Paul gestured to indicate that, no, he didn't mind listening to a story.

"Because that's really how I communicate best, I think. I'm a storyteller. Not a TV media sort. I don't like sound bites. They're too short. I like to have unlimited time." He smiled professionally; his face was youthful yet experienced, his lifelines set in their proper places but not sunk so deeply that he looked dessicated in body or spirit. The guy was handsome, that was all there was to it. "I like a captive audience, too!"

"You like the pulpit."

"I guess I must."

"Here I am," said Paul, spreading his hands apart. "Captive."

"Not quite one of the flock, though."

"As a believer or a voter?"

Code hesitated, as if in minor reappraisal. "You are different than other writers, aren't you?"

Paul felt flattered, obliquely, but fed the reaction through his experience, knowing this, and other things he sometimes encountered in his work—amiability, serendipity, lust—were just calls to be wary.

"How so?"

"Well . . . I'm not sure yet, to be honest. It's what Rachel says, though."

Paul felt a flush bloom up his chest and over his collarbone. "Rachel said that?"

"Yes, and she's not often wrong about things, that girl."

"You must be proud of her. Intelligent and attractive is a good combination."

Code shrugged and angled his head a degree or two toward his shoulder. "'Pride cometh before the fall.'"

"'Reserve your greatest mistrust for the falsely humble.'"

"Hmm, who said that? I like it."

"Harold Buckthorn."

"I don't know his work."

"He's rather obscure. Bit of an acquired taste, to be honest."

Code lightly slapped a palm against the table. "So, where shall I start? The beginning?"

"'In the beginning,'" said Paul. "'There was the word, and the word was God.'"

Code gently put a forefinger into his ear, scratching then removing. He looked at his watch.

"Yes," said Paul. "In the beginning."

"Growing up in rural Alberta in the fifties and sixties was never easy, not for me, my siblings, my parents. My father's father—a failed pastor, incidentally—emigrated from England, tried to farm, and boy, he made a mess of it. I don't know what he was thinking, but he must have thought it was just about planting a few seeds and then pulling grains and vegetables out of the ground five months later. He learned a lot about drought, locusts, winter, dust. It defeated him, the prairie. Well, perhaps not the prairie, but farming. So then he opened up this little tool shop in Quantree. My father took that over and kept it open during some pretty hard years—this was around when I was born. But he made it work and eventually he moved and opened up Code's Hardware in Black Hills. It's still there, you know. My father just retired last year. Have you been up to Black Hills yet to see the store?"

Paul shook his head no. Code leaned his head back and paused just long enough to suggest Paul might be a writer in dereliction of his duty.

"Anyway, my father still goes in a couple of days a week, arranges stuff on the shelves, flaps his pie hole—as he calls it—with the customers. But my older brother is the one that runs it now. If you go—and you really should—let me know, or rather, let Rachel know, and she'll give you the names and numbers of some people you should talk to, some friends and supporters throughout the years, the real flock, as it were, people who've been at my side for years now. Anyway, we moved from Quantree to Black Hills in 1968 when Dad opened the store there, and that's where I grew up. Of course, I still keep a house in Black Hills, because that's where my federal seat is. I go back and forth."

He stopped, took a sip of coffee, went on.

"Strangely enough, ours wasn't a particularly religious household. And I talk about this only because . . . because I know you have no choice but to make my faith a part of your profile. That's normal. I'm used to it. We were Baptist. My mother, though, was always complaining about one aspect of the service or another, about getting all dressed up for church, about how her time could be better spent doing other things. Still, she would always say that she had no doubts there was a God somewhere, and that Jesus had definitely existed, but did that mean he was the son of God? Stuff like that. She wasn't a disbeliever, just a skeptic, I suppose. Always asking questions. That was her way. But it got to my father. He finally told her to stop coming to church if she didn't want to. She said, Fine. And she never went again. After I was about thirteen or fourteen, I never saw my mother in church. It was always my father and my brother and me.

"My father was different than my mother. He believed more in the protocol of faith than 'faith' itself. He never seemed that pious to me, or even interested in matters of faith. But I think he thought church had something to do with morality and living a good life and setting a good example for your children, all that sort of stuff. He was—is—a very moral but moralizing man, a man of his era and place. This was the situation I grew up in—kind of strange, really—a father who insisted on the structural value of church but had no passion for understanding his faith, and a mother who was always trying to understand what she believed in, but who never went to church. Hard to say who influenced me more. Probably my mother. In any case, it became irrelevant when I was seventeen."

"Irrelevant?" said Paul, writing the word down in his notebook with quote marks around it, doing so specifically to allow Code to notice he'd highlighted the word. "Why did your parents become irrelevant?"

"I didn't say my parents became irrelevant. I said their influence on me, as it relates to faith, became irrelevant." He pointed at Paul's notebook. "You have that distinction recorded accurately, I trust."

Paul looked at his notebook purely to satisfy Code, though he resented the request. "Yes, I do. And so . . . ?"

"Because when I was seventeen I was chosen."

"Excuse me?"

"I was chosen. In the twelfth grade. Of course, I don't mean chosen in the way of being chosen by God or some other power to do something unique or be something extraordinary. I don't mean chosen as *elect*. In fact, I mean chosen in quite an ordinary way. I was simply chosen to believe. That's all. You know, handpicked."

"And how did you know this? That you were ... handpicked?" Paul made a conscious effort to use a tone of voice free of inflection or implication, despite the fact he was mentally shaking his head.

"This is always where it gets sticky with the media." Code smiled. "Why aren't any of you Christian, anyway? Why is that?"

"How do you know we're not?" said Paul, smiling. "We can't play favourites, you know."

"Oh, of course, how silly of me to have forgotten that."

"So you were chosen ... ?"

"And how did I know? Simple. The Lord Jesus talked to me."

Paul let his pen rest on his notebook.

"See," said Code. "Sticky."

"I'm just not sure I quite understand," said Paul, frowning.

"What's not to understand? I told you. Jesus talked to me."

"So ... you had a feeling of ... peace?" asked Paul, using the language he'd heard from other believers, one or two of them politicians. "A sense of newness. Purpose. You felt something beautiful enter your heart? Like that?"

"You're not listening, Paul. Jesus spoke with me. I was at home back in Black Hills, laying in bed one spring morning, lounging a bit, thinking about getting up for school, what to wear, some homework I'd forgotten to do, that kind of thing. And just like that Jesus was sitting on the edge of my bed, smiling patiently, His hands in His lap. I wasn't surprised, wasn't scared. He told me who He was. He was patient and calm, but direct. I introduced myself and He smiled at that. 'I know who you are,' He said. And then He reached out and put His palm against my forehead, like this." Code reached out and put his palm on Paul's forehead. It was dry and warm against Paul's skin, and the physical sensation of it was not entirely unpleasant, though Paul immediately fretted about trying to explain it to some nosy Rotarian; his secondary feeling was one of professional exhilaration—he could use this. Code withdrew his hand.

"He left His hand there for a few seconds, like He was checking to see if I had a fever. And then He said, 'Daniel, I have chosen you.' 'For what?' I said. 'To lead *and* follow,' He answered. I knew He meant to lead others but to follow Him. I said, 'Thank you, Jesus.' Then He said, 'Thanks be with you, too, Daniel, for I have no glory except that which resides in my believers.' And then He was gone. I got out of bed, brushed my teeth, got dressed, ate breakfast, went to school. In fact, it was at least a week before I even told anyone or did anything about it. There was no rush, no fear, nothing to doubt. It wasn't ecstatic in the way that I've read others have experienced such things. It was just—and I know Jesus himself was this way—it was just being filled with this sense of quiet and unhurried confidence."

Code stopped speaking and sat back, his eyes still on Paul, his lips joined in a peculiar sort of satisfaction; Paul might have almost called it serene, if it weren't for the blue-eyed stare jabbing into his head accusing him of lesser spiritual understanding and pitying him for it. As Code finished speaking, Paul felt creeping through him a sub-genre of sadness he'd never known before, a new strain of emotion in his system that caught him off guard. It was so unusual that it took his subconscious a few seconds to catalogue and shelve correctly. He was sad, he realized, because he did not dislike Code, yet he now also knew the man was not fully mentally sound. How could someone who claimed to have heard and seen Jesus Christ speaking to him be sane? Additionally—and not insignificantly—Code had to know Paul would quote freely from this conversation in his profile. How could he not? In what possible way could Paul spin it so that Code appeared rational—if for some reason Paul even felt inclined to spin it that way? Why would he tell me this? thought Paul. What possible purpose could it serve? What goal was being achieved? Daniel Code did not appear stupid, despite the retrograde nature of his politics. Yet he wasn't sane. How could he be? And he was so preposterously and utterly certain of it all, of who he was, what his life meant. There was only one thing, one alone, that Paul did not doubt in this life, and that was the existence of doubt.

Code was going to win the leadership of the Democratic Alliance, Paul felt sure, if for no other reason than that enough people in the west, and particularly in Alberta, didn't mind a little God with their politics. But Paul was sad because the man was going to get eviscerated by the national press and they would use as a weapon their own brand of self-righteousness—namely, their secular cynicism. Paul knew he was deep inside the circle of those ready to hand Code his head on a platter, and this made a part of him melancholy.

Not that that meant he would let Code off the hook. Sadness and empathy only went so far.

With a brisk sniff, Code turned his full attention on Paul, who said nothing, but waited, expectant, a little downcast.

"What matters, Paul? To you?"

Paul gave Code a squint, but felt his heart miss a pump or two.

"In your life? What is it that matters to you? I want you to tell me. And then I'll explain why I want to know." He sat back, crossed his arms, tilted his head a notch; it was, thought Paul, the self-possession of upper management trying to 'help' an employee who hasn't quite bought into the company's ethos.

"I'm not sure how this matters. I mean, not that I mind talking in this way, but it's not really why we're here."

"Why are we here, then?" Code asked in quick reply, with an impatience that took Paul aback.

"Are you asking me a metaphysical question? Or a political one?"

"Are they so different?"

"Well, yes. I mean, of course they are."

Code uncrossed his arms and clasped his hands together on the table in front of him. "Now you're avoiding me."

"How so?"

"What matters to you? In this life?" He shrugged. "I'm asking you."

Paul decided to play along. He was eating a danish with an amiable, harmless lunatic—unless he became prime minister—but even though Paul felt the situation to be fundamentally comic, flickers of irritation ran along the skin of his forearms. It was his role to ask the questions, not answer them; a held question was power, an answer a form of surrender. There was noise from the front of the room, as a stocky old Rotarian was awkwardly removing the lectern Code had used, dragging it across the linoleum floor like a hitman hauling a body out to his car trunk. The man needed some help, Paul thought. Where the hell were those other guys?

"I don't know," Paul said, turning back to Code. "What matters to me? The normal things, I suppose. Love, health, family. Gratifying work. Various pleasures. Food. Reading. Entertainment. I don't know. There are a lot of things that matter to me, I suppose."

Code stuck out his bottom lip. "That's a very good list. Mostly balanced. You're a healthy individual . . . to the naked eye."

". . . Meaning?"

"There's one thing you didn't mention. I knew you wouldn't. Which was precisely why I asked the question." He actually pointed at Paul, not aggressively but just to emphasize the precision of his insight. "Not for one single second did I doubt that you wouldn't include it in your list of things that mattered to you."

Paul ran a finger down the mental page of his taxonomy of pleasures and values and couldn't come up with anything to match the significance Code was looking for. Sure, he valued many things in life he hadn't mentioned, and wouldn't: TV, sturdy bowel movements, music, popcorn with lots of butter, sex (as best as he could remember), badgering his sister, wine and beer and chilled vodka and single malt scotch—the list at this level of the table was as endless as it was minor, but he couldn't think of anything major. He shook his head. "I can't think of anything else that's really that significant."

"You didn't mention faith."

"Faith?" Paul very nearly laughed. "Well . . . I guess that's because it's not a big part of my life. You said to say what mattered."

"I think faith *is* a big part of your life." Code's eyes had begun sparkling, which made Paul uneasy. Did the man think this was some sort of conversion? "In fact," Code added, tapping the table with a forefinger, "I *know* it is."

"I assure you it's not," said Paul. "Not that I'm disrespectful. Not at all. I really respect the faith of others. In fact, sometimes I'm even a bit envious of people who seem to have a real faith of some sort, but like a dry faith, you know what I mean, a light faith—it looks like it's kind of comforting if you've got it. But I just happen to be an agnostic, that's all. I believe in God in the same way I believe in poetry: I'd be depressed if it didn't exist, but I just don't participate."

"Agnostic?" said Code, making a face like he'd been forced to utter the word *pedophile* or *masturbator*. "And what, in your opinion, is an agnostic?"

"One who suspects, or hopes, that there is a higher power, a 'God,' but who isn't sure. At least, that's my understanding of it. My interpretation of it. That the absence of reliable evidence precludes full commitment."

"And so this is your position?"

"I suppose it is," said Paul flatly, hearing his voice echo slightly against the far wall. He looked that way. They were now alone in the room. Where had all those Rotarians gone? Shouldn't they have said something if they were going to leave? And who was going to lock up?

"In other words, the whole of your spiritual life, your entire spiritual existence, past, present, and future, is founded on a hope, a shrug, an 'I'm not sure'?"

"Why are you asking me these things?" Paul asked, a little surprised to hear the obvious irritation in his voice. "Why does any of this matter? You don't know me. I don't know you. I'm writing about you. You as a politician. How is any of this relevant to that?"

"Because this is what matters, Paul. You'll write your story. I'll win or lose my race. Then what?"

Paul felt his irritation shift into impatience, of suddenly wishing he were elsewhere. It rose up inside him like hunger. It was not unlike being back in the confessional booth at St Luke's when he was a young teenager, so desperate to have it done with, though he'd still never entirely forgotten the strange pleasures of passing words through the bamboo screen that separated priest from sinner, the filter that made every word different and somehow more important than would have been the case had they been spoken outside of that double upright coffin.

"Then what? I move on to my next piece. You . . . you do whatever you have to do. Lead your party. Meet your constituents. Go to church. I don't know."

Code sat back and served Paul an expression Paul had seen on some of his professors' faces when he'd done the minimum to get by in university, a look of disappointed exasperation—the slight tilt of the head, the pursed lips. When this look emerged on his teachers' faces he didn't resent it, since it implied they thought he had horsepower in reserve. But Code's expression didn't deliver to Paul the same current of inverse satisfaction. He was being judged today, and had been found heavily wanting.

"Let me ask you something," Code carried on. "Have you ever lost anyone close to you? Imagine they're gone. Your mother, your father, past girlfriends you've loved? Are they really gone? Does love just die? That's just too awful, Paul. Faith overarches all the things you mentioned because it accommodates them all. It takes them in. Otherwise, it's just the void, and our lives mean nothing. Surely you don't believe in that, do you? You don't believe in the void. I know you don't. . . . It's okay, Paul. You don't have to say anything. I don't need your acknowledgment to know I'm right."

A Rotarian clattered through one of the rear doors leading into the small auditorium, fracturing what had become, Paul realized, an intimate conversation, which didn't necessarily make it something he'd been enjoying. The Rotarian waved at them. "Stay as long as you like—not an issue, my friends," he half-shouted. "I'm locking up, but just close the door behind you when you leave. They lock automatically."

Code waved over, smiled professionally. "Nearly done, Larry."

"Thanks again," said Larry on his way out. "You're our man."

Paul looked back to Code, who had dropped the smile. "I assume he was talking to you," said Paul.

Code didn't laugh, still wouldn't smile. After sitting in silence for a few seconds, Paul looked at his watch, closed his notebook, stood, and then extended his hand. "I appreciate you giving me the time," he said slowly. "I'm away for a day or two. I'll touch base with Rachel when I get back."

Code took Paul's hand and shook it in a casual man-to-man way. ". . . I went where I shouldn't have. You're upset."

"It's not that," said Paul, shaking his head, though it partly was that, and if his research and interviewing had been complete he'd have said so—he'd have told Code to look somewhere else for followers, to find other sources of reassurance for his own faith. "There's no need to apologize."

Code stared at Paul from where he sat. "I wasn't planning on apologizing."

SIX

Montana

A few kilometres from Turner Valley a small animal broke suddenly from the bushy ditch, and before Rick could brake or swerve, the right front bumper had caught it on the rump, flipping it onto the hood. Paul threw his hands in front of his face, instinctively, as a tan blur rolled up over the windshield and thumped once on the truck bed. By the time Rick skidded to a stop on the side of the highway, the deer lay still, thirty or forty metres behind them. Paul got out and went to the animal crumpled near the edge of the road. He saw by the angle of the head that its neck was broken. If it hadn't been killed by the initial impact, landing on the pavement would have finished it. Paul knelt, ran a palm over the small bowl of the animal's skull, gave it a gentle scratch between the ears. Antler buds the texture of walnut shells were beginning to show through the fur and skin at the top of its head. Red-black blood trickled into fissures in the tarmac. He looked up. Rick stood with his hands burrowing into his pants pockets.

"That's fucking awful, man."

"Yeah, poor thing," Paul said, again running his hand over its head. "I love the feel of that. The skull. Those little antlers."

Rick hesitated, looked up and down the highway, as if checking for traffic coming either way. "You miss hunting? I don't, I don't think."

"I sort of do."

"I really only ever did it to hang out with Dad." Rick nudged the dead animal with the toe of his shoe. "We should move this poor fucker."

Paul exhaled loudly. "Yeah." They each took a hoof and hauled it into the ditch. Rick lit a smoke to get the animal smell off his hands, then walked to the front of the truck. The headlamp was broken and there was blood speckling the bumper.

"Dad'll be pissed about his truck."

"Wasn't your fault," said Paul. "We're lucky this is all that happened. Could have been game over for us."

Paul had one more look at the deer in the ditch. He hated hitting animals like this, on the road. It was a waste in every way imaginable. Road kill meat tasted rank to him; something to do with the nature of the killing blow, he figured, the toxins released by such a blunt shock to the animal's system. Who knew what went on underneath the skin when a life was put under such sudden trauma. Some years before, he and his father had tried to eat the meat from an elk they'd plowed into on their way to Rocky Mountain House. "Don't even have to shoot anything now," Paul's father had joked as they threw the carcass in the back of the truck. But the steaks stank in their mouths, and none of them had touched road kill since.

When they were back up to speed, now an hour out of Calgary heading due south, Rick glanced over at Paul. "You know . . . I wrote a story in jail. About hunting with Dad and you. That's mostly what it's about, anyway."

"Really?" Paul turned to look at Rick, his eyebrows hoisted in surprise.

"Why are you shocked?"

"Well . . . I'm not. I mean, I'm not surprised you were writing. Or maybe I am."

"I was good in English, don't forget."

"Better than me."

"Damn right."

Paul started to laugh, but when he saw that Rick wasn't laughing with him he was able to stop himself. He didn't want Rick to think he was being condescending or unsupportive, even though the fresh thought that Rick might try to find work as a writer was alarming to Paul, on numerous levels: it was hard to get established and make a living, no matter how good you were, but, in any case, as soon as the notion of Rick as a writer came into Paul's head he knew Rick wasn't the right kind of tough. He'd give up, or, more likely, get confrontational the first time an editor told him he'd gotten a story wrong, or that his thinking was fuzzy, or that he had the material down but wasn't making the most of it, or that he needed to go back and get more detail. Editing, Harold often told Paul, was a dialogue, not a standoff. But that wouldn't float with Rick. He didn't do dialogue.

"Why don't you show it to me?" asked Paul. "The hunting story. I'd like to read it."

"I almost sent it to you. Last year."

"Why didn't you?"

"Ach, you know. Too much pressure. You can't win. You criticize, you're not being supportive. You gush all over it, that's what you're supposed to do because I 'need the support.'"

"I'm sure you could handle my opinion. It's just feedback from an honest reader. Isn't being honest the same as being supportive?"

"That what you think?" asked Rick. He'd moved his hands up on the wheel, so that only his wrists and lower palms were resting on top of it; he began to lightly drum the edge of the dashboard with his fingernails and as far as Paul could tell Rick seemed to be enjoying the drive and the conversation. Paul was enjoying it, too. It felt good to be alone with his brother, albeit on this strange mission to retrieve a woman neither of them had ever met, yet who would soon be living in their house.

"So how's it going? You know, being out. I mean, I know it's only been, what, not even a week. But is it weird, hard, good, bad? What?"

Rick seemed to think about it for a moment or two, pushing his lips together and pouting them out, and then he pointed out both the east- and west-looking windows. Paul was not sure what it was exactly that Rick was trying to identify. He saw only a stern beauty in the west, the David Range of the Rockies, a line of glowering, serrated peaks with another seven hundred kilometres of mountains backing up that line. East, the Porcupine Hills, beyond which were thousands of kilometres of prairie. Paul imagined that Rick, in pointing, was only trying to highlight what he'd missed in the Alberta landscape over the years, what he hadn't had access to.

"Yeah," said Paul, still looking out the window. "I guess I know what you mean."

"No. You don't."

"I don't?"

"It's about borders. There aren't any." Rick looked out the west window and then east. "I mean look at that. Look how far you can see. It's not like that inside. Everything has a line around it in there. Time. Space. Movement. There aren't any lines out here."

"Doesn't that feel good?"

Rick stuck out his bottom lip. "I have to get used to making decisions again. I'm out of practice."

"It's not that hard."

Rick scowled at Paul. "Not for you, maybe." He pointed out the window again, this time to a gravel turnoff they sped past. "That," he said. "Side roads."

Paul turned to the view the gravel road, which snaked over the foothills and looked to disappear into the towering mountains, twenty kilometres distant, the peaks of which were now a shimmering pewter under the hot white sun. Incomparable, thought Paul. There wasn't any way to look at it except with marvel in your heart.

"What you're looking at," said Rick, pointing out the window again. "That's what you don't have inside. That's what's hard to adjust to. There are so many different roads you can take out here. It kind of fucks with you."

"But if you have a place to go, side roads just make it take longer to get there. I don't always take side roads, even if they're there."

Rick smiled half-heartedly. "That's because you probably don't go anywhere unless you've got a place to go to. That's good for you, I guess."

"You don't make it sound that good."

"I'm just jealous, that's all. I wish I had the kind of direction you and Lisa seem to have. Must be nice." Rick sniffed, as if he didn't think it was a nice thing at all.

"You don't actually think we know what we're doing? Well me, anyway."

"That's how it looks."

"It's not how it feels."

"Try looking at it from where I'm sitting. You . . . you say, Okay, I want to do this, and then you just get on with doing it."

"It's a lot more complicated than that, but, okay, say that's mostly true. Why is that any different from you? What's stopping from you doing that?"

Rick nodded his head in emphasis with every word. "You really don't get it, do you?"

"I don't know where you're going with this. You're out. You have the chance to start over. Sure, there are barriers, *lines*. I'm not saying there aren't. But does that mean you just hit a fence and turn the direction it sends you? That doesn't seem much like you, or much like the way anybody ought to act, whether you're just out of jail or not."

"That right there, what you just said, shows you don't understand what it's like."

"What what's like? Why are you being so obscure?"

"To show you that you don't know the mind-set."

"Of who? Of somebody who's just gotten out of jail?" Paul turned his head toward his brother. "No, of course I don't. How could I? I never claimed I did."

"Then why are you talking like you do?" Rick took a hand off the wheel and gestured at the inside of the truck, as if that explained it all, though it explained nothing to Paul.

"I'm not talking like I know the mind-set, Rick. For Chrissakes."

"You know, you think it's normal, like it's standard procedure to own your own person, your individuality or whatever. Well, it's not."

"I don't think it's 'normal.' I didn't say that. I just think it's essential, that's all."

"So do I, but in a different way than you."

"How so?"

"Because I know you." Rick tilted his forehead toward Paul. "I know what you write about."

Paul paused before speaking, so that he could make sure he didn't let any more of his gathering frustration leak into his voice. "I have no idea where you're going with all this."

"You write about authority."

"I do?"

"Oh, come on, you sent me a subscription to 2.2.4. the whole time I was inside. I read every issue. Maybe sometimes you could say your writing is technically about something else, but you're always writing about authority at one level or another. Abuses of it. Challenging it. Holding it accountable. Well, listen up. One thing I came to understand inside is authority, alright? And it's cool that you write about it, that you want to challenge it. That's great. But you have a boss. You report to people. You have to do what other people tell you to. You do it."

Paul thought about that as he fixed his eyes on the road—they were coming up on the steeply rolling set of foothills just north of Longview. He'd never have characterized his relationship with Harold as one with rigid lines of authority, but the way Rick was representing it was not totally unfair. Harold *was* his boss. And although Harold would never have overtly channelled him to write in a certain way, Paul knew he would be as likely as not to fall in step with a line of thinking if Harold was strongly in favour of it.

"You're sort of right. I do listen to Harold. And he is my boss."

"But that's okay, if you see what I mean. You are an individual in a real way. Lisa is the same. She's an individual, but she still has to report to people, her advisor, her committee, whatever the hell that stuff is—she's got to make other people happy. Right?"

"I guess so, though I imagine she'd have a reply to that."

They both laughed. "But," said Rick, poking his chest with a forefinger, "I'm different."

"You're not an individual?"

"I'm more individual."

"More individual? Is that right? *Extra*-individual. *Ultra*-individual. Wow. I didn't realize I was driving with such a special person."

"As usual, missing the point. You challenge authority from where you sit, and that's great. It's theoretical. But for me, it's more direct. It's real." Rick paused, seemed to concentrate on driving for a moment, then he continued in a softer, almost tender voice. "I decided inside—in jail—what being an individual means. I can't listen to the bullshit anymore, Paul."

"I'm still not quite following you, Rick."

"I don't want people telling me what to do anymore. Here. Now. Not theoretically. I mean me, today, tomorrow. I can't stomach any more of it. You know?"

"But Rick, that's *totally* theoretical." Paul looked ahead as he spoke, holding his palms out in front of him, as if one held *theory* and the other *reality*. "Okay, it's philosophically cool. It'll sound great in the bar when you're shooting pool with your buddies. But it's unworkable. You say it's real, but it's not real at all. Not only that, it's . . . well, *egotistical* isn't quite the right word. It's like you're making yourself the centre of the world. It's arrogant, don't you think. I don't think you really mean it, anyway."

"Why's that, Aristotle?"

"Because you can't escape all that, all that stuff you talked about. That's the way society works. People tell other people what to do. It's part of the social lubricant. The social order. The rule of law. Does that mean you won't obey a red light because a person other than you decided to put it there? Or that if you get a job you won't report when your boss tells you to, because you just don't want to? I mean, how is that going to work? Surely, the point is to choose your battles. Why drive on the right side of the road? Why drive the speed limit? You're just posing."

Rick shook his head and chewed his bottom lip, as if disappointed in a child's manners. He sped up slightly without saying anything. They came to the crest of a hill from which the road ran downhill for at least two or three kilometres. The line of pavement, thought Paul, looked like a black rope stretching out away from them, thinning, taut, pulling them toward some unknowable but tantalizing adventure, like they were water-skiers and the future was a boat. Rick let the truck pick up speed naturally as they came down the hill, but at the bottom he gunned it, so that they hit the trough and shot out along the bottom as if on a roller coaster. He kept his foot to the floor. Soon they were twenty, thirty, forty kilometres above the speed limit, rocketing along the highway.

"Right," said Paul, hoping his voice didn't betray him. "A gesture. So what? Don't be so literal."

Rick said nothing, just stared straight ahead, his foot pressing down. They were shooting insanely down the two-lane tarmac. Paul put his hand on the door hold and pressed his feet against the floorboard.

"Rick," Paul half shouted. This was real fear. "It's not funny. Slow down. I don't want to die because of some point you feel you need to make. And more importantly, *you* don't want to die because of some stupid point."

"Stupid?"

They picked up even more speed. Paul began to feel and hear a shimmying from beneath, as if the road had taken on a washboard quality.

"My point, Paul, is not theoretical." Rick looked at Paul for too long, then turned his face back to the road, took his foot off the accelerator, and let the truck's speed gradually die off. "It's more important than anything. My individuality. That's all I have. Sure, I'll get a job. Sure, I'll stop for red lights. But there isn't anybody that is ever going to tell me what to do again when it matters. Ever."

Paul saw how calm his brother was, how unrattled he was by his own stunt, a composure Paul didn't share. "I just told you to slow down, Mister Individual, and you did that."

Rick glared at Paul and hit the gas hard with his foot, almost slamming it into the floor, so that the truck practically lifted off the pavement and shot forward. Paul felt his colon seize up and he shouted out, "Hey!" Rick immediately took his foot off the gas and turned to his brother cackling and hooting.

"You fucker!" Paul leaned over and punched Rick as hard as he could on the upper shoulder, meaning it. "You absolute bastard."

"Hey, hey," said Rick. "Don't screw with me, buddy. I had lots of free time inside." He lifted his shirtsleeve to reveal a bicep Paul saw had to be twice the size of his own. Five minutes later, they hit the steep crest of Longview Hill and saw the small town of Longview at the base. "Gas now I figure will get us all the way to Stennets." At the station, Paul leaned over in his seat and reached for his wallet.

"Forget it, buddy."

"It's only fair. You paid when we left town."

"I asked you to come."

"Not just to share gas?"

Rick smiled. "Not just to share gas."

Through the southern pass, Highway 22 to Highway 3, then through a corner of British Columbia along the 93 to Montana, Rick spoke little. Once pointed west, they took the snaking Crowsnest Pass through the first of the Rockies, past the abandoned and dilapidated coal mines, through the massive granite field of the Frank Slide, where a hundred years earlier the side of a mountain had dropped onto the town of Frank. Paul felt claustrophobia descend on him like a bad mood; he sometimes felt this way in the mountains, which he usually preferred to admire from afar. They were too big, too tall. And look what could happen. The Frank Slide. Something as solid as a mountain—something you could never imagine would betray you—could just collapse and fall on top of you. Paul opened his mouth and took a breath to the tips of his lungs.

"Four thousand people?"

The boulders were the size of cars. The upper face of the mountain where the rock had sheared away was as smooth as a cleft brick of cheese. How long had it taken? Two seconds? Ten? Could a world end that quickly? And what had they left behind? It was underneath that rock, whatever it was. If a rock slide covered me and my house, thought Paul, what would the world know or remember of me? Did it matter who knew what?

"Four?"

"I don't know. I didn't see the sign. Maybe we'll stop at the info booth on the way back."

"I wonder if anyone saw it? Witnessed it?"

"All of them."

Paul smiled. "Seriously."

"We could ask Tammy. I bet she'll know."

"I can't wait to meet her. It's kind of wild, don't you think?"

Rick hesitated, then grimaced hard, as if fighting off a stomach cramp. "Would you be worried if you were me? I mean, it's crazy. Fuck! This isn't going to work, is it? Should I turn around?"

Paul didn't know what to say, and, anyway, he could tell Rick wasn't really looking for answers, that he might have been asking the same questions out loud even if he'd been the only one in the truck. Rick made to pass a semi-trailer once they got past Frank Slide. He sharked out into oncoming traffic and gunned past the slower vehicle. Once past, he seemed in a greater hurry to get to the border, speeding, forcing himself into tight spaces when passing. Paul said nothing. He wouldn't have driven that way, but he wasn't doing what Rick was doing. You had to cut him some slack.

They passed through Fernie on 93, which across the border became US 37. It was only here that it occurred to Paul again to wonder if crossing the border might be a problem for Rick. In the new world order, terrorism, profiling, concerns about the porous border, crossing over into the United States was not the smiling Have a Nice Day pleasantry it used to be, particularly if you'd just been out of jail for a week or two. Paul even wondered if it was legal, if Rick might be violating his parole? Or if he even had a passport, though Paul knew technically you didn't need one for a surface crossing? Just when he was thinking of asking Rick these things, when they were within about ten kilometres of the border crossing at Roosville, Rick abruptly turned onto a secondary road, one he seemed to know. He drove a couple hundred metres down a long bend before stopping.

"What's going on?"

"You're taking over," said Rick.

"What? Why?"

Rick undid his seat belt and opened his door. "You're driving. Border guards always focus on the driver. Just tell them you're picking up Tammy Vine in Stennets. Pretend she's your girlfriend. Here." He handed Paul a piece of paper. "Tammy's address and phone number in case they want to call her or bring up her data. That's the kind of shit they do."

"But that's lying. I'm not going to pick her up. You are. I'm just along for the ride."

"You're not lying. Just tell them what we're doing.

"But . . ."

"I thought you said you were coming along to help me?"

"I am."

"Well, this will help. If I'm driving they might give me some grief."

"Are you even allowed to cross?"

"Yeah . . . pretty sure. But these guys have a lot of power. More than any other policing force. Did you know that? They're motherfuckers. One of them might decide to not let me through because he's constipated, or because he doesn't like my shirt. Even prison guards don't like crossing the border. Too unpredictable, especially now. Flying I wouldn't do, but driving, we'll probably get through."

"Great." Paul looked out his side window and then back to his brother. "This is great, Rick. Fuck me."

"If you're going to shit your pants, we'll take one of the logging roads. There's a few I know down this way."

"Oh, yeah, that would be a *lot* better. How do you know about logging roads, anyway?"

Rick ignored him. "In fact, there's one about five miles down this road. But it'll be a couple hours slower. Don't want to ding Dad's truck anymore, though."

Paul undid his seat belt. "Let's just go."

Rick and Paul changed seats. "Like you said, Paul. You take direct routes. You avoid side roads. I'm just helping you be true to your own nature. I'm facilitating."

Paul didn't laugh along with his brother. He could feel his face turn red as they approached the border crossing. The soft fleshy parts at the bottom of his ears felt like hot wax about to drip onto his shoulders. He cleared his throat repeatedly before pulling up to the booth.

"Morning," said the border guard, a heavy-set man with a walrus moustache.

"Hey," said Paul, certain the guard would see his veins throbbing from jawbone to collarbone.

"Canadian?"

"Yes."

"Where you headed?"

"Stennets."

"Stennets?" He ran a cupped hand over his thick moustache. "What's in Stennets?"

"Going to pick up a friend. She's Canadian, but she went down there to help out her sister, who just died of cancer. We're basically coming right back."

The guard nodded: "Where to?"

"Calgary."

"What's your name?"

"Paul Munk." Paul handed the guard his driver's license and passport.

"And your friend's name? Not that guy"—he pointed at Rick—"the woman in Stennets."

"Tammy Vine."

"Okay. . . . Now you can tell me who that is," he said, gesturing into the truck cab at Rick.

"That's my brother, Rick."

Rick pulled his wallet out of one back pocket and his passport from the other and made, Paul saw, a subtle show of giving them to Paul exactly so the border guard would see him doing it. The guard looked further into the truck, but didn't ask for Rick's ID. After pulling back a bit, he looked into the bed of the truck.

"Mind if I have a quick look through those duffel bags?"

"No, go ahead."

The guard unzipped the bags, poked around, zipped them back up, and returned to the window. "Got any luggage or bags behind the seats here?"

"No sir."

"Who'd you say you were visiting?"

"Tammy Vine. You want this?" Paul offered him the slip of paper with Tammy's name, address, and phone number.

The guard took the paper. "Just a moment, please." He slipped inside the booth.

Paul faced straight out the front window, and took as deep a breath as he could manage and let it out slowly. Rick leaned over and took his wallet and passport off Paul's lap. "Jesus, I'm hungry," he said. "We ought to grab something in Eureka."

The booth window shot open, and without coming back outside, the guard handed Paul his ID and the sheet of paper.

"Enjoy your stay in Stennets," he said without inflection, closing the window.

Paul eased the truck into gear and slowly pulled away. His fingertips were tingling; he made a fist of one hand, then the other, pressing, releasing, pressing.

"I didn't enjoy that. Don't do that to me again."

Rick looked over, pushing his lips out. "Side roads," he said. "You might learn something if you took one every now and then. Anyway, you were a pro."

A pro? At what? "And where'd you get a passport so quick?"

Rick grinned. "It's my expired one, just a few years old."

Paul looked over at his brother. "You *are* joking?"

"Relax. You're all tense, man."

"I wonder why."

After eating at a local diner in the little town of Eureka, then passing through the scalped, burned-out forest of northwest Montana—a place that seemed stark and alien to Paul compared with the forest on the other side of the border—they pulled into Stennets along the Clark Fork River, where there hadn't been as much logging and that seemed to Paul as physically appealing as his own part of the world. The mountains didn't feel as oppressive as being in the Rockies. He imagined living here, the hiking, the hunting, the fishing; it would be paradise for some. But only for some. Along the main strip was a convenience store, liquor store, hardware store, and three low-slung bars with the kind of creamy neon beer signs flickering in smallish barred windows that Paul had always associated with the random, senseless violence of movies about rootless drifters. They were in America. It was a different barometric pressure; Paul felt he could have closed his eyes and still known they were no longer north of the border. They followed Tammy's directions, making a turn by the Mercantile convenience store into a neighbourhood hard against the Bitterroot mountain range bordering the southern edge of a town that couldn't have been made up of more than a couple of hundred buildings. Rick drove slowly as he looked for the address. They briefly got stuck behind a slow-moving vehicle, a pick-up with a bumper sticker that read, IF IT'S "TOURIST SEASON," HOW COME WE CAN'T SHOOT 'EM?

"Nervous?"

Rick was leaning forward, chest near the wheel. "Should I be?"

"*I* am."

They pulled up in front of the house with the same address as that on the slip of paper in Rick's hand. It was an industrial part of town, where a few mechanics and plumbers had their workshops, but it was the last stop before the wilderness. On the east side was a dense wall of forest, but the house—if you could call it that—was long and low and clearly had not been originally constructed to act as somebody's residence. It looked like a car repair shop. Along the partially sided west flank hung a long black strip of tarred insulation underpaper, the end of which was flapping in the breeze like the heraldic banner of some defeated medieval army. The building squatted like a big grey brick, with two drapeless front windows that stared out dead-eyed. The "lawn" seemed as if it might once have sported grass, but it was now a kind of low-rent driveway and parking stall surfaced with gravel, weed, and crabgrass, though there were two lawn chairs near the door. It was hard to believe this was someone's house.

"This is where she's been living?"

"This is Palmer's place."

"Who's that?"

"Palmer is . . ." Rick hesitated. "He's a friend of hers. Gave her a place, sort of . . . I guess helping her out. Place to stay while she helped her sister. You wait here," said Rick, his voice thin. "I'll see if she's around." Rick turned his gaze away from the house and back to Paul. The skin of his throat was mottled, like he'd just been caught out in a small and pointless lie that betrayed a larger character fault. "I . . . I don't know . . . I've never felt like this before. I don't know what to do."

Paul reached over and put his hand on his brother's shoulder. "Come on. This is a great thing you're doing. Go on up. I'd go with you but then she'd see I'm better looking and call it off. Come on. Go. You'll be fine. We'll laugh about it later over a beer."

Rick tried to smile. "Okay." He opened his door and hesitantly made his way to the front of the building, peering at the windows. The main door was at yard level, so Rick simply stepped forward and in one motion, as if trying to sustain his forward momentum, put a hand to the bell. He waited. Put his finger to the bell again. After a minute, he turned and looked to Paul, raised his shoulders up, then retreated from the house, trying to look again through the front window.

"Nobody home," he said, back in the truck.

"She was expecting us—you—today, wasn't she?"

Rick nodded, pulled another slip of paper from his wallet. "She gave me the address of where her sister used to live. Maybe she's down there."

"Well, let's run down and look. Can't be that far, can it?"

Rick looked at the house again. "No, you wouldn't think so . . . how about you wait here, just in case, so she knows we're here if she suddenly shows up. I'll be back pretty quick. If she's not at either place, we'll just wait here, I guess."

Paul glanced past his brother, to the house. "At least there's a couple of lawn chairs," he said, smiling. "I'll wait, and you go to the other place." He took his knapsack and got out, then leaned in the window. "Don't leave me here."

Rick drove away. Paul ambled up to the chairs, put his knapsack in one and sat down in the other. It felt good to not be driving. The chairs were in the shade, and as he sat there, hot yet cool, he tried to keep his frustration in check. *Don't judge.* It didn't work. *Okay, judge, but keep your mouth shut.* He was pissed off at Rick for his border stunt, but now that they were in Montana, on this quixotic mission, Paul began to feel more acutely, and with more sympathy, why Rick had wanted him to come along. To supply the familiar. Something known, a handrail in the dark. At least, Paul wanted this to be why Rick had asked him. He'd want the same thing. It was okay. It was normal.

He took out his book, and had been reading for maybe five minutes when he heard a scream from the house—a child's scream, partly in glee, partly in torture. Tickling taken to sadistic extremes, he thought immediately, the kind of tickling Rick used to inflict on him. He shot to the door, found the bell, pressed it, heard the chime. The screaming stopped. He rang the bell again. His cheeks were pinpricking with confusion and worry. In the queer leftover silence, Paul heard steps on the other side of the door. A shuffling. He took time to try to adopt a friendly expression, but what was he supposed to say now? *Hi, I'm Rick's brother, except he drove away and left me here.*

The door didn't open. Paul nearly put his eye to the spyhole, but the thought of seeing another eye staring back at him was too creepy. He decided to stand his ground. He put his finger to the bell again and the door jerked open, the chimes ringing out onto the yard and into the street. He snapped his finger back as if he'd touched a live socket. A woman was standing in the doorway, and something about her expression Paul found immediately mystifying, a sad projection in the eyes, the gaze of someone who has waited a long time for a thing she knows she'll never receive. Was this Tammy?

"I'm Paul. Uh, Rick . . . Rick Munk? He's my brother?"

The woman continued to smile delphically at Paul, batting short sparse eyelashes over reddish brown eyes. He might have been a salesman she was kindly enduring. She had thick lips and parted them slightly. Paul hesitated, trying to parse out who this woman was. Silently, she hiked her shirt out of her pants and lifted one side of it as high as her shoulder. She was braless and showed Paul one breast.

"What are you . . . doing?" He looked from her face down to her large breast, at the heavy aureole gathering to form a thick brown volcano of a nipple. Two or three crinkly black hairs sprouted from the base of the nipple. He returned his mute stare to her face. She was smiling at him the same way, but still had not spoken. She lowered her T-shirt. A child, a boy of twelve or so, poked his head around the corner of the entranceway, as if he'd been hiding there the whole time just to see what happened. "Who are you?" said the kid. "Government? Or what?! Selling something?" He cackled, his voice high and uncertain.

"Rick Munk is my brother?"

The woman seemed to stare at Paul's mouth, then moved her lips. Garbled sounds escaped, not quite gibberish, but more the speech of someone talking with a mouthful of steaming hot food. She kept the same grin on her face. Paul stared hard at her lips, trying to make out the words. She was pudgy in a delicate, cream-fed way, as if she might still grow out of it, though the plentiful, bristly hairs along her moustache line made it impossible for Paul to accurately guess her age. She might have been twenty or forty.

"Rick Munk," he said again to her.

"She's deaf," said the boy smartly, still mostly hidden behind the wall of the entranceway. "D-E-A-F. Deaf. Get it?"

"Oh." Paul turned to the woman. "Sorry," he said, before realizing what he was doing. "Can she lip-read? I mean . . . can you lip-read?"

"She's a retard, too."

"That's not a very nice word."

"Well, it's what she is. A retard. Like you." He burst into a cackle again and licked his lips as though he'd been messily eating candy. He had big teeth with gaps between them and brown buzz-cut hair, and appeared severely emaciated to Paul, as if eating was not much of a habit.

"Do you know where Tammy Vine is?"

"Yeah." He smirked and made Paul wait. "She's grocery shopping."

"Groceries! Why?" asked Paul, almost adding, *. . . if she's leaving?*

"Gee, I don't know. Why do people usually buy groceries?"

"We're supposed to meet Tammy here."

"Rick better be nice."

"Huh?"

The kid stared at Paul, no longer grinning. He seemed older, tired, when he lost the grin and cackle. "Dad was out back a while ago, but he might have gone to the hardware store . . . I wrecked his Robertson digging for gold. Maybe he knows when Tammy'll be back." With that the boy disappeared behind a wall inside the long, low, dingy house; Paul turned to the woman, who was standing much as she had been when she'd opened the door. Her sienna eyes were open, but it was plain they were now shuttered from the inside. She stared at him, mute, dull, no longer smiling. The lamp was out.

❦

The skinned frame of a truck was hoisted up on blocks beside a small Quonset hut, which Paul assumed was the garage, but which was more the size of a large garden shed. There were no wheels on the axles and no cab on the frame. It reminded Paul of a vehicle from a science fiction movie he'd seen recently in which the future had become a post-apocalyptic wasteland, but there was also something shameful about this denuded truck, as if it were an innocent prisoner stretched naked on the rack. Two steps led up the back door of the house. Paul sat down on the top step and cast a skeptical eye across the yard between the house and garage. To one side was a large vegetable garden, but strewn across the rest of the scabrous lawn were dozens of toys, most of them so smashed up they might have been shards of field shrapnel. *Dad? Did the kid mean Palmer?*

Paul stood up, thinking that before he went knocking on any garage doors he'd talk to the mouthy little kid one more time to find out who was who around this dump. There was no back door bell, so he put his hand to the doorknob with the intention of opening the door and yelling into the house. The door was unlocked but stuck, and just as he put some weight into it, a voice attacked him from the yard. "What in hell's name you doing?!"

Paul's heart turtled and only came out again when an axe didn't fall across his neck. He turned and was met by a large man with black and grey hair sprouting from the neck of his filthy green T-shirt. He was holding an intricate piece of machinery about the size of an adult human head, and it fit comfortably into his huge oil-soaked hands.

"I'm looking for Tammy Vine," Paul said, stepping back to yard level. He coughed and cleared his throat. "Are you Palmer?"

The man stood in front of Paul, assessing him as if buying livestock at the fair. He abruptly hefted the machine from his right hand to his left, freeing up the right, Paul imagined, for the maximum delivery of violence, should it come to that. There was anger in the air around this guy, like a bad body odour, which, it turned out, also happened to be in the air. He was a big man, with a stout gut and greying hair straggling well past his ears except for where a rubber band had gathered most of it in a messy ponytail. He was just some kind of animal. Paul felt the big muscles in his legs sag. The man stared at him, apparently making calculations in the back of his head: the numbers weren't adding up. He said nothing for a long time. "Tammy," he finally said. "Really."

Paul analyzed the yard, glanced back toward the gate leading out to the front. He began making best-guess measurements involving distance, body weight, fitness, and the superiority of his own footwear over that of his soon-to-be pursuer. Paul reckoned the odds to be slightly in his favour, particularly if he could get five feet of ground between them before the man could react. Paul's thighs began to squirm. His breathing quickened and he moved his weight to the balls of his feet. "I'm Paul Munk. My brother is Rick Munk."

"Rick?" The man diluted his scowl. "Hunh. So where's your bro' then?"

"Umm . . . buying something, I think. Gassing up. He said he'd be back in a few minutes. Actually, he might be checking Tammy's sister's place, too."

After another moment of skeptical inspection, he thrust a dirty hand toward Paul. "Palmer."

The hand was the size of a book, and impossible to encircle. Paul tried to match Palmer's masculinity, pumping a couple of times, but on the second pump his hand slipped out of the larger paw. Palmer looked at his hand then dragged it across his filthy overalls, a gesture that, given the griminess of Palmer's hand, Paul felt he ought to be performing himself.

Palmer smiled for the first time, and the whiteness of his teeth stood out in startling relief against the filth covering the rest of him. "Paul Munk . . . Rick sent you in to do a little recon, did he? Doesn't surprise me." Palmer was grinning widely now, and seemed delighted by his thumbnail-sketch of events. "Sounds like him."

"He rang the front bell first, about ten minutes ago. Nobody answered."

"I got the bell rigged up to my garage back there. I didn't hear nothin'."

"Maybe it's not working. I mean, you didn't answer it when I rang a few minutes ago."

He stared at Paul for so long, Paul almost wanted to laugh. "The bell's working," he finally said. "Morton answers it when I'm out back."

"Okay . . . well, Rick should be right back."

"Can't wait to see the ol' jailbird. Been a few years, I guess."

"Isn't jailbird, like, an *escaped* convict?"

Palmer angled his face toward Paul's jaw, and then raised his eyes to Paul's. ". . . Thanks for clearing that up."

"Well, that's only what I thought."

"Uh-huh. So, you're from the family, hey?"

"Family?"

"She'll be staying with?"

This was the first time it had really been stated so bluntly to Paul. Palmer was right: Tammy was going to be staying in their house, or at least the house Paul had grown up in. Tammy. A woman he'd never met. A woman who had some sort of relationship to this man, Palmer, and to the people in this house. Who was this woman, anyway? Her name was Tammy Vine. She was a potter. She wrote to criminals, and had apparently fallen in love with one. Her sister had died of cancer. She was from Stennets, where she lived in a shithole of a house with some sociopathic ten-year-old and a deaf disabled woman and with half a truck on blocks out back and a hairy, filthy mechanic in the garage.

"Hey, don't look so overjoyed about it all. She's not so bad. Listen, just park it on the porch there, Mister Munkey Boy. She'll be here pretty quick, I'm guessing. Must have been something important made her late. Ricky Dick'll be right back, won't he, if he's only gone to gas up? Or was that to check at Tammy's sister's?"

Paul parked it where he was told and watched Palmer go back into the garage. During his six years working for the magazine, Paul had met hundreds of people he needed or wanted information from immediately upon meeting them, and through experience and simply paying attention he'd learned his gut instinct almost never failed him when it came to assessing them—what their essential character was, what he could expect to get out of them, what they thought of him; he trusted his gut here, too, but he was still a bit surprised that he didn't feel more apprehension around this guy, this whole situation. Why was that? Palmer and Rick seemed to go back some, perhaps that was it. Palmer returned from the garage carrying the same piece of machinery, as well as a wrench that seemed much too large to be applied to the piece under consideration. When Palmer made to sit down beside him, Paul bum-shuffled over a couple of feet, ostensibly out of politeness, but in reality to avoid coming into contact with Palmer's greasy overalls.

"Thanks," Palmer said. He pulled a silver, puck-sized tin from his pocket. "Chaw?"

Paul gaped at the tin of menthol chewing tobacco. He bared his teeth.

Palmer shrugged and packed a wad between his lower teeth and lip, and set to work on the machine in his lap. Paul watched intently as Palmer removed two bolts from what appeared to be a lid.

"What is that?"

Palmer loosed a thick stream of chaw juice from between his lips. It hit the dusty ground with a dry splat and quickly mutated into a narrow black turd laying beside the porch. It sat compatibly within the overall aesthetic of the yard. "What do you think it is?"

"I don't know. An engine?"

"... Engine?" said Palmer. He grinned at Paul, then turned his mouth into a tight sour hole to launch another stinky black gherkin onto the lawn. Paul could smell the minty dirt flavour. It was revolting.

"So are those your kids inside?"

"That's right." He took a small flathead screwdriver from a chest pocket and scraped it along the underside of his heavy chin through his beard, as if he were considering having a shave with it. Only when Palmer was scratching his chin did Paul notice his fingernails; they were chewed to the quick, raw and red, as if rats had been at them during the night. Rick had the same problem, or at least he had since coming back from his first time in jail: often he reduced his nails to such worried nubs they started to bleed. Paul wondered if a woman would, could, ignore it or even find it attractive? If Tammy, who, of course, had never laid eyes on Rick—and never might, depending on whether he ever returned—would see his nail gnawing as significant or symbolic? It was one of those things people rationalized with. This made Paul wonder more about Tammy, about who she was and about her taste in men, since nail chewing was, he hoped, for Rick's sake, not the only thing she was looking for in a partner. Rick and Palmer didn't seem much alike to Paul, except that in Paul's early assessment of Palmer he appeared to share with Rick a kind of *Fuck You* confidence, a take it or leave it self-assurance. But then, Paul wondered, how could Tammy truly know even that much about Rick, having never actually met him? Paul heard noises from inside the house, and turned back to Palmer.

"You know, for a second I wondered if the woman, your daughter, the . . . I mean, she's deaf, I guess, I wondered if she was Tammy."

This caused Palmer to laugh so hard he nearly choked on his chaw, and was forced to sloppily cough it out of his mouth onto the porch where it sat glistening like a freshly skinned mouse. He sawed a sleeve across his face and kicked at the wad, sending it into the yard, where it disappeared amongst the clutter. Paul laughed along with Palmer, though, in truth, he wasn't sure what they were laughing about.

"No, Debbie's mine alright."

"And the boy, too?"

"'Fraid so." Palmer laughed. "Morton. He's a pain in the ass, that little pole of shit." Palmer glanced behind him to the back door, as if worried Morton might be listening. "Ah, he's an okay kid. Just in a phase . . . since the day he was born."

This time, Paul laughed first. Palmer slapped Paul's knee goodheartedly, the ease and bonhomie of which Paul appreciated until he looked down and noticed a painterly smear of grease stropped across his jeans. Palmer put down his tools and pulled a toothpick and a small penknife from his shirt pocket. After briefly testing the sharpness of the toothpick, he removed it from his mouth and used the knife to whittle it to a needlepoint. Then he worked it back in between a couple of teeth and put the knife back in his pocket. After a moment or two of intensive research with the toothpick, he produced a speck of tobacco chaw between his lips that he spat briskly into the air.

"So, you like Stennets?" said Paul.

"What's not to like?"

"You don't feel sort of isolated? It feels pretty remote here."

"That's why people come here, Munkey Boy," said Palmer, his attention on the machine in his lap. "You can do stuff. Be left alone. Big places are just collections of strangers, that's all. Weirdos. You know what I mean. Different types. Cities are sewers. I don't mean that in a negative way, acourse."

"People are just people to me."

Palmer smiled at Paul like a teacher listening to a student trying to fake his way through a subject he knew nothing about, waiting patiently for him to bury himself. "Is that right? *People are just people*. I'm gonna have to remember that."

Paul was thinking how to respond when a truck pulled in off the alley and came to a stop out of sight behind the garage.

"There's your gal," said Palmer. "Or do I mean Rick's gal." He turned and applied a broad theatrical stare to Paul. "*Is* that what I mean?"

"Sure. I guess . . . if that's what she wants. What they want."

"She says she does. Asking me . . . I figure she'll be back. Call it a hunch."

Paul ran a couple of fingers across his hairline and forehead to direct some sweat away. "Umm . . . so . . . who are you, anyway, Palmer? I mean, like, to Tammy."

Palmer removed the toothpick from his mouth, examined the now slightly dulled point. "Husband."

Paul's intestinal tract seized up. A vehicle door closed shut behind the garage.

"How do you mean?"

Palmer ignored the question. Tammy came around the corner of the garage, dropped something, bent over to pick it up, and then waved heartily, as if she simply could not wait another second to return to the scrappy but warm bosom of her fucked-up Stennets family. She had frizzy brown hair and a big, friendly smile, and though she wasn't overweight her faded jeans were so tight Paul could see even from where he sat the way the middle seam of the crotch separated the lips of her vulva. Palmer waved back to her with the screwdriver in his hand. Paul looked at the head-shaped machine cradled in Palmer's lap, then cast a sidelong glance progressively upward until he reached Palmer's face. He was watching Tammy approach, but noticed Paul looking at him.

"Got a problem, Munkey Boy?"

"No," said Paul. "Not me."

SEVEN

She handled each playing card with ease, expertly shuffling, cutting, and dealing out the deck. Waiting for their lunch on the patio of the Grin and Bear It Diner on the banks of the Clark Fork River on the northwestern edge of Stennets, Paul watched Tammy and Rick play cribbage. Tammy's long, ringless fingers, the dexterity in her wrists as she flicked cards across the table, the angle at the crook of her elbow in relation to the weight and delicacy of the thing in her hands; it all spoke to her way with materials, her comfort with an object in her palm. To Paul her hands seemed functionally yet elegantly constructed, like a small tight whisk, a simple and perfect shoe, an ordinary light bulb. It wasn't hard to believe she might be a fine potter. She had a sense of humour; he knew that much just from the mug she'd given Rick with the jail key handle. He was curious to see what she would make in Calgary. Already she'd talked hopefully about a kiln, a studio, getting a distribution deal with local artisan co-ops.

Rick laid his cards down when he was supposed to, but all his attention was on Tammy. "Fifteen-two," he said, looking up to Tammy and grinning.

"Oh, you bum," she said, paying close mind to her own cards.

Paul watched them both, trying to absorb it all. They were comfortable, intimate, and at ease with one another. What had she said in those letters? What had Rick said back? Paul found it hard to imagine that what he was seeing right in front of him was even possible. They were sitting there playing crib like some old couple on the porch who'd just seen off a passel of grandkids, but they'd only met a couple of hours ago, in a scene so muted and matter-of-fact that Paul could only assume they'd prearranged to make it that way to avoid any awkwardness, with Palmer or themselves. After that, Tammy simply said good-bye to the kids and then to Palmer, giving him a breezy hug and kiss, promising to write. Palmer didn't seem that broken up about her departure; he nodded, hugged her back, and said, "Drive safe." He shook Rick's hand, and they even shared a tight smile; it seemed to Paul they had an understanding of some sort, as if one was grudgingly entrusting to the other the safekeeping of a valued object.

She and Palmer had only lasted a year, Tammy had explained in the truck. She'd met him about eight years ago, when she had been down visiting her sister. Palmer was a friend of her sister's husband. But she and Palmer had failed "spectacularly" she said, without elaborating, except to say that he had "issues" and "opinions" she'd never be able to live with. After ending it with Palmer—amicably, she said—she had then gone back to Calgary, only to return two years ago when her sister got cancer. Palmer, she added in a soft voice, had been generous in letting her use his house as a base while she cared for her sister. Now that her sister had passed away, she was ready to get on with her life. Paul reasoned that Rick had to have heard or read a lot of this already; he didn't seem surprised or even interested, except for when she alluded to Palmer's issues and opinions. A couple of times he made noises of approval at the way Palmer had supported her.

"What about Debbie and Morton?" Paul said. "Palmer told me they were his kids."

"His first two marriages." Tammy was silent for a few seconds and turned more serious than she'd been to that point. "Palmer has always needed help raising his children," she said thoughtfully. "He just wasn't going to get it from me."

After they finished their crib game, which Tammy had suggested so as to "help things feel normal," she got up to go to the bathroom. This gave Paul a chance to talk to Rick alone for the first time since they'd arrived in Stennets. The patio was empty. "You know, Palmer said you brought me down here just to case the joint, to loosen things up before having to come in yourself."

"Huh?"

"When I was back there talking to him, feeling like a complete idiot, he snickered and said that was the only reason you brought me along."

Rick laughed. "What kind of guy did he seem to you?"

"Excuse me?"

"Palmer. Did you like him?"

Paul thought about that for a minute. Considering the way he felt the instant he saw Palmer and the way he felt when he first saw Tammy, his impression was not all bad. Paul was about to say that Palmer was not really a guy he'd ever be friends with, but given their differences he didn't seem like such an ogre. Before he could answer, however, Tammy came strolling back, arriving at the same time as the waitress. The short, bulky woman put a BLT with fries in front of her.

"There you go, Tam." The waitress was wearing a tag that said Noelle.

Tammy looked up and smiled. "I'll miss you, sweetie. You'll be good, won't you?"

"'Course." She grinned. "It's not me that's the problem. But we'll soldier on."

"I'll visit."

"We'll be here, you know that." Noelle laughed, walking away.

"What was that all about?" said Rick, through a mouthful of burger.

Tammy waved a hand in the air, then put it to her lips as she chewed. When she'd swallowed her bite, she said, "Noelle's boyfriend. He's . . . well, he's had some trouble with the law. Oh, sorry, hon." She put her hand on Rick's arm. He smiled. "I just mean, ongoing trouble. He's a bit of a folk hero down here. Palmer knows him, too. Run-ins with the government."

"Northwestern Federal Guard?" said Paul. "USMA? Montana Free Militia?"

"You know about those?" said Tammy, her brow crimped like the edge of a piecrust.

Rick laughed. "He's a journalist, Tammy. Remember?"

Paul laughed along with his brother. "And I'm from Alberta. The landscape isn't the only thing we share with Montana."

"I don't think it's very funny," said Tammy flatly. "I don't like it. Lots of people down here are into it, in one way or another. Or at least it feels that way sometimes, especially up in this part of the state. Palmer, too, though I have to say all I ever saw was a bunch of guys sitting around drinking beer and bitching about stuff until they passed out on the couch."

Paul wasn't surprised to find himself thinking about Daniel Code. It was hard to imagine Code would ever be supportive of the men and causes Tammy was talking about—not openly, anyway—but there had been flare-ups now and then of supporters of the Democratic Alliance Party saying or doing things that put them in bed with the radical right. Paul had often wondered what it was that connected all these people anyway? There wasn't one word for it. And what made any of them decide one cause was worthwhile and another not—and how far did you have to go to let positions bleed outside the frame to become extreme? What turned conviction into intolerance? When did a belief that the government overtaxes the public turn into becoming an antitax outlaw like Gordon Kahl, the North Dakotan who died for his cause? When did a belief that your government was too lax on immigration turn into bigotry and racial caricature? When did pride in your own heritage tumble headlong into denying the Holocaust? How did someone like Randy Weaver, who didn't want anyone telling him what guns to own, turn into a guy in a shootout? What was it—solipsism, frustrated individualism, insanity? There *were* fulcrum points; he was going to argue that again with Harold. Paul made a mental note to give it more thought when he got home, and to grill Code on both the question of belief system turning points as well as the views and actions of some of his more radical and outspoken Democratic Alliance colleagues. Already, Paul was curious to hear how Code would spin it, but he turned his attention back to Rick and Tammy.

"Aren't they kind of whacko?" said Paul. "All these guys. Bobby Greitz, John Vannmen. And Weaver, that standoff guy whose wife and kid got shot by the ATF at Ruby Ridge a few years ago."

"Why do you think they're whacko?" said Rick.

"Who?"

"Greitz, Vannmen, Trochman, Pitner, Weaver. All those guys. You don't think maybe they've got a point about a few things? Government's way worse back home. I don't see what makes those guys so crazy."

"Hmm, let's see. Maybe because they tend to be religious separatists, white supremacists, antitax extremists, antigovernment scaremongers, cultists, bigots and proto-Nazis. Other than that, they're probably a pretty good bunch."

Rick nibbled on a French fry. "Lisa was right about you."

"Who's Lisa?" said Tammy.

"I mentioned her once or twice in my letters," said Rick. "But I wouldn't be in a rush to meet her, if I were you."

"Our younger sister," said Paul. "And what do you mean by that? What did she say?"

"No, no. It's nothing."

"Bullshit," said Paul, smiling, putting down his sandwich. "Come on. What did she say?"

"Why do you care what she says?" said Rick. Tammy had joined in the laughter, cottoning on to the family teasing.

Paul hesitated briefly. It was a good question. Why did he care what Lisa thought? He knew the answer, and figured he might as well share it. "I care," said Paul, trying to be serious so that Rick would know he was giving a real answer, "because she sees things clearly, that's why. But don't tell her I said that, or I swear, so help me God, I'll pile-drive you."

Rick held up both hands in mock surrender. "Hey, trust me. I don't want to fuck with her either. But I'm not sure I should tell you. It'll go to your head."

"I've never met this woman," said Tammy, "and even I want to know what she said."

"Okay, okay. She said that Paul may not be very bright, and that he may not be very good with girls"—Tammy slapped Rick on the arm and then patted Paul on the shoulder, saying, *I'm sure that's not true*—"but that on things that mattered, he wasn't afraid to stand up and say what he thought."

"Wow, she said that?" Paul sat back. This was information worth having. After all, despite the differences in their sensibilities (his softer) and in their intelligence (hers greater), he just plain old liked his sister, even if he'd harboured reservations about getting close to her. Actually, he suspected she'd have hesitations about getting close to him.

"I want to meet your sister," said Tammy.

"No," said Rick. "You don't."

Tammy gave Paul a questioning look. "Why don't you want your sister to know that you respect her? Isn't that a good thing, a nice thing? If I had brothers, which I wish I did, and if they respected me, I think I'd be happy to know that."

Rick and Paul silently peeked at one another, as if each were waiting for the other to wade in. They broke into broad grins at the same time.

"Maybe we'll get married," said Rick. He was smiling at Tammy, but Paul found his expression hard to read. Tammy also looked confused, baring her teeth in a nonsmile. "If we do," Rick continued seconds later, "ask Lisa to be one of your bridesmaids. See what she says. I can't even imagine the look on her face if you ask her to wear some frilly gown. That would be priceless."

"*If* we get married?" said Tammy, poking Rick hard but affectionately on the shoulder with her forefinger. "That's a big *if*."

EIGHT

Calgary

The sign in front of the One Shepherd Parish near Paul's parents' house had changed for the third time in the last week. A fertile period, thought Paul. For a couple of days the message board had read, ASPIRE TO INSPIRE BEFORE YOU EXPIRE. But today there were no cheap words of wisdom, no moralizing tropes, no plumbing the shallows of the human condition: instead, DANIEL CODE FOR DEMOCRATIC ALLIANCE LEADER. CHART! Speared into the lawn underneath the message board was a sign supporting the Democratic Alliance Party.

Paul pulled around to park in the alley. The garage door was open, so he went that way, nearly tripping over a ski pole. Kicking it against the wall, he hit the switch to the automatic garage door opener, initiating the downward movement. Typically he'd have waited to make sure it closed properly, but this time he went straight inside.

Already, after not quite a week with Tammy around, there was a differentness to the house, a change in breathing patterns, an irregular pulse. It felt profound to Paul, as if the mood and emotion and energy and life of the house had been taken outside, torn apart like some play doll, then shoddily reconstructed before being brought back in. But, of course, there were more parts now, and it all felt a bit off to him, everything the same but for that extra ear sticking out of the rib cage or that third big toe stubbily attached to the forehead. Part of the problem was Tammy's disposition. She was so eager to make a good impression, and was so open-natured, that she turned their quiet, reserved house not so much upside down as inside out; she was regularly speaking out loud what she was feeling, and that was not normally the way things were done in the Munk home. Though Paul's father hit it off with her almost immediately—which was not surprising to Paul, given his father's disposition—his mother remained polite toward her, rather detached— also not surprising to Paul, given his mother's disposition. Lisa seemed to get along well enough with Tammy, though after the first evening in her presence described her privately to Paul as an "emotional octopus."

No one was in the kitchen. This was unusual, since Lisa or their mother could usually be found there; Lisa eating and reading, their mother fussing about a shopping list or talking on the phone to friends. Paul heard the TV from the family room in the basement, which helped put things back in order. He was about to go downstairs and see who was there and what they were watching when his father came down from the upper level of their house. "Hello, hello," he said. "How's life?"

"Good." Paul glanced toward the stairwell leading down to the TV room and lowered his voice as he spoke. "How are things going?"

Paul's father hunched slightly and made a fifty-fifty gesture. "I like her. She's a sweet girl," he said in a loud hoarse whisper. "Lisa." He rolled his eyes. "You know. Not as bad as you might have thought, though. Your mother . . . likes her, I think, but is having some trouble with them staying here, though she hasn't said so to anyone but me."

"What about Rick?"

"What do you mean?"

"You know, Rick and Tammy. How is it going? Are they getting along? Does it seem okay?"

Brian straightened up a little. "Have you seen problems?"

"No, no. Just making sure."

"Oh. No, seems fine so far."

"So where's Mum?"

Brian cleared his throat and assumed a theatrical voice that made Paul want to laugh out loud. "She's in the laundry room," he half shouted. "Have a beer. I'm barbecuing some steaks. Dinner in about an hour."

Paul reached into the fridge, pulled out an ale from a local brewery his father liked, and went downstairs to the TV room. Rick was slouched on the sofa—the same posture he'd assumed every time he'd sat in that room over the last couple of decades. Tammy was beside him. Rick was holding a half-empty beer, and Tammy had a glass of what looked like iced tea.

"Paul!" she said. "How are you?"

"Hey, man," said Rick, turning his attention back to the screen. They were watching baseball. Paul sat down in the big chair that used to have the coil sticking out of it, until his father had had the chair repaired a couple of years earlier. It felt odd to sit in it. Though this was the seat they'd fought over as children, Rick had usually ended up with it. It felt like Rick's chair, but of course Rick couldn't really sit in it now, not with Tammy around.

The three sat and talked before dinner, Paul and Tammy doing most of the talking. Rick tossed in an occasional comment but seemed more interested in the game. Paul asked Tammy about her pottery, what kinds of things she wanted to make, her long-term plans. She spoke further about wanting to run her own store and co-op, but only after she had children, a statement that brought Rick out of his ballgame trance.

"Seriously? Kids?"

This caused Tammy to slap him on the shoulder. "You only read the parts of my letters you wanted to hear."

"I'd like to have children, too," said Paul, surprising himself that he said this so easily, so quickly. It seemed a dangerous admission, somehow; luckily, Lisa hadn't been there to hear it.

"Really?" said Tammy, smiling broadly. "That's great." When she smiled Paul saw that it caused her eyes to narrow slightly, which somehow made her appear to be both interested and hopeful for him.

"Yeah," said Rick without taking his eyes off the TV. "That's great. But personally, if I were you, I'd focus on getting a date first."

Paul scratched the bridge of his nose with his middle finger. Rick didn't see it because he was still focussed on the TV, but Tammy laughed. The talk of kids reminded Paul of his first conversation with Daniel Code, and so Paul told Tammy about Code, his background, his looks, his weirdly genuine manner and his belief that Jesus had literally spoken to him. He didn't mention Code's daughter.

"One of the weird things, though," said Paul, "is that I actually kind of like the guy, despite everything he stands for. It's freaking me out a bit." He listed off Code's views and stances: advocate of capital punishment, extreme pro-life, opposed to entrenching gay rights, dedicated to dismantling universal health care, flat tax. Tammy shook her head in disapproval, but Rick, whom Paul thought hadn't been paying attention, said, "My kind of guy, except for the seeing Jesus bit."

"You can't be serious," said Paul. "I know you're joking."

Rick looked away from the ballgame. "Do you?"

Paul ignored his brother and said to Tammy, "Don't worry, he's just joking."

"No, I'm not." Rick sat up from his slouch. "I mean, okay, I don't agree with all those things exactly. But you're like some freaking left-winger. I'm an individualist. A libertarian. So is Code. You got a problem with that?"

"Individual? Here we go again. Good thing we're not in the car."

"At least he's not afraid to hold opinions," said Rick, his face turned back to the game.

"But that's morally neutral, isn't it? Having strong opinions and being willing to say what you think isn't automatically a good thing. Doesn't it depend on the actual opinion?".

"*Morally neutral!*? Spare me."

Paul made a show of sitting back and spreading his hands, then looking at Tammy imploringly, as if to say *Help me out here*.

"I get what you're saying, Paul," she said, bobbing her head earnestly. "But I hear Rick, too. There's having an opinion, and there's stating an opinion. Aren't there good and bad in both?"

Paul was unsure if the question was directed to him or to Rick, or to them both, but in any case Rick seemed to have lost interest in the discussion. The baseball announcer had gotten worked up about something and the man's braying sucked all of Rick's attention back to the game. A couple minutes later Paul's mother shouted down the short set of stairs that if they wanted dinner it was hot now but wasn't going to stay that way forever.

☙

Paul's father had charred the steaks just the way he liked them. The edges of the pieces of meat were as black and rough as mascara, little skirls of carbonized flesh. For decades this had been the sign to Paul's father that the meat was properly, or at least safely, cooked. Inside, the meat had no traces of pink at all, or of any colour that suggested it had once had blood and life coursing through it. This was a good thing, he had always insisted. Sure, the meat's a bit tougher, but at least you weren't going to catch some disease—or, worse, get worms. *Remember what that's like*, he'd say, his tone sepulchral, referring to the time as early grade schoolers that Paul and Rick had to be wormed out by their mother, bent over her lap, pants down, asses in the air, a suppository delivered straight up the poop chute. It had been sufficiently traumatic—for all of them—that, while growing up, Paul would go to any lengths to avoid another such session. His father would bring in hamburgers so black and hard that they jokingly (but, accurately) referred to them as pucks, and yet Paul would still ask for reassurance from his father that they were fully cooked. Paul had grown up believing that raw meat was nothing but a host for grubs and worms and maggots, and that the only way to ingest chicken, beef, and pork safely was to char, broil, or fry it double the recommended time. The one time in his life he'd visited Paris, with Emily, as a planned break from backpacking they had treated themselves to a nice meal in a fancy restaurant along the Right Bank. He ordered steak Tartare, thinking it was a steak that came with tartar sauce. In a mix of English and the one or two words of French he spoke, he requested that it be well done, a request that brought a thin smile and a nod from their gaunt, laconic waiter. After the waiter had placed the purple weeping ball of raw meat in front of Paul and flamboyantly cracked an egg into its concave roof, Paul very nearly fainted. Emily, a veteran of many Munk barbecues, cried with laughter, and the two of them sprinted from the restaurant after tossing down two or three hundred francs.

"Mmm, delicious," said Tammy, working her jaw as if she'd just taken on too big a ball of bubble gum.

"We like it well done in this house," said Paul's father, sawing into his meat.

"You know, you can get cancer from eating carbon," said Lisa, happily tucking into her steak like the carnivore she was. As often as not she passed on dessert to have an extra helping of meat. "Or anything barbecued for that matter." She paused and considered the piece of steak she had on her fork. "That actually makes it taste better somehow, knowing that."

"How's work, Paul?" his mother said gaily, which meant she was less interested in the question she'd posed than in changing the subject. "What's your latest article?"

"Busy," he said. "It's good. Doing a political piece." He tried to imagine how much of this conversation he wanted to get into. His parents were intelligent, and liked to talk about politics, and about what their children were up to; he credited them for this, and wanted to remember it when he had children of his own. But to take a topic he was still processing in his mind and put it on the table in front of Lisa was like setting a wriggling little pig in front of a crocodile. Not to mention Rick, fresh on the outside, living with his parents, trying to build a relationship, no work yet. Paul decided to stick to generalities, benign and safe statements that weren't false but that didn't make him liable to provide details—a little like a campaigning politician; he noted the irony and pressed on. "Yeah, no shortage of things to write about."

"I just think that's so interesting," said Tammy, putting down her knife and fork, as if that was going to help her pay closer attention. "What you do, Paul. I think it's great. I'd love to be able to write things like that."

Rick swallowed a mouthful of baked potato. "My marks in Grade 12 English were better than his."

"That's true," said Paul's mother. "Rick had excellent marks. In every subject."

"Does anyone remember what my mark was in Grade 12 English?" said Lisa, affecting a questioning expression. "Oh, right," she said. "One hundred per cent. Provincial medal. I almost forgot."

"Are you serious, Lisa?" said Tammy, trying to be friendly in her awe.

Lisa jabbed her fork into a piece of steak. "It was my worst subject."

"That doesn't mean you can write things people want to read," said Rick. "I'd rather go back to jail than read Foucault."

"Foo-who?" said Tammy.

"French guy no one reads," said Paul. "But who has apparently influenced everyone. Anyway, Rick is right. His high school English mark was higher than mine. He was a good writer."

"Was?"

Paul smirked at his brother. "Is?"

"Well, his letters sure were beautiful," said Tammy, leaning over and giving Rick a rub on the back of the neck, which made him blush and the others briefly look somewhere else.

Later, after his parents had gone to bed and Rick and Tammy had gone to a movie, Paul went downstairs to sit and watch TV with Lisa. She was sitting cross-legged at one end of the couch, her small frame wrapped up like a twist tie, although she didn't seem uncomfortable to Paul. He sat on the other end of the couch from her. She glanced at a book on her lap between dips into a bowl of white, yogurt-coated raisins while she rapidly surfed up and down the television channels. An old black-and-white movie. A music video with a bunch of rap artists jangling large gold chains. A tall pale man making dried fruit strips in a cumbersome white machine. Four sexy young people sitting around a table laughing and talking.

"Why do you do that?" he said.

"Do what?" she asked, without bothering to look over at Paul.

"You don't even know what the show is, and you're switching to the next one."

She absent-mindedly popped a couple of raisins into her mouth. "You wouldn't understand."

"Wouldn't I?"

"It's about messages and images," she said, swallowing her raisins and then turning to Paul.

"But not the story, of course?"

She let out a bored, vaguely exasperated lungful of air, as if she just didn't have the energy to go through showing the class simpleton how to tie his shoelaces again. "It doesn't have anything to do with the narrative. I'm not interested in the story. I'm interested in deeper meanings, cultural signifiers. I know that's hard for a journalist or non-fiction writer or whatever it is you're called, to understand. It's about subtext."

"But how can you understand the hidden meaning, or the cultural whatever, if you don't understand the story first? Don't you need to know what's happening above to know what's happening below?"

"Will knowing the colour of people's eyes tell you what's in their hearts?"

"Will knowing the make of an engine tell you whether it's powering an SUV or a minivan?"

She gazed at her brother in a plain horizontal stare and toyed with the zipper of her purple hoodie, which made Paul want to smile; it was a sign—she was enjoying herself. "Does the shell matter when the engine is what powers the journey?"

"Isn't the narrative the engine?"

"Holy high school, Batman."

"You're bored, and you don't have the ability to concentrate, so you're trying to make your short attention span sound cool and important."

"It's just so sad." She curled a few strands of her mousy blonde hair behind an ear, and then looked at Paul sidewise, as if she'd only just then become aware of something. "I think I actually feel sorry for you."

"You like to control the remote, so that you can play me like some fish, get me hooked on what something might be, let me watch it for ten seconds or so, and then once you sense I've zoned in, you flip it instantly. Like some fly fisherman. It's sick. Do you enjoy it? I bet you do. I bet that's the only reason you watch TV when I'm around. So that you can grab the remote and control the situation. Is it fun for you?"

Lisa turned to her brother, paused. "Yes."

They both turned back to the screen, and as soon as Paul allowed his eyes to rest on a program, Lisa switched it again. The phone rang. Lisa picked up the cordless, sat down again, hit the mute button on the remote (which she kept in her lap) and pressed the Talk key on the phone. Paul didn't mind, since he was just as happy to listen in on her call. In fact, part of him couldn't quite believe that she had even stayed in the room to take the call. She rarely spoke on the phone with anyone present.

"Hi Roger," she said, starting to riff through the channels again. She was smiling as she spoke, though she kept her eyes trained on the TV. Occasionally, she would stop at a program for longer than two seconds, at which point she would utter something gnomic. After a few minutes, Paul clued in to the conversation: they were comparing notes but in a challenging way, almost sparring. A shot of a TV drama with a well-dressed and attractive woman holding a clean, cute baby. "Classic conservative values," she said into the phone. "Or maybe something subversive, like the feminist interpretation of the trap of motherhood. We'd have to stick around to find out, and it's not worth the trouble."

A game of rugby. "No way. Homosexual subculture. Just look at the shape of that ball. And those sweaty, huggy scrums. I mean, please."

A children's show with turtles living human lives. Laughter, then, "No kidding. It's so obvious."

A log sawing competition on an outdoor channel. "Castration anxiety? Could be. You tell me."

Eventually, Lisa hung up and resumed her wordless flipping through the channels without even looking over at Paul. She was fiddling with her zipper again, but Paul noticed this time she was slowly moving it up and down the length of the hoodie.

"And who was that?" he finally had to ask.

"One of my fourth-year students." Lisa popped a raisin into her mouth and began chewing it loudly, open-mouthed.

"Evening tutorial?"

She let out a soft little burp that she covered with the back of her hand. "Nice try."

He grinned.

"So, don't you want to hear what I noticed? About Tammy. You haven't really asked me my opinion yet."

"You know," said Paul. "I look at you and I can't help thinking we're all just lab rats in some experiment you're conducting."

"Will you just shut up for one minute? She's not what she wants us to think she is."

Paul shifted positions so that he was facing Lisa with both legs stretched out on the couch. "What do you mean?"

"She was acting. She was scared shitless, but kept it together. That's what it looked like to me." Lisa nodded. "I thought it was fairly cool, actually."

"Is that genuine emotion? An authentic human connection? Are you feeling okay . . . wait a second . . . Who are you and what have you done with Lisa?"

"Oh, shut up."

"I think Tammy's quite nice, if you want my opinion."

"I'm not saying she is or isn't, as if that even matters." Lisa put a raisin in her mouth and sucked on it briefly before chewing and swallowing it. "I'm just saying she feels alone, you know, like she's hiding something, like she's got to keep her finger in some dyke or everything will come spilling out all over the place."

"Such as?"

Lisa was now looking intently at Paul, which he found somewhat unnerving. She had greenish hazel irises, but in the low light of the downstairs family room—which with its dark brick and small windows had always felt like a bit of a bunker to Paul—her eyes were an all-seeing ebony. Paul imagined what it would be like to be a person—a student, a lover, a friend—who disappointed Lisa. That would not be pleasant.

"Well," she said, "what about the husband thing?"

"Palmer?"

"That's freaky. I mean, come on."

"He's an ex. People have ex's."

"Was that guy ever in jail? Is he a criminal right now?"

"How do I know? I didn't exactly become friends with the guy. He looked pretty tough, though."

"But that's the thing, right?" She moved the book and raisins off her lap and swivelled herself to face Paul. "I mean, you could see it with Tammy tonight."

"See what?"

Lisa stared, pursed her lips with exasperation.

"Stop looking at me like that! I'm not a psychic. How about for once you talk so a normal person can understand you?"

Lisa crossed her arms. "She's a rescuer."

"A rescuer?"

"Sure. She already thinks she's the one who saved Rick, and who's going to make something out of his life. It's pretty twisted, when you think about it, like an inverse neediness. And Rick's participating, enabling it."

Paul considered this. "That doesn't say much for Rick's free will."

"It's not really about Rick. It could be anybody who's fucked up. It's just a theory. I need more information. But the way she was ogling him tonight, so . . . protective. And possessive at the same time. Like she was saying, *He's mine now*. She thinks she's going to change him, and then she'll be the hero because she took this criminal and made him into something. No, no. That's wrong. Not change him, exactly. Save him! That's it. It's a salvation complex." She paused, pursed her lips. "Hmm, that's pretty good. Salvation complex."

"She was kind of protective of him on the drive home. Yeah, sure, maybe. But is that a bad thing? Don't you want to be protected by the people who . . . okay, okay, wait a minute. I take that back. I forgot who I was talking to. Don't you think most people want someone to protect them? Or save them, help them? *Support* them?"

"But it's not about Rick wanting or needing saving or helping. It's about her defining herself as the one doing the rescuing. It wouldn't matter who it was. Rick, anybody."

"I don't believe that."

"Why not?"

"Why would she change her whole life around to try and save some guy she's never met, who might not need saving anyway?"

"Hey, I didn't say it was psychologically sound. I'm just trying to help you understand the way things work. Anyway, it doesn't sound like she was giving up much back in Montana."

"Help me understand, please."

Lisa laughed. "I still can't believe Rick left you sitting there."

"*You* can't believe it? I thought that guy was going to strangle me for a minute."

"I can just see your face. That would have been hysterical."

"Yeah, hysterical. Actually, he wasn't such a bad guy. I kind of liked him."

"That's your problem . . . or at least one of them. You kind of like everybody."

"Everybody except you."

Lisa went quiet for a minute, and seemed to be giving all her attention, or what passed for attention, to the TV, but then she turned back to Paul. "Think about it. Her ex in the house with her. Those kids. Yeah, okay, they're his, but still. And she's a potter. A potter? And not that I don't love Rick, but this Tammy writes guys in jail. I mean, who does that? Do you want to date some woman that writes guys in jail? And by that I mean criminals."

"You mean, people like Rick?"

"She needed a project. Raw material."

"Like Rick?"

"So, what's the answer? Would you want to be dating a woman that writes guys in jail?"

"I would if I was the guy getting out of jail. Actually, I'd date anyone right about now. Even you. If you weren't my sister, that is."

"You can't take anything seriously."

"So you don't like her?"

"Stop saying that. Jesus Christ, you're simple-minded. Actually, in a weird way, I think she's kind of cool. I haven't got her figured out yet. I'll keep you posted."

"You've known her a couple of days and haven't figured her out? You're losing your touch."

"No, I'm not. I'm just . . . maturing. I'm not rushing to judge like I used to."

"Maturing? As if. You're living in your parents' basement."

Lisa scowled at Paul. "Like I want to? Find me the money and I'm outta here tomorrow. And anyway, look who's talking. At least I have the excuse of being in university and not having a job. What's your excuse? *Oh, I'm having my dishwasher fixed. They're changing my light bulbs.* Whatever."

Paul laughed out loud at his sister, who was laughing along with him. He pointed at the phone. "Poor Roger. Or whatever that guy's name is. Does he have any idea? What he's getting into, wandering into your path?"

Lisa turned the corners of her mouth up slightly, an expression that signified such a privately pursued carnality it almost made Paul want to hug her. Almost.

"He's clueless, isn't he? This Roger. He has no idea what a cauldron he's stepping into."

"Well," said Lisa, puckering her lips then bringing them back into a sly grin. "He knows as much as he needs to."

NINE

Many of Paul's friends and colleagues, either at 2.2.4. or at other magazines across the country, complained regularly about the amount of email they got and how difficult it was to stay on top of it, to regulate it, to discipline themselves so that they didn't spend hours every day reading and responding. Not much spam got through to Paul's desktop, but what did get through invariably gave him pause. "She won't leave you if you have a BIGGER PENIS!!" Such a concern seemed a bit of a luxury to him; at least it meant you were getting laid. How big was big enough, anyway? How did guys already hugely-endowed react to that? Were they just as neurotic as every other guy? Maybe it was like being anorexic or greedy; there was no finish line, no hope of ever fully scratching the itch.

In any case, excessive email was not a major concern for Paul, a fact that, therefore, concerned him. His friends, and other writers he knew, talked about receiving twenty, thirty, sometimes forty emails a day. He might receive five, eight. Rarely did he get more than ten emails a day, and at least half of these were from Harold, who couldn't be bothered to walk down the hall or pick up the phone. What were all these other people up to? Who was contacting them? What electronic conversations were they having, and why wasn't he part of them? It was worth worrying about.

Today, there were three emails waiting for him when he opened the program. One was from *CampCode, Rachel*, and the subject line read "Hi!" The other two were from Harold. One subject line read "InfoTrue Group." The other, "Code." Paul clicked the message from Rachel first, easily drawing a picture of her in his head, the dark brown hair, the long face with intelligence radiating from it like a deep tan. Her message was brief, blunt at first reading, and left him a bit bruised by its businesslike manner. She merely wanted to remind him about the TriGlen fund-raiser later that day and inform him of another couple of events he might be interested in. Also, she wondered if it wouldn't be prudent to schedule one last face-to-face interview with her father prior to the weekend of the leadership vote, since he was likely to be very busy during and after that time. Paul read through the email searching for the slightest scrap of warmth or interest in him as a person, then instantly chided himself. It was pathetic. What a serious magazine writer had to possess in nearly equal parts to talent, sensitivity, and determination, Harold always reminded him, was detachment—keeping the boundary.

Rachel signed off with a cool "Best, R. C." He responded right away with a thank you, saying he'd be in touch with her soon about dates and times.

Harold, in his "Code" message, wanted an update, and particularly wanted to know if a roughed-out sense of structure and direction was beginning to form in Paul's mind. Harold always sent him an email—he never did it in person—when Paul was in this middle phase of a profile, waist-deep in the research, conversant with all the issues, familiar with the personalities, but still not quite ready to begin writing. This was less about obtaining genuine information than it was about Harold helping signal to Paul's subconscious that outlines could begin to be drawn. It always worked. In every instance Paul was amazed—and relieved—that a structure, like the roughed-out frame of a house, always seemed to be there waiting for him when it came time to find it.

As an addendum, Harold told Paul he'd been out for dinner with oil patch buddies the night before and the talk turned, inevitably, to politics. Harold had remarked that the magazine was doing a profile of Daniel Code, and one of Harold's fellow diners said he remembered that Code Sr., Daniel's father, used to write a column somewhere, for some prairie farmer's magazine, decades ago, possibly even as early as the sixties or early seventies. Harold's friend couldn't remember the name of the magazine. "Might be worth a trip to the library," wrote Harold to Paul. "Might not. Just thought I'd mention it."

Harold's other message, "InfoTrue Group," was cryptic and unsettling. He said reports had filtered down from Toronto that the word in the InfoTrue Group about their meeting was that it had "not gone well," and that Stranga was "pissed off." Harold told Paul not to worry if he heard any rumors. This was just enough information to make Paul worry.

He looked back to his desk and the folder of photos he'd been trying to sort through in the hope of deciding which to include in the album he was making for Rick as a welcome-home gift. Perhaps a hundred photos were in the folder—holiday shots, pictures taken around the house, recent pictures, pictures of childhood, of family. The album was something he thought he'd enjoy doing and was sure that Rick would enjoy, but it had not been a light task. He'd originally got the idea when Rick still had a couple of years to go, but Paul naturally procrastinated. Even though Rick was now out, Paul decided to go ahead anyway; Rick could flip through it in freedom, even if it no longer symbolized the beacon Paul had originally envisioned.

Paul looked at the photo he was holding. The family: Paul, Lisa, Rick, their father, standing on a beach, Long Beach, on Vancouver Island. Presumably it had been Paul's mother who had taken the picture. Paul's father was holding a leash, at the end of which was their dog, Cracker, who was sodden and sorry-looking after a dash through the pounding surf. Everyone in the photo appeared to be smiling about something, though Lisa was doubled over laughing—which may have been the last time she laughed that unselfconsciously. Paul put down the photo and picked up another, a picture of the family around the dinner table. The kids were teenagers. Rick was holding a steak knife in the air in mock threat, Lisa was cowering in her chair like a silent movie heroine. Paul and his father were laughing, but he recalled that as soon as his mother had clicked the shutter she put the camera down and immediately marched Rick off to his room, informing him that such jokes were not funny, that sharp objects like knives, pens, pencils, scissors, forks, chopsticks, toothpicks, screwdrivers, and tent stakes were not playthings. She'd simply wanted to get a nice family-at-home dinner photo to send her friends and relatives as evidence of the normalcy of her life, and Rick had gone and ruined it. Looking at the photo now, Paul thought it priceless and a little bit poignant, particularly in light of Rick's troubles. He was joking, after all. Couldn't their mother see that? Couldn't she have taken another picture instead of pulling him off to his room in so dramatic a fashion? He was always joking, posing, playing the fool. Their mother knew that. Most family pictures found him grimacing, pinching someone, striking a ridiculous muscle-man pose.

Of all these old photos there was really only one Paul cherished. In this picture (which Paul had duplicated and mounted on the wall in his apartment), all three children were inside the frame. Paul was finishing high school at St. Francis in northwest Calgary; Rick, a couple years older, was studying English at the University of Calgary; Lisa, four years younger than Paul, was in the eighth grade at Father Brebeuf. Paul's mother had taken the shot. The picture was unique for one reason alone in Paul's mind—because they had been caught off guard. His mother had snuck up on them in the TV room before they were even aware she had skulked in. To an outsider, the photo wouldn't signify anything beyond three teenagers with awful posture watching television in a basement family room, but Paul treasured it. By a minor stroke of symmetrical fortune, the three were aligned left to right according to age. Rick was seated in the large brown overstuffed chair at the left edge of the frame. His right foot was out of frame because he'd hiked it over the armrest. Paul, the middle child, was seated more or less upright on the right hand of the long, low-slung sofa that dominated the far wall of the room, but Lisa, on the right edge of the photo, was lying down, supporting her head in her palm, her elbow on the sofa's armrest. Her body was stretched out along the length of the sofa so that her feet were almost touching Paul's thigh.

More striking to Paul, however, than the coincidence of their being seated in order was how the photo had come to signify so much to him about his own and his siblings' personalities, their dispositions. Paul saw himself in that picture very much as he remembered sitting throughout his childhood and teen years, looking straight at the television, eyes focused, saying little. His arms were crossed over his stomach, not to indicate discomfort or impatience but because it was comfortable. It was a position meant to facilitate the watching of television; that was his purpose for being in the room, that was why he was there.

Lisa's expression in the photo was caught in what Paul always believed to be her default expression, a mild sneer that was a hybrid of contempt and confidence. She was just fourteen in the picture, maybe even thirteen, Paul couldn't quite remember, but now he could look back and see it all: her self-assurance, her self-proclaimed (and, Paul had to admit, real) intellectual ability, her glee in not only not suffering fools but publicly outing them. She was horizontal on the sofa, grinning about something. She'd likely finished making some smart-ass remark, and was visibly happy to be where she was, doing what she was principally there to do—comment on the programs and make the act of watching television irritating for her brothers. Enjoying the actual program was likely fourth or fifth on her list of priorities, if it was there at all. Even at that age, she was there to mock her brothers for not being smart enough to know what *The A-Team* or *Twin Peaks* or *Alf* were really about. She was in that room to tell her brothers why they were there, why the show was there, and what it meant for them to be sitting down together to watch it. Though Paul and Rick did their best to ignore her, now Paul wished he'd listened more closely, as he always, though surreptitiously, listened to her now. Not that this was something he'd ever admit. Then she might never shut up.

But it was Rick's facial expression that always brought Paul back to the picture. Rick's eyes were on the TV, but his head was angled toward Paul, as if he'd been watching his brother only to have an image or sound grab his attention before he could actually turn his head square to the screen. To Paul, there was an unsettling yet somehow flattering conclusion to be drawn: Rick had only seconds before been looking at him, not the television. Something about Paul had been of more interest, even if only for a few seconds, than what was on TV. What had it been? Paul had often wondered, staring at that picture.

He got his answer during the stretch between Rick's two stints inside. He'd come over to Paul's apartment to drink beer and watch a hockey game and had seen the photo on the wall, framed. Paul asked his brother if he remembered what he'd been looking at. "I was looking at you," Rick had said, "and you were watching TV, but the thing was, you were watching it, I mean, actually watching and liking it. That was all. It was enough for you. Lisa was busy picking the shit out of it. I was scheming about something or other, not really paying that much attention—what was it, anyway, *L. A. Law* or *Remington Steele* or some stupid fucking show—and then I looked over at you, and I knew you weren't doing anything but watching the show. I could see it in your eyes that you were just watching the show, that was all." Rick had paused, stared again at the picture, and then continued speaking, half dreamily, as if he were back in their family TV room, both of them teenagers again. "I remember it. I wondered what that would be like, to be sitting there watching a show. To be doing something just for the enjoyment of it, without thinking about the day before, or the day after."

"I'm not sure that's right, Rick," Paul had said. His memories of those years in the TV room were of watching TV and enjoying it, sure, but of always being conscious he was there with his brother and sister and often his parents, that they all talked during commercials or even sometimes during shows, that they laughed at the same things, that it was where their friends spent time when at their house, that they three kids often conspiratorially snuck back in to watch more TV after their parents had sent them to bed, that all these things somehow made time in the TV room time well, if not exactly properly, spent. In other words, that he, Paul, had not been in the bubble Rick seemed to want to put him in. "That's maybe just how you saw it," Paul had added, as he and Rick stood in front of the framed photo, "Anyway, I was only there most of the time because that's where you and Lisa were."

Rick had turned away from the picture, and looked at Paul for a second or two before he responded, smiling, Paul thought, a little too patiently. "Whatever you say."

Daniel Code's TriGlen fund-raiser was near the university, so Paul decided to go there first and stop in at the library later, since there was no telling how long it might take to find and pore over a decade's worth of old magazines with writing by Code Sr., if such writings existed at all. The CHART the Course for Code fund-raiser was being held in the boxy fir-green Community Hall in TriGlen, one of the northwest Calgary suburbs in the shadow of Nose Hill Park. From the parking lot—so full, Paul noted, that he had to park illegally at the far end of it—one only had to look a kilometre north to encounter the majestic hills, gently pushing against the dusty blue sky. It seemed to Paul that his whole life had been lived within sight of this park, these hills, and that this was a good thing.

Inside the hall, the speeches had only just started. A local organizer, wearing a dark blue suit and vest despite the hot weather, was at a microphone extolling Daniel Code's virtues, pumping up the crowd. The lunch aspect was evidently over, and volunteers scurried around, picking up paper plates smeared with chili and coleslaw and chucking them into green open-mawed garbage bags, stacking cups emptied of juice and water, tossing cutlery into a big grey square tub. Paul did a quick demographic survey and found it exactly as he'd imagined—grey hair and white skin. Here and there in a crowd of perhaps two hundred he saw exceptions: one man in his twenties, a woman holding a young child, a couple of teenagers leaning against the wall. Toward the middle of the room near the front were an East Asian couple, and two tables to the left, a Chinese family. These people were almost certainly plants, found in the community and press-ganged into service by the organizing committee in case the broadcast media started panning their cameras from Code's podium POV. To be fair to Code's team, Paul had to admit that Calgary was hardly Manhattan in the range of its ethnicity, but it wasn't nineteenth-century Helsinki, either.

Code was sitting at the front, placidly listening to his introducer. Paul looked closely at the tables near Code to see if he'd been accompanied by his media liaison, and when he was unable to find her, he realized that his enthusiasm for the event changed in a way he knew it should not have.

"Daniel Code," the navy blue suit at the podium was saying, "is a man of rare courage. How many politicians speak clearly about a subject? How many politicians nowadays can you get a straight answer out of?"

The crowd were shouting out, "None!"

"That's right," said the man. "Except for one. That's who we're here to listen to today. This is a man . . . this is a man I respect. If I ask him a question he will tell me what he thinks. He has the courage of his convictions, and the will to act."

Fair enough, thought Paul. But so did Hitler.

"Please join me in welcoming the man I'm sure will be the next leader of the Democratic Alliance Party, the man to change things in Ottawa, the man who is topping the CHART, Daniel Code."

The crowd rose to its feet, applauding madly. With a gracious smile and a tilt of the head, Code moved to the podium, where he shook the hand of his introducer. "I'm delighted to be here today," he began, after the crowd had taken their seats. "And I particularly want to thank Bernie for that wonderful introduction. I didn't realize I was such an impressive person."

The crowd tittered and Paul saw a few women lean their temples toward one another and whisper words back and forth while grinning. Paul knew what they were talking about: Code had an easy smile, a hint of a tan, impeccable posture, and, Paul couldn't help but note with some envy, the languid physical grace of a natural athlete. When Code walked, he seemed to glide across the floor. When he sat down and crossed his legs, he looked comfortable and flexible. He was probably a great dancer. What a gift sex appeal was for men running for office (in a way that was rarely the case for women). And if you had it you had no option but to let it happen, especially because the more you downplayed it the hotter it burned. Code had it, bad.

"But you know," said Code. "It's quite interesting to me, as a person interested in history, to hear Bernie talk about conviction and the will to act. I was flattered to hear him talk about me in that way, and I do like to think I have the courage of my convictions and that I'm not afraid to act on them. However, we need to be careful in this life because, well," he paused for effect, "they said the same thing about Hitler."

The crowd hooted and guffawed, and though Paul was simultaneously pissed and impressed (pissed because a potential line of his was gone, impressed that Code had the guts to make the joke), his first sensation was unease. Paul couldn't decide if it was brave or stupid of Code to make the remark and of the crowd to enjoy it so much.

He took out his notebook and began writing down these thoughts as he leaned against the back wall. *Hitler, Code, laughter, brave/stupid?, policy/speechwriter?* Code launched into his usual speech detailing the nondetails of Conscience, Honesty, Accountability, Responsibility, and Transparency. When Code had reached Transparency, Paul felt a hand drop on to his shoulder and rest there lightly. He turned and saw Rachel Code. She was smiling at him, but half-looking at his open notebook, which Paul closed immediately.

"Hey there," she said quietly, smiling calmly as if she'd been expecting to see him and was pleased to see that expectation met.

"Oh, hi. Hi," he said, keeping his voice low. "How are you? Where were you sitting? I looked for you. I mean, I didn't see you in the crowd."

Rachel kept smiling at him, though with her mouth tighter, as if she were for some reason pleasantly amused by Paul. "I was just in the kitchen, helping clean up."

"Cleaning up?"

"You know, media liaison, dishwasher. You name it."

"Multitalented."

"C'est moi." She flipped a hand into the air, diva-like. She was wearing jeans and a gauzy black t-shirt, and had her long auburn hair pulled back in a tight ponytail, though she'd also needed, apparently, six or seven plain hairpins to keep rogue strands under control. There weren't many things more ordinary than a hairpin, thought Paul, but somehow in her hair they were jewelry.

He cleared his throat. "So, I'll need to catch up with you to schedule that last sit down with your father."

"When do you want to do it?" she said.

It? thought Paul. He heard Code's voice in the background, still droning on about the CHART.

". . . The next interview, that is."

"Right. Well, I'm pretty flexible."

"Okay, let me check with him . . . and I'll get back to you. His time is pretty good on the weekend, especially Saturday. It's going to heat up in the next couple of weeks for one-on-one time, of course, but we should be able to fit you in. Naturally, you're also welcome to attend any function you see fit."

Paul had been glancing at Rachel's lips as she talked. She had a long, narrow face, and thin lips, too, but they were set across a wide mouth. Her lips made unusual shapes when she talked, sometimes bunching up, sometimes revealing her irregular teeth, sometimes unconsciously exaggerating the popping-out motion made by the letter M. She licked her lips a lot, too, Paul noticed, because of the dryness, obviously, but the saliva made her mouth shine.

"Sound okay?"

"Yes," said Paul. "Very helpful, thank you."

"That's why I'm here."

She turned her attention back to her father, who had begun wrapping up. Paul turned that way, too. Code was making a significant number of hand gestures, but none were choppy or cutting; every gesture was silky, comforting, guiding rather than directing, beguiling rather than coercing. It was a seduction. Code was trying to woo, to convince with charm rather than substance, which was hardly unusual, but meant, thought Paul, that he was trying to distance himself from something, trying to hoist up scrims of image and perception. But from what was he trying to distance himself? What was behind the scrim? Any strain of extremism was possible, even likely. But then again, thought Paul, pretending to look at it from the point of view of the people who'd flocked here to see Code, maybe he was just a decent man who happened to hold deeply felt but "old-fashioned" views, a skilled performer with a sense of humour and a sincere ability to communicate, a politician who wanted to contribute and truly wasn't concerned with the trappings of power. Perhaps he was simply a man making an honest attempt to stay true to the beliefs of his upbringing.

"What's so funny?" said Rachel.

"Mmm? Oh. Nothing. Just . . . something private."

"Oh," said Rachel, staring up at him, the downturn of her mouth suggesting she felt more slighted than uninterested. Paul noticed that in the indoor light her eyes were almost grey, not the very light green he'd taken them to be on the sunny patio at Bravada. "You know," she continued slowly, still looking up at him. "I sort of feel like there's something worth saying right about now. I hope it's okay to just . . . I'm just going to say it."

"Sounds ominous."

She looked at the floor. "No, not at all," she said, bringing her eyes back up to Paul's. "It's simple, really. It's just that I want you to know you don't need to be worried . . . or afraid."

Paul looked at her, his eyebrows drawn together, his underarms greasy.

Rachel waved a hand across the room, out to where her father was making his closing remarks. "This is all going to pass, right? This campaign. Me helping my dad. It's just one thing in our lives, in my life."

Blood poured into Paul's head, filling it, pushing his eyeballs forward, making his temples throb. He felt sick to his stomach and yet at the same time hungry and empty as if he'd not eaten for days. "Rachel, I don't think I want to hear that. Not now, with what I'm doing."

Rachel nodded. "Just don't be afraid of me." She turned and went back into the kitchen.

There was no Q and A afterwards, and Paul didn't stay to observe much of the meet and greet. The gathered crowd was so enraptured with Code it was unlikely he'd be subjected to any pressure greater than having to avoid sloppy kisses from postmenopausal groupies. After finishing his stump speech, he moved through the crowd shaking hands, making eye contact. He laughed at every single table, and left each person flush with a kind of pride and satisfaction after he'd moved on, like they'd actually meant something special to him, as if they had somehow managed to convey to him a piece of information or a scrap of energy that would make a difference. Paul had witnessed hundreds of politicians of all stripes make exactly the same kind of rounds; it was something they had to do, day in and day out, city after city, speech after speech, meal after meal. It couldn't be avoided. The road to public office was paved with flesh, the rote pressing of it, and Paul had long since come to the conclusion that the majority of the men and women who sought political power viewed crowd work not so much as a necessary evil but as a job you simply had to do and keep on doing. One donned the requisite protective gear—toothy smile, extended hand, agreeing nod—and waded in. But Paul had also come to believe that a few of these people, a very few indeed, viewed it not as the dull fibre of the political diet but as something nourishing in and of itself, possibly even as the actual point of a political life. That the reason for being in politics was to meet, know, and adequately represent the concerns of your fellow citizens. Of course, no member of this species ever achieved any real power. That kind of authenticity, in even the smallest doses, was almost always relegated to the back benches by leaders who recognized it as a virus that needed to be quarantined.

 Paul watched Code taking time with every person, smiling, laughing, shaking his head in some mild disagreement, playfully snatching a bite of pie from an old gent, who afterward looked as if he might run out and have the plate bronzed. It can't be, thought Paul. Code seemed to be having fun while also treating the job seriously; he wasn't even in a hurry to leave. It was a mirage, a political trompe l'oeil.

 He closed his notebook and was about to fish out his car keys when Code spotted him halfway down the hall. He said a quick word to the person he was talking to, then gave Paul a big wave and a mock military salute. Paul, for no apparent reason, saluted back. When he got in his car and looked in the rearview mirror, he caught sight of his face. He was still smiling, as if he'd left the apartment of a particularly humorous friend. He couldn't help it. It was true. Part of him liked Code.

 For a second or two Paul experienced something like that flutter of lightheadedness when one stands up too quickly, though in this case it was related to the regret now rinsing through him. It was too bad, a shame, really, that he was going to have to take Code down; the man was dangerous. Paul pulled out of the parking lot, leaving his smile behind.

After the rally, Paul went to the University of Calgary library to cross-reference the name Emmett Code with obscure Alberta magazines from the 1970s. The search came up positive, but the magazines in question were part of Special Collections. He had to wait in the Reading Room. After five minutes a stack of about sixty *Across the Plains* magazines were placed in front of him, twelve issues a year for five years through the early part of the seventies. A place to start, though he reminded himself that he didn't quite know what he was looking for. This fact was less a bother than a lure, though it didn't take much more than ten minutes to find what he was meant to find.

Byline: Emmett Code.

One column. He read the piece from start to finish. "Holy shit," he whispered to himself. Picking up the last few issues, he saw that there were more columns by the same author, one per issue. He couldn't wait, just simply could not wait, to have them all copied, in one pile, in chronological order, in a file folder, and with a coffee on his desk, so that he could sit down and read every last word this disturbed man had written. Paul's lips parted, and he felt his neck and ears ignite, felt a slow smile rising up from his chest and onto his face.

When he'd finished photocopying all thirty or so of Emmett Code's columns, Paul left the library. To get some lunch at a sandwich shop he liked, he ended up driving past his old high school along Northmount Drive, a giant low-slung pumpkin-coloured building that always made him think of mental hospitals from the 1960s: two storeys tall, with windows spaced every thirty feet, windows he used to stare out, wondering when his life was going to start. St. Francis was the biggest Catholic high school on the north side, and with some two thousand students, it naturally had a variety of gangs and cliques, though Paul didn't fit comfortably into any of them; he wasn't particularly athletic, he wasn't blown away by drugs or drinking, he glazed over when talk turned to cars, he didn't have a girlfriend, and in the only course that interested him—English—he was demonstrably better read and a better writer than the teacher, an aging spinster with wattles of veiny fat dangling from her upper arms who would sit on the desks of brawny, mullet-haired football players and recite Shakespearean sonnets. So complete was Paul's nonidentity that he wasn't even enough of a loser to hang out with the herd of official losers—the dorks who typically huddled for safety near the school office or the teachers' lounge at recess and lunch. Paul recalled that Rick didn't help or even try to help him gain entry into any of these constituencies—and Paul didn't really want to be part of them—but Rick's reputation, and sometimes Rick himself, protected him from the abuse he might have suffered otherwise. Rick was well-known. He played varsity basketball, though he wasn't a starter. He did his share of drugs, which gave him passage in the back hallways. He drove his own car (a rusty '78 Honda Civic their dad had given him), which made him popular in the parking lot. He didn't have a girlfriend, and only slept around a little bit—and he was good-looking in an eighties pop star kind of way—all of which made him coveted by different subsets of girls. And to top it off, he got good, sometimes exceptional, grades, particularly in English. This endeared him to his teachers, since Catholic high school teachers valued nothing more than an all-rounder, a student that made them look good on more than one front; it validated the existence of the Separate School Board—proof that a Catholic way of forming minds and souls paid dividends.

Paul slowed as he passed his old school, and looking at it now, now that Rick was out of jail, he thought again, as he sometimes had in the past ten years, of his role in his brother's life, about how much he might have been able to change things. They'd never truly had anything like a conversation about it. Maybe Rick knew Paul had always felt divided as to whether he had anything to apologize for. Paul turned his gaze from the school to Nose Hill Park a kilometre or so to the north, the hills Paul knew as if he'd mapped them himself. It had been an unusually warm Friday in early spring, near the end of his grade twelve. Paul had tagged along with Rick and a couple of Rick's friends out driving. He got asked along sometimes, usually because Rick had been badgered by their mother into taking him to keep "building their friendship," she said, though more likely she just wanted some peace and quiet around the house.

They drove to the liquor store, threw beer in a knapsack, then went up to Nose Hill to drink and watch the sun go down. After a few beers—Paul nursed a single—one of Rick's buddies pulled out his camera film container of hash and an ornate pipe he'd brought back from a trip to Guatemala. It was a night no different than many before, except possibly in the quality of the hash. Rick's friend claimed it was exceptional. "Fucking *packed* with resin," he'd said, putting the pipe to his lips. Everybody nodded sagely, including Paul, though he had no idea what that meant.

Walking down the hill about an hour later, as night was firming up, Rick tripped and hurt his ankle, but he said it was nothing and insisted he could drive, though Paul offered. They drove down into Brentwood, where Rick failed to stop at the first stop sign, barreling through the intersection and clipping the rear bumper of a pickup truck, shearing it off, and forcing both vehicles against the far curb. No one had been hurt and the damage was minor, but the driver of the pickup shot out of his cab. He was a few years older than Rick, but still of university age. "Fucker!" he yelled over and over. "You stupid fucker! That was a stop sign, you moron. You could have killed me!" Inside the car, Paul thought that Rick looked terrified. The engine was still running, and Rick at least had enough sense to shut it off and ask if everyone was okay. But when he got out and started to absorb the abuse the fellow was throwing at him, Rick's fear seamlessly tipped over into rage, the way even the smallest shift of a radio knob turns sense to static. The man came nearer to Rick, angry and gesticulating, not so much in threat it seemed to Paul, but as if he were trying to attract the attention of more witnesses, though there weren't any nearby. He strode close to Rick and shouted out, "I want to see your insurance and registration, you dumb shit." Rick kicked the guy straight in the balls. The man fell to the ground. Rick jumped on his neck with one foot and put the other foot on his face, grinding his heel in. Everybody beetled from the car as if it were about to explode, and they ran the twenty paces to where Rick was standing on the guy. They pulled him off. The man was prostrate, unconscious, his face pulped up. Blood was trickling from the ear Paul could see. The man's head was angled away from the base of his neck so grotesquely—not backward, but forward, like a miniature step had been put in his spine—that Paul could never later rid himself of the memory. Given the state of the man's spine, the cord ought to have been severed. If it had been, Rick would still be in jail, instead of the four years he got, two and a half of which he served. Last Paul had heard—which was a few years ago—the man Rick assaulted was still in an extended care facility and would never be fully active again, though apparently he'd almost regained the ability to walk without an aid.

The lawyer told Rick to tell the judge it was a fight, that both men knew a fight was coming. It was a given that Rick had caused the accident—and okay, for that he would pay his dues—but if they could make the case that what happened after was an implicitly agreed-on fight, then Rick stood a good chance of getting a suspended sentence, or at least a shorter sentence, which would mean, significantly, provincial time instead of federal. "You don't want to do federal," the lawyer said, cryptically. Rick's friends, both of whom had been sitting in the back seat, told Rick later that they had stated to the cops the man had come at Rick straight on and in a hurry, which was not untrue. Paul didn't know what to say. He knew what he saw.

His mother and father, though they used similar words, told him different things. "Say what your heart tells you to say," said his mother, leaning toward him as she spoke. "Tell the truth," said his father, speaking with his arms crossed.

Paul told the truth. Rick had attacked the man.

Rick never blamed Paul, or if he did, never said anything directly about it. "It's okay," he'd told Paul the first time they all went up to the jail to visit him. His tone was not convincing and he looked at Paul's neck as he spoke. "You did the right thing." Those words didn't make that first car ride back from the jail any shorter. Paul remembered it second by second. His parents said nothing, to him or to one another, just smoked and silently listened to the radio for the length of the drive, past the early seams of the badlands, through the flat brown prairie, finally arriving in the foothills embracing Calgary. They got home and pulled in to the garage. Paul noticed with a glum eye that the shelves along the right-hand wall were jammed with sports gear he and Rick had used all throughout their childhoods, but which was now mostly forlorn and dusty with neglect; brown, stiff leather ice skates with rusty blades, splintered hockey sticks, tennis racquets with broken strings, mismatched golf clubs, crusty baseball gloves, and a soccer ball and basketball, both of which were lumpy and uninflated, forever out of round.

After eating his lunch while reading the rest of Emmett Code's columns, Paul poked his head into Harold's office. "Busy?"

Harold held up a sandwich, pointed at a messy pile of papers in front of him. "Yes."

"Oh, good," said Paul nodding, making his way in.

"I thought I just said I was busy," muttered Harold, turning his attention back to the papers on his desk.

Paul ignored him and stepped inside the office, an action that always felt a bit like crawling right inside Harold's head. The room was crammed with so much information heaped in such insubordinate piles that a librarian might prefer to set a match to it all rather than be forced to bring rule to it. Books, magazines, reference texts, manuals. Art photo collections, videos, CDs, DVDs. Ream after ream of manuscript pages of documents unknown to Paul. Two large white boards on the wall stocked with long-dead ideas written in what Harold hadn't realized at the time was permanent marker ink.

"No, no, seriously," Paul said, smiling. "You're not going to believe this."

Harold sat back, and took an impatient bite of his sandwich, but then when he looked at Paul his expression changed. His eyes widened. He put his sandwich on the pages in front of him and did an exaggerated little rubbing of his hands. "Ooh, I like it when you have that look."

"Wait here."

Paul went to his office and got the photocopies he'd made at the library. "Have a look at these," he said, walking back into Harold's office and putting the pages on his desk.

Harold took the first of the pages. "What am I looking at?" he asked through his bite of sandwich.

Paul couldn't help but grin. "Emmett Code, columnist."

Harold nodded and read while he worked on the food still in his mouth. Slowly, he stopped chewing. By the time he was halfway down the first page he was dead still but with full cheeks, like some kid working on two jawbreakers. When he got to the end of the column, the first in the series, he muttered through a mouthful of food, "This is un . . . believable."

"I found it at the library. In Special Collections. This magazine went under sometime in the midseventies."

"Look at this shit. Listen to this: 'and while visiting Detroit for a day from our relatives in Windsor, it became clear the American way has failed horribly, what with mud people everywhere. I recalled that the Lord made just two human beings, Adam and Eve, and they were both of fair skin. Being in Detroit felt like being in the darkest heart of Africa, and I can say to you honestly that I feared for my life walking those streets.'" Harold paused, scanning. "Or this: 'and of course we know what happens when sex education is introduced into schools. Let's just look at Quebec, where abortion is de rigueur, as they so smugly say, and worse, where sodomites freely flaunt their own brand of deviance.'" Harold looked up from the pages. "This would be funny if it weren't so frightening."

"The whole stack is full of it."

Harold then picked up Emmett Code's review of *The Protocols of the Elders of Zion*, which, Paul first explained, was a piece of virulent anti-Semitism used by hate groups purporting to have uncovered evidence of a worldwide Zionist conspiracy to rule the world. It had long ago been exposed as a fraudulent and blatantly racist text, but Emmett Code nevertheless pronounced the book an "essential document" in understanding the problems inherent in allowing Jews to gather power and influence.

"My God." Harold shook his head. "I wonder what little Danny Code was doing the whole time his father was enlightening the world?"

"Good question," Paul said. "Research assistant, maybe."

Perhaps it's a Code family trait, thought Paul, as he sat waiting for Rachel Code to arrive. She was now possibly thirty minutes late, unless he'd misunderstood the message on his cell phone. He listened to it for the third time since he'd sat down with his rapidly cooling Americano. "Hi Paul," the voice on the message said. "It's Rachel Code. Listen, I've got a slot free later today and I'm just going to sit at Café Beano for a while and then push off after an hour or so . . . probably around two. If you're free, come by . . . if you have any questions, or, you want to talk about anything, the campaign. You know it, Beano? Seventeenth Ave and Ninth Street? You don't have to phone back. I'm taking some paperwork and going anyway, so don't worry if you can't make it, or don't need to. Bye."

He turned his phone off. Looked at his watch. 2:20. It was slightly unclear if she meant 2 PM as her arrival or departure time, so he showed up at ten minutes to two. She wasn't there. The place was not crowded, and at the counter he asked a young woman with green hair if anyone had just left, such as an attractive brown-haired woman who had been sitting alone for an hour doing paperwork. The green-haired girl knocked open a goofy smile, revealing a pea-sized stud screwed through the fleshy middle of her tongue. "No. Why?"

"Possible mix-up," Paul said, forcing himself not to look at the tongue stud. The only reason women got them—Lisa had told him, groaning at his naïveté—was to give better head, and he'd never been able to get that out of his mind. He never wanted to be caught looking at the stud, because if they both knew what it was for—and both knew he was looking at it—both would know what he was thinking of at that moment. No other possibilities were available, were there? How could this not be the logical assumption? It brought out the former altar boy in him, roiling in a state of pre-sin that featured all the guilt and none of the fun.

Rachel came in at 2:30, just as Paul was about to leave. "Paul!" she said. "You're here. Hi."

"I was here before two," he said, meaning it playfully but instantly regretting it. Rachel's face, happy at seeing him, dropped, enough for Paul to see it was the wrong thing to say. It occurred to him, not for the first time in his dealings with women, that he had a talent for taking someone else's lapse and in one stroke turning it into a point against himself, a strip of birch to whip himself with.

"I mean, that's okay. I was taking notes." He pointed at his notebook. "It was actually really relaxing to have the quiet time."

"Oh . . . do you want the company, then?"

"Yeah, yeah, of course."

"I'm so sorry. Darn. I just didn't think you'd actually show up. Then something else came up that I had to deal with, so I did it over the phone in the truck. I should have come in and checked." She pointed outside to an old grey pickup parked across the street. Paul had had his nose in his notebook and hadn't even noticed it pull up. "Can you believe it? I was just sitting out there for the last twenty minutes."

Paul waved a hand, attempting to brush it away good-naturedly. "Let me get you a coffee. What do you want?"

"Café au lait. Thanks."

At the counter, the green-haired girl smiled puckishly without saying anything while she prepared the coffee.

"Thank you," said Rachel, as Paul set the coffee in front of her. "So how's your article going?"

He shrugged, felt short of breath. This was not what he wanted to talk about. But then, if he didn't want to talk about that, why was he here? "Still researching, really. It's going to be a longish story, so I'm collecting a lot of material. You know, fairly new party. And your father, he's . . . he's an interesting man."

"He sure is," she said, raising her eyes from her coffee, her tone implying that Paul was writing a story designed to portray her father in a flattering light. Surely, Paul thought, she didn't see him as an ally? But if not, why was she being so nice to him, why was she co-operating so fully? "Anyhow," she continued, "I'm looking forward to reading what you have to say about him." She laughed softly. ". . . I think."

"You know, Rachel. I am writing for an independent magazine." Paul hesitated. "I mean, you seem . . . I don't know, pretty relaxed about the whole thing."

"My father is who he is," she said, using both hands to curl her hair behind her ears as she spoke. "I'm sure you'll be honest and thorough. I've read your stuff. What more can we ask for?"

Paul hesitated, wondered how best to proceed, if at all, along this line of conversation. It couldn't lead anywhere worthwhile, but somehow it didn't seem right to change the topic without giving her a little more information. He realized right away what he was doing—candour, though not yet complete honesty, was his only option here. He couldn't lie to her, but he couldn't tell her the truth. And he was embarrassed for himself, embarrassed he was letting his loneliness even start to become a factor in how he was thinking about his piece on Daniel Code. Not that he planned on tempering any of his opinions or observations. If anything, he'd do the opposite, just to doubly assure himself he wasn't caving in. But what if he then did a hatchet job on Code in trying to prove to himself that he wasn't getting played by his own emotions? Marvellous, he thought. Something new to worry about. The funny thing was, he could imagine Rachel losing respect for him if he *did* moderate his conclusions in any way, since he had no doubt she'd be able to spot it. And he couldn't even imagine what Harold would say if he pulled even one or two punches. Actually, he could. Harold would say, *We're not running this.*

Right now, though, Paul knew he had to be direct without being informative. Only when the article and leadership race were over and done with could he even allow himself to think about Rachel, though it was unlikely to matter by then. But . . . here she was. It was intoxicating, this feeling, and so palpable; she was in front of him, looking at him, talking with him. The fall line of her hair draped across her cheek, just like that, had such life in it, such simplicity.

"Are you familiar with Janet Malcolm, the writer?" he said.

"I've heard of her."

"She wrote a book called *The Journalist and The Murderer,* and the first line of the book reads something like, 'Every journalist who is not too stupid or too full of himself to notice what's happening around him knows that what he's doing is morally indefensible. He is like a confidence man, preying on the vanity, loneliness and stupidity of other people, gaining trust and then betraying them.' Something like that."

Rachel drew her nose and eyebrows close together as if fighting off a bad smell. "That sounds awfully cynical." She paused, then took hold of her pen and daytimer, and made a note in it. "I'd better read that. Thesis, you know."

"I don't agree with all of it, but her point is that journalists, especially magazine journalists, which is what she is, are in a position where they can't possibly *not* manipulate their subjects and material. That it's impossible to be totally honest and impossible to be totally objective."

"Let me see. . . . I wonder why you're telling me this?" She picked up her spoon and stirred her coffee. "Sounds like an inoculation, for both of us."

"I suppose I want to give you a . . . a broader understanding of what I'm doing. I don't know. To tell you that these things are complex. Writing about any politician is complex. He's your father, so it's not as complicated for you. But from where I'm sitting . . ."

Rachel swirled her coffee, took a sip, looked at Paul with lightly pursed lips and a long unchanging stare. "You know, you may need to attribute a little more sophistication to the people you have these kinds of chats with. You're not teaching a first-year class, you know. My father has had unfavourable things written about him in the past. And he will in the future."

"I know that."

"But he's also had many positive things written about him."

"I know that, too."

"Sometimes I actually think he's rather naïve. An innocent. But I'm not."

Paul nodded. "That's a good thing. That you're not, I mean."

"You're a free agent, Paul. The magazine you're in, and the writing you do, I read it. My father doesn't, much. He's vaguely heard of the magazine. He's more concerned with TV coverage. He doesn't think many people read magazines."

Paul laughed and instantly thought of Boar and Stranga. "I'm afraid he's right."

Rachel laughed, too, then looked to her side, across the space of the coffee shop, as if taking the time to think about what she wanted to say next. Paul studied her face in this half-profile she was giving him; she had smooth, clean skin except for a small mole just below her cheekbone. He noticed through a flutter of loose hair that she wasn't wearing earrings. She turned back to face him.

"You know, I told my dad it would be good to participate in this story, for this magazine, and with you as the writer, precisely because you are a free agent. I'm much better read than my father, much more involved in the culture. And I think you're a good writer, and that you have a way with profiles, with capturing character, with a political sense. And don't be flattered. I'm not saying these things because I like you. I mean, I do like you." She stopped and Paul swore he saw her blushing ever so slightly, a sight that made his balls tingle, a delightful sensation that, regrettably, did not last long. "Paul, you're trying to be 'honest,' though not as honest—or at least as direct—as you could be, though I don't blame you for it. But since you're making the attempt, or going this far anyway, I might as well be honest with you. You think you're trying to warn me of something, or that you're trying to cushion the blow for when we read what you write, which I'm sure will be something between high praise and the guillotine. That's okay, that's normal. But I think maybe you're missing the point in some ways, if you don't mind me saying. Do you really get why we're participating in this article? Why I recommended to my father that he give you so much time, and that we give you so much access to so many things he's involved in?"

Paul was sitting with his back against his chair and his arms crossed. "Well . . . because he wanted the coverage, and because he, like every politician, feels he has something to offer, and he wants this offering, this message, to be disseminated to as wide an audience as possible."

"Sure, that's part of it." She took hold of her pen and turned it in slow circles on the table in front of her, looking at Paul almost as if she were apologizing to him. "But I'm mostly just curious, that's all. That's why we're doing it."

"Curious?"

"Everybody knows how liberal 2.2.4. is. It hardly meshes with my father's platform. He stands a good chance of winning the leadership. Sure, it's a fledgling party, but he'll still get a lot of national coverage, even though most of the national media is left-leaning. Will he get taken apart in some of them? Maybe. Probably. But he's never had a major profile in a national magazine before, at least not a respected magazine like yours. I'm basically curious to see what happens, how he comes off, how he looks through that particular filter."

"That doesn't quite make sense to me, Rachel. What if I were to do a takedown? A hatchet job? What if I used my six thousand words to take him apart? That seems like a heavy price to pay to satisfy your curiousity, which, now that I think of it, sounds rather calculated, maybe even, oh, I don't know, academic?" Paul uncrossed his arms and wrapped his fingers together on the table in front of him. "No connection to your grad work, by any chance?"

Rachel ignored his last question. "A hatchet job?" She smiled, seeming to enjoy the phrase. "That would be fine."

"*Fine?* How would that be fine? I mean, I'm not going to do that, at least not necessarily—that's not the way I work. But how could that possibly be something you want? How could my writing a negative article be helpful?"

"My father is a good man. I know this in a way you never will. Sure, he has strong views on some things. Views I know you don't agree with, and that a lot of other people don't agree with. In fact, *I* don't agree with a lot of what he thinks. I'm not religious, at all, and I'm more middle of the road socially—you know, soft on gay rights, abortion, capital punishment, but to the right on taxation. My father is different, sure, an openly, *proudly*, unreconstructed conservative, but those are just his views, Paul, that's all. He's not a hater of others. He never cheated on my mother. He raised us on his own. He never beat us. He's not an alcoholic. He doesn't have a gambling addiction or make fun of the homeless. You can go after him all you like on his views, but that's precisely why we can't lose with you writing about him. *Because* you're as honest as you are." She emphasized her last point by lightly karate chopping the table.

"I'm still not sure I'm following you, Rachel. I'm sorry. I get how you feel about your dad, and I think that's wonderful, but . . ."

"You think you hold all the cards when it comes to writing your profile; but honestly Paul, and I'm sorry to say it this way, it doesn't matter *what* you write—in terms of how many votes he'll attract—because it will only help us. If you attack my father, it's a tool for us to energize our base."

"'Look at how the kneejerk liberal media portrays us.'"

Rachel raised a palm as if holding a tray. "And if you say anything positive, it's doubly valuable, because then we can say, Look! Even the 'liberal' media have some good things to say about my father."

"You're making it hard for me to feel good about doing my job."

Rachel grinned, then waved a hand expansively across the café. "Forget everything I just said. This message will self-destruct in ten seconds."

She was funny, and Paul was beginning to adore every single thing about her, but as she spoke, he came to understand she had no idea about her grandfather's career as a magazine columnist with *Across the Plains*. She'd never be sitting here so confident, so flirtatiously sure of herself (and damn it was sexy), if she knew her grandfather was a published racist. A coil of sympathy wound up Paul's throat; he was sad for her. He'd been wrong before when he'd first met her, thinking that she wasn't exactly beautiful; she *was* beautiful, very much in her own way, how she wove together her intelligence and humour. She was even more beautiful because she was also going to be wounded, badly, by him.

"The press has ruined many a politician's career, you know."

"Stupid politicians," said Rachel. "Besides, you won't do that. You can't. You're fenced in by your magazine's reputation and small readership, and anyway, you're too much a real writer. You're not an attack dog, like the newspaper press. You won't do a hatchet job because you're interested in ideas—even the ones you don't agree with. Which, by the way, is the main reason you don't have a big readership."

"Flattery will get you nowhere."

She nodded. "Can't hurt to try."

"So why should I even write the article? Why not focus on something else, a new topic? Why should I even bother writing about your father, if it doesn't mean anything?"

"I never said it didn't mean anything. I'm only telling you that we have different agendas, that's all. Don't tell me that comes as a surprise."

"No, no, fair enough. But what if I didn't write it?"

"That would really be a shame, no matter what you say in the piece. Speaking as a reader, I can say that because I'd be interested to know what you think of him, from the angles you take—the person, the politician, the meaning of the symbols, the agenda and how it's made manifest. You'll write it because he's a great subject, and it will be a great read."

Paul sat still, pressed his lips together and bit them on the inside. Rarely had such flattering words been directed his way, but never had praise made him feel so low. He had to admit that Rachel's take on it all was, in theory, savvy and sound, but her take was based on possessing full knowledge of the subject, a knowledge she thought she had. Her confidence and his correspondent sadness brought on a kind of melancholic dreaming about what might be, or might have been. She was going to detest him once his article appeared. But, perhaps he was wrong. Maybe she had higher interests, and truly did, and would, see the value of what he was doing. In fact, he thought suddenly, maybe he even ought *not* to be thinking about Daniel Code as a moral throwback, as a dam on the river of human progress—an approach that would solve certain problems, principally, that Rachel was soon going to hate him.

He awoke and gave himself a figurative slap on the side of the head.

"You know, Rachel, all the stuff you've just said, it makes me realize, again really, that so much of what I write about is just my own attempt to understand. To make sense of things. I guess that's why I do it. And that's probably why I don't worry about having so few readers."

"It takes courage to sort out thoughts in public. It's a risk. I'm doing the same thing in a way, only it's more protracted."

"You have to meet my sister someday. Lisa. She's the one doing her PhD. She would have loved being part of this conversation, even though she'd have probably told us by now how we both were missing the point."

Rachel leaned her head a couple inches toward her left shoulder. "I hope to meet her, someday. That would be nice."

Paul felt the tingling again, the stirring of his physical memory; to have someone warm beside him, naked, breathing hard, reaching out, wanting what he wanted at that moment and afterwards too. "Well," he said, "you seem pretty clear-eyed about the whole thing. I only hope you'll still talk to me after, even when I publicly disagree with some of your father's views."

"*I* disagree with some of his views. Lots of them. I mean, I don't even believe in God. How do you like that?"

Paul coughed up a bit of his coffee. "Excuse me?"

She shrugged. "He respects my views, and I respect his. Simple as that. I believe in him, not Him. Surely you're not so simple-minded as to think I'm his parrot?"

Paul was about to speak when the green-haired girl came by. "Gab gab gab," she said. "I thought you were going to do paperwork together?" She laughed at Paul, revealing the stud, which he instantly transferred to Rachel's tongue. It was almost too much to bear.

"Do you guys want another coffee? It seems to me you don't want to get up and since it's not that busy I'll get you one if you don't want to come to the counter."

"Yeah, thanks, two more," Paul said, smiling for her. The girl left and Rachel turned to Paul for something like an explanation. He said that when he'd arrived he had asked if there had been an attractive, long-haired woman sitting by herself, doing paperwork.

"Attractive?"

"Purely objective description. Just to help her differentiate from the other patrons."

"I thought you said before that writers can never truly be objective?"

"I did?" After a pause, he smiled and added, "Then I guess that makes the description subjective."

The next morning, Paul finished his shower, dried off and looked hard into the mirror as he combed his hair, putting on a little lotion where his face was already beginning to dry out. The late part of summer had turned abnormally hot, and with it came a burning wind dehydrating everything in its path, a wind that in winter would be a welcome chinook. If a chinook arrived in the middle of a frostbitten January day, it could hoist the temperature thirty degrees in an hour. Paul was always inspired by chinooks, even though they never lasted more than a day, and you always knew they were going to quickly fade away. He finished in the bathroom, the basement bathroom in his parent's house, and then changed to head into work, vowing as he did to call up Stelio just to see how the renos were coming along. It was getting time to think about heading back to his own place—whether the work was complete or not.

Sitting at his desk at 7:15 AM before anyone else had come into the office, Paul was admiring the sun when his phone rang. The shock of it made his legs twitch out. No one ever phoned this early on his personal line, though it was easy enough to navigate through the magazine's directory outside of office hours. There was silence on the other end, but he could hear tension crackling like a bad connection.

"Is this Paul?"

The voice was recognizable but not familiar. He knew it from somewhere. "Yes. Who's this?"

"Okay. I'm glad it's you, man. That's what I was hoping for."

"Who is this?"

"You don't have much of a memory, do you, Munkey Boy?"

"Palmer?" The image of tobacco juice splashing into the dust came into Paul's head, and the stink of those minty little turds rose up into his nose as if one were sitting on his desk right in front of him. "Why are you calling here?"

"To check up on things, is all."

"What do you mean?"

"What do I mean? What do you think I mean? I'm calling to check up on things."

"What things?"

"Fuck's sakes, Munkey Boy. Tammy."

"Tammy? Well, then why are you phoning me?"

"Do you think she'd tell me if things were going south on her grand plans? Who likes to admit they fucked up? Think about that. And trust me, she'd be the last person on earth to admit she made a mistake." The tight, violent silence returned.

Paul said nothing. He concentrated on listening to Palmer's silence even as he gazed out his window, where he saw the street gradually filling up with people, stepping off the bus, getting their coffee, heading into their workplaces.

"Sorry," said Palmer. "Didn't mean to get angry. But hey, I care. So sue me. But I just figure . . . well, she's alone there, right? Not that it matters to me. But I still care about her. We're still close . . . friends."

"If you're still close, why wouldn't she call you if she needed help?"

"Because she is so fucking stubborn, you have no idea. She's a mule, that one."

"Well, they look happy to me, if that's what you're calling about. Rick's started working, delivering stuff for the hardware store at the mall. Tammy's looking for studio space. Things seem okay, as far as I can tell."

"Yeah? Really? Everything's alright?"

"Well, that's how it looks to me."

Palmer truly had a way with silence, a gift for turning it like a gem to expose this or that facet. He rotated his quiet to a sharp disappointment, sending it down the line through the tone of his breathing, through the way he turned an exhalation into a murmur.

"Didn't want to hear that?"

"Don't be an asshole, Munkey Boy."

"You asked me what I thought. I'm telling you."

Palmer laughed, but it was forced. "Okay, listen, do me a favour. Don't tell her I phoned, alright?"

"Why not?"

"Just don't, okay? I care, but I don't want her to think I'm worried. Or that I'm interfering. And I do not want to have that woman pissed off at me."

"Why would she be mad that you care?"

"I need to hear a yes, Munkey Boy. Now that I know things are cool, I'm all straight. I've got business up Medicine Hat way every now and then, sometimes in Fernie, sometimes Kimberley, and if you thought a visit from me would help, I'd be there in a shot, right? But I'm not coming all that way for no reason. Right? Am I right?"

"I guess."

"So, in your opinion, a visit is not required?"

The formal language sounded almost comic to Paul, and he had to stop from sarcastically imitating Palmer with an equally formal reply. But after he thought about it for more than a couple of seconds, he wasn't quite clear what Palmer was asking of him. "You'd make that kind of decision based on my opinion?"

"Who else have I got up there to ask? I mean, besides Tammy."

"Fair enough."

"So we're straight?"

Paul paused, and knew there was conflict to be had no matter what he said. "Sure."

"That's the right thing to say, Munkey Boy."

Paul said good-bye and hung up the phone. He was sweating, with a damp feeling at the small of his back. He took a couple of deep breaths, stretched out, and waved his arms around to hack away at the thick tangle of mossy vines that had somehow occupied his office. He got up and went down to the water cooler, hoping to soothe the burning at the back of his throat.

TEN

The fact of Tammy's letters to Rick, held like a single complete thing built of so many unique but similar components, was almost moving for Paul. It was like looking at a pyramid built from all those single blocks of stone. The same envy he'd felt the first time he saw the stack of letters bit into him again. Of course, it wasn't these letters in particular he wanted, as much as he craved what they signified—a relationship, having another human being invest in you, demonstrating affection through the effort required to produce such a wealth of material. If there was an arc to the way people found one another, gained trust, became friends, lovers, spent lives together, Paul suspected such an arc, or at least half of it, was inside Tammy's letters to Rick.

He was standing in the basement bedroom Rick and Tammy had been using. The stack of letters he was holding was neat and tidy, much as it had been when Paul first saw it on Rick's lap during the drive home from Drumheller. Rick left it sitting on his dresser in front of the mirror. He'd gone away that morning for "a couple, three days," he'd said, to do some catching up with some old pals in Rocky Mountain House, back near where they used to hunt and camp, though Paul didn't recognize any of the names Rick mentioned. He'd invited Tammy along, but she said she wanted to stay and "get set up." She was out looking for studio space. Paul had come back after work to find the house empty; he didn't know where Lisa or his parents were.

In his hands were fifty, maybe sixty letters. He rifled through them quickly and saw again that they were numerically ordered with a small number in each bottom right-hand corner, though he noticed that one had been pulled from the stack and placed on top, out of order. One they'd been revisiting, possibly. But every letter had the same stamp, the same printing of Rick's name, the same return address of the house in Stennets. Each letter was opened across the top, carefully, with no tears or rips, in the same manner each time; this was, Paul imagined, indicative of the way Rick received and read them, and the importance he accorded them. After all, every article of faith, every piece of evidence that another life existed for him in the future, was something he'd no doubt cherish and hold on to inside.

Paul saw this image so clearly—this picture of his brother holding these letters and treating them with such tenderness and value—that the shabbiness of his own grasp of the stack, holding it like some grave robber with family treasure, brought on a thickening of his tongue at the top of his throat. These letters were something Paul knew Rick took pride in, and at the moment he made the final decision not to peek into any of them, Paul realized Rick probably wouldn't even hesitate to let him read them. It would only take a little courage on Paul's part to ask, to state his curiosity. That was all. In fact, he was sure Rick would even tell him what *he'd* written to Tammy, what he'd said that had so inspired her to write him the way she had, and which had made her fall in love with him through their letters.

He fingered through the stack one last time, smiling for his brother, sending him his love and hope, when he saw an envelope that was slightly different in both shape and weight. It was thicker than the others and his heart backed up on itself when he saw *Paul Munk* written on the face of the envelope, with the address of his apartment below his name. There was no stamp on it. Sealed shut, there was no way to tell when it had been written. It could have been years old, or days.

"See anything interesting?"

Paul started with fright and lost control of the stack. "Fuck!" He grasped at the letters fluttering to the floor. Before he had a chance to look, he knew who it was not only by voice but by the choice of words.

"You think that's funny? Well, it's not. You scared the shit out of me!"

Lisa stood leaning against the doorjamb, arms crossed, her hazel eyes incandescent with joy. "Look at you," she said, emphasizing every word. "Who would have thought?"

Paul was bent to the floor picking up the letters. "You're a witch. That scared me."

"Lost in thought, were you?"

Paul had the letters in his hands again and began to sort them, making sure they were all face up and oriented properly with the return address in each top left-hand corner. Thank God Rick numbered them, he thought. Then he remembered. There had been one letter on top that was out of order.

"I was just looking at them. I wasn't going to read them."

Lisa laughed again. "Oh, I believe you . . . I do."

"It's true."

"I didn't peg you for a snoop," she said, frowning theatrically and shaking her head. "Of course, you *are* a so-called writer. I guess that makes you unable to help yourself."

"I wasn't snooping. I was just looking."

"You crack me up."

"Lisa, I'm serious. I was thinking about them. Looking at them. I wasn't going to read them, honest. I mean, that's so private. It's, like, sacred."

"Actually," she said, reassuming her default above-it-all expression, "I couldn't care less about the letters. I'm sure it's just page after page of Rick and Tammy babbling back and forth. There's a pretty low ceiling on how interesting that could possibly be. What's more interesting to me is that you're in here casing the joint."

"*Casing the joint.* Been watching a lot of cop shows?"

She ignored him. "So what do they say?"

"I told you, I didn't read them."

"Okay, whatever."

"I mean it. And Lisa, come on, you can't tell Rick I was in here. I was just walking by, going to watch some TV, and saw them on the dresser. I'm serious."

"Whatever. Don't have a coronary."

Paul continued to reorganize the letters. Lisa watched her brother for a moment before speaking again. "He's pretty fucked up. And he's got no one to go to. That's why he wrote her. It's also why she wrote back. You know that, right? You understand that?"

"You know, Lisa, I don't like to place myself in the position of deciding who's fucked up and who isn't."

"You don't know what you're missing."

Paul smiled, shook his head. "And who, in your humble opinion, is someone he can go to? Who do you go to? Or is there anyone worthy enough to hold that distinction? What about Mum and Dad? Or . . . Roger? Is that his name?"

Lisa's expression changed, not towards melancholy, exactly, but to a sad sort of acceptance. Her mouth dropped into a straight line, her eyes turned down to Paul's chin. "I ended it."

"What! Why?"

"Because he's smart. If I sleep with him and then give him a good grade, both get compromised. I won't enjoy the sex and he won't enjoy the grade."

"Oh. . . . Sorry, I guess. Am I sorry?"

Lisa stared flat-lidded at her brother. "I'd go to you," she said.

"Me?"

Lisa paused, exhaled. "You're not the only person who's lonely, Paul. You might think you are, but you're not. It's not a death sentence, you know. It's just a learning curve. Don't romanticize it. If you do, that's what you'll fall in love with."

She turned and left, and Paul heard her walk into the family room. The TV came on with the volume up high. The sound of channels rapidly changing funnelled down the hallway to where Paul still stood. The cacophony of it, the random noise and compulsory twitchy substitution of one channel for another and another and another, was more heartbreaking than any sound he could imagine in its place.

He stood in the bedroom of his brother and future sister-in-law, holding the paper trail of the first two years of their two-year-and-three-week-old relationship. He put the letters back on the dresser where he'd first spotted them, burying the letter addressed to him roughly in the middle, and hoping he'd remembered correctly which letter belonged at the top of the stack. There was nothing he could do about it now. He accepted that. If Rick said anything, Paul would tell him that he'd gone into his room after seeing the letters from the hallway, that he'd held the stack, that he'd even briefly considered reading them but decided it was wrong. Rick would accept that. As he was stepping out of the room, Paul caught himself in the mirror. The face was drained, drawn, but he tried to gaze evenly and dispassionately into the eyes behind his glasses, into irises glistening like rough nuts of newly mined coal. Lisa *could* come to him if she ever needed to. And so could Rick. It would be okay. It would all be okay.

⁕

Harold wanted to know how the Code profile was progressing. They were seated in Harold's cave, as Paul sometimes called it. Harold did not look well to Paul, though this was relative, given that Harold's normal appearance sometimes caused off-duty paramedics to stop and ask if he was okay; today his eyes were pushed back deep in his sockets.

"Nail him to the wall," said Harold.

"I'm starting to wonder if that's really what's required here."

"Oh, no. Look at you. You're softening. That's why he's doing it. It's classic. He's creating a relationship, something you can't extricate yourself from. He wants you to make him a person first, instead of a politician first. It's classic. Standard. And he's making his daughter—his sexy, young daughter, who says she likes you, I might add—part of the equation."

"No, Harold, it's more complicated than that. He really doesn't care, I think. I think he really does believe I'm going to take him down."

"Then don't disappoint him."

"It's almost too easy. What'd P. J. O'Rourke say about criticizing born agains . . . *shooting dairy cows with a scope and a rifle.*"

"There's no such thing as 'too easy' when you're dealing with fools. In fact, sometimes it takes even more concentration."

"He's a lot of things, many of which I don't like, some of which I even despise, but he's not a fool."

"Hold on . . . it *was* you, wasn't it, who told me that one of your sources said at a town hall meeting in Crawford Way that Code announced to the crowd that the earth was seven thousand years old because that's what the Bible said? And that man walked with the dinosaurs?"

"Yeah." Paul sat looking out the window. He let a few seconds pass. Harold was right. Code was a subject, a thing to be profiled, that was all. Paul didn't want to like or dislike the man; he wanted only to assess him disinterestedly. That was the point, the purpose. Otherwise, his profile would be nothing more than another in the long line of slabs of propaganda that passed for journalism across every political orientation. This thought alone was horrific enough to Paul that today's spurt of empathy had already been leached from his bloodstream, but he let Harold continue. He seemed to need the outlet.

"I know you as well as I know anyone in my life, Paul, and this guy would paste that canned smile on his face and happily wreck everything you value in a society—equality, distribution of wealth, universal health care, the value of the intellect, the separation of church and state. If we let him remake society, every member of it would be a white, gun-carrying, greedy religious zealot who only mated with one member of the opposite sex in his lifetime and then died the day after he retired so that the state wouldn't have to pay for his failing health. Come on, Paul, you know this guy is a Trojan horse. You know it. He gets in with the soft sell, maybe a little of the old bait and switch with the faith bullshit, and then nutjob ideas are going to pour out of him like cockroaches. Look at what we know about this guy. Stop and think about it. He's a homophobe. No argument. He's a rabid pro-lifer, and has even flirted with not prosecuting those guys that shoot abortion docs. No argument. His father is a racist, and we know the branch never falls far from the tree. No argument. He has said publicly that the earth is seven thousand years old. No argument. He thinks the Bible is a phone book, published for reference and information. No argument. He wants to reinstate the death penalty. No argument."

Paul had been nodding in sober agreement with each point. When Harold finished, Paul grinned and said, "Yeah, but he's got a cute daughter."

Harold sighed and let his shoulders slump. "My life's work is a waste."

"If I'm your life's work, then it *has* been a waste."

"It's over, isn't it?" said Harold, muttering to himself, dejectedly scrutinizing his desk as if searching for one last thing, anything, he could hold and trust. The performance made Paul smile. "It's just . . . it's a lost cause."

"Relax," said Paul. "Listen, it's just that it's complicated. That's all I'm trying to tell you. Don't go opera on me. I'm going to be accurate and unbiased. You know that. Conclusions will be based purely on their pertinence to the questions of the campaign and his leadership abilities. I'll assess only the available evidence. Induction will be my compass. Fair-mindedness my wheel."

"So you'll do the hatchet job this clown deserves?"

"You'll have a draft by Friday."

ELEVEN

The simplest of tasks always gave Paul tremendous satisfaction. Vacuuming. Ironing a shirt. Even standing around doing the dishes, as he was now, alone, listening to the radio, taking his time. After dinner, his parents had gone for a walk. Lisa had gone to the university. Tammy had secreted herself in the basement room she and Rick were using; Rick was due back the next day from his buddy trip.

Paul had the dishwasher fully loaded and burbling along, a sound he always found reassuring and that made him feel purposeful. He was scouring the large cast-iron pan in which his mother had razed the pork chops, but it was hard going. She used too many spices, too much oil, too much heat, and cooked them for too long; the result, fused to the pan, was a new kind of alloy—black, carbon-based, and roughly the thickness of tooth enamel. He was just finishing chipping away at the last of it when Tammy surfaced from the basement. She sat heavily at the kitchen table. "Need some help?"

"You should have asked twenty minutes ago."

"Oh . . . sorry."

"I'm just joking. I sort of like doing it."

Tammy smiled. "You're a freak."

Paul shrugged. "Some things can't be helped." He placed the pan in the drying rack, wiped his hands on the dish towel, and sat down opposite Tammy. "So what's cooking?"

"No more pork chops, I hope . . . was that what they were?"

"Mum tries."

"She does?"

"Well, cooking never interested her that much. Still, she fed us for years. That takes commitment, to do something you don't like to do, every day for twenty years, just because you love your kids."

"Alright already. What a guilt trip. All I was saying was, they were dodgy pork chops. Not that I'm some French chef or anything myself."

"Yeah, they were a bit overdone." Paul laughed and stood up. "Tea?"

Tammy nodded wearily without really looking at him.

"So fill me in," said Paul, plugging in the kettle. "How's it going? How is this whole thing going?" He waved his hands around the house and toward the basement to indicate what he was referring to. "I really admire you guys for it. It can't be easy."

"That's sweet of you to say," said Tammy. "I mean it. No one's said that to us yet."

Paul smiled. "Not even Palmer?"

"Palmer?"

"Well, he still seems pretty supportive of you. Especially for an ex-husband. Or should I say husband?" Paul said it lightly, almost teasingly, trying to walk the line.

Tammy snapped a look at Paul, a look without malice or antagonism but that conveyed a quick sense of reconnaissance, as if an unknown scent had been detected.

"That's the word Palmer used in Montana. Not ex-husband. 'Husband.' You weren't there, so I had to talk to the guy. I mean, Rick just dumped me there."

"What do you mean *dumped* you there?"

"I don't mean dumped. I'm kidding."

"No, you're not."

"He went to look for you at your sister's house. That's all. He tried the door and there was no answer, and so he asked me to wait there. We told you that. I remember telling you that while we were playing cards."

She leaned her head back slightly to look down her nose at him and inhaled while keeping her mouth closed. Paul could smell the crisp lilac scent she'd worn in the truck home from Montana. He'd found it overbold at first, as if she'd simply put too much on, but now he associated the scent with her and liked it. The electric kettle came to a boil and flicked off.

"Chamomile? Earl Grey?"

"Either."

After letting his tea steep for a minute or two, Paul dropped a glob of honey in his transparent glass mug and swirled his spoon around in a tight circle, watching the honey quickly melt away until it was fully dissolved. This small action always fascinated him—just by looking at it you wouldn't know there was anything but tea in the cup, and yet the tea was different than it had been a minute earlier. There was no reversing it. Paul offered the honey to Tammy.

She shook her head. "You know, it was Palmer that sort of introduced us. Me and Rick, that is. Rick ever tell you that?"

"No!" Paul was surprised and he didn't try to hide it. "He didn't tell me that."

"Through letters. The introduction, I mean. Me and Palmer had broken up long before, but like I say, we still saw each other a lot once I went back down there to look after Penny. He was really good to me. I'll never take that away from him. Anyways, he told me I should write to this guy Rick, help him not be so lonely in jail, that's all. From Calgary, and so on and so forth. Palmer knew I was from Calgary. I think he thought it would get my mind on other things besides Penny. So I wrote Rick, and—" she stopped, then grinned.

"Well . . . that's, that's sweet, I guess. But how did Palmer know Rick? From before, I mean?"

Tammy stared into her tea mug, then shrugged. "I don't really know. They met a long time ago, from before Rick was in jail second time around. They did stuff together. Between Rick's times inside. They both fish. Maybe that."

"That's odd Palmer would have acted like that about Rick with me. Maybe it was just because of you and Rick and all. Being an ex, maybe. That had to be weird for him. I thought he was a pretty funny guy, though." It was the truth, though far from a summary of what Paul thought of Palmer. "But nope, Rick never told me he knew Palmer. Just dropped me off there. Palmer scared me at first, but then he lightened up, seemed okay."

"He's just another guy with a big cock."

Paul coughed on his tea, scorching the nib of his tongue. "Pardon me?"

"Balls down to here." She held out an open hand as if trying to gauge the weight of a small grapefruit.

"Do I really need to know this?"

Tammy laughed. "Aren't men interested in that kind of stuff? Comparative information? Stats? Figures? Numbers? For God's sake, if I ever saw another one of Palmer's charts about banking and government, the UN. All those arrows. He used to pore over the sports pages, too. I mean, for hours. Isn't it the same thing? He was always doing football and baseball pools with his pals. Isn't that what men do? Compete? Compare?"

Paul adopted a severe and philosophical expression. "As a matter of fact, we're tormented."

"Excuse me?"

"Ripped apart from the inside out by our competing desires to protect, nurture, and conquer. We're unable to set our hearts free, obsessed with an instinct for species survival that overwhelms any chance for intimacy."

"Yeah, whatever. Men keep score. I've never met a man who didn't keep a list somewhere of every grievance and every victory. It's the only thing they can remember."

Paul squinted and wrinkled his nose up. ". . . Balls down to where?"

Tammy laughed again. "You don't want to know."

"Anyway," continued Paul, "what do you mean, charts and banking and arrows? I thought Palmer was a mechanic?"

"He is. Anyhow, I wish you guys hadn't shown up so early in Stennets. I wasn't expecting you until later in the afternoon. I wasn't quite ready. Not that I'm embarrassed or anything. He is my ex. That's the truth. I still like him, I suppose, though not in that way. He's . . . well, he's not a good man. I almost said he was. But he's not a bad man, either. He's just got to get some things worked out. And not with me. That's all. That doesn't make him bad or good, just . . . well, just a work in progress?"

Paul snorted. "That's what Lisa calls me. I'm pretty sure she doesn't mean it as a compliment."

"Then maybe she should meet Palmer. You seem about as different a man from Palmer as two guys could be, I'll say that much. You're also pretty different from your brother."

"Is that a good thing or a bad thing?"

"Why does it have to be measured by that yardstick?" She frowned and all of a sudden seemed exasperated to Paul, overly so, like she'd just come in from some other discussion, an argument she'd lost. It occurred to Paul that she wished she'd gone with Rick instead of staying behind, and was upset with herself, and lonely. He would be.

"Good thing or bad thing?" she continued. "Why can't things just be different? There's no prize, you know. We're not doling out first place ribbons."

"Fair enough."

Tammy sat silently considering her surroundings, looking at the table, the counter, the windows, almost everywhere except at Paul. There was something very serious yet comical about it, and it almost made Paul grin; it was as if she were seeing her environment for the first time, and trying to make a snap judgment the way someone might measure a hotel room right after checking in for a long stay. She was assessing something, it was clear, but her manner was coy, almost playful; Paul was anxious to hear the verdict.

"I want to tell you something," she finally said. "If that's okay." She glanced at the chunky, leather-banded watch on her wrist. "You going out, got time?"

"I've got nothing but, especially for a bedtime story," said Paul, teasing her. "Maybe I should go get into my pyjamas."

She dropped her head slightly, and gave him a brief but unmistakable look of such frank physical appraisal that, unnerved, he sat up straight in his chair and cleared his throat like a schoolboy called to order. Tammy was so often to be found chatting in what seemed like aimless pitter-patter, or appear to be listening deeply only to ask a follow-up question utterly unrelated to the conversation at hand, that Paul had on occasion fallen into thinking she was quite seriously scatterbrained; not unintelligent, precisely, but wildly, almost hopelessly unable to channel her intelligence in any way useful to herself or anyone else.

"Well?"

"Yes, of course, tell me the story."

"It's about my sister. Well, about both of us, I guess. Has Rick told you this story, about me and her? There's some similarities between us, and between you and Rick."

Paul shook his head. "He hasn't told me."

"We grew up in Calgary, actually just outside Calgary, in a little town called Well Creek, up north and west of Cochrane."

"I've driven by it. The mountains are huge from there."

"Yeah, it's gorgeous, quiet." Tammy used a fingernail to pick at something on the table. "Anyways, well, my parents split up when Penny and I weren't that old. I was maybe six, Penny was seven. Dad, who was American, like your dad, well, he went home."

"Draft dodger, too?"

"Yeah. He was from Portland. Anyways, he went back home. Said he missed the rain. I guess he figured the war was over, and so on. Nothing ever did happen to him, I don't think, least not that we heard about."

"You don't know?"

"I only saw him a couple of times after that, and one of them was when he was just about dead. That was like ten years ago. Anyways, he went back to Portland, did whatever—I think he worked as an insurance salesman—but then about a year after he went back, he started writing to Mum. Started saying how lonely he was, how he was never going to remarry, how it was all so unfair that he was alone, and that she had both daughters, on and on. And so he says that he thought he should get one of us, one of his daughters to raise, that that would only be fair."

"You can't be serious? He left the family, then starts saying that?"

Tammy nodded. "He was like that. The world's most confident man with the least reason to be confident. So Mum said. Anyways, people around Well Creek, like my granny and some other mums around there, they start saying things like, Well, yeah, it's going to be tough on you, Kitty, raising two little girls, not much work, hard to find a new husband, on and on."

"Kitty? Your mother's name was Kitty Vine?"

"How 'bout you shut up for two seconds. Anyways, so guess what?"

"She sent Penny to Portland."

"Yup. Seven years old. Sends her off to Portland to live with him."

"He was your father, though."

"Yeah, some blessing that was. Of course, what he did next was get Penny down there, all legally signed over, get her all on his side, and then he met someone, married her, some rich thing, and she didn't like Penny, or at least the idea of Penny. So Dad sent Penny off to live with his mother, our other granny, halfway across the country, in Flint, Michigan. That was where Penny grew up. In Michigan, of all places. My mum was furious, but she'd signed the custody papers to him. What could she do?"

Paul sat back in his chair, ran a hand through his messy hair. "No offence, Tammy . . . but I can't believe your mum did that. I mean, Jesus Christ."

Tammy folded her arms under her breasts. "It wasn't until a couple years after she died that I could admit to myself I wasn't ever going to forgive her. Penny felt the same. We stayed in touch all those years, and it was weird, but I swear it made us closer. We wrote each other every week, phoned each other whenever we could."

"And then she got cancer. That is so sad, Tammy. What a sad story."

"I didn't see her from the age of seven until I was twenty-two. Fifteen whole years. She was my sister, and I didn't see her for fifteen years. Oh, you've never seen two people so happy to see one another when we finally met again. It was like we were just, I don't know, like lovers or something. We just couldn't stop hugging." Tammy stopped and gazed at the table as if a picture of her sister was right in front of her. "That was the happiest moment of my life, easy."

Paul reached over and touched Tammy's hand.

She looked up and though her eyes were wet she was smiling. "And that's maybe why I think you and Rick are a bit like that."

"Me and Rick?"

"Because you were separated."

"Well . . ."

Tammy ran a forefinger under each eye. Paul saw her eyeliner was running slightly, so he got up and got a tissue for her from the counter. "And I know how close you two were when Rick went into jail. He's told me. He told me all about it in his letters to me. I think that's partly why I was so attracted to him, just through his letters. Because it was so beautiful, so true. You guys were close as brothers. I can still see that. And then for him to go to jail, that must have been so hard for both of you. I guess I could relate."

"You and Penny were a lot younger though, right?" Paul felt his stomach muscles contract. He shifted in his chair.

"Yeah, we were. But the point's the same, don't you think? You get separated from someone, and it hurts. But that's not only what it's about. It's not just the hurt. Because the separation, especially when it's something awful like that, like when your mother gives you away, or when your brother goes to jail, it's not just about the hurt. There's something really powerful about it, too. Something that's stronger than being apart. It's not even good or bad, not like that. It just is. It's like, like . . . like you're sharing a destiny together, like you're more permanently together because you're forced apart."

"You think Rick and I share a destiny?"

"Well, when you say it like that, it sounds kind of corny, but you know what I mean."

"I think I know what you're trying to say, but I'm not sure I totally agree. You mean, we'll always have that bond, right, that connection? Okay, that I can see. But it doesn't go much beyond that." Paul looked over the sink, crossed his arms in front of him. "I mean, we are brothers, after all. It's not that abnormal to be close to your brother. That's not destiny, Tammy. That's family. Just family."

Tammy wiped her nose with the tissue Paul had given her. "Now you're mad at me. Or you think I'm being too intimate, too familiar, that I have no right to talk like this."

"No, don't be silly."

"You crossed your arms."

"So? You crossed yours five minutes ago."

"Now you're being defensive. It's basic body language. You're closing off. You won't be able to talk about it now. I shouldn't have told you my story."

Paul consciously tried to uncross his arms, but couldn't. "Don't be silly, Tammy. I'm glad you told me your story. I can see why you'd want to find similarities between you and Rick. That's normal. You guys *are* similar. That's great, isn't it? For a relationship? And I'm not closing you off. This is just a comfortable position, that's all. Don't read stuff into things. I will tell you this: Rick and I *are* close. We always have been. But it's complicated, you know? You can't understand what it's all about, because you've only been around for a few weeks—I mean, you've known Rick longer than a few weeks, mostly through letters, and that's okay, I'm sure you feel like you know a lot about him, and about me and about our family. But it's not that straightforward. . . . I think it's wrong to compare us to what you and your sister went through. That sounds like something awful that could have easily torn you apart. It's amazing that it didn't happen." Paul broke off because he felt the need to breathe deeply, but he couldn't. He tried to offer up a light smile, but felt sure his face betrayed him. He felt like he was going to have to perform a tricky bit of stick handling, like trying to break up with someone you didn't want to hurt. He wasn't offended by anything Tammy was saying. That wasn't it. It just didn't feel like her business. Tammy had been watching him calmly the whole time, her face increasingly impassive as his went hot, and probably a patchy red. Would he ever be anything other than utterly readable?

"He told me all about it, Paul."

"All about what?"

"About his first time inside, I mean, why he went in."

". . . For assault."

Picking up her cup and swirling her tea, Tammy let the silence collect around Paul.

"Well, isn't that what he told you? That he went in for assault?"

"He told me you talked to the cops."

"And he told *me* I did the right thing."

"Well. Yeah. That's because he loves you. Anyways, my point is that you two have something Penny and I had—a past, a past that makes a bond that isn't even about love or support. It's about a thing you can't ignore, almost like a duty. I mean, I loved Penny, but looking after her down in Stennets wasn't always about love. There were times I would have done anything to run away from her, the sickness, the neediness, that pull."

Paul was sitting back in his chair, arms still crossed, his top lip curling under his bottom lip so that he could suck on it.

"Do you feel that about Rick sometimes?" Tammy said. "You missed him, didn't you? But now he's back, and actually being around someone isn't quite the same as *wanting* to be around them."

"I did miss him . . . I still miss who he used to be." Tammy didn't look even slightly shocked by what Paul had said, though he himself was. He felt his eyes water and crinkle, and he tried to blink the tears away. "So then what was it about, with you and your sister, if it wasn't always about love? Aren't you going to tell me? What is that thing, that bond?"

Tammy stood up and took their teacups, placing them quietly in the sink. She did not sit back down, but stood over her chair.

"Just before Penny died, when she was in bed all the time, skinny as a rake, no hair, she said to me one day, 'Come closer, I have something I want to say to you.' Just say it, I said. I'm right here. 'No,' she said. 'I'm too embarrassed. I want to whisper it.' So I went and stood by her bed, and I leaned over, and I put my ear next to her lips, and I could hear her breathing, in and out, in and out, like every breath was work, which I guess it was, since she died a few days after that. Anyways, I put my ear there, and after a minute or two of just breathing, she whispers, so soft, 'I just wanted to tell you something now, in case I forget, or in case I die tonight. I want you to know that I always felt it, even when we were so far apart.' Felt what? I whispered back. She was quiet again for a few minutes, like she was catching her breath. 'No matter where I was, with Dad or with Gram, being shuttled all over hell's half acre, Well Creek, Portland, Flint, feeling like Mum just cut me loose, all that time, Tammy, I always knew, I just knew, that you were on my side. That's all. You were on my side. I never once doubted it. And I loved you for that. Now move away from me so we can talk normal.' I stood up and we cried our faces off. She died a couple days later."

Tammy pushed her chair in and left the room, briefly putting her hand on Paul's shoulder. Paul stood, went to the counter, rubbed his eyes. He stared for a moment at the two cups in the sink before going downstairs and turning on the TV, looking for something strong enough or vulgar enough or stupid enough to grab him and take over.

Paul sat up, opened his eyes, still drowsy from his unexpected mid-afternoon wolf nap. The easy heat of the day had gone deep inside him as he lay on the prairie shortgrass with his baseball cap over his eyes. He felt content and full, not with drink or food, but with sun and air. He turned his gaze east and south, across the length of the plateau. There were quite a few people up on the hills today, some of whom were standing along the top edge of the park, silhouetted against the blue sky like ramparts on a castle. A few hundred yards away, a woman was walking back down, toward the city. She walked like Rachel, loose-limbed, about the same height, with the same brunette hair. He shouted out, loud enough to be heard, but the person kept on walking. He shouted her name one more time, but she disappeared over a blunt dip, then reappeared further down the hill, now well out of earshot. Paul briefly considered sprinting after her, but if it had been her surely she'd have seen him. He was planted in broad daylight on the side of the hill, in plain view.

He looked to the city below, to the giant towers clustered in the basin along the Bow River, to all the neighbourhoods stretching for miles in every direction. Never—not once in his life—had he failed to be mesmerized by the breadth of the view from the top of the park. You could almost see the curve of the earth from up here, and he imagined Montana as visible on the edge of the southern horizon. His favourite time to be on the hill was dusk, with the western sky bleeding off its light and the eastern horizon a black void, when a paling spectral flush of illumination hung directly over the city. It made the hill an in-between place, a place of dark and light. Calgary at dusk had a meaning, truthful yet mysterious, that he hadn't fully uncovered, but that would always be part of the way he tried to understand and explain the place he lived.

"Hey," came a voice from Paul's left, from the northeast. He glanced over to see Rachel lurching toward him in an awkward side hill gait, as if one leg were shorter than the other.

"Well, hello."

"Hi," she said, smiling widely, standing over him briefly, then sitting down beside him.

"Why were you coming from that direction? I thought you'd come up the fall line from the parking lot."

"I parked over on the other side, you know, the Fourteenth Street parking lot."

"You're kidding," he said, his voice rising in an admiration he wanted her to hear. "That's got to be three or four kilometres."

"Which would explain why I'm all sweaty and my feet are hot. God." She pulled her shoes and socks off.

"Well, I'm glad you came. I didn't know if you would."

She shrugged. "I didn't know if I would, either. But . . . here I am."

"In the flesh."

"Apparently so . . ." She looked around the hill, down to the city, then back to Paul, and the light was so clear and she was so close to him that he could see exactly how her irises were flecked with tiny arrowheads of gold. "How's it going? How's the article?"

"The article? You know. Just . . . yeah, just beavering away. It's going all right." He bunched up his lips and bobbed his head up and down.

Rachel laughed. "Boy, you're still just getting all bent out of shape, aren't you? Really, Paul. You're not consorting with the enemy here. You are allowed to talk to me. I know what you're going to write. I wasn't born yesterday. I'm still here, right? I'm somehow managing to deal with it, unlike someone else I know."

Paul made to speak, but then stopped. The other times he'd seen Rachel she'd been wearing a clean burgundy lipstick, fairly lightly applied. There were remnants of it on her lips now, but for whatever reason—having eaten lunch, perhaps—the lipstick had dulled somewhat, and was pallid and uneven. Paul found this less aesthetically appealing but quite a bit more arousing than when it was carefully applied. The thought of having sex with her rumbled somewhere deep inside him, as if a thunderstorm had begun to growl over the back side of a ridge of hills.

"Ohhkay," said Rachel slowly, grimacing in her attempt to change the subject, "I haven't been up here in a while. It's so beautiful." She swivelled her head from one side to the other, to take in the panoramic view, and it was only then Paul noticed that not only was she not wearing earrings again, her ears were not even pierced.

"Your ears aren't pierced. I just noticed that."

She looked back his way, though not straight at him. "No," she said. "My father wouldn't let us."

"You're joking," said Paul, starting to laugh.

Rachel smiled along with him. "I'm not. I'm serious. I was desperate to get them pierced, around grade seven, I think. All my friends were getting it done. But, he was a single parent, right? My mum had just died. He was a preacher. He didn't know, maybe didn't care. One of my friends had three or four piercings in each lobe, you know, all the way up, and I think that freaked him out a bit." She ran a long finger up the carnation pink C-shape of her ear, a tender motion Paul imagined doing for her. "Anyway, he told me that if I wanted to mutilate my body—that was the word he used, *mutilate*—that I was going to have to wait until I was the age of majority." She said the words *age of majority* in a deep, paternal tone, and when she stopped, she let out a little laugh through her nose, smiling to herself as if it were a cherished memory of her childhood. "I guess you could say he sometimes overstated his case."

"But you obeyed him? You never 'mutilated' your body? He must be very proud of his obedient daughter."

She rubbed the inside of her wrist for a few seconds, before turning her eyes up to Paul and saying, "I waited a bit. Then I just got my piercings where he couldn't see them, that's all."

Paul felt his eyeballs begin to bloat.

"Well, look at that," said Rachel, poking him in the thigh.

"What?"

"You're blushing."

Paul cleared his throat loudly, both because he wanted to exaggerate it for the joke, but also to get some time to pull it back together.

"Paul?"

He felt his colour come down, his skin start to cool off. "Yes?"

"That's just a story, right?" Her voice was small, vulnerable. "The earrings, *mutilate*, all that. That's just a story from me to you, okay?"

Paul knitted his brow.

"Come on, you know what I mean. You won't use that, right? In your article?" She looked across the park and then turned her eyes back to Paul. "I'm telling you that I don't want you to."

"I never would have even thought of it," said Paul. It was the truth, though the moment he said it, he realized it was in fact precisely the kind of hard, shiny character detail he'd love to have in his back pocket. But he didn't possess it. He knew that.

"I'm sorry. I just had to say it."

Paul nodded, leaned back on his elbows. "You didn't have to say it. But I know why you did. It's okay." He let silence sit between them for a moment. "So you used to come here a lot?" he said. "Up to the park?"

Rachel leaned back beside Paul. "I did when we lived right here in the northwest. We only lived here for a year or so, back when Dad was trying to figure out where to live, you know, city or prairie, after Mum died."

"So you came up here for walks and stuff?"

"Usually with boyfriends. Not a lot of fooling around allowed back at the old Code house."

"What a shame."

"Yeah, not much of anything went on at our house. It was all pretty much by the book."

"The good book."

Rachel acknowledged the pun, nodding and rolling her eyes, but she didn't pretend to find it all that funny.

Paul smiled, but then couldn't contain himself any longer. "Rachel . . . why are you working on your father's campaign? Really. I mean, you're an academic. You're going to be pursuing a completely different life than the *doing* of politics, aren't you? To analyze our system of politics, any system of politics, don't you have to be outside of it? It seems to me you can't be doing yourself any favours in either arena. Politicians generally don't hang out with academics, and academics generally don't like to get their hands dirty with day-to-day political activity. And on top of everything else, you don't even really believe in a lot of what your father stands for."

Rachel remained reclined on the brown dry grass. "Boy, you really know just what to say to a girl."

Paul shrugged. "Some things you're just born with."

"He's my dad, Paul. Why is that so weird, to want to help him? He asked me. I said yes."

"But you told me yourself, you don't share all his beliefs."

"I love him, so I'm helping him. I told you before. Loving someone doesn't mean you have to imitate them. Or does it with you?" She gave him a little kick on the thigh, then left her foot near him. Her toenails had been painted red, but little flakes of paint had come off here and there. Paul took her foot and placed it in his lap, held it in his hands. The veins and tendons that mapped out the top of her foot were all so perfectly arranged, so balanced and true. Her eyes were closed, and Paul turned to gaze at her face, at the underside of her chin, which was strong and long, and sculpted so tightly that he was sure the bulge in the bottom middle was the lower part of her tongue. His forefinger would fit in that dip between the bulge and her jawbone, it was just that size. He could see the full outline of her nostrils: sad black wells the shape of pendant jewels, of tears. He ran his palm over top of her foot and then along the underside, across the ball, scooping out the hollow of the arch, stopping to grasp her heel as if it were a small mandarin orange.

"That feels nice." She kept her eyes closed. "You've done this before?"

"Just to Emily."

"Emily?"

"Girlfriend from a few years back. Quite a few years, actually."

"Hmmm," mumbled Rachel. "What happened to her?"

What was there to say without sounding melodramatic? The sadness had long since gone, but the maudlin nature of the admission—and why did it feel like *his* admission?—hadn't. Years had gone by now. Last April was the tenth anniversary, if that was the right word. Emily's parents were away on vacation on Vancouver Island, and when Paul couldn't find her for a couple of days he called them. They came back, set up search parties. She'd been depressed in high school, garden variety, it seemed, and appeared to have pulled out of the emotional trough, enough that the two of them—they'd met in first-year university—had gone backpacking together through Europe. There were no traumatic events, at least none Paul saw or could remember, and then she simply fell back into a debilitating depression. For days they looked. There were no guns. No cars with hoses running from tailpipe to window. All her pills were still in the medicine cabinet. There had been no reports of bridge jumpers, and no bodies had washed up in the river past the zoo, where suicides sometimes tended to eddy. There was no note. The police questioned Paul then left him alone. It wasn't until her parents had been back home for four days that they finally needed to get something out of their old relic of a chest freezer in the basement.

The coroner determined that she'd let the locking lid fall shut, which would have been the only way to ensure the latch closed on the outside. There was no inside release, and no way to change her mind once the lid had come down. For two or three years afterwards Paul had nightmares of her trying to get out, clawing at it, screaming, begging for someone to come and help her and open it up because she made a mistake and didn't mean it. In this dream her voice simply faded into nothing. He read a magazine article during this time about people who jumped off the Golden Gate Bridge and survived, and how the only thing they had in common—these lawyers, carpenters, kids, seniors, Mexicans, Germans, it didn't matter—the only thing they shared was that after they'd jumped, on their way down, they all thought the same thing, which was, *I wish I hadn't jumped*. But maybe, Paul had thought then, maybe that was why they were the ones who survived the leap. Because they were ambivalent. Had Emily been? Maybe. It wouldn't have mattered anyway, locked in like that.

Paul looked over at Rachel. She was still leaning back, enjoying her foot rub, a dreamy half-smile on her face, and she didn't seem in too much of a hurry to hear anything about some ex-girlfriend of Paul's. He gazed off across the northwest neighbourhoods spread out at their feet, down towards Brentwood, where Emily used to live. He could almost make out her old house from where he sat. Although he hadn't felt the urge for a few years now, Paul sometimes used to go by there. He fought with the desire to ring the bell and ask the new owners if he could go down to the basement for a few minutes and be alone, alone where that freezer used to be, and where the owners probably had their new freezer since it was the only suitable place to put one. He wanted to stand there and look. He wanted to open the lid. Pull her out. Make her breathe. Hold his warmth against her so that the cold chill of her pain would fade away and change into heat, life.

"What did you say happened to her?" asked Rachel, softly, as if waking up. "Emily?"

"She passed away ten years ago. Suicide."

Rachel sat up, whispered, "Oh my God."

This was where it always got awkward, and Paul's experiences with girls after Emily drove him to avoid bringing it up anymore. It all sounded meaningful enough, a piece of serious experience, somewhat romantic in a bleak, novelistic kind of way and even a bit existential; this was how it sounded in theory. In reality, when he talked about it, not one single romantic or positive or existential thing could be drawn from it. It was simply sad without being conclusive because, well, what could you say? There were no answers. It was the kind of thing you never got over but that did, he had to admit, get easier to compartmentalize as the years went on. It had long ago ceased to be an excuse or a reason for anything.

"What happened?"

Paul told her, everything, as much as he could remember. He didn't mind. In fact, he found he wanted to. He ticked off details as if there were a list in front of him: emotional, physical, practical. He ran through it as comprehensively as he could. The particulars of her suicide. The aftermath. The love he'd shared with Emily, but more than that, the fun they had together when she was feeling well. His confusion and helplessness when she wasn't. The way she would make a joke and keep an utterly straight face, then burst out laughing, her fingers on the tip of her nose. Everything.

When he was done, Rachel looked at him with big eyes and tender lips, and Paul knew she was about to say something standard and blandly supportive, and that was okay, because that was what he expected, from her, from everyone he'd ever told, even though such words were really just signals to ease away from the topic.

But Rachel said, "You must have felt so guilty. Like you could have stopped it? Did you feel that way? That's how I think I'd have felt."

No one, except Lisa, had ever asked him that question so directly before. He almost laughed. Such a cleansing draught of frankness, a spring breeze through a window opened wide after a long, dark winter.

"No," he said. "Not at first. At first I was shocked, then sad, then angry. Not guilty. But then I felt guilty for not feeling guilty, and even though I never really thought it was because of me, or even that I thought I could have prevented it, I walked around feeling guilty."

Rachel put her hand on Paul's, shook her head at him. "Catholics."

"A Pentecostal Baptist wouldn't have felt guilty?"

"A Pentecostal Baptist would have accepted that they *were* guilty and moved on. A Catholic'll keep the guilt alive and nurture it for twenty or thirty years." She laughed, as if to herself, face to the ground. She'd had pulled a long stem of fescue grass from the ground and was running her thumb and forefinger up and down the length of it. "You were nice to her Paul, I know you were. I don't need you or anyone else to tell me that. I feel bad for her that she couldn't stay alive, and bad for her that she didn't get to be with you." She got to her knees, then squatted on her haunches before Paul, hands splayed on her thighs, as if she were an elementary school friend readying herself to point a finger at him and scold him for some playground transgression. She leaned forward and kissed him lightly on the cheek, then straddled him, held his hips with her thighs, and kissed him again on the same spot.

"Is that okay?" she half whispered.

He could still feel the imprint of her lips on his cheek. He had an erection and she was sitting right on top of it. "No, probably not."

"Why?"

Why? He looked into her eyes, felt his heart scamper up into his throat where it pressed against his windpipe and made it hard for him to speak in a clear voice. "It *is* okay," he said, kissing her on the lips. He put his hands together on the small of her back and held her tight. "It's okay."

She brought her face near his and rested her forehead against his neck between his ear and shoulder. Her hair was drifting and wafting across his cheek, her skull against his chin. He could see through her soft, fine, deep-brown hair to her scalp, which was white and clean, scrubbed-looking. It smelled of green apples. She had gone quiet but he could hear a living huskiness in her throat as she took air in and out. Paul took a deep breath in synch with her, and he let her weight press him down against the ground.

The next morning, Paul sat in his office staring out the window, contemplating a couple of minor changes he was going to make to his profile of Daniel Code. The majority of the research was complete. He'd interviewed everyone he'd hoped to interview. The bulk of it was written. To Paul it was clear Code would never be prime minister or anything close to it, due to what he termed the "Trojan horse factor" of Code's views, views that appeared severe though still within accepted societal parameters, but that were, in fact, stepping-stones from a hard conservative belief system to the far shore of intolerance and bigotry. At least, this was Paul's thesis. But even though it was plain to Paul that Code would never hold the top job, the man had every chance of affecting the tone of the debate, of forcing the powers that be—whether it was the Conservatives or the Liberals—to swing further to the right here and there, that he would "hold their feet to the fire," to use one of his favourite phrases. Paul even suspected Code would enjoy playing outraged critic more than he would leader, since governing was always about degrees of compromise and dilution. He couldn't imagine Daniel Code diluting his message.

Gazing out his window onto National Avenue, Paul let his eyes wander up and down the boulevard, as he always did, and his eyes stopped at the End Time Revelation Church, as they always did. A new saying had appeared on the billboard. The nature of the message was, as usual, groan-worthy (FEELING THE HEAT? THEN COME ON IN—WE'RE PRAYER CONDITIONED), but what made Paul sit up straight in his chair was the sight of a man walking back inside the church, carrying a small stepladder and a cardboard box full of letters. Before he even had the chance to think it through, Paul acted, dashing out of his office, down the stairs, juking through traffic to cross the street, and sprinting the half block to the church. He looked for a bell to ring but couldn't find one. The door was plain metal, and when Paul knocked, harder than he meant to, a thunderous noise echoed far inside what sounded like an empty airplane hangar.

No response. Paul knocked again.

Traffic pulsed in spurts up and down National Avenue. He stood there a moment, trying to decide whether to knock again when his mind caught up with his instinct, and he realized he had no idea what he wanted to say or ask. A flight response gurgled in his windpipe, but he fought it, forced himself to pause, not panic; to think about what could be gained and lost. He was about to knock again, but he put his hand on the doorknob and found it had been open all along.

The entranceway was dark and gloomy, but after he hit a switch a stark, clear light burned from above. Paul eased through the swinging doors that led to the main area of the parish, which was lit only by the sunlight passing through the small rectangular head-height windows. He'd not been in a house of worship of any sort in years, let alone one of the evangelical variety. To his immediate disappointment, the main room presented itself as a plain and thoroughly unmysterious space. No creepy iconography, no padding to facilitate rolling in the aisles, no translation tables on the walls to interpret gibberish tongues. In fact, the only reference of any sort to God or Jesus or religion was a small beech crucifix hanging above a table he supposed was the altar. The seating area was not composed of pews, but rather folding chairs. It looked to Paul pretty much like the community hall it had probably once been prior to its conversion into a house of worship. Perhaps that was the point: merely another community association. A community association that thought the earth was seven thousand years old.

A set of swinging doors off to the right opened, and a man stepped through them. "Oh hi," he said. "Can I help you?"

The man was wearing an unmarked ball cap, and a black sweatshirt that matched his track pants. He had a couple days' growth of beard, except for where a smooth, plasticated scar ran along his right jaw line.

"Are you the . . . pastor, the preacher, here?"

The man let his eyebrows climb the ripples of his forehead, bunched under his cap. "Not exactly."

"Oh . . . so . . ."

"I'm more like a congregation manager, I guess," said the man. "Though nobody calls me that. We have a preacher who comes in three times a week, but I manage the building, look after the administration, pay the bills, shovel the walk, clean the toilets. All volunteer, mind you."

"And change the sign out front."

"Yeah, that's right," he said. "If you're looking for service times or prayer group meetings, I can give you all that information, but there's nothing on today, I'm afraid. I'm only cleaning up a few things, then I'm outta here."

"No, that's not it. I . . . I don't really know why I'm here. I work across the street, and for a long time I've been watching these slogans get changed on the board."

"Slogans?"

"Well, you know. The sayings. Sorry. The sayings."

"We call them *Insights*. It's the word we use."

"Right . . . insights. So, there's, like, a pastor here? A big congregation?"

"Yes, fairly large, I suppose. We don't take attendance." The man sniffed. "What precisely is it that I can help you with? I'm assuming, by the way, that you're not part of another church, that you're not saved. This is just a wild guess on my part."

"Lapsed Catholic, I'm afraid."

The man suppressed the gentle smile of a parent watching a young child struggle through a simple problem rather than accept help. "Lapsed? That's even worse than not being saved, my friend."

"What if I don't need saving?"

"We all need saving."

"What if I don't want to be saved?"

The man snorted lightly, as if entertainingly disappointed that this was the best Paul could do. "First expression of a resistance destined to crumble."

"You've used that line before."

"And I will again." He smiled widely, and when he did it brought his scar higher on his jaw, made it more obvious.

Paul stopped. Took a deep breath. "Okay, I'm going to speak my mind. You seem like you can take it."

The man put down his stack of papers and leaned against a desk.

"Well, those sayings. *Insights*, sorry. They're so, so . . . simplistic. I mean, they can't possibly be taken seriously by any person who really wants to participate or explore his or her faith in any real substantial way. Right? Surely they just trivialize faith, lessen the meaning of believing."

"You don't like them?"

"Well, it's not that I like or dislike them. Sometimes I find them pretty entertaining, actually. I write them all down."

"Entertaining? That doesn't sound like a compliment."

"Do you make them up?"

"Sometimes," he nodded, squinting at Paul, as if trying to figure what Paul's game really was. "And sometimes we get them off the Internet. We have a great youth group, and every now and then they come up with a corker. And for your information, my friend, you're being rather condescending. Who are you to say what this person or that person finds inspiring or helpful? Who said you understand the hearts and minds of others? We've had probably hundreds of people stop in over the years because of that sign. It's the best kind of advertising. Not everybody gets it, of course," he stopped and smirked, "but mostly it's a great way of reaching out and connecting. We love it."

Paul saw a folding chair nearby and pulled it over. After sitting down, he motioned to the man to do the same. "My name's Paul."

The man sat down on another chair, held his hand out. "Jon, no h . . . So why did you come in here, anyway? Was it really just to ask me about our Insights?"

"Yes. I guess so. I don't know, really. I just saw you walking back up the sidewalk, and I ran over. Simple curiosity, I guess."

"There's no such thing as simple curiosity."

"Now *that* I can agree with." He looked around the room, at the plainness of it. There was a simplicity here, but a denial, too. The room was almost ostentatiously shipshape; it smelled scrubbed and antiseptic, every book on every table stacked and ordered just so, the chairs not only neatly but also perfectly and symmetrically arranged. In fact, the more closely Paul inspected the room, the more it seemed to him that its decontaminated minimalism was not so much about humility as a kind of reverse smugness, the complacency that comes with certainty. *This is all we need, and it's all anybody ought to need.* The room began to emit light green bubbles of hermetic self-satisfaction, and Paul found himself wanting to pop those bubbles, though he swiftly admitted to himself his Catholic background and general religious skepticism probably didn't predispose him to complete open-mindedness in situations like this. "I'm a writer, and I'm doing a piece on Daniel Code. I imagine you're supporting him."

"Proudly."

"So, what is it about the former Pastor Code that makes you actually believe he's, you know, a guy that could be in charge? Of everything. Is it only because he's Christian?"

Jon sat against the back of his chair, his arms crossed loosely, his fingers jammed into his armpits. "You've got it backwards."

"Backwards?"

"Being saved didn't make him what he is. It's what was inside, the capacity within, that allowed him to be saved. That's why the Lord Jesus spoke to him. He didn't become who he is because he was saved. It's the other way around."

"But, with all respect, that's kind of nutty. That Jesus spoke to him."

"He spoke to me, too."

Paul grimaced. "Why do you say things like that? I mean, how do you expect anyone to take you seriously?"

"Anyone? Who is anyone? And taken seriously by who? By you? As for being saved, you either have it in you, or you don't. You don't. Not now, anyway. It's about growth, readiness, Paul, and you're not ready to be saved. That's pretty obvious. And no offense, but the last thing I'm thinking about when I'm living my life is whether or not you, and those like you, take me seriously. I do wish you peace and salvation, I truly do, but what you think of me or this isn't relevant."

"Relevant to what?"

Jon sat back and laughed softly, before fixing a look of ecstatic calm on Paul and speaking his final three words. He stood up, politely shook Paul's hand, and returned through the door by which he'd entered.

Paul stared after him, feeling somehow unjustly slighted, like an underling publicly denied a promotion he'd never sought. After folding his chair and replacing it where he'd found it, Paul turned to head outside, into the heat, back to the known world. Walking toward the first of the two sets of doors leading outside, Paul's bemusement turned to anger, even resentment, at the judgment Jon had made about him. Who the hell was this guy to tell Paul who he was or wasn't? The need to somehow disrupt this too-orderly rejection of the external world abruptly surged into Paul, and he let his eyes wander with intent as he moved toward the exit, but by the time he arrived at the doors reason had returned. What purpose would it serve? Who would be impressed by it? Nobody, himself included. Near the exit was a large copper bowl sitting atop a waist-high marble plinth and column; possibly a baptismal font, though Paul thought they used rivers for that sort of thing. Still, it was clearly some kind of ceremonial basin, and it was about a third full of water. Glancing behind as he walked, to make sure Jon wasn't watching him, Paul stopped and stared into the water, gazing at his reflection. He put a finger near the surface, then sank it in to the second knuckle, which made his face ripple and distort. He brought the finger to his lips, curious about the taste of the water. Sticking out his tongue, he laid a drop upon it. The water was room temperature, metallic tasting, a touch stagnant in smell. Nothing else. It was water, that was all. He repeated the sequence. Still nothing, just water, and a bit skunky at that.

Seconds later, Paul gained the door and pushed through, but it wasn't until he was fully outside that he felt his blood surging up and down his neck, as if he'd just sprinted madly for the bus and then flopped down on a seat, sweating and giddy to have made it. Why the relief? he thought. What is *that* all about? Maybe, he thought, chuckling, maybe it was relief that Jesus didn't show up and start talking to him.

Standing on the sidewalk, letting his breathing return to a normal pattern, Paul saw afresh that it was another dazzling day in the city on the open prairie. The sun was pouring down on the shimmering skyline and Calgarians were bustling up and down the street in search of their fortune. Paul felt as if he'd somehow just passed a test, or escaped taking one, and so he decided to treat himself to an Americano and maybe even a chocolate croissant. The office could wait.

TWELVE

After the printer had churned out the last of the pages, Paul let the document sit on his desk. He was proud of the article, this clean and yet provocative object he'd created, which he believed to be thorough and professional, written as well as he was able, an insightful weave of idea and character, thematically in sync with his view of working toward a companionable, socially harmonious society—in other words, it was a piece of writing sure to be ignored by everybody except the people who already thought like him. Additionally but no less significantly, he also felt the piece would somehow cause him heartache, though on what levels and with whom he wasn't sure. His mother and Rick would label him a Trotskyite. His father would proclaim it his best yet, as he did with each successive piece Paul wrote. And it was almost certainly going to kill any chance of spending time with Rachel, even *if* that was something he'd be able to figure out at every other level of complication. The one person he knew would read the article from start to finish, word for word, and who would consider every point, take them on open terms, evaluate them, assess his interpretation, and nonjudgmentally tell him what she thought, was Lisa (although she would first clarify for Rick and their mother precisely what a Trotskyite was, and why it was the wrong term in this instance). She would also, naturally, eviscerate the article in the end; that was a given. But she would do it intellectually, devoid of personal bias or character judgement.

He picked up the piece and prepared to give it one last read, clearing his head of everything except imagining he was a reader of the magazine, an intelligent, skeptical, open-minded reader. This was always the last thing he did before handing work over to Harold.

The structure felt right. An opening scene to animate the man and set the tone for a narrative exploration of a political phenomenon and personality. A biographical section illustrated with quotes and anecdotes about his life up to the point where he entered politics. A weaving together of the man's political philosophy, using performance, speeches, writings, the opinions of various commentators, as well as the bulk of the interview material Paul had himself collected during time with Code. Another short anecdote that illustrated the way Code liked to do politics (Paul used the Hitler joke). It would all be summed up by Paul's favourite part of every piece: the section where he tried to make sense of it all at the level of "meaning," where he would try to create for his reader an image not only of what his subject said and did and planned to do, but an image of what that person represented in the broader culture—and, moreover, of what it said about the culture that it could generate such a person as a possible leadership figure.

Paul held the first page in front of him with fingers and thumbs, elbows resting on his desk. He read the title, "Ascension," and the epigraph he'd chosen for the piece, a quote by Camus (*Politics and the shape of mankind are shaped by men without ideals and without greatness. Men who have greatness within them don't concern themselves with politics.*), and then moved to the first paragraph.

> Just northeast of Calgary, outside the town of Black Hills, in the federal riding of Alberta-Merryvale (a riding held by the Democratic Alliance Party of Canada MP Daniel Code), there is an oil well flare stack that stands hard against the east–west flow of rural Highway 412. It is just one stack of thousands, flaring off a variety of toxic chemicals, that loom over the flat Alberta prairie like battlements without a fortress. The well it is connected to has for many years now been pumping oil and generating significant private and public wealth. But this well is different from the others. Arrayed against its scaffolding is a set of bright white lights shaped like the cross on which Jesus, as most around here fervently believe, died for our sins. During the day, you cannot see the massive thirty-foot cross, only the towering steel rig. At night, the radiance of the Lord is visible for miles. The cross seems to follow you as you drive on west into Calgary, into the city that is quickly becoming the power base for Daniel Code, a no-longer practising but still 'licensed' Pastor of a breakaway community parish near in structure and tone to southern Pentecostal Baptist's. Code is a former county and provincial politician, and he will surely lead the Democratic Alliance Party for many years to come. Some are even touting him as a potential future Prime Minister.

Paul traced over the longish section outlining Code's childhood, his upbringing, his first jobs, his faith, the moment he decided to leave his teaching post at a Christian school in southeastern Alberta to enter politics. Taking a sip of coffee, Paul turned a page, moving toward the end of the first third of the piece. But here he began to feel the balance was off somehow, as if the necessary elements were present but not correctly ordered. Right after the section on Code's upbringing and entry into political life, Paul had written a scene involving the moment where Code explained his conversion by demonstrating for Paul what Jesus had done upon arriving in the teenage Code's bedroom one morning.

> "And then," said Code, "He reached out and put His palm against my forehead, like this." Daniel Code then did the same for me, reaching out and placing his palm against my forehead, letting it rest there for longer than was comfortable, perhaps showing me what Jesus had done for him, perhaps trying to *do* for me what Jesus had done for him.

Upon reading it, however, Paul thought it would be a more useful characterization of the man later in the piece, nearer the end, once the reader understood better who the man was today and what sort of power he was seeking, the message being, *This is who Daniel Code is today, not thirty years ago in his bedroom as a teenager in Black Hills, but today, a grown man who wants to be our Prime Minister.* Paul cut that section out and pasted it into the last quarter of the piece, where he detailed following Code on the campaign trail. It even seemed to work better thematically, since it more overtly situated his faith in a political context, which Paul was aiming for.

This change allowed him to go straight from Code's entry into politics to a discussion of the moral implications of his voting patterns in the Alberta provincial legislature. His 1994 motion to ban Steinbeck's *Of Mice and Men* from Alberta libraries because the book "demeaned the name of Jesus Christ." His 1995 refusal to sign a motion to formally recognize *Freedom to Read Week*. Here, Paul took the time to go into some detail regarding what the *Edmonton Journal* called Code's "persecution campaign" against gays and lesbians. These included his stand against including equal rights in the Alberta Human Rights Charter, and his direct hand in creating a policy to ban gays and lesbians from foster parenting, a move that prompted even a local conservative senator to announce that Code's stance was "an embarrassment," and that "Alberta was becoming a backwater." Paul concluded this section trying to understand what these stances meant for Code's future prospects.

> In some ways, the simple truth is that Code cannot win. Either he's a gay-bashing redneck, which wins him votes at home but nowhere else. Or he grows away from it, a move which may enhance his popularity outside his core support group, but which may then be viewed by his inner circle as an abandonment of the fundamental beliefs that first won him support. This is the irony: He may play better in Toronto if he drops his prejudices, but then he might not get elected in Black Hills. As of late, it seems he has tried to deflate the rhetoric. "I do believe the state should stay out of the bedroom of the nation," he said in one of many interviews. "And people should not be discriminated against for their choices of partners. But I will never change my definitions of marriage and spouse."
>
> On the matter of Daniel Code's stand on gay rights, perhaps we should save the final word for John Warburg, owner of the House and Home Centre in Erving and long time friend to Code. "I think he's broad-minded," said Warburg, in his office above the shop floor of his store. "He may have personal beliefs, but he'd keep them underneath. And he'd have no problem giving rights to whoever wants them. But I'll tell you this. He's sure not going to let a bunch of faggots run around downtown with their dongs hanging out. That's just not going to happen."

The next section, just prior to his conclusion, was the one that contained the material of greatest interest to Paul but that made him the most nervous—not for professional reasons but personal ones. It was about Rachel's grandfather. Paul got straight to the point, quoting Emmett Code on the definition of alternative lifestyles ("cohabitating sodomites") and race relations ("sitting in the waiting room in the Edmonton Department of Immigration was like being at a family reunion of the Harlem Globetrotters"). Paul pointed out for the reader that all these musings could be found in a now-extinct journal called *Across the Plains*, a magazine published by a lawyer famous for defending Holocaust deniers.

But sadly, the above is not the full extent to which the elder Code displayed his views on society. In a column written in April 1976 (when Daniel Code would have been a 20-year-old man), the elder Code penned a review essay of an 1887 publication entitled *The Protocols of the Seven Learned Elders of Zion*. This is an ur-text of the anti-Semitic radical right, a book that purports to prove a world conspiracy of Jewish bankers. It is a viciously racist text, one proven a century ago to be utterly fictional, but the elder Code states blithely that it "sheds light on the current state of world affairs." He refers repeatedly to the fact that the automobile magnate Henry Ford considered *The Protocols* to be an "accurate reflection of the world situation." (Though Code has taken Ford's comments somewhat out of context, it is sadly true that Ford himself was an avowed anti-Semite who, incredibly, received the Iron Cross from Hitler.)

Code ends his "book review" on a note of avuncular encouragement to all young people to "educate" themselves and to not rest in a state of ignorance about "the truth of our world as it is and not someone else's truth." Even taking into account the debates surrounding moral and historical relativism—the notion that we are all culturally and historically positioned beings, and must be judged as such—one still cannot help but imagine the education bestowed upon young Daniel Code, and how that education has manifested itself in the grown man.

There was more to come in a substantial conclusion, but it was not yet fully written—Paul wanted to wait until after the actual leadership convention, in case something severely dramatic happened there, though he wasn't worried that it would. He finished reading and put the article back on the desk in front of him. An ember of satisfaction the size of a bottle cap came alight in the middle of his sternum; he felt its warmth begin to radiate outward. This moment, this feeling; this was why he did what he did, why he risked, challenged, wrote. To try and get it right. To feel that he did get it right. It was that simple. With a zipper of a smile, he drafted a quick email to Harold. He attached the file to the email and sent it. Harold wasn't in the office, but Paul knew that he never shut off, and obsessively checked, his home email. Paul almost expected a return email or phone call within five or ten minutes, acknowledging receipt of the file as well as offering suggestions for improving the piece based on the few sentences he'd have read. It was a Pavlovian editorial response Paul found unnerving at first but that he now found endearing, even comforting. When his phone rang a couple of minutes later, Paul nearly snatched it up and said *Hey, Harold*. He didn't do this too often because he was always a little afraid of the embarrassment if it wasn't Harold, and also because the two or three times he had been correct, there had been no indication Harold was amused by or even aware of Paul's amazing psychic gift.

"Hello, Paul Munk."

It was not Harold.

Paul didn't recognize the voice because there was no voice. But he soon identified the silence on the other end and the way it made him feel—as if he was staring at a sealed tank full of hornets, swarming, buzzing, butting up against the glass.

"Palmer?" said Paul. "What are you calling for?"

"Hey, Munkey Boy, good to hear your voice."

"Where are you? Are you in Calgary?"

The silence that was Palmer's own again briefly filled the line, again filled Paul's head. Then, finally, he spoke. ". . . 'Fraid not."

THIRTEEN

Montana

Blood was weeping through the engorged gauzy fabric of the bandages. A sickly sweet warm odour tinged with iron shavings rose off Rick's head, which rested on two pillows at the end of the bed nearest the room's one small heavily curtained window. "Take those old bandages off," said JJ slowly, standing beside a dresser top where he'd arrayed extra dressings, various ointments, and other things Paul couldn't see. "Do it slowly, now," said JJ. "It's already bad enough." Palmer was hovering over Paul's shoulder. He could smell Palmer's mint chaw, but he didn't take his eyes off his brother. Paul picked up a pair of scissors to cut through and remove the bandages, so he could clean the wound and cover it with a fresh dressing. Whoever had applied the first bandage had done so clumsily. Paul slowly cut around the edge and then through the middle. He lifted the lower part of the gauze away. It was sodden, saturated with blood and a glutinous ooze. He removed the top next. It came away easily, but sloppily, pulling some of Rick's hair up with it. A rich rotten stink spirited out from under the skullcap. Paul tossed the sloppy mess into a bucket near the side table on which he'd placed some fresh dry bandages. Rick was groaning through the veil of his semiconsciousness, as if he were dreaming of, rather than experiencing, pain.

"Hard to figure," said Palmer.

Paul shut the gates to his heart long enough to look away from his brother and up to Palmer. "What's that?"

Palmer hitched both thumbs into his beltline, as if he were some dusty sheriff trying to decide what to do about a drifter cowboy lying dead in the dirt. "Never should have happened."

"You still haven't really told me what *did* happen." *Accident*, Paul thought. *Accident?* It was a word that made no sense to Paul at that moment. Nobody's fault? Is that really what *accident* meant? It was hard to imagine this wasn't anyone's fault.

Palmer pressed his lips together and wrinkled his nose like he'd come across a bad smell. He'd said all he was going to say about it. For now, Paul thought, for now. JJ didn't offer any thoughts on the matter, either, and he left the room without saying where he was going. Paul had only just met JJ, whom Palmer described as 'the local doc and such,' but Paul disliked him immediately for the authority he took as his right. Paul took a cloth, dipped it in the bowl of hot water JJ had brought to his side, wrung it out and draped it across Rick's face and scalp line, which, underneath the gluey crimson slop at the top of his head, was where the wound appeared to be. The white cloth turned scarlet, sucking up the blood. Paul repeated the process, rinsing and wringing out the cloth, each time peeling it off Rick's face and head slowly, as if he were removing a sheath of skin he might have to reattach later on. After the third application of the cloth, Paul could see things a little more clearly. In the welter of black and red, white bone was pushing through an area about the size of a dime. The bone was smooth, shiny, slightly convex, like an egg being squeezed out of a chicken. Paul thought he could see the red edges of the hole actually pulsing. Blood began seeping from the wound again, along with a clear, less viscous liquid, which seemed to trickle on top of rather than emulsify with the blood. Both fluids were dribbling down the side of Rick's face. The smell of his scalp hit Paul's nostrils again, and triggered his gag reflex. Rick opened one eye, then the other, but they didn't move in coordination. One stared at the floor, the other at Paul. Neither was focused. He had black, saggy pouches under both eyes. Paul's sinuses filled up, but he held his face tight and closed the opening at the top of his throat to try to suppress the urge to vomit. Some bile snuck past, worming into the back of his mouth and onto his tongue; he swallowed heavily to rid himself of the taste.

JJ came back in the room carrying a large bowl of liquid giving off a steaming, bleachy heat. Setting the bowl on the floor beside Paul, JJ motioned for Paul to move aside.

"Why? What's in that bowl?"

"Just move aside, son. Give me a minute here." JJ smiled, but Paul felt the least warmth from a smile he'd ever known. It was hard to see JJ's lips through the fulsome yet tidy brush of beard and moustache he'd clearly cultivated to give himself, Paul guessed, as close to a Moses-like appearance as possible. It was effective and irritating within the same snapshot of interpretation. Why? Paul wondered. Why do you want to look like that? Who is it for, who is it meant to impress? It was absurdly self-regarding, and it made Paul want to poke him in the eye, punch him, do anything to wipe that authoritative smirk off his thin, greying, hairy face.

"I asked you what is in that bowl?"

JJ was on one knee, waiting for Paul to move. He didn't say anything more, but slowly turned his head to Palmer, and gestured sharply with a nod of the head to the door of the small, dimly lit bedroom. Palmer came up and put his hand on Paul's shoulder.

"Let's get you something to drink. Ol' JJ's just going to put an antibiotic on it. That's all."

"Antibiotics don't smell like that."

". . . Paul. Come on out here with me."

Paul got up, staring at JJ, who ignored him. As Paul stepped away and stood near the foot of the bed, JJ took the cloth Paul had been using and dipped it into the second bowl. He lightly squeezed it out, though not so hard as to remove too much of the liquid, then applied it to Rick's head. The warmth of it, or perhaps something chemical in the mix, made Rick groan sharply, as though he'd been kicked in the gut. Paul shook his head, put his hand to his mouth.

"JJ's the top guy around here, but he's a doctor, too. Don't worry."

"Doctor? He's not a doctor. Have you been to medical school, JJ?"

JJ didn't look at them, but said loudly enough to be heard, *"The fool who persists in his folly will become wise."*

Paul turned to Palmer, lost. "What is that?"

"William Blake," said Palmer. "He's a freak for the guy, knows every word. Thinks they're connected spiritually. Don't you, JJ? But he *is* a doctor. I can vouch for him. He is."

"He is not."

"Okay, well, he's not a 'school' doctor, but he practices medicine around here if we need some. He was a paramedic, and fought in Vietnam. People from all over come see him when he's around. He lives in Troy, mostly. Rick's fine with JJ, though. He'll be alright. Come on."

Palmer opened the door and led Paul through it. Paul reluctantly followed him, out into a poorly lit hallway, a low lengthy space with incongruously sided walls. It made Paul think of the catacombs he'd visited in Rome, when he and Emily had gone through Europe years earlier. Palmer's house from the outside was like Paul had remembered it from when he and Rick had first come down to Montana to pick up

Tammy, but the interior was a revelation to him, though not a particularly comforting one. It was a long, low structure, and the few windows it had were small and covered with curtains. The floor was concrete, with large tattered rugs placed in the traffic areas. To Paul, it was a house custom-built for a serial killer, though logic made him doubt someone of that predisposition would choose to live in a house so obviously identifiable as that of a serial killer. Still, stumbling across a stone circle dungeon hole somewhere in a back room would come only as a minor shock.

Palmer led Paul through a warren of tight hallways back into the front of the house, to a room that had likely once been an office or reception area for a mechanic's shop, but was now the kitchen.

"You know, I built this place myself," said Palmer, twisting the cap off a bottle of beer. He directed an eye down the east wing hallway, from the front door to what looked like a kind of living room; a distance of at least forty paces. "Took a while, but I'm pretty proud of it. Feels good to do things yourself."

Paul nodded, waited a moment, cracked his own beer. "Palmer, have you called the police?"

Palmer stopped the progress of his beer bottle toward his mouth, holding it near his chin. "Why would I call the police?"

"I don't know. To report what happened?"

". . . Oh yeah. And what did happen, do you think?"

"He's seriously hurt, Palmer. Don't you report things like that?" Paul looked at his watch. "It's been six hours since you called me. He could be in a hospital somewhere by now."

"Report things?" said Palmer. "Report an accident to the police? When you take somebody into the hospital back in Canada do you have to report it to the police? Is that what you do? Wouldn't surprise me to know that, actually. But here, we get people help straight away when they've had an accident." He paused, casually tipped some beer into his mouth. "The doctor from Libby was on the phone with JJ this morning, and he told JJ what to do, though JJ knew it all, anyway. And the police. For what? The doctor didn't suggest it. I call the sheriff's office in Libby, the first thing they're going to say is, What happened? I tell them what happened, they're going to say, Thanks for the call, but no way I'm getting in my car driving an hour down to Stennets to look at some dude who tripped over a rock and hit his head on a stump."

"Is that what happened?" Paul took a sip of his beer, though he wasn't really tasting it. "I just don't see it. I don't see Rick tripping over a rock and hitting his head."

"What you're saying is that you don't believe me. That's not a very nice feeling. Anyways, I don't care what you do. I'm trying to help out here, calling you and all, because Rick's in trouble, and he's part of us. But, hey, you do whatever the hell you like. Call the boys up in Libby. Call the cops in Thompson Falls. Let me know what they say. I'd be curious." He stood up and took the phone book off a desk, walked up close to Paul and dropped the book on his lap, hard, from a height, making Paul grunt and draw his legs in to protect his balls. Palmer sat down again. "I can leave if you want some privacy. Phone's right over there."

"I didn't say I didn't believe you, Palmer." Paul lifted the book off his lap. "And I don't need to call the sheriff."

Palmer took a jerky, pressurized swig of his beer, and Paul could see the liquid go foamy as it settled back in the lower half of the bottle. "Good. So stay out of the way until he's better, and then take him home . . . if he wants to go."

"What do you mean by that?"

Palmer shrugged.

"He'd stay here?"

Palmer looked around his house, affecting deep offense. "What's so wrong with that?"

"You know what I mean. What about his new job? He's still on parole, anyway. And what about Tammy?"

"Tammy?" Palmer laughed. "Okay. Whatever you say."

"Anyway, how am I supposed to get him across the border in this state? You don't think they're going to want to know? They'll check, especially if he looks like that."

"Just tell 'em what happened. He tripped. Why shouldn't they believe you? What're they gonna do . . . not let a Canadian citizen go home because he had a hiking accident. Give him a day or two. If you're the nervous type at the border, I'll map you through the Yaak Valley, and you'll come out heading up towards Cranbrook. We keep some of those old logging roads in decent enough shape to get our ordnance through."

Paul laughed at the word, though nervously. "Ordnance?"

"Weapons."

"I know what the word means."

"Store a lot of it up Nelson and Kaslo way, across the border. ATF guys come through here whenever they're bored and looking for something to do. We just stay ready, is all, on both sides of the border. That's what Rick was doing for us. Before, too."

Paul noticed a throbbing in his thumb and looked down to see that he was gripping his beer bottle so tightly the webbing of skin and tendon between the first knuckles of his thumb and forefinger was as taut as a canvas tent. A despair filled him up like a heavy fluid, made him feel grotesque with it, though he understood immediately that his despair was not really for Rick's injury, or even for his brother's involvement with these people, but more that he wasn't even shocked to learn of it, that, in fact, he'd more or less expected it, or something like it, from his brother, something this fucked up, something this *wrong*.

A door closed somewhere down the hall, and Paul heard slow, deliberate footsteps approaching them. Just before JJ came into the kitchen, Palmer leaned over closer to Paul and said, "Maybe I'll explain a few more things to you later."

JJ came in and sat down. He bent his head, then placed his hands together palm to palm like he was about to wash them. He stared hard at his joined hands, then put his forefingers to his lips, as if he were Pontius Pilate giving things a second thought. Paul found the man's affected solemnity deeply worrying.

"Well, what's the verdict, JJ?" asked Palmer.

"You mean, diagnosis."

Palmer grinned and turned to Paul. "Can't get nothin' by this dude."

JJ moved his hands apart, then brought them together again to intertwine them, a different gesture—one meant, Paul thought, to signify expertise rather than commiseration. "Difficult to say," said JJ. "He's drugged up pretty good about now, which is a good thing, otherwise we'd be listening to him screaming. The way I see it . . . no more morphine, just Tylenol Threes to keep the fever under control. I suspect he'll sleep for the next twelve or fifteen hours. Mild concussion, is what I figure. Doc on the phone said he'd come by tomorrow morning if we needed him to. But the boy'll be fine. It's a nasty little wound, but it looks a lot worse than it is. It's really just his scalp, that's all. I don't think there's a skull fracture."

"You 'don't think'? Isn't that the kind of thing you should be fairly sure about? Or doesn't your extensive medical training call for certainty?"

JJ hesitated before speaking and then glared at Paul, his eyes as black as cave holes. "I understand you're upset, son. I truly do. But if you keep talking to me that way, I'm going to fix you up something fierce."

Paul sat back, surprised by how certain he was that the menace in JJ's gaze was not for display only. "I'm worried. That's all."

JJ reached over and put a long, dry hand on Paul's shoulder. It was a warm hand, and when he gripped the ball of Paul's shoulder, it felt like the hand of belief, of someone who thought himself called to God's work—or who thought he was God. "That's what I'd be feeling too, Paul. It's okay. You're in good hands with us here. We take care of people who need taking care of. It's not about who's with who and who isn't." He paused. "Isn't that right, Palmer?"

Palmer started up slightly from his beer. "JJ's right about that. I agree. We all agree."

JJ stood up to his full height. He was a tall man, taller than Paul had thought when he'd first seen him bent over in Rick's room. He had to be a couple inches over six feet. "Paul, you'll do what you think is right, here. But if you're asking me, I'd let him rest a day or two before moving him. He might even be conscious and okay by then, which will mean it won't be hard to cross the border. If you feel going back right away is something you have to do, and he's still incoherent or not conscious, then we'll find a different way for you to get across the border, if that's what'll make you comfortable, though I don't think that's anything you need to worry about. If you feel you've got to get him to a hospital despite what the doctor and me think, well, then, we'll call for an ambulance to come on down here from Libby. That won't be cheap. Either way, son, we'll leave it up to you. You'll make the right decision. *No bird soars too high if he soars with his own wings.* You just let us know. Palmer'll set you up to stay here, like I told him to."

"Got him a room all set up," said Palmer.

JJ nodded his approval. "I'm going now. Palmer knows how to reach me if there's a need to, but I'll be back for the meeting tonight in any case." He turned to face Palmer. "Eight o'clock?"

Palmer nodded.

"That's fine, then." JJ turned to look one more time to Paul. "I respect you, coming down here so quick for your brother. He'll appreciate it, I know that. When he's better, he'll be able to tell you all about us, maybe even make you understand us. I do know from what he's told me about you that that's not likely to happen. But you'll try to understand, I know you will. Palmer and me, and the rest, maybe tonight we'll try. Any smart man will respect what we're doing. I truly believe that."

He reached out and held Paul's shoulder in the same manner he had earlier, gripping with those long, twiggish fingers. But the sense of his grip, if not the power, felt different to Paul this time. It felt human. All too human.

Paul gently pushed open the door and peered in. A single bulb glowed under the brown shade of a lamp on a table in the far corner. The window curtains were drawn. It was late afternoon, but inside this room it felt like the centre of eternal night, a cell holding a darkness natural light could never cut. He gazed around the room, inspected the walls. There was little in the way of decoration: a calendar with mountains on it; a framed poster of a horse; the dresser on which JJ had laid out the bandage supplies earlier but that had no personal effects on it. He softly shut the door behind him and advanced toward where Rick lay. Paul knelt beside the bed, resting his knee on the small blue puffy bath mat. He hadn't noticed when he'd arrived earlier—when he'd come in in such a rush to see his brother, pushing past Palmer, hardly noticing anything at all about the house—that this bed was lower than a normal bed, certainly lower than his own bed at home. A child's bed? Perhaps a teenager's? This could be Morton's room. It could be Debbie's. Where were Palmer's children, anyway?

Rick sighed and turned slightly to one side, but he didn't wake up. Paul looked at him as a parent might look over a child in the midst of a troubled sleep, listening to the laboured breath, the guttural moans. Rick's face was a bit contorted, as though perplexed inside a dream problem. Paul wanted to reach out and touch his brother's brow, run a gentle finger down the length of his nose, but he didn't, thinking it was not worth the risk of waking him. Rick was recovering and his body was in charge. Paul didn't want to disturb that, and so he watched his brother without touching him, watched his chest rise and fall, watched his lips sometimes part then close, watched his head shift from one side to the other.

Then, in one of those moments that came to him all too rarely, Paul saw everything whole. In a swift weaving of the past, present, and future, he understood that his brother was always going to be precisely what he was at that very moment—someone who would need looking after; and that no matter how many protestations of independence or claims of newfound drive and ambition, he was destined to mess it up one way or another. He was a loser. A pathetic loser who would never fully understand who he was, and would therefore never be able to change things in any real way except for the worse. This insight struck Paul as so hopelessly sad, so melancholy, that he had to put fingers to his eyes to hold back tears. Why didn't Rick just get it right? Why didn't he simply work, live a life, mind his own business? Why did he always have to be plotting, forever processing shortcuts to turn things around? Why couldn't he do it slowly, steadily, in steps he could take, toward deadlines he could meet? No. He would always search instead for the big score, the U-turn, the bold, dramatic move that would prove to everybody what he apparently actually believed himself to be: a person to be taken seriously, to be respected, instead of someone who was increasingly a burden to the people around him. And Paul suspected he'd be one of those carrying that burden for decades to come.

Murray. Paul remembered an acquaintance from high school, Murray, the redheaded guy who almost went to jail for selling hash in little baggies during lunch breaks. He was always shooting his mouth off in the hallway between classes, crowing all the time about how the school was really just his office, and that the only reason he ever showed up was to conduct "massive business." He was of the same cast as Rick, at least in that cocky mind-set. But he made mistakes, boasted at the wrong time, and got caught selling his stupid dope. The cops decided to let Murray and his parents off the hook if they promised to send him to one of those disciplinary schools on Vancouver Island, a kind of high school boot camp. It turned out he was even lying about the hash; all he ever sold were a couple of dinky little bags. His parents did as they were told, and when Murray got back a couple years later, he was still a cocky bugger, but at least somewhere along the way he'd learned the one thing Rick had never allowed anyone to teach him: patience. Murray always claimed to hate school, so he didn't go to university. Instead, he got his electrician's ticket, apprenticed for a couple of years, worked for almost nothing, then got hooked up with an experienced guy running his own company, who went on to retire five years later, pretty much leaving Murray the entire business. He got a bank loan and bought the company, and now, fifteen years after getting caught like some dummy selling nickel bags in the wings of the school stage—and having to suffer the embarrassment of not even having the authenticity of being the bad news he claimed to be—he was a success, or at least, he had a life. He had a wife, a couple of daughters, a house not too far from where Paul and Rick had grown up. He was making a hell of a lot more money than Paul was, and for sure he was making amounts that Rick could only dream of. Rick, of course, would have had nothing but scorn for Murray, for the safety of Murray's life, but Rick had never held a real job. He'd been in jail twice. He'd not been able to convince any woman to stay with him longer than six months (except for Tammy, if that counted). Things were getting critical. And yet he remained so confident, so intransigently convinced that his way of doing things was the right way. This wasn't due to stupidity; perhaps it was a missing gene, a critical discrepancy in that synaptic link between ambition and self-knowledge, between being smart and being smart enough to do yourself some good.

As he listened to the debate inside his head, Paul began to feel like Starbuck to Rick's Ahab, the man of safety cautioning the crazed dreamer. But wasn't that simply reality? Wasn't that the truth of it? We all have to do this, Rick, Paul almost said out loud, as he gazed at his brother's quiet face and the bandage that covered his head. We all have to find a floor to stand on before we can start groping around to see where our ceiling is. Where had it started, this instability, the shifts, the tremors, the bad footing? Where was it headed?

He knew the answer to the first question, or at least part of it.

Paul put a hand to his brother's forehead. It was hot, and a thin film of perspiration had come over it. He took a dry facecloth from the dresser and pressed it lightly against his brother's head. Rick didn't move. Paul knew then what he really wanted to say to his brother. He bent forward and stroked his brother's cheek, lightly, barely touching it. "I wish I'd lied," he whispered into Rick's gauze-covered ear. Paul did not ask for his brother's forgiveness, but decided he would later, when it meant something, when Rick would hear him asking.

He kept his hand on his brother's cheek for a moment longer, but it began to feel hotter than it had when he'd first rested his hand there, so he removed it. Paul drew the cloth across his brother's forehead one last time before standing up and glancing toward the door. There were things going on outside this room, things Rick was somehow part of, and Paul wanted to know what they were.

FOURTEEN

"Palmer?" Paul inquired, loudly enough to carry to the furthest reaches of the house. "Are you back there?"

No response. Paul sat down at the kitchen table and looked at the stove clock: 4:08. A note was stuck to the refrigerator featuring a scrawl he assumed was Palmer's. *Munkey Boy—back in an hour.*

Through the small kitchen window a quadrangle of light skittered and rippled across the varnished cement floor. Peering outside, Paul could sense it was a bright day, but the massive stands of pine surrounding the house altered the power of the sun so that the light splintered into dozens of irregular beams, twinkling, shifting gemrays of white and blue. The forest canopy here on the Bitterroots side of the Clark Fork River had to be sixty or seventy feet high. This was a forest that hadn't been logged much. Paul stared for a moment out that small square window, admiring what he could see of the trees. Each in its own way perfect, true, in balance with the world around it. It had only been a matter of hours since he'd arrived in Stennets, but it felt to Paul as if he hadn't been outside in weeks. He wanted to be out amongst those trees, walking through that forest—how freeing a vision that seemed to him at that moment.

The tingling need for release in the muscles of his thighs made Paul realize he was deeply lost—he wasn't sure what he was supposed to do or expected or needed to do. Yes, he could think it through, but this was about more than his mind; it was about faith, too. About making some kind of decision and believing in it. Belief was required, because right and wrong, he was beginning to sense, were not what mattered most here.

Paul made an effort to sit back and close his eyes and let his thoughts gather, coalesce around what he needed to do. This was about intuition, he told himself, gut feeling.

They would stay.

Rick wasn't well enough to travel. Not yet. Even if Paul decided to cross the border somewhere along an old logging or fire road, the bumping, Paul's posture in a car seat, and Rick's inability to help him while driving would make the journey risky. Paul wanted to be able to talk to him. He wanted Rick conscious. The drive would be a chance to spend five hours with him alone, to ask him all the questions he wanted to ask, to say things he maybe ought to have said a long time ago.

In the morning he would see how Rick was doing, then decide. If Rick had regained consciousness at all, he could ask him what he wanted to do; if he remained unconscious, Paul would decide on his own. He would trust himself.

With this decision made, his thoughts reflexively winched his other life out of the well, a world that now struck him as deeply alien. Daniel Code? 2.2.4.? Rachel? What were these things, and how did they apply in any way that mattered today, here? That he could be back at that place, those people, those locations, those concerns in the space of a few hours' driving was a fantastical leap. Was that the attraction to Rick? This place wasn't just a drive away—it was completely across the earth, across the breadth of one's imagination.

Paul, being a creature of habit, saw the phone on the counter and had a kneejerk reaction to it. He needed then and there to check his messages. In his rush to leave earlier that morning, he'd forgotten his Blackberry; anyway, he doubted he'd get a signal out here. He guessed Palmer would have a computer up and running somewhere in this spooky crypt of a house, but the thought of poking around trying to find one was not an attractive option. It'd be no problem to use his calling card on Palmer's phone, but the sour paranoid air of the place had gotten up his nostrils; it wasn't more than a mile down to Stennets' main street. Paul knew the Mercantile between the two bars had a pay phone out front. He didn't want to leave Rick unattended, but it wasn't more than three minutes there and back, plus whatever time he took on the phone. In any case, he needed to get out, to breathe the air from somewhere other than the depths of this house.

Since Palmer wasn't around, Paul decided to at least have a cursory look through the front couple of rooms before going out. Immediately beyond the kitchen was a kind of open-plan office with an old folding-leg table, the sort you would find in the basement hall of any church. It was well-worn, and what looked to be a few decades' worth of graffiti was etched into its splintered plywood surface. *Guns, God and Liberty. shitfuckpisscuntass. Our Father who farts in heaven.* Paul couldn't make out most of the scribbling and scratching. On one wall was a carefully made needlepoint about the size of a piece of foolscap, featuring an amended version of the Prayer of Serenity. It was a colourful and lovingly presented piece, nicely framed, in refined stitchwork that must have taken a considerable amount of effort and patience. It read, "God grant me the serenity to accept the things I cannot change, the courage to change the things I can, and the weaponry to make the difference." A picture of a semiautomatic rifle was sewn into the bottom of the hanging. Paul's initial reaction was to laugh out loud; his second reaction was to ponder, for just a few seconds, the mindset that fashioned this needlepoint first as an idea and then an object. He heard his laughter strangled by the deep silence filling the house, a silence that felt sentient, somehow, as if it had the will and ability to extinguish the sounds of the living.

There was no computer in the room, but on one end of a table hard against the wall was a messy gathering of what looked to be randomly ordered publications, hundreds and hundreds of them, smaller piles stacked on groupings of larger piles, like some crazy ziggurat of information: books, pamphlets, broadsheets, even some videotapes. Paul picked up a few of the pamphlets and leafed through them. *Equipping for the New World Order. How to Manipulate the Media. Citizen Soldier. How to Disappear Completely and Never Be Found.* From farther down one of the outer corner bottom piles he pulled out a videocassette entitled *Pressure Points, Chokes and Sealing the Vein*, a video that promised to show how "pressure points are invisible points on the human body which, if struck, will cause a specific organ or section of the body to cease functioning. A precise touch can cause a heart attack, paralyze an arm, stop the breathing, disrupt the brain or cause instant death. The chokes taught here cause complete respiratory shutdown and if done properly cannot be detected."

On one pile sat a few copies of a book called the *Vigilantes of Christendom* by some fellow named Hoskins, detailing a movement called the Phineas Priesthood. The inscription on the cover read, "As the Kamikaze is to the Japanese/As the Shiite is to Islam/As the Zionist is to the Jew/So the Phineas Priest is to Christendom." Paul shook his head; it was the kind of book Emmett Code might have reviewed for *Across the Plains*. The kind of book for people he didn't want to know. Which meant . . . Rick?

After thumbing through books that detailed the "true" plans of the UN to invade United States soil with Belgian troops, that explained the Zionist conspiracy to control the banking systems of the world, and which explored the "Committee of 300"—the real yet illegal rulers of the world—Paul left the room and went outside, clattering the door open. The purity of the pine-scented air shocked him, as if he'd dived headfirst into the stinging cold waters of a high mountain lake. It was a kind of madness in there, and not a little bit farcical; conviction, too, so much green and glinting passion and patriotism and fever that Paul felt the old pull—there was learning in it. The heat rising in his blood was like the welcome smile of an old friend, even if he was surprised to find it visiting him out here. It was entrenched curiousity, his unfillable need to know. It outweighed nearly everything else about him. *It's not healthy*, Harold had once told him. *Only necessary.*

He went back in, took a copy of the Phineas Priesthood book, the Committee of the 300 book, and a couple of survivalist pamphlets from the largest stacks and placed them in a large brown packing envelope pulled from under the table. He shifted the piles around a bit so that it was impossible to immediately notice something was missing. Before going outside, he left the books on the kitchen table, so that if caught he could always claim he was ready to pay for them. There was no sign of anyone outside. He went back in, took the books off the table and then hid the bag in trunk of his car, secreting it under an old tarp and a dirty blanket. Just as he shut the trunk, Palmer pulled up.

"What're y'up to?" He was walking toward the house carrying a couple of brown-paper bags full of groceries.

Paul glanced at the trunk of the car. "Looking for something."

Palmer nodded like a judge considering a request he was about to deny. He looked at the closed trunk. "Find it?"

"No." Paul felt his toes twitching and he pressed down on the balls of his feet. "Anyway, I'm glad you're back now. I'll check in on Rick again, but I thought I might go for a walk. He's sound asleep. I just need some air, to move around or something, but I don't want to just leave him. Is that okay? Are you sticking around here?"

"Yeah. Making my special chili for the boys tonight."

". . . The boys? Who are the boys?"

Palmer ignored the question and went inside. Paul followed him, then went to Rick's room. He was either sleeping soundly or semi-comatose; it was hard to tell. Paul listened to the ragged yet metronomic respiration for another minute or two, then he shut the door and retreated, heading for his car to go into town to find a pay phone and check his messages, buy a cold drink, walk down main street. The meeting with "the boys" was at 8 PM. He'd be back for that, whatever the hell it was. Palmer's chili, too. His *special* chili. Even something as simple as a pot of chili promised information of some kind, information Paul didn't have and that he felt sure he wouldn't find anywhere else.

FIFTEEN

Two trucks drove by twice as Paul stood at the outdoor telephone in front of the Stennets Mercantile and Gas Bar. He didn't recognize either driver, though he laughed when, after his initial reaction, he remembered the only two people he could possibly recognize would be JJ and Palmer. No messages were on his machine at home, and he tried work next. Three messages.

The first was from Harold. "Paul, call me. I sent you an email, too. The piece is fantastic. We need to shorten it, though, by about a thousand words. . . . Where are you, anyway? Isn't this Thursday? Why aren't you in the office?"

Paul smiled and hit the erase key.

The second message was from Lisa. Paul had hurriedly called her that morning before leaving. "Hey, Paul. I told Mum you were away for work . . . I just wanted to hear your voice so I phoned your machine. Isn't that lame? I know you're not due back from Montana for . . . what? Another day or two? I hope Rick's okay. Tammy wants you to call us as soon as you can. She said she was going to go down, but I told her not to, and she listened. Come straight home, okay?"

He saved the message.

The final message made his throat close up when the voice came over the line. His abdomen began to ache deep down. "Paul, it's Rachel. Hi. How are you? I haven't seen you or talked to you in a few days. I suspect you've probably finished the article on my dad. I wanted to ask if you'd like to get together soon. The convention is next weekend. I'll be there. You'll probably want to come to finish off the last bits of your research. Our numbers are fantastic, and I guess my dad is going to win. But you already sensed that, huh? So . . . let's see, what do I want to say . . . ? Well, I suppose I want to say that I'm not sure I'll go back with my dad to Ottawa if—when—he wins. I'm not sure what I'm going to do. Okay . . . give me a call, alright?"

Paul hit the save key. She sounded so sincere. Maybe she was. But he put her out of his mind, or tried to. He hung up the phone and went inside the Mercantile. A yellow frying-oil haze was suspended in the air at head height, so thick he could taste it on the back buds of his tongue and nearly even touch fatty globules of it drifting around his face. A fryer beneath a glass cover sat at one end of a long counter with a till. Chicken parts, french fries and corn fritters littered the steel pans under the heat lamps. It was revolting, but Paul hadn't eaten since he'd had breakfast in Calgary—was it really only eight hours ago?—and his stomach complained as soon as the smell of the food hit.

"Hey," said the girl behind the counter.

"Hey," said Paul.

The girl looked up. "Oh, not from Stennets, that's right, innit?"

Paul smiled. "Calgary."

She nodded. "No surprise."

"Accent? I wouldn't have thought the Alberta accent was much different than the Montana accent. I can't tell them apart."

The girl shook her head. She looked young enough to Paul that she might still have been in high school, but they sold liquor at the Mercantile, so she had to be twenty-one according to state law. Whatever her age, thought Paul, she needed to do something different with her life in a hurry. He eyed her body from across the counter, at the way her neck already filled out below her ears; she probably ate the food here every day.

"Naw, it's just you look different. You look like someone from the city. I thought maybe you were from Spokane, Great Falls, or something." She handed Paul his change from the Coke he'd pulled out of the fridge. "Why you in town? Fishing? Hunting?"

Paul tried to predict her reaction to the variety of things he could say. "No . . . I'm here to see a friend."

"Really! You've got friends in Stennets?" She seemed delighted and surprised by this possibility.

"Palmer." It occurred to Paul as he spoke that he didn't even know Palmer's last name. "More a friend of a friend, really."

The girl laughed. "Now I know you're lying to me."

"Why's that?"

"Palmer doesn't have any friends! Everybody knows that. And you can tell him I said so, too, that skunk. He still hasn't finished fixing my boyfriend's motorcycle."

"I'm actually a friend of Tammy's."

The girl's expression changed, her cheeks sagging to collect in two pockets of flesh around the corners of her mouth. For a moment she looked angry, but her eyes began to shine near the food lamps of the counter. "Penny was a sweetie. She used to come in here to buy her newspaper on Saturdays."

"I never met her."

"Same as Tammy." She smiled. "Sweet and mean . . . in a good way, if you see what I'm saying."

Paul thought maybe he did, but didn't try to clarify it.

"So you're here to see Palmer then, are you?"

". . . Sort of, why?"

"Help him out, like?" She leaned over the counter in a friendly way, so that her top unfolded slightly.

"I guess so," he said. He thought it was time to cut off the conversation before he ended up with a mascot. "Well, I suppose I'll head out now. I'm leaving tomorrow, so maybe I'll see you then. I'll probably stop by to fill up and get a coffee for the road."

"See you then, I hope. And you have a nice evening, alright."

Paul stopped. *Nice evening?* "What did you say your name was?"

"Christine."

"I'm Paul." He looked at his watch. It was 4:30 PM. "Hey, Christine, are there some nice places to go for a walk around here? I mean, I'm sure there are. I just don't know any. I feel like a little hike, nothing too hard. I've got an hour to kill."

"You can always walk up and down the river. That's okay, but kind of boring. Lots of people walk their dogs there. You could go up to Curdle Lake behind town. Take twenty minutes to drive there. Oh! You could go on the other side of the river, too, over to the falls and the potholes."

"Potholes?"

"The Smock Creek potholes. The creek comes down out of the mountains, and there's a waterfall and then like all these little swimming holes. I wish I could go. It's so hot today." She pouted slightly. "Anyways, you go back across the river, head east towards Thompson Falls, then turn left a couple miles down the highway, onto Fire Road 433. The trail head is a couple miles up. Just park your car and hike in the rest of the way along the old mining road. That oughta fill an hour, depending on how long you swim."

"That sounds great, thanks."

She reached under the counter and pulled out a walking stick, offering it horizontally as if it were a tribal relic transferred from an elder to a younger warrior. "Bring it back when you're done."

"It's okay," said Paul. "I don't need a cane."

"Suit yourself," she said, flicking a fingernail against the bell on the handle, "but I'd never hike around here without a bear bell."

"Bears?"

Christine nodded. "Cabinet Range is full of 'em. Black and grizzly."

Paul reached for the stick.

He came to a halt, dumbstruck, standing at the foot of the Smock Creek potholes, a staircase of the giants, a massive, broken-stoned, water-touched passage, less a group of potholes than a series of nature's baptismal fonts, basins filled with the cool, serene waters of promise. The sun squirted through the canopy and down the gorge's fall line. It looked as if there were one or two potholes near the top, a couple of hundred feet up, then a waterfall halfway down—about ten feet in height—after which another four or five potholes ramped down to where Paul now stood. He squatted, cupped his hands and brought some of the water from the bottom basin to his mouth; it was glacier-cold and stony-tasting. He took another couple of handfuls.

After climbing to the top pool, Paul undressed, toed his clothes into a pile beside the bear bell stick, then stepped into the water. It was frigid, and when he splashed in up to his navel his scrotum shriveled up like a dried apricot and his heart thundered into his neck. Soon enough, after a minute or two, he sensed his body getting the measure of the cold; but, though he began to feel almost warm, he felt as alone as he ever had. He slipped in and out of the silvery pool, watching and listening—to the silence, the glacial stone, the scrabby pines. Looking straight up, the high arrowheads of the conifers groped and swayed like seaweed in a soft tide. The water trickled around him. He listened, as if with an ear up against the earth's ribcage. There was a heartbeat. For the first time Paul felt as if he were touching the earth in some way, was within its rhythm—yet he knew that pulse would go on when he took his ear away. This pothole could swallow him whole, frictionlessly digest him, and the world would not change as a result, not a bit. He held his breath, and soon he felt only the terror of the earth's pitilessness.

The drive home would take five hours and Rick would be in pain, might even sleep most of the way, but when he was awake, when he was able to listen and maybe even respond, Paul would tell him what he'd said earlier. And then he would listen to Rick's response, and he would accept it. It was a start.

Paul slipped out of the pool and picked up his clothes. The day was still hot, though it was nearly five o'clock. He picked his way back down the path to one of the middle pools and waded in, enjoying the first cold shiver of the water. This was the kind of place he instinctively knew Rachel would enjoy, the kind of place Paul would like to bring her to. They would climb up together, stop here in the same spot. She would be naked with him. They would make love on the stone with their clothes under them, or perhaps they would move into the water, her tall slender figure hugging his. They would do it silently, and the silence would only intensify it, make it more urgent. He let the vision linger in his head, and wasn't shocked to hear himself whispering to her in his mind that she was exquisite, a thing of loveliness and grace, the only one he cared for, would ever care for. She smiled for him, stroked the hair at his temple, said she had been waiting for him all this time.

Moving partway out of the pool, Paul put his head back on the rocks and let his hand glide under the skin of the water. He kept Rachel in his mind, but was surprised and not completely pleased to have a vision of chubby Christine at the Mercantile also come into the movie playing in his head. When he sat up, his ejaculate was holding together, swirling delicately in the basin's eddy like a dollop of glue. He slipped further into the water and brushed it along with the back of his hand until it gradually moved to the lip that spilled over the rocks down to the next basin. Paul was taken by the notion that this was a symbol of something about him; not in a moral sense, that was absurd, but in a factual, even circumstantial way of existing, something having to do with the sadness of growing used to loss. He thought again of Rachel and realized how upset he was not to be the biggest part of her life, that in fact he was grieving the loss of something that hadn't even happened, and likely never would.

He was thinking about getting out of the pool when from the silence of the forest came a sharp *crack*.

It was almost theatrical, as if someone nearby had laid a piece of deadfall prone and brought a harsh foot down its middle. He quickly stepped to the edge of the basin and warily looked around, but with the gorge acting as an echo chamber the best he could figure was that the sound had come from right on top of him. He looked at his clothes and saw the bear bell stick. "For fuck's sake," he said. He pulled on his underwear and dragged his T-shirt over his wet torso, grabbing the stick and jingling it for all it was worth. He was certain it hadn't been a gunshot. If someone was walking the path, then why weren't there further sounds? With visions of limbs torn from sockets, he assumed a bear was looking at him right now, deciding when to charge. He remembered reading some book about a hiker discovering the torso of a bear-savaged man stuffed into the empty trunk of a dead tree. Why had he read that book?

"Shit. Shit. Shit," he hyperventilated. He high-stepped it into his pants, socks and shoes, then held up. His body stopped first, then his mind. He understood the noise. There were no bears. No hikers, no hunters. He stared into the forest, then up the length of the stone and water staircase. He stood and looked at the world around him. He'd touched it, and it had spoken back. He had gone the wrong way. His place was somewhere else.

The panic grew with every moment it took Paul to get back to the house, and he hit the catacomb hallway running after flying past Palmer in the kitchen. Rick's door was closed. He put his hand to the knob and took a breath, held it, turned the handle. A body was in the bed, crumpled in the fetal position. Paul touched the hip of the body. There was a movement, a twitch. No consciousness. Paul slipped the cover off the head.

"Rick? Rick?" Paul whispered hoarsely. "Rick!?"

Rick coughed and tried to roll over, stayed asleep.

Paul sat on the floor beside the bed, brought his knees to his chest and his hands to his face, digging his forefingers deep into the space between his closed eyes and the bridge of his nose. Relief surged like blood from his fingertips. He pulled his hands from his eyes, which made his sockets feel gouged out, hollow. The basin in his guts holding his fear and horror emptied out, but it didn't stay empty and he was shocked by what filled it. Rushing back, he'd been terrified by the notion something had happened to Rick and, further, that he should never ever have left him alone, but as he sat now beside his sleeping brother, he understood fear had not been the only feeling he'd been gripped by. The undercurrent was the intensity of finality, its very real possibility. And now he was sickened by it, by what he felt the second he knew Rick was still alive. In a way he would never have admitted to anyone, it was disappointment that had filled him up, a disappointment to find Rick still breathing. He was disgusted by it, his own callousness, his hunger for endings. It wasn't over. It wasn't close to over, this here in Stennets, or anything to do with Rick. That this could have been it—no matter how awful that would have been—was a little brush up against those thrilling, abhorrent things at the core. Part of him had wanted it. But that outcome wasn't there. They were carrying on.

The door opened and Palmer stepped into the room. "What the fuck?"

"Shhh." Paul stood up and ushered Palmer out, following him.

They went back into the kitchen. "What was that all about?" said Palmer. He didn't look at Paul, but picked up a wooden spoon and began stirring a pot of chili, resting his free hand against his hip bone. He put a dab of it on the tip of the spoon, blowing on it first, lightly but pointedly, as if directing a toy boat across a tub. Paul was surprised by the gesture's domesticity. Palmer put the spoon tip into his mouth, then returned it straight into the pot without rinsing.

"I was worried. I thought something happened. I don't know why."

Palmer shrugged. "Oh, yeah." He turned back to his chili, and after another couple of passes with the spoon, seemed satisfied. With a large bowlful, two slices of white bread with thick pats of real butter, and a fresh bottle of beer, he began to make his way back into the room where Paul had earlier seen the stock of books and pamphlets. "Help yourself," he said, nodding at the pot. "Boys'll be by at eight. That's when we'll vote on whether you can join in tonight or not."

"Join in? Why should I join in?" Paul stopped, thought about it. "I mean, I guess I could . . . if that's what you want?"

"It's not what *I* want." Palmer stood for a moment, hovering in the doorway. "Anyway, don't hold your breath. I'll be voting no."

SIXTEEN

They began to arrive fifteen minutes before eight, a few through the back, two through the front. Palmer didn't introduce Paul as he brought men through the kitchen, and nobody seemed all that surprised to see a stranger in their midst. JJ came up to the kitchen through the back of the house.

"I'm going to check in on your brother," JJ told Paul. When he came back, he said, "Resting up okay. High fever, though. Gave him some liquid Tylenol and some water. He choked on it a bit 'cause he's still out, more or less, but he's not bad."

"JJ," said Paul. "I appreciate what you're doing. I do." He tried to find the words that might get Rick the right kind of help, or that would at least put Paul more at ease about his brother's health, but he wanted to do so in a way that was not going to make it harder to navigate their way out of this remote, fucked-up corner of the world. But it was, Paul knew of himself, not quite correct to say he was ready to leave. He was anxious, his armpits had been damp with cold sweat from the moment he'd arrived, he found himself breathing hard even when sitting down, but he'd already admitted to himself his curiousity about these people and about what would draw Rick to them. He was completely out of his element, and had no like experience to draw from, but that was a big part of what made this a place he wanted to leave and not leave. It called for something he wasn't sure he had, and he wondered, worried, if he was up to these people or not. It was something worth knowing.

"I think I'd feel more comfortable having someone else, like a real doctor, look at him, if that's okay." Paul briefly looked at the chili pot, and then returned his attention to JJ. "I really don't want you to take it the wrong way, JJ . . . but I don't know. That's just how I feel."

"A *real* doctor?" JJ paused, seemed to pull back on words partway out of his mouth. "You wouldn't want to do that," he finally said, "if you knew us better. You'd know you wouldn't have to."

With that he returned to the back of the house, to a room Paul couldn't see. They were not in the room with the books and not in the living room area, either. Paul sat waiting, feeling like a schoolboy anxious to hear whether he'd been accepted into a treehouse club. He finished a big plate of Palmer's special chili, and there was nothing special about it except for the fact that it featured four different kinds of beans—kidney, brown, black, and garbanzo. It didn't even taste much like chili, and seemed made, perversely, or maybe specifically, to cause blinding gas. Perhaps that was what made it special. About twenty past eight, JJ came out to the kitchen. "Come on back," he said.

On the inside wall of the living room was a door that had been closed the last time Paul had been in the room. He and JJ passed through it now into a long and fascinatingly disordered space, obviously the drive-in aspect of the repair shop or auto garage where Palmer did most of his work. In the middle of the floor was a large rectangular table with folding metal legs, much like the one holding all the books in the other room. Six men were seated around the table. JJ was standing at the head. He motioned for Paul to sit between two men, one about Paul's age, wearing what looked like camouflage hunting clothes, the other, maybe in his late thirties, early forties, wearing jeans and a grey hooded sweatshirt, who was already scowling. Paul sat down.

"Four votes to two, we decided to let you sit in," said JJ. "For two reasons. One, you're Rick's brother. Two, we know you're not a batfucker."

Paul furrowed his brow.

"Batfucker," said Palmer. "Bureau of Alcohol, Tobacco and Firearms. BATF."

"I think it's a mistake," the man to Paul's immediate right blurted out. Palmer had already told Paul he was voting no; here was the other one. "I don't care whose brother he is. And I don't care what he does in Calgary. Big fucking deal. You're not taking this organization seriously enough, JJ. We have real work to do. I don't think you know what you're doing on this one. You're wrong here."

JJ turned on the man. "Don't you tell me what I'm thinking, Roy. *The tigers of wrath are wiser than the horses of instruction.*"

"So," said Palmer, grinning at Paul. "How 'bout some intros." He went around the table, naming the four men Paul had not yet met, starting on Paul's left.

"Colin. He's a hunting guide out of Libby." Colin was younger than

Paul and bigger, much more muscular. He had longish black hair and he nodded at Paul without smiling when Palmer introduced him.

"Munro. He's currently making himself available to the highest bidder for his services." The others chuckled; a running joke, apparently, about the man's unemployment. Munro looked to be closing in on sixty and was heavyset with a greying moustache and a crazed grid of veins wired into his upper cheeks and nose; a heavy drinker.

"Richard. He runs the hardware store down on main street." Richard did not smile or nod or acknowledge Paul in any way other than to look at him.

"Then, course, you know me and JJ. Last beside you there is Roy. He lives in East Hope, actually, but we let him across the border anyway."

"Where's that?" asked Paul.

"Idaho panhandle, on the way to Sandpoint," said Roy, without looking at Paul. He continued to glare at JJ, his mouth a scrawl. His hooded sweatshirt had a logo on the front that read, "We're getting READY for it." Of all the men, he was the one who most reminded Paul of Rick. Same general age, same general build. But it was more than that. Roy, like Rick, radiated energy, had an aura about him. If it had been something that made you want to be near him, you would have called it magnetism or charm. Even still, you wanted to find out what was going to happen, so you kept looking. Paul could feel Roy's force right beside him, crowding outward, bristling, insisting.

"Right," said Munro, the unemployed drinker. "Let's get started on the meeting of American Eagle One, Western Freedom Front, 21 September." He pulled a sheet of paper from a worn blue backpack, a tattered, shapeless pouch of a thing. "We've got a lot to talk about tonight."

Paul kept his mouth shut and his eyes moving. At the far end of the space was a large roll-up metal door, big enough to drive two half-ton trucks through. Both sides of the room were lined with wide work tables holding small engines, woodworking projects, a chainsaw without a chain, chairs that looked newly painted. Above one of the tables was a 3' x 4' white board; on it, composed in dry-erase marker, was an intricate chart with lines of connection between hundreds of names, some people, most of corporations and multinationals. From a cursory glance, Paul noticed two letters at the heart of the diagram from which everything else flowed: UN. His eyes kept moving. A snowmobile without its hood sat in a corner beside a motorcycle—Christine's boyfriend's, perhaps. At the end of the room opposite the garage door was floor-to-ceiling pegboard holding dozens of power tools, screwdrivers, hammers, chisels, power cords, drills, and two chainsaws with chains attached. Whatever else he felt about Palmer, Paul had to admit it appeared as though the man worked for a living. This was a room teeming with smells: engine oil, paint, pinewood, the thin reek of varnish and stain, the grasping stink of glue—all of which commingled into what for Paul was a truly pleasurable scent. It smelled like labour, and that was a good smell.

Munro kept working his way through agenda items. "Right. Palmer, you were going to update us on the numbers from the Cascadia Patriots lecture you and JJ delivered in Spokane last month."

"Pretty good. Fifty people or so. Not as good as I'd have hoped, but pretty good. Cleared about six hundred dollars. Real good crowd, though, wouldn't you say, JJ?"

JJ nodded. "I'd go so far as to say sympathetic."

Munro made a notation in his papers. He was clearly a secretary, a record keeper. None of the other men deferred to him in any other way or showed him particular respect.

Paul sat still and said nothing, and had nothing said to him, as the meeting continued on in this way for perhaps half an hour, with Munro going from man to man checking in on various areas of responsibility and jurisdiction: publications; formal membership ("just under two thousand paid," said JJ); tracking various instances of contact with the local authorities and what happened, if anything, as a result (Palmer had gotten a speeding ticket, Roy had been in an argument with a sheriff in Libby about openly carrying a handgun, Colin's mother was refusing to remove a sign from her front lawn that read KILL THE PRESIDENT.); updating the web site (the address of which Paul made a mental note); correspondence; and finally, revising "areas of convergence" with what Paul assumed were other militias and antigovernment groups around the Pacific Northwest and the western provinces of Canada. The tone and process of the meeting, and even some of the content, seemed to Paul less like an armed group of antigovernment survivalists than the local Elks Club.

After finishing with what seemed routine agenda items, Munro called for a break so he could have a "slash." JJ also left the room. While the two men were away, Palmer got more beer. Roy twisted the cap off his bottle and said to Paul matter-of-factly, "No offense, really, about not wanting you here. I consider what we do important . . . and think it ought to be covert, or at least a hell of a lot more discreet. JJ disagrees with me. We have what you might call a difference of opinion."

Palmer was slouched in his chair, drinking his beer, gazing lazily at Paul. "I agree with Roy."

"I'm not offended," said Paul, looking at the salt and pepper stubble of Roy's angular chin. He wanted to look Roy in the eye, but couldn't quite bring himself to lock on. It wasn't that he was afraid of Roy, exactly, just that Roy was a different man than the rest. Paul realized he had begun to actually start thinking of these men not just with, but as, weapons. Palmer was a shotgun. JJ a long knife. Roy? An axe.

"Not that we've got nothin' to hide." Roy pointed the snout of his beer at Paul. "A sheriff could march in here this minute"—he waved his bottle around the room—"and I'd still carry on talking about what we're talking about. All this is perfectly legal. Armed militias have the right to form. It's in the Constitution. Look it up. First Amendment."

"I bet he already has, because that's just the kind of thing he does," said Palmer, smiling as if he were a Paul specialist explaining typical behaviours of the species. "Hey, anybody hungry? Got some chili left, unless Munkey Boy ate it all up."

"There's lots left. I was pretty hungry, though, after smelling that fried chicken down at the store."

"Where? The Mercantile?"

Paul nodded. "Stopped in to get a pop."

"I wouldn't eat that shit down there," said Roy. "Fried shit. Stuff'll soak up all your blood and your blood turns into grease. That's proven. It's science. I'd eat Christine, though. A little sippin' from the furry cup." He sniggered, and so did the other men around the table. Paul didn't particularly appreciate the image, even though he'd had something like it in his own head a couple hours earlier, but he thought he'd better laugh along, so he bared his teeth and moved his head up and down a couple of times.

"Hey, Munkey Boy," said Palmer. "You know why they don't serve niggers down there?"

Paul let his mouth open slightly. He wanted to bark out a laugh of incredulity, knowing that Palmer was testing him in some way, prodding him for a reaction, but he also wanted, more than ever at that particular moment, to just leave these people behind and be gone.

Palmer turned to Roy, grinned, then looked back at Paul. "'Cause the grill ain't big enough!"

Roy had clearly heard it before, but he chuckled along the way friends will.

Paul's first thought was that he should ignore it, to stay out of the way and not become the focal point. His second thought was to shoot out of his chair and call Palmer and Roy racist dickheads and storm out and throw Rick over his shoulder and get in the car and peel off. He waited, took one deep breath, then followed his first instinct. Fear leached into the consideration of his second thought, of whether that was something they would even let him get away with. *Let.* The word hit him hard as he thought it. That was the truth of this situation right here, right now. He was not in complete control of what he and Rick were going to be allowed to do—now, tonight, tomorrow. With his gut throbbing, he got up and walked over to the white board on which was drawn the giant chart he'd noticed earlier. Above it was an epigraph he hadn't been able to read from the table, a saying by Edmund Burke: THE ONLY THING NECESSARY FOR THE TRIUMPH OF EVIL IS FOR GOOD MEN TO DO NOTHING. "What is this, this big chart?" He thought his voice sounded high, reedy.

Palmer answered while looking out the room's open door; he must have been wondering, as was Paul, where JJ had gone. "Everything you need to know about who really runs the world is right up there. It's basically what we're up against."

"Meaning what?"

"New World Order," said Roy. He pulled on his nose with thumb and forefinger. "UN-controlled. Our government, and it goes without saying, your pathetic government, and most other western so-called democracies, have capitulated, and are participating with the Jewish-bankers to let a one world government take over." Roy must have noticed the mix of alarm and surprise Paul felt on his face, because he kept on. "It's not about racism, it's about heritage, about integrity. They're trying to wash everything out of us that make us individuals." Paul took note of the word. Roy kept on, counting on his fingers as he made each point.

"Homeland Security is gonna put microchips in all of us. *Fact.* They're making a musical out of Rumsfeld's speeches to brainwash people. *Fact.* Your government, the Mexicans, and ours here in the USSA are joining up to make identity cards we all have to carry everywhere with information about us hidden on them. *Fact.* You don't believe me, I'll give you every piece of evidence you need. Got it all documented, if you want." He stopped briefly, and kept his flat gaze on Paul. He tipped the last of his beer down his throat, swallowing slowly, with satisfaction, almost as if he was regulating it with his big pointy Adam's apple. "Just let us be, is all this is about. We'll take Montana, Idaho, Washington State, BC, and Alberta, make things right. We'll call it Cascadia. Except for Seattle and Vancouver, of course. Full of homos. Anyways, I don't know why we're wasting our breath talking to you."

Paul licked his lips.

"You're not even hearing me. You think we're stupid as shit."

"I don't think that," said Paul, hearing the lie in his voice.

"Doesn't bother me," said Roy, his tone suggesting it bothered him a lot. "It's okay. So does everybody else. Being underestimated is the best camouflage."

Paul was about to protest—though he wasn't sure in what way—when JJ re-entered the room, carrying a bag full of papers and books. He went straight to Paul. "Just wanted to let you know, son, that I checked up on your brother. The head is just fine, it seems to me. I changed the dressing again, real quick, and there's no blood. It'll close over good, I think. You might want to check the bandage again before bed. His fever is a bit higher now, too, so I gave him some more Tylenol. When you check him, if he's real hot, give him another spoonful of that Tylenol. He'll swallow it, even if he's not awake."

In this mad and lonely neck of the planet, Paul wanted to thank JJ, to say he appreciated the concern. But then again, Paul reasoned, how could he possibly transfer some of his being to a guy caching "Meal in a Tablet" pills in the woods and who was using his brother to smuggle weapons into the hills of the east Kootenays? "I appreciate it, JJ," was all he could manage.

When Paul turned back to the room, assuming the meeting was about to get started again, he saw that Palmer and Roy had their heads together, and were discussing something under their breath. Munro pulled his sheet of paper out and began to scan the list of things he wanted to cover.

"New business," said Roy, turning back to the group.

Munro looked up. "Huh?"

"I got some new business to put on the agenda."

"I've got new business listed as the last thing we do. It's always the last thing you do at a proper meeting."

"Tonight's different."

Munro stared at JJ, who said nothing.

Roy pointed at Paul. "Why is he in here, JJ? I mean, truly. Say it straight up. For me, because I'm a dumb shit and I need to hear things said plain. I mean, I know it, but I just want to hear you say it and I want to talk about it, because it ain't about him at all, is it?" Roy again jabbed a thick, dirty finger at Paul, which made Paul flinch inside, and then he waved a hand at the other men around the table, excluding Palmer and Paul. "You talked people into letting him in tonight, and maybe these need to know why, too, cuz I sure as shit got it figured out."

"We had a vote," said JJ, his eyes half-lidded.

"Oh, fuck the vote! Stop with that. He shouldn't be in here. This is not a democracy. We live in a 'democracy,' and look at it. This is a militia, JJ. Don't you read your own fucking essays? Well, stop writing it and start living it. I don't want some knobhole publicizing us. I don't. It's not what we're about." He glared at JJ. "You aren't taking this seriously."

"Roy," said Paul hastily, turning to face him. "I don't plan on writing about this. Anyway, didn't you say a few minutes ago you wouldn't care who walked in here? Even a sheriff. Come on, all I want is to get Rick home. I didn't even know about any of this. I swear to God. I don't even care about any of it."

"Really? Is that right? You don't care? You don't care about politics? About the state of nations? About what's happening to your country up there, and to ours, too? Shit, all you have to do is listen in to that Communist Broadcasting Corporation. It's all anyone talks about. The 'state of the world.' And you don't care about any of that?"

". . . Not like this. Not to do with this way of thinking."

"That's peculiar," said Roy, affecting confusion, his black, thick brow scrunched up and lowered, "because Rick told us you write about politics a lot, that that's all you care about. He told me you're obsessed with authority figures, and that you're writing some hotshot thing about Daniel Code."

"You've heard of Daniel Code?"

"He seems a good Christian," said JJ, pulling on his beard. "Potential president, we hear."

"Prime minister."

"Yes, well, maybe he'll start to fix up that awfully peculiar country of yours. *The human question is not how many can possibly survive within the system, but what kind of existence is possible for those who do survive.*" JJ paused for effect, then stared gravely at Paul. "Feel free to use that if you want to, son."

"Um . . . thank you. It's already in, though. The piece. Submitted I mean. I can't change it or anything. Not that I would. I mean, all this down here doesn't have anything to do with anything. I don't want to write on this. I don't plan on it. That's crazy. Why would I?"

Roy exhaled hard and pointedly turned his chair to face Paul. "You are so stupid. You think JJ's actually worried you might write about him? Come on, Sherlock. Wake up. He *wants* you to write about him. That's his whole deal. That's the only fucking reason you're sitting in that chair right now. Am I right, JJ? Or am I wrong? Hey? Right or wrong?"

JJ was staring hard at Roy, but said nothing.

"You get it yet?" continued Roy, turning back to Paul. "Some of us are serious. Some of us want to be ready." He stopped and made a show of looking at JJ. "And some of us are just out treating it like a fucking hobby. Well, you go ahead and be a weekend fucking warrior, but not me."

"Ready?" said Paul. "Ready for what?"

"Ol' JJ," said Roy, ignoring Paul's question. "He's busy trimming his beard up nice. He wants to be on CNN. Huh? Notice that beard? Nice and long, but always so trimmed up. Looks good on you, JJ. It'll look good on TV."

"But . . ." said Paul. "Isn't some of this illegal? I mean, storing arms. Planning insurrections. Talking about all these things, the UN, and Ruby Ridge, and 9/11, all like they're actually reasons to own a semiautomatic weapon. Why would you want to be known for that? Why would you ever want me or anyone to write about that, especially when you know what it's going to make you look like, which is a bunch of whackos?"

Paul instantly wanted the words back inside his mouth, but they were gone, skipping across the table in every direction. Palmer laughed out loud at Paul, delighted, and Roy said, "My point exactly," but before he could say anything more, JJ spoke up in a loud voice.

"*When I tell the truth, it is not for the sake of convincing those who do not know it, but for the sake of defending those that do.*"

Roy shot up out of his chair, which clattered to the floor behind him. "I swear to God, JJ, if you quote Willliam fucking Blake one more time I will personally break your fucking neck, do you hear? Use plain English, and use it so that it means something to me. Stop acting like you're some goddamn prophet, because you're not, okay? Stop with the pseudo-mystical bullshit, or I swear I will walk out of this room and never come back, and trust me, you do not want that, you do not want me back in Sandpoint and Spokane telling everybody what a bunch of fuckups you are. Is that what you want, JJ? Because if it is, tell me so right now and then we don't have to go through all this. It's been three years of this shit."

"You know," said Palmer, addressing Paul with a calmness that only increased Paul's apprehension, "it was JJ who thought it would be good if Rick brought you down here some day. Expand. Inform. How could it hurt? said JJ. But he, Rick, I mean, wasn't sure. He thought you wouldn't respect it, wouldn't respect him."

"It doesn't matter if Rick was right or not," said JJ, who was standing up, still glaring at Roy. "When you have a cause, you tell people about it. You are not afraid. I'm not afraid of anyone knowing. I want to talk about it. But you, you're afraid of something, my friend, and I don't even know what it is. Why are you so afraid? Why is that? Why are you so afraid and I'm not? Tell me, Roy, King of the Action Heroes."

"That's enough," spat Roy. "I am gone. This chapter is corrupted. Everyone is going to hear about this. Eagle One . . . bullshit." He went for the door, not angrily, not in a hurry, but as though this were something he'd rehearsed, a sensation Paul felt even more strongly when he stopped and turned to face the group. "Palmer, you I'll call. The rest of you can go ahead and strategize about your 'message.' I'll be working with someone else. Hear that word, JJ? *Working.*" He pulled the door open swiftly, surely—again, it seemed to Paul like he'd thought it out beforehand. "Fucking amateurs." He slammed the door shut behind him.

Everyone in the room was silent, except for Palmer, who was chuckling softly to himself. He got up and began stacking plates messy with dried over chili. JJ was chewing on his bottom lip, looking angrily at the door Roy had just walked out of. Paul looked to Roy's chair keeled over on the floor beside him. He reached down to lift it upright and saw his fingers trembling.

The close heat in the room wasn't helping Rick's fever. Paul found a window behind a heavy purple curtain, but it wouldn't open. It was past midnight, and JJ had decided to stay the night after a long hard talk with Palmer following the blow-up earlier in the evening. JJ said he wasn't going to leave until things were "sorted proper." He told Palmer he wasn't worried so much about losing Roy ("No room for that kind of volatility . . . when misapplied," he'd said), but that he, Palmer, was still someone JJ had to have on board. This was the only portion of their conversation Paul was party to. Then they had asked Paul to leave the room.

He'd spent the next couple of hours sitting with Rick, running a cool, damp cloth over his brow, whispering to him, watching his face contort with pain and fever dreams. Twice Rick's eyes opened and he looked around in a state of confusion. Both times he shut his eyes again, pressing hard, falling back into a stupor without responding to Paul's words. His breathing was regular and, as JJ had said, the wound seemed to have stabilized. A straw-coloured fluid leaked steadily from Rick's nose, and almost made it look as though Rick was weepy or emotional, despite being unconscious. Paul changed the head dressing once, and the egg that was pushing through Rick's scalp twelve hours earlier had changed colour. No longer the porcelain whiteness of wet bone, it had taken on a pallid grey and pink glaze, vaguely translucent.

After JJ and Palmer finished meeting, both men came into Rick's room. JJ checked him one more time, administered a half dose of Tylenol and said that he'd be surprised if Rick wasn't fully conscious by tomorrow, though that didn't mean, he reiterated, that he'd be ready to travel. JJ said he himself was tired, didn't want to drive, and didn't mind staying to keep an eye on Rick, in any case.

Palmer stood by the door with his arms crossed while JJ examined Rick. He held an envelope, and after he placed it on the dresser he told Paul that he'd appreciate it if he passed it to Tammy.

"What does it say?" asked Paul, not caring how it sounded

Palmer reached behind his head and released his hair from its ponytail. He ran a stiff-fingered hand across the top of his skull and then briskly scratched side to side, so that his long, slightly greying hair draped down on either side of his head. Paul wondered how Tammy could have ever found this man attractive.

"What does it say?" Palmer said, half-sneering. "Maybe Tammy'll let you read it when she's done. 'Course, maybe you'll open it yourself. Or maybe you'll just chuck it in the river. Whatever."

"Maybe I'll let Rick give it to her."

"Maybe you will."

An hour later, as Paul was giving Rick's face one more wipe with the cool cloth before going to bed himself, Rick woke up. He didn't move his head or neck, just opened his eyes and said, "Water."

Paul quickly got him a glass of water from the kitchen and put it to his lips. "Oh my God," said Paul. "I can't believe it. I can't believe you woke up."

Rick took a sip of water, and tried to rotate his head to see Paul, but winced and returned his head to its original position. "Oh, fuck, my head. Oh, God. Paul. Paul, you're . . ."

"Palmer called me. You're hurt."

Rick nodded. "Okay."

"You've got a bad wound on your head. You fell running in the woods, I guess, though Palmer hasn't really told me quite what happened."

"I don't remember that," said Rick slowly. "I was running. Why?"

"Palmer said you fell, hit a tree stump, out doing something in the woods, I don't know. Palmer said he was running behind you and saw you trip."

Rick screwed up his brow and this action seemed to cause him a lot of pain, because he groaned again, from deep inside, and the fact that he was awake making this sound made Paul feel it along with him.

"That's not what happened." He waited a moment. "So, you know? About this."

"Yes."

He closed his eyes, rested.

"Rick, this . . . it's not you." Paul wasn't sure what to say, how much to say, when to say it. There was no precedent, no inner guide. "We'll just get home, I guess. See Tammy. See everybody else. Go from there."

Rick slowly opened his eyes. "I know you looked at my letters," he mumbled.

"Rick." Paul touched his brother's arm. "I didn't look."

"They were out of order." Rick let his eyelids come together. "But it's okay. It doesn't matter."

"Yes, it does. I want you to trust me. I held them, but I didn't read them. You can trust me."

"You can't fool me, you know," said Rick, his voice a slow hush.

"What?"

A crescent smile surfaced on Rick's lips. "Paul, this is real. Here." He dropped his voice to a dull, energy-conserving monotone, a low, steady train of words heading away from Paul, toward a horizon, beyond which was sleep, rest, healing. "What you do. It's hiding, that's all. You always have. I don't hide." He paused, closed his eyes. "But it's okay. All of it. I forgive you."

"I don't know what it is you're forgiving me for."

". . . 'S okay," whispered Rick, the train disappearing over the horizon. "I do."

SEVENTEEN

Paul's dreams were nightmares of inky diffusion, of nothing he could remember or wanted to remember, only a sensation of claustrophobia, of shallow breathing. When he awoke, the quilt Palmer had given him was over his head, and when he lifted it off it was so damp and heavy with his sweat he felt as if he were pushing the lid off his own sarcophagus.

Debbie, Palmer's disabled daughter, was sitting at the table eating a bowl of cereal when Paul went out to the kitchen. She smiled and a dribble of milk ran out of the corner of her mouth. Morton was standing at the counter, pouring cereal into a giant mixing bowl.

"Well, hello! Where did you two come from?"

Morton turned around and grunted out a hello. "Dad said you and your loser brother were around."

"What are you doing here?"

Morton looked around the house with an exaggerated expression of confusion. "Maybe 'cause I live here."

"Where were you last night? And where's your dad?"

Morton sat down beside his sister. He reached for the sugar and dumped four tablespoons into his cereal. "Dad's out back on the paths down by the river, walking the neighbour's stupid dog like he does every day. We stayed at her mum's house in Heron last night." He pointed at Debbie. "She dropped me and her off this morning so she could go to work."

Paul looked at the oven clock. Nearly nine. He decided; they were leaving, no matter what state Rick was in. Back roads, border crossings, no matter. They were going home. "When's your dad going to be back?"

Morton shrugged. "He goes along the river, through the forest a ways, then back. Hour, maybe."

Paul's stomach began to rumble and he went to the counter. Morton had left the cereal and milk out, but there were no bowls to be seen. "Where are the bowls?"

Morton's face was stuffed, so he pointed to the cupboard left of the stove.

Paul sat down. Debbie stared at him, smiling. She was eating quietly, happy. A door closed from a far part of the house. Paul looked up. "Your dad back already?"

Morton shook his head, and when he spoke a dribble of milk slipped out onto his chin, which he wiped off with his shirtsleeve. "That's probably JJ."

Paul had forgotten about JJ; when he brought the image of JJ's face into his mind's eye, the events of the night before returned. Maybe I lied to Roy after all, Paul thought. Maybe this *is* something I'll write about.

After the first door closed, a similar sound followed—a door opening and closing—but it was a different door, the bathroom, probably. Paul returned to his breakfast, and five minutes later, as he finished his last mouthful, he heard steps that stopped behind him. A hand came onto his shoulder. Long probing fingers, a hand that had been there before. He looked up from his cereal bowl and what he saw first, before turning around, was Morton half sneering in confusion, as if he were seeing something that he wanted to ridicule but that was strange enough to make him hesitate.

Paul swung around in his chair. JJ was standing over him, his face blank, except for his eyes, which were twitching and blinking.

"Paul."

"What? JJ?"

JJ turned his eyes to the floor. *"The grave is Heaven's golden gate, And rich and poor around it wait; O Shepherdess of England's fold, Behold this gate of pearl and gold!* I believe we'll be forgiven, Paul. I truly do."

The chair met JJ's knees as Paul shoved it out from under him. He ran down the catacomb hall to Rick's room. The door was open. Rick was flat on the bed, hands laid across his chest, eyes shut. Paul knelt beside the bed and put his face near his brother's.

"Rick. Rick? Come on."

The body did not move. He put a thumb to his brother's right eye and pried it open without a flicker in response. He felt for a pulse. He put his palm under his brother's shirt, against the bare, cold skin over his heart.

"Rick. Wake up. Please. Open your eyes. Open your eyes, we'll go home. Come on. Let's just go. Okay?"

"I laid him out like that. When I came in he was curled up like a tiny baby, sleeping away, a gorgeous little baby waiting to be picked up by his heavenly Father."

Paul turned and through the distortion of his tears saw JJ standing at the doorway. He was standing with his hands clasped in front of him.

"Hematoma, I suppose. I am sorry, son. My God, I am."

Paul stroked his brother's cheek, his ear, down around his cold chin. He tried to imagine his brother smiling, radiating his unique grin that was magnetic and annoying in equal parts. He couldn't do it, couldn't picture it. It was just a face now. It was Rick's face, but it was missing something, something besides life. In his stillness, Paul saw his brother's face without its anger. It was gone. But to where? A levee broke wide open inside Paul, and everything built up behind it spilled through. He held his brother's hand in his own, stroking it, squeezing it, running his palm up and down his forearm. Kneeling over him, Paul put his face against his brother's neck, between his chin and collarbone, and wept hard. The room collapsed into the space where Paul had his lips pressed to his brother. He kept them there, and let the saltwater from inside him warm his brother's skin.

"Awwwww."

Paul swiveled his head around ready to lash out, at Morton, at JJ, but it was neither of them. Standing in the door was Debbie. She had her hands at her sides, and she was weeping freely. Snot was running down the space between her nose and upper lip. She raised one hand to her face and didn't clean away the tears and snot so much as work them in together.

A hand appeared on Debbie's chubby shoulder, a boy's hand. Morton gently squeezed his sister's collarbone and neck, and without looking at Paul, he moved his sister backward, out of the room.

Paul ran to the back door and shouted Palmer's name into the forest. There was no reply, and without having to look hard or go very far, maybe a hundred metres, he found the path along the river, the one Morton had said Palmer would be on. It was well-used, though still rock-strewn and uneven, and it followed the river for half a kilometre before it cut away from the water and pushed into the forest. Paul was half-running, and he shouted Palmer's name every couple of minutes. He could feel his pulse clattering in his ears, his eyes watering, his legs rubbery yet flaming, as if he'd pinched a nerve somewhere in his lower back. Soon the forest to either side was so dense Paul could not see twenty feet into it before the greens and browns became a two-dimensional dark khaki barrier.

"Palmer!" he shouted. "Palmer. Where are you? Where the FUCK are you?"

A dog barked from a distance up the path. A movement in the brush. The wind shuffled through the trees in the canopy, but on the forest floor the air was still and thick. He could hear his own hard breathing, but nothing else. Paul jogged quickly up the trail, toward the bark. The path was slightly uphill, bending to the left, but after a couple minutes along this direction, it straightened out and then there he was, Palmer, standing at the far end of a long stretch. Paul's stomach jumped, but before Paul could shout again, Palmer disappeared to the right. Paul advanced slowly; he felt his senses subtly rearranging themselves, as if his brain had shrunk to make room for something else, a newly activated organ that caused his skin to tingle down his right side. He scratched and pinched his right arm where it tingled. When he got to the spot where Palmer had evaporated he stopped. He looked left and right, concentrating his vision into the forest, to see where Palmer could have gone, and where he might come out. Nothing. He saw nothing. He bit his top lip, hard, and knew at that moment that he needed to go backwards, immediately. Slowly, holding his breath, he turned around.

The dog, a black lab, came galloping out of the trees twenty metres away, barking and whining, but then stopped running. It went to the middle of the path and stood there, tail straight out. Paul quickly went back toward it, looking for Palmer to come out of the treeline, but he wasn't there. Near the dog, Paul slowed, and like a wraith, Palmer materialized from the trees rushing at Paul and swinging his walking stick at Paul's knee, though Paul saw at the last second that it was a rifle. Palmer caught him square on the kneecap, felling him to the ground, where he shrieked in pain and put both hands to his knee. The dog ran up to Paul and licked his face. He tried to bring a hand up to get the dog away, but there was too much pain for him to take his hands away from his leg.

"Don't you EVER do that again," hissed Palmer. "Do not *ever, ever, ever* chase me like that again or it'll be the last time you ever do it."

"Rick's . . . he's dead!"

Palmer stood back, holding his rifle in the crook of his arm. He made a little kissing sound and the dog went back to his side. "Yeah."

"Oh Christ, my knee." Paul sat up, then stood, despite faltering and wincing at the lightning strikes of pain that flashed from his knee into his hip and the small of his back. He didn't need or want to step back from what he now knew: he hated Palmer, and he let it out from behind the walls he'd built to protect Rick, to protect himself, while in Stennets. "You fucker! Why did you do that? Do you know what you just did to my fucking knee?"

Palmer straightened up as if surprised. He took his ball cap off and put it back on. "Somebody's pissed."

"I said, Why the fuck did you do that?"

"Why the *fuck* are you chasing me?"

"Palmer, what happened? To Rick?"

"He died. Isn't that what you just told me?"

"You piece of shit. That's it? That's all you've got to say?"

Palmer changed his attitude with the rifle, so that he wasn't resting it on the inside of his elbow, but was holding it in his right hand with the muzzle pointed to the ground. "I found him that way this morning when I went to check on him."

"What?!"

"I figured I'd let JJ handle it. He's the doctor." He sucked on his cheeks for a minute and squirted out a strand of black, minty goo at Paul, splashing it onto his pants.

It didn't matter. None of it mattered. He was going home or he wasn't, but he couldn't hold it in anymore. "He's not a fucking doctor! Stop saying that."

Palmer shrugged. "Doesn't matter much if the patient's dead, does it."

"You're lying to me."

"What?"

"You're lying. You did that, didn't you? Whatever it was, you did it. Or Roy. Rick's dead because of you. Because of—all this."

"I killed him?" said Palmer, grinning, as if genuinely amused by the thought. "Why would I? Stupidity is no reason to kill someone."

"Stupidity? What's that supposed to mean? And anyway, why wouldn't

I go and report this, Palmer? Why won't I call the sheriff in Libby?"

Palmer stopped grinning and stared flatly at Paul. "I already did. This morning."

Paul felt his lower jaw start to shake and tremble. He clenched his teeth, but it wouldn't stop. "You're lying again. You killed him, and don't tell me you didn't. Why did you do it? Because Tammy left you and your stupid goddammed ponytail? You're a liar, Palmer. A fucking liar."

"Stop saying that."

"Goddamn you. Goddamn you all. Shit. You jumped up phoney. Playing around at your stupid games. And look! Look!" He was yelling at Palmer, letting his voice soar through the spaces around them. Then he felt himself begin to heave and moan. He had trouble drawing breath. "You don't . . . you don't even get one single thing . . . you ignorant fucking . . ."

Palmer stepped toward Paul quickly, raised the butt of his rifle and brought the flat end of it down onto Paul's breastbone before Paul could process the fact that this man was doing such a thing. No immediate pain, just a heavy blunt thud and he was down.

Paul was on his back, looking at the sky, into the bright sparkling sun that made his eyes go fuzzy and pointy at the same time, little needles making incisions to get deep inside his head. A shadow fell over him. Palmer was standing astride him, so that the toes of his boots were touching each side of Paul's hipbone. He was holding his rifle, the snout of it three feet from Paul's forehead. Palmer couldn't miss. Paul squinted, shut his eyes. There was another noise like a messy spit, and Paul felt a jammy glob of something land on his upper chest. The smell of mint and tobacco began to rise up into his face, and he could sense the weight and wetness of it on his T-shirt. He heard the laughter, a low snigger. Paul opened his eyes. Palmer was looking down his rifle barrel, laughing and shaking his head, as if he'd just seen something amusing, and which fulfilled some sort of private expectation. The black lab whined but didn't bark. Paul stared up the length of the barrel. He could see Palmer's head framed in the pines and spruce above, with the light pouring through the cracks in the forest canopy, through the upper boughs that swayed and danced around one another. Palmer's strangely benign face floated down on top of Paul, through the dust motes sighing within the light, through the sticky scent of pine, through the heartbreaking beauty at the end of every passage. The sun shifted, found a seam, and moved directly behind Palmer's head, so that the details of his face disappeared. The only thing left for Paul to see was a corona, a smudged crown of light that somehow managed to camouflage everything it circumscribed.

EIGHTEEN

Calgary

After the funeral, Paul stayed at his parents' house for a few more days, even though Stelio had phoned to say the painting and recarpeting had been completed. The first night, he sat up watching TV with his father. Lisa had gone out, without a word. When the phone rang around 8 PM, Paul let it go, thinking his mother might answer it in her bedroom, but she didn't. Paul went into the kitchen to check the message. It was the sheriff's office from Libby, a Sheriff Pruman. He wanted Paul and his family to know they were entitled to request a formal inquiry if they so chose, but that he was closing his own file. It seemed clear to the coroner in Libby, the sheriff said, that Rick had died of causes related to his head wound, which they were accepting had happened in a "hiking accident . . . according to local sources and eyewitnesses." The official cause of death was a hematoma that likely would have occurred whether Rick had been taken to a hospital or not, "if that's of any comfort," he added. Paul listened closely, but couldn't decipher anything from the sheriff's tone, any hint of whose side he was on. The sheriff said charges were being laid against a Mr. JJ Pearl for the illegal dispensation of narcotics and prescription medications, but that he'd likely escape with only a fine, since the sheriff's department had also concluded Mr. Pearl's actions had not contributed to the death, and since Mr. Pearl had, in fact, phoned a doctor in Thompson Falls for assistance. "And I want to pass along my deepest condolences," said the sheriff at the end of his message. "We are very sorry that Mr. Munk has passed away, and we hope that the good Lord provides you with some relief and some ability to make sense out of this awful circumstance."

Paul thought the sheriff sounded honest, or, at least, professional. He wrote out the contact information and saved the message, but he knew his parents would not pursue further action. They were broken. They wanted it over. There would be no inquiry.

When Paul came into the kitchen the next morning, Lisa was sitting at the table, reading a book and eating a bowl of fruit and yogurt. She turned her face up to him as if caught in an illicit act, and any other time—with her comical stuffed cheeks—Paul would have made some crack, but not this morning.

"What are you doing today?"

Lisa shrugged. "You?"

"Finishing things off. Get ready to go to the convention tonight. I'll go in to work first. I don't know. The usual."

She nodded. "The usual."

Paul sat down beside her. "Any word?"

Lisa swallowed what was in her mouth. "She phoned yesterday."

"She did? Why didn't you tell me?"

"I'm telling you now. I had to go out last night, and I didn't want to leave a note."

"And?"

Lifting her eyes from her book to Paul's face, Paul could see that his sister hadn't been sleeping. He'd wondered how all this would manifest itself, in what ways the strain was going to break out of her.

"She sounded sad. Lost."

"She was sad and lost at the funeral. You could tell by looking at her." Paul fiddled with the small ceramic salt and pepper shakers on the table, moving them around like chess pawns. "She should have come over and said hello. She should have stopped."

Lisa nodded. "It's not like she said much on the phone. She just said not to worry."

"Where was she calling from?"

"I don't know. It wasn't a collect call or anything. I didn't get the sense that she was somewhere else. I assumed she was calling from Calgary."

"Did she ask to talk to me?"

Lisa gazed wearily at Paul. "And what would that mean if she did?"

Paul felt tears forming along his lower lashes. "Why can't you ever give someone a straight answer? Why is that? Why can't you stop needing the upper hand every time you deal with another human being? Hey, Lisa? Why is that?"

Lisa stopped chewing and seemed to be having trouble swallowing what was in her mouth. She jammed the last few pieces of fruit into her mouth while staring into the bowl, then stood up. "Sorry," she said, her voice a hoarse whisper. She picked up her dirty dishes and pushed the chair into the table. "And, no, she didn't ask for you."

Harold came into Paul's office, a move that so shocked Paul he immediately assumed something was devastatingly adrift in Harold's life. Harold had never done this before. Once or twice in the past he had stuck his head in the door and requested a quick meeting "down in my office." Paul suspected that Harold found his office too bright and organized, as if it exposed him in some way, placed him in too sharp a relief. They had already talked briefly on the phone about Rick, and Harold had been at the funeral, but once he'd found a chair in Paul's office, Paul told him everything about Montana, about what he'd seen and heard. Every detail he could remember.

"Why?" asked Harold. "Why do guys like that get involved? What's it about? I'm not sure I understand it."

"When your life isn't what you wanted it to be, you blame someone else, right?" He shrugged. "Immigrants, Jews, the government. All that matters is that you don't blame yourself. But then one day you wake up and the accusations, the blame, well, the paranoia, really—it controls you, instead of the other way around."

"I think they want a day of reckoning," Harold said. "To prove they were right, that their hate, paranoia, whatever, was justified all along. That's just human. We all want to be right, in the end, when it counts."

Paul widened his eyes. "Day of reckoning?"

Harold scratched the back of his neck. "Don't you think?"

"Well, yeah, I do, but that's exactly what that guy across the street said to me, the one who always puts up those sayings at the End Time place. Jon, no H. He used the same phrase when I asked him, well, I guess when I asked him why he believed what he did, the way he did. *Day of reckoning.*" Paul glanced out his window down to the message board of the End Time Revelation Church. Today it read, THE DOOR TO THE HUMAN HEART CAN BE UNLOCKED ONLY FROM THE INSIDE. He tried to take a deep breath, but had to stop halfway through the let the pain in his breastbone subside.

"My theory," said Harold, quietly, following Paul's gaze out the window, "for what it's worth—and it goes for all of them, your brother, these extremists, even evangelicals like your man Code—is this: It's about emptiness."

"Emptiness?"

"We need filling up. Our souls require it. People that don't have anything to fill them with rummage around. They might not even know it, but they project it, too. Empty souls get found, and get filled. Some actively, some passively. And not very often with the right thing."

"It's the optimist in you I've always loved," said Paul, smiling wearily. "Anyway, I sure don't feel like I have much filling my soul."

Harold kept staring out the window. "Paul . . . it's an awful thing to tell you this now . . . your story on Code is going to be our swan song."

"What?"

"November is the last issue."

Paul crossed his arms and looked with Harold out onto National Avenue. Hundreds of people were dashing here and there, up and down the street, zipping into the liquor store, stopping at the coffee shop, meeting up with friends for lunch. Normally, the mere sight of all this perfect, messy human variety thrilled him and gave him hope and made him thankful in a prosaic and therefore profound way, but today, seeing all those people going about their business simply made him angry. Didn't they care? Did they know? Didn't any of what went on in this office matter? Harold was doing it for *them*. Harold had spent his life trying to give each and every one of them a few ideas worth holding on to. It was a gift, given without request for reciprocity, as any true gift had to be. Yet not one of them gave a damn. You could tell just by looking at them, at the way they scuttled around, chasing their own pleasures and nothing else.

"I'm sorry," said Harold. "I am, Paul. What a time to have to be telling you this."

Paul waved away Harold's concerns with a shake of the head.

"How are you doing, anyway?" said Harold.

Paul could see that Harold really didn't want a long or detailed answer. "I'm alright. Breathing. Eating."

"These are positive signs."

"So," continued Paul, trying to put Harold at ease, the task that forever falls to the grieving. "InfoTrue. I guess 'Ed' is not much of a friend anymore, shutting us down." Paul nodded toward the other offices.

"All for tax purposes. It suits him. He'll fund a new magazine if I ask him to. Don't worry, he won't leave anyone out in the cold. Everybody in the office with a full-time contract will get a job somewhere else in his empire. Then, in a year or so, when I'm done writing my memoirs, you and I will start over again, and we'll do it even better."

Paul couldn't help but grin at his dear friend. "Your memoirs?"

"You could ghost it for me? Might be a way to extort some money out of Ed we can funnel to you." He pushed his chair back a bit. "Anyway, you're not done here yet. There's the leadership convention. You're going, I assume?"

Paul nodded.

"Not that anything too surprising is going to happen, I'm sure," said Harold, standing up. "The polls have Code by a mile. I'm curious to hear his acceptance speech, that's all. But you'll want it for colour to add a paragraph or two to the end of the piece. Then we'll put it in production on Monday. That'll be enough time for you to write a couple paragraphs, I assume?"

"Yes, Harold, that will be enough time for me to write a couple of paragraphs."

"Good." He made to leave, but stopped at the door.

"What?" said Paul.

Harold looked at the floor, out the window, back to Paul. "It's a great piece, Paul. And I, uh, hope whatever I do . . . I hope you're there, too. If you want to be there, you will be there." Then he left Paul to himself. Paul wanted someone else to come into his office, his phone to ring, anything, but there was only quiet and stillness. He looked out his window. The End Time Revelation Church. "Insights," he mumbled. "Amen."

⁂

A young boy, a teenager almost certainly still in high school, approached Paul. He was nicely dressed and had his hair slicked back. Youth Wing, thought Paul. They're always the worst to get stuck talking to. Paul was standing at the back of the crowded hall, where he typically liked to hang out at conventions. The kid stopped in front of him. He was wearing a CHART=CODE button on his breast pocket.

"Are you Paul Munk?"

"Yes."

He held out a narrow pinkish hand. "Bruce McCarron. I run the 'Faith and Politics High School Working Group' for the Code team. I'm also in charge of running all the Messages and Deliveries for the whole convention. Well, I mean, for the Code team."

"Hello, Bruce." He reached out and took Bruce's hand, and got the 'dead fish' in return—young Bruce needed a handshake lesson from his political mentor.

"Um, I hear you're doing a big profile of Mr. Code for 2.2.4. *Magazine*. Actually, he told me that. Well, Rachel did. I mean, Ms. Code."

"Yes, it's done, but I thought I'd come around and see his speech. And the reaction to it."

"Oh, right!" He grinned. "Anyways, Mr. Code is back in the green room. You know, the green room, where they wait for stuff. He told me to see if you'd picked up your press credentials, and if you did, to find you and send you over to see him."

"Send me over?"

Bruce looked at the floor, then back up. "I mean, like, ask you if you wouldn't mind going over to see him."

"I'll go over."

The teenager's smooth face lit up. "Excellent!"

"Is Ms. Code with her father at the moment?"

"Um, no, I don't think so. I was in there about twenty minutes ago, and she wasn't there . . . so, do you want me to take you over? I know where it is, and I sort of promised him that I would, I don't know, I guess bring you there."

"It's okay, Bruce. I know where the green room is. Tell him I'd be happy to see him. I'll be there in a few minutes."

Paul waited until Bruce got lost in the crowd, which was beginning to compress toward the stage in anticipation of the results. Party officers were scheduled to announce the numbers in thirty minutes. Paul pushed himself off the wall and felt a hot narrow slash across the breadth of his kneecap. The hairline fracture had not yet healed fully, and never might. *It's like a piece of china*, the doctor had said. *You can glue it back together with the best glue, and it will look and feel as if it's perfectly healed, but it's never going to be as strong. It will always be a little bit weaker.* Paul allowed himself a slight limp, easing the pain. He cut around the outside of the throng, to the left along the huge black curtains, closed to contain the crowd and allow room for the camera crews. At the backstage area, security teams stood rigid and scowling. Paul flashed his media badge.

"No media," said the guard, stopping him.

"Since when? Media have always been allowed full access."

"Not at this convention."

Paul grimaced. Did it never end? "And why is that?"

"Do I look like I'm the one making the rules?"

"I was asked to come by. Daniel Code."

The guard said something into the lapel of his coat, then stared into the distance as a reply came through his ear bud. "Green room, third door to the left."

"Thank you for all your help," said Paul, with excessive politeness. "Much appreciated."

The door to the green room was closed. Paul knocked gently and went in. Code and a couple of his staff were slouched in corner chairs, discussing something in low, weak voices. It had been a long campaign.

"Paul," said Code. "Thanks for coming by." He indicated a chair nearby. The two staff moved off to the coffee table. "How are you?"

"I'm looking forward to your speech. You must feel pretty confident right about now."

"What happens to me is one thing. But how are you? I know about your brother. I am deeply sorry." He reached out and touched Paul lightly on the shoulder, and Paul felt sure that had they been standing, Code would have leaned in and given him a hug. He would not have resisted.

"Thank you."

"It's devastating, I'm sure."

"How do you know about it?" said Paul.

"Well, I read the obituary in the paper, of course. I was out of town during your brother's funeral, and I am so sorry, Paul. Please know that I would have gone had I been in town. It's all very sad. Rachel told me it was a moving ceremony."

"Rachel?"

"She was there, but left as it ended. I think it was highly emotional for her. She said your eulogy for your brother was quite powerful. When she told me about it she wept." Code paused and seemed moved himself by the thought of his daughter's tears. "Your brother sounds as if he was a man who . . . had challenges in his life, but met them squarely, and with courage. That's to be admired. That must have been tremendously difficult, Paul, to deliver that eulogy. That too takes courage. Great courage. I know about these things. I gave my wife's eulogy."

"It didn't feel courageous," said Paul. "More like shame, guilt, I don't know."

Code nodded gravely, eyes to the floor, as if he understood precisely what Paul was talking about, and that this shared knowledge somehow bonded them. He looked up. "True courage often chooses to disguise itself as other things, Paul."

As had so often been the case, Paul couldn't decide whether to admire or dismiss Code's axiomatic gift. What he'd said made some sense and sounded as though it might be true, especially since it seemed like wisdom earned through experience, but the words were stated with such certitude it made Paul doubt their value. It could have been a saying up on the board at the End Time Revelation Church.

"I hope you and your family come through it okay. I will be thinking of you. Of course, I'll be back and forth a lot between here and Ottawa. But—and I say this with true sincerity—I hope our paths continue to cross."

Paul smiled wryly and imagined Code's quiet time at home, away from the lights, the cameras, the crowds, when it was only him and no one else, sitting down to read Paul's article. He tried to imagine Code's reaction, the body language of his response, twisting in his chair, adjusting his reading glasses, crossing his legs. "You have to realize, the—"

Code stopped Paul with a half-raised hand. "I know. It's going to be negative."

"It's not an opinion piece. It's going to be unbiased, fact-based."

"*Unbiased*. Oh, yes, of course. That's the word the press always use when it's negative."

"That's a bit cynical."

"Paul, I don't mind. I stand by what I say. To speak with a clear conscience is the greatest gift one can possess. Nothing anyone can say can change that, and it allows me to understand the pressures others are under when they make choices different than mine." He bent his head toward his shoulder and smiled tenderly while searching Paul's eyes, like a lover waiting to be understood. It was a moment Paul found touching, if perplexing. "One man I know in my heart," Code continued, now sitting up straight, his hands joined together in his lap, "was tolerant to the worst around Him, perhaps even most tolerant to the least sympathetic. He forgave those who didn't agree with Him."

Then Paul saw. He got the narrative, whole, that from the start Code had been using to interpret, and therefore quarantine, both Paul and their relationship. Paul let it seep in for a moment, admired the simplicity of it, its distorted psychological convenience, its armour-plated irrefutability. He even wondered for a second if Rachel had supplied it.

"You know, you're mixing things up, Daniel."

Code slightly lowered his brow.

"Before the betrayal, Judas was a disciple. He was part of the fold to begin with. I've never been part of the fold."

". . . You sound quite sure of that."

An aide came over and stood beside Code. "Sorry to interrupt but . . . makeup wants you. Things are getting going and they're up on stage right now getting ready to announce the results."

Code nodded politely. He turned back to Paul. Without getting up, he held his hand out in an informal and warm gesture, one man to another. "I do hope we'll see you afterwards, when you've moved on to your next victim, and you'll feel free to be yourself. I'm sure I'll enjoy that person."

Paul said nothing. He took the warm, dry hand in his own and shook it slowly and firmly, letting go only when Code relaxed his grip.

≈≈

An hour later, immediately after Code had finished delivering his victory speech, Paul limped down to the press room, and sat at the chair assigned him. He fingered the credentials hanging around his neck. Signs, signifiers—but of what? Of who he was? What he did? Yes, he supposed, though it felt much more complicated now than it had before.

The room was almost empty. Only the volunteers were there, sitting behind their tables, waiting for the inevitable onslaught of the media hordes, which would come, Paul guessed, in about forty-five minutes, after Code's press conference.

"Paul?"

The voice went up the side of his neck like a moist tongue. He hesitated a second or two, then turned his chair around. Rachel had pulled a chair up beside his. She sat so that they were seated close; to an observer they might have looked like strategists conferring about the next move. Paul breathed in her delicate sandalwood perfume. Placing a hand on Paul's thigh, just above the kneecap, she gave a light squeeze. Paul winced sharply.

"Oh! I'm sorry. Is there something wrong with your leg?"

Paul shook his head. "Accident."

"Montana?"

"Story for later." Paul spoke not quite at her face, but above and beyond it at the wall-mounted message boards behind them. *Media Hotel Transportation Schedule. Messages. Lost and Found.*

"Paul, I'm so sorry about Rick. I just . . . I just can't believe it. I'm really sorry."

"I didn't know you were at the funeral. Your dad told me. Just tonight."

"Are you okay?"

"You know how it is. You go on, right? What else do you do? You must remember . . . from your mum."

"I guess. I really don't remember it too well." She reached out for his hand, and he gave it to her. Her palms were soft and smooth, and she placed his hand between her two.

"Hey," Paul said, trying to smile. "I'm out of a job."

"What?"

"The magazine is folding. Corporate masters have other plans."

She let her mouth drop open. "You're joking."

"I'm not."

"How could they close the best magazine in the country? That's so wrong." Rachel hesitated. Paul knew what the question was, so he answered it.

"Yes," he said. "The article will still run. It's in the farewell issue."

"And so . . . what are we going to do?"

"About?"

"I have to get back to Toronto sometime. My father wants me in Ottawa with him, to work in his office. He says I can finish my PhD. from there. . . . I'm not a huge fan of Ottawa." She'd turned her face away from Paul and finished her sentence while looking at the rows of tables around them, the stacked pages of press releases, the ranks of chairs, the phones, the computers, the wires, all part of the machinery, Paul thought, of what she was in the process of studying. "I guess I could finish it here if I wanted to. I guess I could finish it anywhere."

"Rachel, you need to wait a few weeks . . . before we talk about—"

"I don't care what the article says, Paul. I mean, I do, but I don't."

He put his hand to her cheek and stroked her jawbone, lightly, tenderly, as if testing the grain of the fine hairs along a newborn's scalp. He decided, in the skip of a pulse, to tell her what he'd written about her grandfather, but when he opened his mouth he didn't tell her anything. He went to speak—intent on telling her to prepare for the shock and pain—and no words came; he only felt sadness toward himself. He'd thought, *What's more important?* and then hurt himself with the answer.

"I'm not him. You're too smart to make that mistake, so don't." She stopped, let her mouth open to reveal her teeth, those white and irregular teeth Paul had fallen in love with the first time he'd met her and that he so badly wanted to run his tongue across.

"I do know that, Rachel. I do . . . I can't believe he said what he did up there, at the end of his speech, announcing how important faith *ought* to be in politics."

"Why?"

"It won't win him votes, to say *faith in politics is like faith in the Saviour.* You know, *believing is will, and will is what creates change, so believe in me and I'll be your will in government.* Think it, sure, but don't say it. That won't fly in Toronto or Ottawa or Vancouver. It's demagoguery."

Rachel angled her head to the side slightly, as if trying to see a sore ear Paul was hiding. "You know, this whole time, I thought maybe you understood. Not agreed with. But understood."

"Understood what?"

"Why he's doing it."

"He's doing it because he likes power. And public adulation. And influence. That's why politicians become politicians. If they wanted to 'contribute' but didn't want power and a spotlight, they'd become teachers or social workers."

She shook her head slowly.

"No?"

"You didn't get to the bottom of him, Paul. I thought you would. But you didn't. Or haven't, yet."

"What if there is no bottom? No middle? No top?"

Rachel took her hand away. "If you mean that the way it sounds, that's a hurtful thing to say about my father, Paul."

Paul exhaled. "We're not talking about your father, Rachel. We're talking about a political candidate. Maybe he's someone else when he's your father."

"I want you think about it, Paul," she said in a quiet but insistent tone. "You think about what you've missed. And then you call me."

A vast yet physically satisfying exhaustion stroked its tender hand across Paul's brow, down the middle of his breastbone, and made his toes twitch. "I'll call you either way."

". . . Okay."

"There are a lot of things, Rachel, not just the article."

"I understand that," she said. "I've been thinking about you, and about your family. But I might not be around in a few weeks."

Paul reached out, took her hand. Rachel stood. She was still holding Paul's hand, but released it and smoothed his hair a little on one side, bent over, kissed him on the lips, and then she left. Paul's impulse was to put his own hand to his hair, to tidy it his way, but he stopped. He left it as it was, and gathered his things to leave.

NINETEEN

Paul had not changed his mind, and neither had Lisa. Nose Hill Park was not crowded as they made their way up, and they soon found the spot they'd talked about, along the upper ridge between the second and third hill on the southern edge of the park. Two thickets of buckbrush sat hunched at an elbow in the terrain, forming a tiny amphitheatre. Paul pulled a garden trowel from the plastic bag he'd been carrying. Getting down on his knees, he touched the small shovel to the ground, then glanced at Lisa. She nodded, turned and sat facing down the hill. He began to dig. The topsoil was dry, hard, and crusty, and he had to chip at certain spots as if he were breaking a block of ice. Soon, he'd opened a hole the size of a dinner plate. He heard the occasional chink of metal against stone. A mound rose incrementally beside the crater. He imagined the hole as immeasurably deep, a shaft sunk past his ability to picture it, but one that at a certain point had to butt up against some intractable layer of fundament, something deep and basal, bedrock—the truth.

Paul took a break to collect from the hillside a dozen or so small boulders, which he then arranged around the perimeter of the hole. He resumed his digging, and once he had the hole to a depth of six inches, he sat down and fingered through the letters one last time, searching for the one still unopened. Not for the first time since Rick's death, Paul thought that maybe he shouldn't read the letter Rick had never sent him. Would a better person leave it unread? He didn't know, and didn't have the energy to answer the question. He carefully opened the envelope and took out a number of pages, one in longhand, the rest typed. The handwritten page was undated.

Hey Paul,

You're the writer, but I guess I've had some time in here! Hey, don't ever forget who got the highest mark in English 30. (Well, okay, it was Lisa, but I mean between you and me.) Anyways, you're always sending me your writing (which I always show off to the thugs around here), so I thought I'd send you some of mine. Why not, hey?! The worst that can happen is that you don't like it. I'm not sure I like it. It's sort of about us, and Dad, and hunting, I guess, but I wouldn't quite call it a true story. I'm not sure if it happened this way or not. I just listened to my memory . . . I do that a lot in here . . . and this was what came out. I guess it's partly, or even mostly, true, though I know there are a couple of parts I imagined. I don't know what you call that . . . truth, fiction, I don't know . . . I'll leave it up to you to figure out. And I hope you like it . . . and respect it.

Anyway, I hope you're doing good out there in the world. I watch TV. I read the newspaper. I get time on the Internet. And even though it just seems to me that the world is a pretty fucked up place out there, I still miss it. I can't wait to get out and do things, things that matter, like you and Lisa are doing. I miss trying. I miss you, too, and Mum and Dad . . . and even Lisa . . . but don't tell them I said that. I'll tell them myself. Take care, Paul.

Your brother,
Rick

Paul folded the letter and placed it back inside the envelope. He felt his stomach start to shake, and had to spend a minute or two concentrating on his breathing before he could look at the other pages.

Crown Shyness
by Richard Munk

Rick is with his father and younger brother, the very last time they hunted together. Their exact location is unclear to him. It is a cool morning in the high foothills of southwestern Alberta, not too far from the Montana border, though he knows the chill won't last long, that soon he won't feel so cold. He knows they are somewhere near the Rocky Mountains, but not yet quite in them. The ground heaves and rolls all around. Fir, larch, pine, all green towers to him, surround them, except for when they break out into a high, flat and small clearing. Here his father looks across the misty valley with binoculars.

The long plastic strap dangles from his head, sways like a rein below his jaw. The earth under their feet is spongy and damp. Rick's boots are dirty, and clots of mud are wedged between the treads. He can see breath steaming out of his little brother's mouth with every lungful of air he lets go, like it's been fired from him. The season is fall, but Rick is not aware of the day, month, year. He thinks October is right, but he is a child, twelve years old, and dates don't mean much to him. Tracking the passage of time is something he leaves to his father.

Rick can see the mountains in the west, grey, snow-topped. The sun is in the east, rising slowly, unmelting itself into existence above the flatness of the far horizon. It's so gorgeous. They are in the most serene and beautiful place on the planet. Rick's father has told them this, and although Alberta is the only place Rick has ever lived, he knows his father is telling him the truth. From the foothills, where they are, he can tell the sun is going to be warm and bright this day. The simple act of feeling it heat up and seeing it turn yellow takes some of the shiver out of his shoulders. But still he's cold, and he tells his father this.

His father says: Be quiet and stay still.

His father is crouched ahead of them, looking in the direction of the mountains. His rifle is horizontal in front of him, but he's carrying it at chest height. Rick and his brother are holding their rifles with one hand, muzzles pointed at the ground. They are standing behind their father. He is moving slowly toward the mountains, and does not see the sun, which is now almost completely above the horizon.

There, says Rick's father.

Rick and his brother turn their eyes the same direction as their father's. They are standing together on the crest of the hill. Across the valley, up the side of the next hill, is an animal. A whitetail deer, with antlers extending from the two posts of bone sprouting out of its skull. A huge rack, they can tell from where they are. The deer is far away, but looking in their direction.

Rick's father whispers: Don't move.

The animal and Rick's father stare each other down. Rick and his brother look, too, but the animal has no interest in them, no fear of them. They do not exist.

His father slowly raises his rifle to his shoulder. The animal remains motionless. Rick is squirming with excitement, but still he wants to shout and tell it to move, to run. Doesn't it know what is going to happen? Why doesn't it run? His rifle steady, Rick's father peers right-eyed through his scope.

Line up for me, he whispers. Line up for me.

His breathing is quick, but now he calms his chest, takes a deep breath, makes a small "O" with his lips, and squeezes the trigger of his rifle during an exhalation. He squeezes slowly, as if savouring that instant of inbetweenness that straddles before and after, an animal square in your crosshairs, when the animal is both alive and dead. The hunter's endless present moment.

The rifle sounds. The boom cracks the clean plate of silence hanging over the valley, and the animal falls as though boneless. It does not dance in pain or plead to the sky to be given back that time when it could have escaped. Rick would have given it that chance back. But it drops.

The father whispers: My God, I got him.

They begin scrambling down the hill and across the narrow valley floor. There is a stream at the bottom and they have to wade through it. Cold water gets in Rick's boots, soaks instantly through his wool socks and makes his toenails throb. There is bush to break through before they can start up the hillside. The sun has broken the crest of the hill, and yellow-white light leaks into the bottom of the valley.

As they approach the whitetail, they see it is a huge thing, chest like a sofa. The legs stick out from underneath like snapped twigs. One of the legs moves slightly; Rick's father puts another bullet into the buck's chest. There is no more movement.

The head is small but supports a perfect 14-point rack. Two tines are at least ten inches long, and the two smallest sprouts of antler near the base sit perched like tuning forks. The spread is a good two feet, but Rick looks away from the rack to the face. A tongue like a rough, grey cucumber hangs from the deer's mouth. The eyes are dead, open, still staring, but not at Rick's father. There is a neat wound above the shoulder blade, through the thick part of the neck. Blood seeps out slowly, trickles like thick purple gravy, winds through brown fur.

Rick's father says: What a beautiful animal.

He runs his hand across the top of the deer's head and scratches between its ears. He pulls his green canvas pack off his shoulders, and removes a long knife from its sheath and an axe from a side strap. From inside the pack he pulls out four tent pegs and four short lengths of rope. Rick and his brother and his father roll the deer onto its back, and his father says to Rick: Go back to the truck and get the meat bags. Paul and me will work on the deer.

Rick returns the way they came, down through the valley, across the creek, up the hill. At the top of the far hill, near where they stood twenty minutes ago, when his father had yet to kill the deer, he stops, turns and looks back. His father has the body belly up and spread-eagled, the four legs roped to tent stakes planted in the ground around the body. He is working the knife under the skin, slitting it from anus to throat, preparing to disembowel the animal. Rick turns and keeps on moving toward the truck, which is about a mile away.

On his way back, carrying the cheesecloth meat wraps, he stops in the same place as before. His father is holding an axe now, working with it, raising it over his head, gripping with both hands near the butt end. He brings it down across the rib cage of the animal, causing the body to ripple with the blow. He raises the axe again, delivers it, hacking at the bone and cartilage, working hard. Rick's brother is standing still, watching. Rick imagines his father sweating, and wonders what his face looks like as he takes apart something that was alive an hour ago. Curious, Rick raises his rifle and peers through his scope to see his father's face.

His father is breathing heavily, concentrating. His body, and his face in particular, tremor with each drop of the axe. His lips are moving, like he's talking to Rick's brother. Though his father's hair is brown, it looks gold with his sweat and the early light. Suddenly he stops, puts the axe down, stretches out his back and runs his sleeved arm across his forehead to sop up some of the perspiration.

He sees his son across the valley, and waves. Rick doesn't wave back, because he's holding the rifle to look through the scope. "Hello," he says, though his father and brother will never hear it. But he says again, "Hello. Hi, Dad. Hi, Paul."

When Rick doesn't wave back, he can see that the look on his father's face changes. His father can see that Rick is holding a rifle. He doesn't move, just waits, with an animal's head at his feet, separated now from its body. Blood moves freely down the hill to the stream cutting through the valley. Rick and his father stare at one another, and Rick can see him so clearly. They watch one another until Rick lowers his rifle and then his father waves. Paul waves. Rick waves back to them and then makes his way across the valley and up the hill, and is back beside them in ten minutes.

Why were you pointing your rifle at us?

To see you, says Rick, through my scope. I was looking at you. Watching you cut the deer up. I saw you like you were right in front of me. It was cool.

Rick's father nods and looks at his son. Then he smiles, widely, and Rick smiles back at him. His father messes up his hair with his big, thick-fingered hand, and Rick realizes how happy he is. His heart swells with love, a balloon only his father can inflate. Rick wants to be an adult, soon, so that he and his father can be friends together.

Paul stopped, stared at the pages for a moment without really reading any of the words. He licked his lips, could feel his heart fluttering like a rabbit's. "This is a story," he said to Lisa, his voice husky. "It's a story about us hunting, me and Dad and him, I mean. He told me he'd written a story, but he never sent it."

"Hunting?" said Lisa, without looking back up the hill. "Why didn't he send it?"

"Don't know," said Paul, exhaling as he spoke. "I'm not finished it."

Lisa nodded, didn't say anything more. Paul looked at his sister, saw how small she seemed holding the pain on her slender back, her rounded shoulders. He turned back to the story, the clean lines, the simple black and white on the page.

> The animal is lying in pieces on the ground; two huge shoulders, the massive rump, ribs like the roundness of a rain barrel. The earth around their feet is black with blood. The skin of the animal sits rumpled up off to the side, the gutpile a steaming mound in front of them. Heart, lungs, kidneys, other things that Rick doesn't know about. The gutpile looks almost alive, glistening, sighing, a soft whiteness rising off it like from their own sweat in the heavy walking at dawn. Flies are buzzing and landing all over it.
>
> Rick's father says: We better get a move on. Bears'll be around.
>
> After they have the meat stored away in the bags, they haul it back to the truck, throw it in the bed, make room for the skin and the head. They go back to the kill site. Rick takes the skin, wrapping it over him like a blanket, bloody side out. Paul carries some tools. Their father picks up the head and rack, and hoists it over one shoulder so that the antlers are pointing behind. The animal's eyes are still open. Rick is behind his father on the trail and the animal looks at him while they walk. He still has part of the animal surrounding him, and he says to it, softly, "You could have run. You didn't have to be there. If you'd done just one thing different this morning, one thing, none of this would have happened."
>
> Rick doesn't say these things too loudly, because he doesn't want his father to think he's not happy to be hunting. He is happy to be hunting. He stops to catch his breath, and when he does he looks up into the sky to see where the sun is. It's hard to find, since they are now walking through a grove of tall spruce. It's gotten windy, and looking skyward, he sees the trees sway like tall men listening to slow music, but he also sees the branches of the trees moving around, lilting, dropping, waving, but, it seems to him, never touching, as if they were avoiding one another on purpose.

Look, he says to his father and brother who have stopped to wait for him. Those tree branches never touch, up there at the top. See that?

His father stands beside him, also looking up. Crown shyness, he says. That's what they call it. Survival thing. At the top of the canopy, the branches don't want to hurt one another, so they developed this way to not touch at the tips when they're growing. Even in rough weather, they sway and blow all over, but they'll never damage one another, or at least not much. It's one theory, anyway.

Cool, says Rick.

Paul stares up, saying nothing.

Back at the truck, they arrange the animal skin in the bed. Their father puts the head and rack on top of it, wrapping the antlers with the skin as if it were a tarp. They get in, their father starts the truck.

The sun is now directly above them in the sky, even moving a little bit off into the west. It is warm and the mountains glow a fine blue and slate under the clear light. They rise like a wall, forcing them to take the only available route out, a badly maintained road. The truck bounces and jiggles from the washboard ruts in the road, and Rick can feel his big heart slapping against his ribs. Soon, he starts to laugh from the sensation. His brother laughs along with him.

His father says: What's so funny, you two?

Nothing, says Rick, giggling. It just feels funny, bouncing around.

His father laughs, too, and then starts to play around with the steering wheel, snapping it left, then right, increasing the sensation of being out of control. They are not travelling very fast, and he is in command of the truck, but Rick and his brother Paul whoop and shriek. The truck hits rut after rut, and it seems as though their father is increasing the speed, so that at some point Rick begins to believe they are actually out of control. But he feels so safe, so much where he belongs, that the thought comes into his head that if they were to go into the ditch, have an accident, and die, that that would be fine, that they would die together, that he would still be with his father and brother. When the truck stopped rolling they would still be together. They would be alive or dead. It wouldn't matter which. Either would be okay, as long as the same thing were to happen to all of them.

The thought that this could be their fate makes him giddy. His father fiddles with the wheel, laughing. Paul is laughing. Rick keeps laughing, too, but now he starts to think about actually having such an accident. He closes his eyes tight and hopes for a crash, into the ditch, rolling and flipping, their bodies crushed and torn apart, like the animal in the truck bed behind them. He can see it, he and his father and his brother, lying side by side, dead, smashed and broken and bloody; all of them together forever. This thought makes him happy. And though his eyes are closed, Rick just knows that his father and his brother can see him smiling. Smiling big and wide. And from this they will be able to see that he is happy.

Paul looked up, forced air in, ran a hand through his hair. The colours of fire, red and orange and a yellow-brown, filled the valley, erupting fiercely against the fading green of the long snaking strips of parkland inhabiting the farther reaches of the city. Everything had changed. Gazing over the long valley, to the city's freeways, he could see the failing of light all around him, the diminishment of heat that powered it. At the edge of the city, Paul could make out planes landing and departing. He looked to the sky. No jet streams; the air was getting heavier. The feel of it on his skin was different, the way it lingered longer and denser than the light, hot summer air. Snow was coming. Not now, but soon.

"Do you want to read any of them? . . . The story he was maybe going to send me?" He heard the quaver in his voice, and knew Lisa would hear it, too.

She shook her head.

". . . And Tammy was sure she didn't want them?"

"That's what she said yesterday, that she had Rick's letters to her to keep and that was enough."

Paul folded up Rick's story and the letter, making the folds neat and clean. Rick had never sent it to him, but in Paul's heart it was his. He would show it to his parents, someday. And he would take it with him when he went to Toronto. Lisa watched him.

"I'm going to let Rachel read it."

"If she'll see you."

". . . If she'll see me," Paul said, nodding. "Either way, I don't think I'll be gone long."

He picked up the rest of the bundle, the fifty-odd letters Tammy had sent Rick, then he placed the thick packet in the earth bowl he'd surrounded with stones. The air soon stank of liquid lighter fluid. After the flames had died out, a cool fall-bearing breeze dipped into the basin and swept a few ashes out and across the grass. Paul waited another couple of minutes, then poked a stick into the belly of the grey ash pile. Satisfied, he stood up, and with the toe of his shoe nudged every stone into the centre of the bowl, so that it looked simply like what it now was: a hole with some rocks in it. He looked around and took his bearings; he knew he would come back to this exact place.

Lisa was sitting partway down the hill, facing away from him, slender arms around knees she'd brought to her chest. The wind was playing with her long, dirty blond hair, switching it back and forth like a little kite's tail. She appeared small but unbreakable, made of some otherworldly element, so strong, eternal; he wished he had it in him to say this to her, but he didn't—not yet. He stopped next to her. She rose, gazed across the city, took a long, heavy breath, and started down, stepping delicately, as if guarding a tender ankle.

"Lisa."

She stopped and glanced his way, though she didn't turn. Paul went to her, touched her on the shoulder, and clasped her hand briefly before letting go.

"Ready?" she asked.

Paul nodded. "I think so."

Acknowledgements

Thank you to those many friends and colleagues who offered advice, assistance, and support. I would also like to acknowledge my debt to the Canada Council and the Alberta Foundation for the Arts; both provided time for me to work on this book. I'd also specifically like to thank Ruth Linka, Wendy Schmalz and Michael Wilde for their energy and dedication. To Jack Hodgins, thank you for your insight, skill and enthusiasm. Finally, to Cathy, Jessica and Grace, thank you . . . for everything.

CURTIS GILLESPIE won the Henry Kreisel Award and the inaugural Danuta Gleed Literary Prize for *The Progress of an Object in Motion*, and was a finalist for the Grant MacEwan Prize for *Playing Through*. His magazine writing on politics, sports, travel, science and the arts has earned him three National Magazine Awards from fourteen nominations. He lives in Edmonton with his wife and their two daughters.

Acknowledgements

Thank you to those many friends and colleagues who offered advice, assistance, and support. I would also like to acknowledge my debt to the Canada Council and the Alberta Foundation for the Arts; both provided time for me to work on this book. I'd also specifically like to thank Ruth Linka, Wendy Schmalz and Michael Wilde for their energy and dedication. To Jack Hodgins, thank you for your insight, skill and enthusiasm. Finally, to Cathy, Jessica and Grace, thank you . . . for everything.